Shona Ramaya was born in Calcutta, and grew up in Calcutta and Delhi. She was educated at an Anglo-India convent (from which she was nearly expelled for sliding down the bell-rope of Delhi's main cathedral). After working for a time in Delhi television and radio, she left India to study in the United States. Later, she lived in England for a while and she now lives in New York, where she teaches and writes.

Shona Ramaya

FLUTE

FOR BECKY

AN ABACUS BOOK

First published in Great Britain by Michael Joseph Ltd 1989
Published in Abacus by Sphere Books Ltd 1990

Copyright © Shona Ramaya 1989

Reproduced, printed and bound in Great Britain by
The Guernsey Press Co. Ltd, Guernsey, Channel Islands.

ISBN 0 349 1 0077 2

Sphere Books Ltd
A Division of
Macdonald and Co. (Publishers) Ltd,
27 Wrights Lane, London W8 5TZ

A member of Maxwell Pergamon Publishing Corporation plc

Acknowledgements

I absolutely have to thank Tula for 'believing', Sally Daniels for moral support and helpful criticism, Professors Jerry Goodisman and Harry Brumberger for allowing me to be a constant nuisance in their x-ray lab and using their computer to write the book; but most of all, I thank Raghu for his incredible patience and understanding through this 3-year ordeal.

'It sounds crazy,' she said automatically, and the young man sighed and shrugged. 'In any case,' he said to Blanford, 'your novel about the matter is finished: it only remains for you to see if we are going to live it according to your fiction or according to new fact, no?'

Sebastian, Lawrence Durrell

Northern India

Prelude

When Nikhil looked at the river from the stone terrace of the Phulgarh temple, the hot pearl sun of September was still behind damp clouds that spread across the horizon. Crossing the terrace, the pale, thin young man entered the inner recess and smiled at the woman arranging flowers at the altar. Her head bowed, and partly covered by her green *sari*, she touched the marigolds, tuberoses, frangipani and the gold-vermilion gul-mohrs as if they were wounded. As she began to thread the flowers into garlands, Nikhil smoothed his hair, removed a gul-mohr from the pocket of his white *kurta* and tossed it at the feet of the idol on the altar. The long orange stamens quivered for a few seconds. The woman looked up and saw a pair of dark eyes staring at the gold flute that the god held against his mouth. Placing the tray of garlands and the plate of petals on the altar, she left.

There was a frailty about the slender indigo form that stood on the altar with his ankles crossed, eyes half closed, wrapped in blue silk from the waist down. The god's body curved from the waist upwards as if he had frozen in a moment of movement, a dance maybe. There were gul-mohr blossoms in his black stone hair, which glinted with gold lights from the lamps all around.

Who could play the flute like Krishna? thought Nikhil. Who could so entrance, captivate for ever? In a garden, among the waves of the river, where? Somehow to wrench him from that altar. He has to come, he's supposed to come again. Come as you are here, not as Kalki, come as enchanter not as destroyer. Your face neither man's nor woman's, but such – such – no, not beauty.

Nikhil turned away and walked towards the low parapet of the terrace.

3

'Nikhil!' He looked down. A woman stood under a neem tree wiping her sweating forehead.

'Tulsi, what are you doing here?'

'Go to the bazaar, *jaldi*,' she said. 'Heera Lal wants you to help him with his fruit stall. I've got you a job.'

'But I don't want to work!'

'Go right now,' Tulsi yelled, adjusting her dirty orange *sari*. 'I won't feed you if you don't get some money in. Either you work or find some other place to sleep.'

'But I take care of your kids while you're at the construction site!'

'Money,' she smiled, '*paisa lao, pyaré*,' and, turning her back on him, left.

Nikhil came down the wide stone steps slowly. The neem trees were quivering green-gold. Hundreds of tiny, oval, pale yellow fruit skins lay scattered on the white dust. Nikhil popped a hollow pod with his toe. Bitter, bitter fruits. Only parrots eat them. Maybe other birds eat them, too. Only parrots – what a myth! Bitter, bitter tree, and so cool under here, the green-gold-white-dust-shade. And the river out there, so bright now. The flute in the Yamuna.

Nikhil turned and looked up. He saw the columns of the inner recess framing a darkness. What eyes would be like your eyes? What colour? The river so bright with the light of water.

The Countess of Ravinspur lightly rubbed the calluses under her feet. All those exquisite shoes into which we squeeze our feet. Leaning back against the comfortable cushioned berth of a first-class train compartment, Caroline stretched out her legs, smoothed her green silk dress and looked at the closed bathroom door. What was Dane doing for so long? How long would the smoke curl from these sausages? She patted her bobbed auburn hair and reached for her cup of tea. You should never wait for your children who take too long in the bathroom just when the train slows down so that the passengers can breakfast in peace. Putting down her cup, she opened her green velvet purse and removed a tiny ivory object. Two inches high, an eighth of an inch thick, exquisitely carved, a miniature temple gateway stood on her palm. She looked at it for a few seconds, then put it away. Dane takes so

long in the mornings. Not Julian though – the adorable stepson – well, well, the sixth Earl of Ravinspur, two years now.

A fairly lacerated face smiled wryly at the mirror. 'Now for
the other half,' said Lord Dane Hartley, and raised the shining
steel blade. Long cuts and specks of blood followed each stroke
of the razor. 'Blast.' His almost-indigo eyes narrowed and his
jaw tautened as the razor swept up his throat. ' "Accidental
suicide in a train bathroom, somewhere between Bombay and
Delhi," hah! And Julian with his smooth face will read it in
The Times and laugh. How was I to know that I'd have to shave
myself some day in a train bathroom in India?' He wiped his
face tenderly with the white towel hanging over strong
shoulders.

Trying to take his mind off the stinging after-shave, he
looked at the morning brightness rushing outside the window.
Julian had a smile like that years and years ago – like morning
brightness rushing across, rushing away.

Saw him twice in the last three years. Twirling that violet
ostrich feather, slender and frail in a purple velvet jacket, he
ran up the long flight of wide stone steps of Ravinspur that
summer. Will you come to India? Mother thinks you will. And
Ju, when have you ever kept any promises?

Breathing in the aroma of Darjeeling tea, Caroline closed her
eyes. I'm your friend – she could hear herself twenty-eight
years ago, kneeling before a six-year-old boy, a boy whose
face felt like a mask. That same little boy had screamed in
excitement a year later, is that my brother? Ooh, he screams
and scowls! And for years and years, Dane: Ju this, Ju that!
Then Winchester, Cambridge, a different Julian, a different
smile, and constant pushing away. So will you come to India?

'Bon Voyage' – a card with a peacock feather clipped to it you
sent from Paris. 'Will come, I promise.' Dane smiled and
brushed his dark brown hair back from his forehead, then
wiped a speck of blood off his cleft chin. Well, Ju? Don't know
what to make of anything any more.

So many stories about him from different people – seen at
Montmartre, playing a mandolin surrounded by models, silk

shirts and silk scarves. Then the Monte Carlo business! The Baroness von Halkein. The baron found them in the Blue Salon . . .

Dane put his cream shirt on and tucked it into his grey trousers. What about that club on Fitzroy Street – what had really happened?

Wilde's been arrested! Harry Winston had caught Dane after breakfast. God, ten years ago? Tell Julian right now. Why? Dane had stared stupidly. They're turning Fitzroy Street inside out.

Julian had shrugged and turned to the window. Maybe you should leave London. And Julian left: once-a-year Julian after that. A few days in London during the season; a day or two at Ravinspur.

In the green woods of Ravinspur; or alone in your room, cursing Crowley, your champagne head bowed over those cards, whispering, monsters, monsters, monsters, all, all, run, run, run. Caught unawares, get out of here, you snarled, your skin tautening over the fine bones of your face, your blue-grey eyes hard as lightning.

And that morning, Father had stood with his head against the mahogany panels of the library. I'll speak to Queensberry, he said. Too late, said Mama. Julian's in Europe. It'll die down.

It's that club, and all those lies, I said, Ju. All lies.

Will you come? As Dane lightly massaged his left shoulder, he felt the train speed up with a jolt.

Six men stretched their bodies out on the wooden benches for oil massage at the hands of native boys and Thomas Sherley moved away and sat down on the white-dusted courtyard of the Talkot cantonment. His shirtless body was as golden-brown and strong and young as the bodies fifteen yards away. But as a native boy approached him, carrying a bowl of mustard oil, Sherley turned him away with a curt 'No'.

Hands moved along shoulders, arms and legs, relaxing muscles, making skin gleam and smart pleasantly with slaps. 'The D.M. of Phulgarh wants to arrange a cricket match with us some time,' Sherley heard one of the men say. 'They'll lose – innings defeat certainly!' laughed another. Sherley closed his grass-green eyes for a few seconds, then looked at his raised knees, around which his arms were clasped. His jaw muscles flexed tightly for a moment, then relaxed.

'Hate it; hate this, hate this. I'll hate for ever, waiting for nothing,' he said under his breath.

The boy came back again and said, '*Saab*?'

'I said no!'

Very toned his slim body was, and dark brown, almost black. His shoulders, a little bony, collarbones prominent; a ridge ran down his chest, past his navel, and vanished under the dirty white cloth wrapped around his waist and legs.

'Not today,' Sherley said. A similar ridge ran along the boy's spine.

'God, do I hate this,' Sherley whispered again.

The bathroom door opened and Dane stepped into the compartment.

'What have you done to your face?' his mother asked, almost dropping her toast. Dane sat down and served himself four cold sausages.

'I wonder if Harry's gained weight,' he said.

'Are you sure he'll be there at Delhi Station?'

'Yes, Mama, he'll be there with that carriage he wrote about. Winston's not that irresponsible.'

'What's Harry doing in Phulgarh anyway?'

'Leather business or something. Just spending his inheritance. Good he happens to be there.'

'Yes.' They ate quietly, looking out of the window occasionally.

Wiping his mouth with the starched white napkin, Dane set his empty plate down on the table in front. He stood up, flexed his shoulders, stretching his arms behind him, and picked up his grey felt hat. Caroline watched her son walk to the mirror and try on the hat at different angles. 'This is how Julian wears it sometimes,' he said with a half-sigh and pulled the hat low over his left eye. Caroline smiled. 'Do I look silly in hats, Mama?' Dane asked the mirror.

'You look incredibly handsome in anything, dear.'

'But not like Ju.'

'Why would you want to look like Julian?'

'So that I can think his thoughts.'

7

'Now you're being silly.'

'Sure. Why did we come to India, Mama? We had nothing to run away from this time.'

'Just what is that supposed to mean?'

'I figured out a sort of a pattern – I mean, every time you, Papa and I went off on one of those exotic trips we were running from some awful mess Julian had got into.'

'Don't be silly! Charles loved travelling. Wasn't Cairo wonderful, and Alexandria and Luxor and Baghdad and Athens and —'

'Yes, Mama, of course, but don't tell me travelling was the only thing on Papa's mind! We fled to Cairo because Ju went to Lady Brenton's masquerade in a black velvet cloak with not a stitch underneath.' Dane threw his hat up and caught it. ' "I went as myself," Julian explained later. Oh, God!'

'Oh, Dane —' Caroline covered her face and laughed. Dane smiled and sat down opposite her.

'Now tell me,' he said, 'please, why have we come to India?'

'Julian will come,' she said, serious all of a sudden, adding just a half-smile.

'And what will happen if he comes?'

'When he comes.'

'What then? I find it very difficult to talk to him . . . now . . . for the last ten years . . . I wish we hadn't run off to Athens then, y'know, when they called him names. Of course he left, too.'

'Names?'

'L–like Wilde – y'know what I mean. All lies.' Dane stood up and began to pace. 'He won't come, Mama.'

'Yes he will,' Caroline said firmly. 'He will come because he is curious.'

'He doesn't like being together like this, you know that. We've implored him to come with us before, to Athens, to Cairo, Baghdad . . . oh, you know he hates being with us! I don't see why you're being so hideously optimistic about him this time.'

'He'll come; he's run around enough; he knows that.'

'What if something goes wrong here?'

'So far from home – who cares?'

'I do. But what's the point anyway? Oh, damn Julian!'

'This time, Dane, we've come away . . . in order to go back . . . together.'

They looked at each other silently. The brightness rushed by whistling, flashing against the corner of Dane's eye. Ah, running through those green woods of Ravinspur at Julian's heels. Wait, wait, Ju, wait for me . . . Stay, Ju, please, don't go away again . . . I hate you, Julian, hate you, hate you . . .

'Why d'you love him so much?'

'Because he is not my son.'

Dane lay down and placed his hat over his eyes. 'I love him, too, Mama,' he said, 'but does Ju care about us? Does he care about anything at all? Ah, God bless the sixth Earl of Ravinspur, wherever he may be now, in whatever state, ahh – I'll take a nap I think. I'm stuffed.'

Caroline stared out of the window at the flying smears of greens and browns, the blurred bodies of men and cattle. You couldn't concentrate on anything really. What shall I think about in this strange country with its different smell, warm, damp, salty, and why have I come here?

India? Dane had choked over dinner. What on earth for, Mama?

Because Charles loved India? Twenty-nine years ago, or thirty? Charles had fled to India. Two oceans between his self and his guilt. And for one whole year a child with vacant eyes waited and waited, wandering through empty rooms. Can picture it vividly somehow. A horse tearing through the woods; torn stirrups; a slim young body flung into the air. His first wife had been killed in a riding accident, she had been told when they met. And they met like all others met, at a ball; under moonlight, a stroll; fountains and gardenia. But they had been slugged by the same loneliness and boredom. They turned to each other desperately and married within six months. And after the cold little boy responded to her touch, life was wonderful. But Charles could never meet Julian's eyes.

What will I think of in this strange land? No, not quite so strange. So many of us here, trying to create another home. What is the house like? One of the *nawab*'s bungalows, Harry Winston had written. Will have everything in order. Phulgarh – citadel of flowers. Let there be flowers.

*   *   *

The noise grabbed them roughly, pushed them around. The train stopped with a shudder in Delhi Station. Bodies poured into the train, bodies poured out of it. The countess straightened her wide-brimmed straw hat in front of the mirror.

'*Coolie memsaab*?' '*Garhi chahiye*?' Loud voices shook her.

'Just wait in here. Mother. I'm going out to find Winston.' Dane stepped into the late September afternoon. Hot, but not unbearable. Suddenly he was swamped.

'Coolie! Coolie!'

'Oh, get out of my way!' He scattered the dark faces.

'Dane! By George, you look splendid!'

'Harry! Harry Winston!'

'How's Harriet Selwyn ... and Belinda Hartnett ... and Madame Yakashova? Tell me about London! Oh, this is going to be like old times. Wait till you see the *naach*-girls!'

'Harry, you rascal! *Naach*-girls! Madame Yakashova! Why you had to jump out of her bedroom window when ...'

'Here, let's get the coolies. Where's your mother? Come on, come on, my carriage – wait till you see it –'

In the glaring sunshine stood a vermilion and gold horse-drawn carriage, with parrot-green trimmings all over. The *sahees* and his guide were dressed in vermilion and green uniforms. The spacious and comfortable interior had walls lined with bright pink satin; the seats were turquoise with yellow satin cushions. Caroline nearly fainted with shock. Dane staggered into a corner. Harry tugged at his sandy hair and his collar.

'Do you like it? Do you like it? Isn't it gorgeous? Designed it myself. Came to Delhi for all the satin. It's the talk of the town! Love bright colours. This country's full of bright colours. All the howdahs on the elephants are orange and gold, y'know, the rajahs and *nawabs* always travel in dazzling coaches. See, it's shaped like a landau, and I had six men work on it, fixed really sturdy wheels, and er, and er –' Caroline kept her eyes shut. 'We'll be stopping for the night,' Harry informed them happily. 'There's a pretty habitable bungalow three hours from here. The Company's taken pains to keep it quite up to date. We'll start off tomorrow, stop several times on the way, so that everybody's comfortable.'

'Harry' – the countess opened her eyes – 'your dear mother is very worried about you. She really had the Foreign Office in mind.'

'Oh – um – yes – but – what I mean is that I love doing absolutely nothing and I mean we'll all have an absolutely splendid time here. I say, Dane . . .'

As the two young men dived into that world they had left behind, Caroline turned to the window. Dear, responsible Dane. So lighthearted now. Looking after the estate for the past two years since Charles's death, while Julian vanished into the Continent. But now, the time's come to face each other, accept each other for what we are. Take charge of your own individual lives; not Julian running and Dane waiting and hurting. Dane to lead his own life – not just the life of waiting for a fallen hero. Julian's no hero; just human, and in pain, to be sure, with all the running away.

The fresh green of the wheat fields eased her eyes that had stared long enough at the glaring colours of the interior. The white dust swirled and blended with the fading sunlight. The sky was turning from blue to a warm rose. The green grew softer and softer. The white dust clung to the rose-gold of the approaching evening. It was a different twilight. She rested her head against the cushions and let the rushing landscape pull her along with it.

They settled down among the cane chairs and the night which spread out fragrant with the white flowers that flickered in the darkness. Suddenly the past vanished. Only the taste of the dinner lingered, and the smell of fresh sheets in the fairly comfortable rooms of the *dak* bungalow. On the veranda, now, they lapsed into the present. Strange – such darkness should have been accompanied by a rich silence. But the distant bark of foxes and the constant buzz of insects against the wire screen covering the veranda kept them tuned to the foreign darkness that surrounded them. When the high, melodious piping of a flute crept through the night and wrapped around them they forgot to be startled. Those haunting tones seemed part of the darkness – inseparable.

'Hear that?' Harry pointed at the darkness. 'Probably the

mali playing the flute – the gardener, that is. Quite common here. Quaint, isn't it?'

Nikhil sat under a neem tree behind the Phulgarh temple and looked at the flute on his lap. A slim bamboo flute. Fireflies spun around before him, like some god's emerald eyes in a forgotten temple deep in dark woods. There was a moon, too. The night was too bright. He closed his eyes and leaned his head against the bark. That other darkness – the darkness of Krishna. Nikhil touched the flute and gently stroked it. No, he couldn't play it. He wasn't supposed to play it. He didn't want to play it. An other to play the flute, an other who had that darkness in his eyes, beyond the river-brightness. He would find him and make him play the flute. He will come because the garden is waiting. And they would touch, flute and mouth, feet and hands, flowers and hair. That other's breath in the flute's hollow body. A love taken a touch too far, a sound taken to the river's edge and returned to the waters.

PART ONE

The Citadel of Flowers

Chapter 1

'Move away,' cried the women to the children splashing mud and water too close to the wet clothes. 'Move away and play further down the bank. Or we'll have to wash *memsaab*'s white sheets and *saab*'s white pyjamas all over again.' The children laughed at the chiding and slid down the muddy slope of the river bank. Numerous dark hands tried to grab the river over and over again. The Yamuna slithered through wet fingers and wrapped around the ecstatic bodies rolling in her folds. In dived more dark bodies and the water flashed up against faces and burst into gold glitter catching the last rays of the sun. The women slapped the clothes on the rocks at the edge of the river, scrubbed them, rinsed them. And the children continued to splatter mud and tear at the water.

It was then, against the setting sun, that Harry Winston's brilliant equipage rolled into Phulgarh. Caroline looked at the women washing clothes and the children playing with mud and water. And they stared back at the travellers. 'New *memsaab* and *saab*,' they whispered and giggled. She smiled at the children. She couldn't help herself. There was something happy about them. Dane looked at the women curiously; funny, the way they grouped together. No men around. Some bathing, totally oblivious to the strange eyes that had appeared suddenly. The children came running towards the carriage. '*Paisa! Paisa!*' Harry threw a handful of coins. Laughter and squeals and fast-moving legs and hands. Then like quick tadpoles the children slipped back into the river.

Along the river, then away from it. Through meandering roads, past open spaces, past the bazaar, past men selling mangoes and bananas and pomegranates, the old men with withered skin roasting peanuts and corn. Then they reached the temple. The air, thick with the smell of incense, oil lamps and trampled flowers. This was no private communion. The noise was overwhelming; people laughing, talking, quarrelling; children screaming; women cursing in exasperation. '*Puja* – worship,' Harry said. 'It's like this practically every evening.'

'What's going on?' Dane touched Harry's elbow as they raced away from the temple towards new territory. 'Slow down. Want to see. What's that? Those wall-like things?'

'The construction site – the District Magistrate wants a new High Court. Can't slow down. Sorry, ol' chap. This is the Indian section.'

The carriage moved into the quieter section of the town. 'There's the Collector's bungalow,' Harry pointed, 'the D.M.'s over there – the Lyndons – and there, the Police Station, the jail, and that's the hospital run by Dr Morel – and oh, here we are!'

A red-brick bungalow stood draped with bright magenta bougainvillaea against a dark-rose evening sky. The white wrought-iron gates were flung open by two men in loose white clothes. Wheels and hooves crunched along the gravel drive and the *sahees* brought the horses to a full stop in front of the long white veranda that ran across the front of the house. Rolled bamboo shades, potted palms, cane chairs and bougainvillaea, and, oh, my goodness, thought Caroline, marigolds, chrysanthemums, dahlias, roses, gardenia, jacaranda, tuberoses, jasmine . . . !

'Here we are!' Harry jumped out. Dane helped his mother out of the carriage. 'The servants.' Harry waved at the five figures standing at attention on the steps. 'Zulfiqar, your cook, *khansama*, that is. Here – Jugnu – get the bags – will wait at the table, and, Dane, he'll take care of your stuff. Pretty well-trained, the boy. The *mali*, and the fourth chap, just an extra hand, when you entertain, etcetera. Ravi Singh, OK? For Julian perhaps, when he arrives. OK everybody, get to work, get the bags, come on.'

'Who is the woman?' Dane asked.

'Christ! How could I forget? Meena —' Meena stepped

forward and touched Caroline's feet. Caroline moved back, startled.

They trooped in surrounded by bustling servants. Crossing the veranda, they entered an ante-room, wood-panelled, with coat racks and hat racks and potted plants in brass holders. The living room, brightly lit, made Dane and Caroline gasp. Gleaming brass, Persian rugs, teak furniture, velvet upholstery, huge stone vases of flowers, an enormous chandelier, and a royal Bengal tiger spread out snarling on the wall opposite them stormed their senses.

'You must have spent a fortune, Harry.'

'I wanted you to be comfortable. And besides, it was the *nawab* who did the place up, not I. I just bought the bungalow from him on your behalf, servants and all. How about some tea?'

As Jugnu served tea, Dane and his mother looked at the sandalwood and onyx bric-à-brac scattered on table-tops and on shelves that ran along the white walls.

'Let me show you the house,' Harry said, and showed them the antelope heads on the walls of the dining room. 'That's a mango tree,' Harry pointed, leading them to the back, 'those are banana trees. And those, the servants' quarters. Woods out there. And flowers.' Harry scratched his head. 'I happened to mention to the Collector's wife that you were coming. News here spreads like cholera. You can kill me when you tire of the visits.'

Dane scrutinised his room, liking what he saw. Lying on the large bed with its rust raw-silk spread, he looked at the ceiling. 'Harry, what's this thing hanging over the bed?'

'A mosquito net. You'll need it when the time comes.'

'I want to talk to you 'bout something.'

'What about?'

'Is that a balcony over there?'

They moved into the quaint crescent-shaped balcony as Jugnu unpacked. 'Well, what's the matter?' Harry asked.

'What have you said about us?'

'What d'you mean?'

'What have you said about Julian?'

'What – nothing really – what's there to say?'

17

'You know what I'm talking about! The Fitzroy Street fiasco, that whole business.'

'Dane! I never talk about my friends! Besides, that's nearly ten years ago. Who's interested in that now, anyway? And I never quite knew what to make of it.'

'Mother's really worried about Ju. He's been away for nearly twelve years now. Of course, he comes home for a few weeks every year, but we've sort of lost touch, after that awful fight over Helena, and all the trouble with that club. I don't know what happened to Julian after that.'

'Worrying about him still! After all these years! You idiot, forget about all that, about him. You didn't come so far to sort out the past – you've come to enjoy yourself.'

'I've been quite the Labrador, haven't I? Just waiting for Julian, taking care of his responsibilities while he goes on Sindbad's voyages.' Dane turned his face away.

'So you are bitter after all.'

'Not quite as much as I'd like to be. Forget it – I'll fall into the arms of your *naach*-girls and drown my sorrows!'

'Good. Now listen, there's this *naach*-girl you've got to see. This one's special. She's the prince's mistress.'

'What prince?'

'The *nawab*'s son – Salman. You've got to come to Talkot, to the *kota*, and see her dance some night. You'll meet the subalterns from the cantonment there – splendid fellows, not like the old bores at the club here. They just do what they want and have an absolutely ripping time. The *kota*'s the only place for real fun. The native women, the dances, the intrigues! You'll see. We just have to be a little discreet, that's all. God, when you see the women at the club dances and the tea parties, you'll drop dead. What faces, what conversation! Enough to make you want to hang yourself.'

'And what exciting verbal intercourse do you manage to establish between a native dancing girl and yourself, pray?'

After Harry left, Dane threw his coat on the bed and pulled his tie off. Sitting on the bed, he began to unbutton his shirt. Jugnu reached for his shoes. Dane felt a little awkward. But once Jugnu's experienced fingers massaged his feet, Dane lay back on the bed and relaxed his spine.

* * *

18

Caroline sat down and examined the rosewood writing desk in her room. The drawers were empty and clean and had a faint musky odour. Its dark maroon leather surface was a little scratched. She placed a blue diary against it and closed her eyes for a few moments. Removing a silver pen from inside the diary, she began to write.

Dear sister – she scratched it out. Dear Lorna, she wrote, I remember you in your mauve silk dress, standing against dark trees and clouds. I have wanted to talk to you so many times. About Julian. Cousin Alison used to say Julian keeps all his hurt squeezed inside his ribs. Why? Because he likes to show off his dry brittle smile. Well, now that we are here in this alien land where Charles found peace, we wait for Julian.

I have talked to Alison about the past; but after Alison died, I have not spoken to anyone.

No, the past is not the only thing I want to talk about. I want to share with you – India! We're here now, and I'm not quite sure why. I want us to be here together, learn to live together, go back together. Understand each other, accept each other, here, far away from all the messes. Maybe Julian will share with us his hurts, his unknown longings.

Must I talk of Julian? Alas, you see, Charles's eternal question has become mine now: what is Julian, what is he? We have shared him without knowing him. Now, I want to share the past.

Looking back at all that has gone before, looking back from so far away, I feel I have to tell you the emotions that came out of the events. The events are dead. The past matters in its feelings.

Charles blamed himself for the death in the family and ran off to India. Motherless, Julian, at six, wandered through Ravinspur for a year. Julian and Charles were strangers after that.

It took me a year to touch the tips of Julian's fingers. Oh, Lorna, what is the point of churning the past when what we all really want is to shake it off like snowflakes? I want to live in the present, not in the past and in constant contemplation of the future – what will happen, what will happen when Julian comes? How differently can one look at the past really? It doesn't change; we force ourselves to say, oh, that's over. Is it? Julian isn't over. How will Julian look at this country, how will Julian look at us in this alien country? What shall we say to each other after ten years of silence? Dane says Julian will not come.

Alison said Julian is a little boy who has half grown up. I said Julian doesn't want to feel. She said, yes, that's why. Julian has scared all of us from time to time. After that awful Fitzroy Street scandal, they said Julian was like Oscar Wilde and Bosie Douglas, and he might have ended up in prison had he not left England. Dane was furious and called them liars. Got into fights with people. We didn't know what to think. I don't care what people say. I just don't want my stepson, whom I love, to live like a stranger amongst us. I can accept it all, but I can't stop the questions.

As the District Magistrate aligned his body over the billiard table, Dane looked out at the copper sky through the french windows of the club. Before the night took them by surprise with its dazzling brightness, the sky waited in copper. He felt Harry touch his elbow. 'Dane, Cyril Trevors, from the Talkot cantonment. Lord Dane Hartley.' Something about cricket, horses and *naach*-girls. Dane found it difficult to keep his eyes off the sky outside. He wanted to catch the night as it fell. See it happen in slow motion. But the voices stood in the way. More men, more voices.

'At the *kota* in Talkot,' he heard. 'Gorgeous dancing girls. Bells around their ankles. Songs. Music.'

'You enter through iron gates. The *kota*'s a big white-washed house. Three storeys. The dancing takes place in this enormous hall with marble floors, black and white marble. Chandeliers, incense, roses, wine, sweets. You can stand against the columns that surround the dancing area, or you can sit on velvet cushions. But we don't do that, because then we'd have to sit with the Indians. You have to throw money on the floor after each dance, and at the end you tell the Begum which one you want and they come to you. We don't spend nights there. The cantonment's a pretty convenient place.'

'What's it like inside?' someone asked.

'Long corridors, with rooms on either side and a courtyard at the back. You never go there alone.'

'Do you get what it is, the *kota*?'

Dane looked at the sky again. It was bright with stars. It had happened suddenly — the darkness — and escaped him once more. Julian under that sky. What would Julian say about this sky? He wanted to hear about the Taj Mahal. The ultimate symbol of love they call it; love perfected in death. He wanted to touch its white marble surface.

You know, Lorna, our first feel of India: a wicked, wicked cobra! And a Dr Morel who reminds me of old Dr Chatham who used to tell great-aunt Penelope about the maids! Dr Morel's the only amusing person, really. We've been here a few days, and he has introduced us to a cobra that danced to a snake-charmer's pipe, a baby elephant, and told us incredible stories about exorcisms. He makes the club evenings thoroughly enjoyable.

The District Magistrate's wife, Roanna Lyndon, keeps her husband on tenterhooks with her outrageous flirting. The men run from her. 'Robbie, dear, a gin and tonic, please. Oh, Mr Trevors, doesn't your uniform look absolutely marvellous!' The subalterns from Talkot come to the Phulgarh club very often. Mrs Lyndon has been trying to corner a strikingly handsome subaltern called Thomas Sherley the last few times. He has the most indifferent emerald eyes I've ever seen. Anyway, the Collector, Mr Bancroft, is pompous but bearable, his wife, bearable. He throws too many tea parties. There's another one coming up soon.

At club events and parties here, I notice that everybody laughs a lot; sometimes for no apparent reason, it seems. Dr Morel said otherwise they would cry. What a man! He asked me when 'his lordship' is arriving. I said we aren't sure that he is, just hoping. He said, So he believes in uncertainty, does he? Does Julian? He's a charming devil, I said. I'm sure, Dr Morel said. Never been in love, has he?

Dane has, or so he says, been in love with that conniving, social-climbing Helena, who left him for Julian in a week. Thank God. And Julian left her in two weeks. I was terrified then that I might be saddled with Helena for a daughter-in-law. How Alison laughed!

God bless Julian.

Lorna, I said I want to talk about the emotions of the past. Perhaps Julian is the emotion of the past. Who knows what an emotion really is?

I overhear the men in the billiard room often, their voices getting intense as they begin to talk about a place called the '*kota*' in Talkot. Roanna Lyndon put in her two bits as usual. 'It's a house full of dancing girls,' she said. 'All our men go there for the native women.' The ladies turned away from her, but she rattled on. 'Oh, Robbie's been there, too, and the Collector *saab*, oh, everyone! It's a brothel really. They don't call it that – they call it a *kota* so that it seems exotic instead of sordid. Men! Ask the servants.'

I don't want Dane to go there.

This place, Lorna, it's dark. I mean, slow-moving. No, I mean like the ocean bed.

Dane and Harry galloped along the river, past the people who come to the river in the morning. They went up grassy slopes and dry, rocky inclines.

'Stop,' said Harry. 'Take a look. Look down.' Dismounting, Dane stared at the mixture of rocky surfaces and grass plots, mud huts with thatched roofs, the stone points of the temple, red-brick bungalows and some whitewashed ones, patches of wooded areas and a wide, wide river that seemed to throw its protective curve around the small town of Phulgarh. 'Do you see that – there?' Harry pointed at a tiny fortress in the distance. 'That's Talkot. A castle-like palace at the centre of a lake and a small town around that.'

'And that's where she is,' laughed Dane.

'No, not in the palace. She dances at the *kota* there.'

'What's a *kota*?' No, he shouldn't be asking that. That's all they talked about at the club. The *kota* had been described to him to its last whitewashed brick. Harry looked at him, surprised. They stood there silently and looked at the shadowy rose palace.

'By the way,' said Dane, 'what's her name – the special *naach*-girl's?'

'Sakhi.'

Spurring the horses they rode back to the house. They didn't look at each other. Dane didn't feel like talking. He unbuttoned his shirt to the waist; he was hot. He could feel the horse sweating against his legs. Reaching the white wrought-iron gates, they smiled and parted.

Dane walked by the *mali*, who had opened the gates, without even noticing him. He walked slowly up the drive, crossed the veranda, the living room, and went upstairs. Jugnu came running after him. Stretching out on the bed he stared at the mosquito net. Jugnu began to pull his boots off. He honestly didn't know why he'd come to India. He came with his mother because Mama shouldn't travel alone. What was he doing here? What had he been doing in England? Looking after Ravinspur. Moving across floors to whatever music was playing. Hands he had held, faces he had kissed.

'Sakhi,' he said, 'Sakhi. What a strange name.' Jugnu started and looked up, boots in his hands.

'*Jee saab?*'

'Have you heard of Sakhi, a *naach*-girl?'

'*Zaroor saab!* Sakhi — we call her Talkot ki Shehzadi because she's the prince's *aurat* and rules his heart.'

'What is she like?'

'*Khoobsurat hai, chaku ké mafiq dilon ké tukré kar deti hai!*'

'Oooh, fill the tub with cold water.'

Like a knife, said Jugnu. She cuts like a knife. The water was pleasantly cold. Dane rested his head against the edge of the tub and closed his eyes. Jugnu prepared to shave him. Dane rubbed his chin. 'Go ahead,' he said, and motioned with his forefinger, 'shave.' Jugnu lathered Dane's face and then, very efficiently, took the stubble off stroke by swift stroke. A strange pleasure swept through Dane as the cold steel scraped his face and throat.

I wonder what Harry and Dane talk about in hushed tones sometimes. Lorna, I'm afraid Dane is going to get introduced to that *kota* soon. Shouldn't worry. He can think for himself. He can take care of himself. But I have this sick feeling inside me that something is going to overwhelm Dane. If only Julian were here and Dane could talk to him like he used to when they were boys. However much he may say that we are better off without Julian, I know he loves Julian intensely. That's why he turns away from Julian — he won't get hurt that way.

He blocks Julian from his mind and Julian blocks us. Walls, walls, walls!

Harry keeps Dane entertained. Cricket in the afternoons with officers of the Raj, with the subalterns from the Talkot cantonment. Chatting about old times in the evenings, sitting out there on the veranda. Riding in the mornings. Oh, maybe everything is all right. I worry, that's all.

Jugnu and Ravi Singh sat under the mango tree in the back yard. It was cool under the glossy leaves. 'He's always late,' Jugnu said, making a face. 'It's past two-thirty, and I have to go help *saab* dress for Collector *saab*'s party.'

'Be patient,' said Ravi Singh. He cleared his throat and spat. 'The *mali* has three children to take care of. It's difficult without a woman. More work to do. You only polish shoes and fill tubs.' Ravi Singh scratched his head and tugged at his greying hair. A lean dark figure, in a muddy *kurta*, appeared from the side of the house.

'There you are, *sala*!' Jugnu yelled. 'We've been waiting for hours! Where's the *ganja*?'

Dark fingers stuffed a conical clay pipe. Eyes closed, pulling deeply, Jugnu sighed. 'Ah! This clears my head. *Khush ho, khush ho. Mera dil-diwana*, my heart-love.' The two older men smiled and leaned their heads against the tree. '*Saab* asked about Shehzadi,' Jugnu said.

'Sakhi?' Ravi Singh sat up.

'Yes. *Shayad* he'll go to Talkot, to the *kota*. *Chhoté nawab* is in Jaipur now, so who knows what might happen?'

'*Chup sala*,' Ravi Singh growled, 'we don't need trouble.'

'Hartley *saab* is stronger than Salman. Later I can say my *saab* screwed Shehzadi in spite of Salman. I bet the Collector's *khansama* will pay to get the story from me!'

'*Hut sala*.' Ravi Singh sent Jugnu sprawling with a kick.

'*Oy chutiya!* What d'you think you're doing?'

'Go lick your *saab*'s boots, *sala*. I'll break your bones if you spread any stories at the bazaar.' Jugnu got up and dusted himself.

'Wonder where they'll fuck? *Saab* can't spend nights at the *kota* and Sakhi can't come to the bungalow . . . hmm . . . big problem . . . is there a place they could hide?' Jugnu took the pipe from the *mali* and took six long drags, holding his breath in each time till he choked. He sank down against the mango tree and closed his eyes. 'Oh, where will they do it? Think, Ravi Singh, think! This is a desperate situation!' Ravi Singh grunted and retrieved the *chillum*. 'The old temple!' Jugnu sat up. 'Ah, the old temple in the woods back there . . . oh, yes! Four times a week. She will feed him pomegranates.'

'Pomegranates?' The *mali* rubbed his eyes and frowned. 'Why pomegranates?'

'Her favourite fruit,' Jugnu snapped, 'everybody knows. Ah, how exciting things will be . . . Salman will find out . . . sword fight . . . racing horses . . . the chase . . . cliffs . . . everybody die . . . ohh . . . the grief, the passion . . . bodies . . .' His eyes grew heavy.

Dane tucked his shirt in and looked at his watch on the bed. Five to four. Where the hell was Jugnu? He fixed his tie and stared at himself in the mirror. White shirt. Everybody wore white shirts. Even the servants wore white *kurtas*. He screwed the collar studs on. Where the hell is that idiot? How could it possibly take two hours to polish a pair of shoes? He paced around the room. The Collector's tea party. Probably turn out to be a frightful bore. Going to Talkot tonight. No, I'm not. I'm backing out of it. He ran his fingers through his dark hair. Wish I could ask Julian what to do. Often wish I were able to ask Ju what to do.

Sounds of running feet, and a red-eyed, dishevelled Jugnu in an orange *kurta* burst into the room clutching a pair of black shoes to his chest.

'*Mafi saab!*' he gasped. '*Galti ho gai.*'

Dane looked at him witheringly. 'I hope this will never happen again.'

'*Nahi saab, kabhi nahi.*'

'Good. Now get out. Just a minute. Come to the Collector's bungalow at six-thirty. Don't come in, wait outside, and get two horses. Now – out. Go see if the Collector's *garhi* has arrived.'

Cucumber sandwiches, weak tea, health problems, problems with the water supply, the dissipation among the natives, the

25

fantasies of the servants about their white masters and mistresses, the dissolute life led by the subalterns at the Talkot cantonment . . . The Collector and the D.M. rambled on about the new High Court, the problem with the lighting in the billiard room. A tom-tom began pounding in Dane's head. He drew his watch out. Five-thirty. There was Mother, cornered by Dr Morel on the veranda, thoroughly amused. Dane walked away from the crowd chatting on the lawn. There was a cluster of trees at the far end. He moved into its darkness.

Dark leaves above his head. Dark grass flattened out under his feet. A strange smell, warm, damp and alive. He became aware of the noise above him. Birds were rioting with leaves. He stood there and looked up. The sun had been able to penetrate at some points. Long needles of light fell on the ground. Shreds of sky, very gold through the dark-green leaves, the sky glowed gold. Must go back now, don't want to be missed. He hurried out. Suddenly, he slipped on a muddy patch. He reached out desperately and managed to clutch something. Regaining his balance, he looked at his support. It was a creeper growing around a tree. It was very strong. He let go slowly and walked out into the lawn bright with the last rays of the sun.

Jugnu waited outside the Collector's house with impatient horses. He felt silly standing there with two horses. He moved away to the side of the house. Dropping the reins, he lit a *biri*.

So *saab* is going to Talkot. Where else? All the beautiful women were there. And Sakhi. He had seen her only once, peeping through a window while she danced. And he had been caught and beaten up. Only rich men could afford to go there. Hartley *saab* can walk right in and fling coins at her feet. Even the Collector had been there, he had heard from the District Magistrate's *khansama*.

'Where the hell is that boy?' Jugnu started. He stamped out the *biri*, grabbed the reins and hurried towards the voice. 'Here you are!' Dane took off his coat, tie and collar, and handed them to Jugnu. He slipped the pearl studs into his pocket. Harry did the same. They mounted swiftly and, kicking the horses, rode off.

They reached the *kota* shortly. Trevors stood before the gates leaning against his horse. A dark-haired young man stood next to him. As the horses were led away by two boys, Dane shook hands with Thomas Sherley.

'Lord Dane Hartley,' introduced Harry.

'Lord,' murmured Sherley, his green eyes narrowing, and rendered a mock salute.

'Join us for drinks at the mess, maybe dinner, too, later, wha'd'you say?' Trevors suggested.

Dane wrinkled his nose. A copper evening heavy with the scent of roses and horse-dung.

Jugnu entered the kitchen through the back door and cleared his throat. Meena, who was sweeping the floor, looked up. 'You!' she gasped. 'It's past midnight – where've you been? Ravi Singh went looking for you. *Memsaab* angry – you did not fill the tub at nine. Ravi Singh had to carry buckets of hot water upstairs. He'll kill you tomorrow, *harami*.'

'I was busy,' Jugnu muttered.

'Doing what?'

'Want to know what I know?' Jugnu removed the broom from her hands. 'Sit – I have a story.'

'I have work,' Meena laughed, 'go to bed.'

'*Chhoté saab*, Meena, *chhoté saab* went to the *kota*, and I followed him.'

'What!?'

'Yes! Last time I went to the *kota* I got caught and beaten up. This time I was cautious. I saw through the window, saw Sakhi dance! And she looked at my *saab* and fell madly in love, right away, like that! She looked at him as if spellbound. Their eyes met and there was magic! His indigo eyes – she's never seen eyes like that, like the rain-washed sky, free and blue! *Chhoté saab* is mad with love, too. Now they'll run away, Salman will chase them, sword fights, bloodshed, death! They'll meet in that old temple back there in the woods and —'

'*Chup, sala*, get out of here and let me finish my work. All this nonsense. *Bakwas*. Get out of here and stay out of Ravi Singh's way tomorrow.'

*   *   *

27

Dane knocked on his mother's door at two in the morning. 'What's wrong with you, d'you know what time it is?'

'I just wanted to say goo' night.' He leaned and kissed her cheek.

Back in his room, he took his clothes off and lay down on the bed. Jugnu put the clothes away and left.

Dane rubbed his eyes. The *kota* was just as they had described. Right now there was a big blur of colour in his head. He could hear the wine gurgle into his glass from the crystal decanters held by boys in brocade vests. Pistachios and those sweets wrapped in silver paper, and leaves called *'paan'* containing spices. The Indians chewed those leaves constantly. Women in silk and satin whirled over the marble floor kicking velvet purses aside, trampling over roses and coins flung at them. And the bells around their ankles ringing like rain against window panes.

Then a slender figure in white and gold walked to the centre of the dance floor. 'Sakhi,' Harry had whispered. Her hair was piled high on her head. A few wisps escaped to throw shadows on her face. Her wide, slanting eyes were lined with kohl. So dark, her eyes, almost like mud. Her skin was the colour of sandalwood. She threw a mocking salaam at the men, and with a one-sided smile snapped her fingers at the musicians. The bells around her feet were like the hush of rain.

Rain, rain, rain. There was a terrible storm and Ju went to his room. He sang with the storm. What were those songs? And she sang too. What about? There was something awful about the sound of those bells. Dane had turned away. Almost impossible to look away. It seemed men's eyes were transfixed on her, moving with her movements as if bound by a spell.

After the performance she stood there, her head flung back, as the men threw money and flowers. She walked away with slow deliberate steps. She didn't notice anybody. She didn't seem to care. He stood there, all six feet two inches of him, but she didn't notice. Why not? How could she ignore the gaze of so many eyes? Blocking all. There was hard polished hate in the slippery surface of those eyes, and disgust. Such violence in those eyes, in a woman's eyes. To cleanse all that hate from her eyes. Was there need for that hate? He didn't fling money at her. Not at her.

'I'm not going there again. No, I'm not going back there again,' he spoke out loud. He felt very tired. His eyes hurt.

'Dane! Wake up.' He was being shaken. 'Come on, man, it's noon. Get up.'

'Oh, God.' Dane clutched his head. 'Oh, God.' The sunlight forced its way into his consciousness. 'What's the matter?'

'This,' Harry said, waving a sheet of paper in front of Dane's face. 'Your mother asked me to wake you up with this.'

'What the hell is it?'

'The Earl of Ravinspur will arrive in two weeks.'

'Julian! Give that to me!' Dane snatched the letter. 'Why, this was written six weeks ago!'

'That's how long it takes the mail to arrive.'

'Let's see now — he decided to join us a week after we left. Well, um, the dogs are fine. Meet me at Delhi on . . . He's sailing from Le Havre. Can't believe it!'

'Excited?' Harry asked.

'Christ, yes.'

'Then how about going to Talkot again, eh?'

'OK, you bastard, I'll come along.' Dane buried his face in the pillow.

'Why don't you want to go there?' Harry asked.

'Don't know,' came Dane's muffled voice, 'just a funny feeling.'

With the passing weeks, Dane becomes tense and fidgety, Lorna, and I'm not so sure if it's only due to his thinking about Julian. He comes home in the early hours of the morning, mud-spattered, agitated, sometimes breathless. I hear him run up to his room and crash on the bed. Harry took him there. I know it. That place in Talkot, it's affecting Dane. In the evenings, at the club, Dane keeps looking outside, almost waiting for the darkness. I can't ask him what's wrong because it would embarrass him. I want to comfort him, tell him not to go there again. Maybe Julian will help him, maybe he'll help Julian.

As boys, Julian took such pride and pleasure in taking care of Dane. Teaching him how to swim, then cricket, of course, hunting and all that, all that trust. So close they were. I think

Julian was trying to make Dane an equal companion; but Dane wanted to adore and follow.

Dane dismounted while Jugnu held the reins. The bells pounded in his head. So many days in a row. Standing against a column, the same column every time, and shaking inside as she danced. Those lacerating bells. Must stay away. He would never go to the *kota* again.

Dr Morel and his mother were waiting. Dane muttered, 'Sorry,' and sat down for dinner. He was glad Dr Morel chatted non-stop and kept his mother entertained. What was that he said? What was Dr Morel talking about?

'. . . the present *nawab*'s great-grandfather, y'know, was obsessed with a certain *naach*-girl. Shut her up in a tower overlooking the lake. Never touched her, I believe. Would just look at her through a silver mirror. Then a doctor turned up. Had left his wife and son behind in England. The *nawab* developed some kind of a liver problem, quite common among them considering the amount of alcohol they imbibe, and our doctor was summoned to fix his majesty's liver. Well, I don't quite know how, but our romantic young doctor found out about the dancing girl. He bribed a few servants, I guess, and managed to get a glimpse of the "prisoner", and as you can expect, fell in love and got it into his head that he had to "save" her. He did. With the help of some subalterns and bribed servants he got her out of the tower and ran off with her. Nobody ever heard of them again. The *nawab* had scores of servants beheaded, then went mad with grief and anger and jumped into the lake. They fished him out but it was too late. His *begum* took care of Talkot till the young prince came of age. The interesting tangent to this story is this version, spun by the natives no doubt, that the doctor hid the dancing girl in an old temple. Now – ready for this? The ruins in the woods back there – that temple! Servants claim on full moon nights you can even see the lovers' ghosts.' Dr Morel placed his hands on his lap and looked at the countess squarely. 'Don't ask me if it's true!'

Dane blinked at Dr Morel a few times. 'Who told you that story, sir?' he asked.

'I'm not quite sure,' Dr Morel said with a laugh.

'But surely you must remember where you heard that — who told you — I mean, you must know — it's important to know where things come from!' Dane struck the table lightly with his fist.

'Where things come from, hmm.' Dr Morel watched Dane unclench his fingers. 'Where do things go — have you wondered about that ever, young man? To know where things come from, what power does that give us, really? None at all. It's where things — inside our heads — go from these germs, that's the real power. It's that place — you become a place where that germ happens and develops —' Dr. Morel stopped and reached for his wine. Dane got up and excused himself. His head was throbbing frightfully.

Dane had no idea how long he had been sitting in the dark on the Persian rug below his bed, his chin on his knees, his hands clasped around his ankles. When Jugnu had knocked on the door hours ago, 'Go away,' he said, 'don't need you.' All noises had ceased now.

He closed his eyes. It could happen now if only he let it. But he was a little afraid to let it happen. He could be lost for a long, long time. However, this was a different place where getting lost was all right. She had looked at him, he was sure. Her eyes on his face were like a stunning slap across the mouth. He had felt sick to his stomach. Even the column hard against his back had moved away for a second as he slipped on mud somewhere. The sound of the bells around her ankles cut into him. It had to happen. Julian, Julian, please help me, Julian. Yes, this is the way it is. A slight sound. The door of his room opens. A dark form enters and closes the door. Eyes as slippery as silt. She walks straight up to him. There are no bells around her ankles and no sound of rain.

In the back yard, Meena rinsed pots and pans and dishes under a running tap. Jugnu scrubbed them with coconut husk and ash. It was dark and quiet. A lantern glimmered a little away from the splattering water and fireflies pulsated among banana and mango leaves.

'Can you hear the river?' Jugnu asked.

'Hmm, sort of, because it's so quiet now.'

'I'm tired,' Jugnu said, making a face.

'Tired? How? You do nothing the whole day. Just polish shoes and fill tubs.'

'That's why I'm tired – tired of doing nothing. I've been flying kites all afternoon. Cut my finger, too, on the string. See.'

Meena laughed and shook her head. Taking the next scrubbed frying pan from Jugnu, 'This is working for *saabs*,' she said. 'Not enough work to occupy you because they hire too many servants. Anyway, it's better this way, now that my *aadmi*'s taken off with some *bazaari aurat*.'

'Don't you have any kids?'

'Had two. One died of typhoid, the other at birth.'

'Are you going to cry now?'

'Don't be silly,' said Meena rubbing her eyes.

'Be my mother,' said Jugnu, banging a pot on the cement.

'Shh, they're sleeping.'

'I want to sleep, too. Want to sleep in Shehzadi's arms. *Chud*, I'm sleepy.'

'Go sleep. I'll do the rest.'

'No – o – o. Can't sleep. It's the quarter moon up there – takes my sleep away.'

'Then go dream,' Meena said with a laugh.

Chapter 2

A slender white man leaned against the rails of the deck and looked at the land mass that stopped the Arabian Sea. The breeze ruffled his blond hair and moved it back from his forehead. A faint smile flickered in his blue-grey eyes, squeezing a little warmth into them. The smile travelled to his mouth for a second, then returned to his eyes again. He straightened up and walked along the deck sliding his left hand on the rails, never turning his face from the blue waters. He sniffed the air with a nose which had stopped short of being fully aquiline, as if a finger had touched it and made it pause suddenly. Rubbing his chin, he looked at Bombay harbour with his head flung back.

A young steward came running up to him across the deck. 'Everything is packed and ready, m'lord. I've left your beige suit in the closet. We're going into port in half an hour.'

'Thank you. Pack the suit, too. I won't be changing.' The steward blinked at the man in the open-necked violet silk shirt and pearl-grey trousers. 'That,' the man said, pointing at the shore, 'what does that smell like? Any particular taste, or smell, can you tell me? Any certain sound out there?' The steward kept his hands against his sides and looked down. 'I guess you don't understand – hmm.'

'Afraid not, m'lord.'

'Thank you.' The steward clicked his heels and retreated.

Julian Hartley, the sixth Earl of Ravinspur, smiled and began to roll up his sleeves, the late afternoon sun on his back.

Dane shifted his weight from one foot to the other. The train should have arrived an hour ago. He looked at Harry sitting on a bench and reading a paper. 'Harry, I'd better warn you now

33

– I don't know how Ju's going to react to your precious carriage.'

'Why, what's wrong with it?' asked Harry, without lifting his eyes from the paper.

'What's wrong with it? It's a bloody monstrosity!'

Dane walked further down the platform. Everything will be all right now. A different place, a change – we all need a change. Dane twisted his watch chain around his forefinger. And Sakhi – what about this dream? Impossible to stop – to stop making love in one's mind, constantly. To think, all the time. Not to make love was torture, to make love, crucifixion. To think in those words . . . A giggle escaped him like a burp. Dane started. Why did he do that suddenly? Where did that giggle come from? Don't think.

But now what – with Julian here? Are we going to take Ju to the *kota*? Why do women run after Julian? Something dangerous in his face, said Helena. No, not possible; Julian was too weak.

'Hey, Dane, here comes the train,' Harry yelled. 'Are you dreaming or what?'

The train screeched to a stop and the squeal of the whistle faded. Delhi Station was galvanised into action. Dane and Harry rushed towards the first-class compartments. Where was Julian? They looked around. What to say to Julian, what to say to him?

'Dane.' A mildly hoarse voice. There he stood, at the door of a coach, a wolf-grin on his face.

'Julian!' Dane ran up. 'Christ, you're brown!' They stood looking at each other. Dane took in his collarless shirt and ruffled hair. Whyever were they staring at each other like two dummies? 'Hello, Ju.'

'Hello, Dane.' Their hands met. With one swift tug Dane pulled his brother off the train. Julian sprang back laughing.

'Come on, let's get your stuff. And here's Harry.'

'Why, hello, Winston. Didn't know you were here.' Harry had been quietly watching the two brothers. He stepped forward awkwardly.

The mid-October sun was warm on their faces as they walked towards Harry's carriage. Harry hurried the coolies on to organise the suitcases. 'What's this?' Julian growled.

'This is what we're going to travel in.' Dane suppressed a smile.

'You must be out of your mind. Winston – were you totally marinated when you got this?' Julian stuck his head inside and reeled back.

'Shh – he designed it.'

'Why, I'll have to keep my eye-balls in my pocket! So how many hours inside this bloody inferno?'

'Six.'

'You don't say!' Julian grabbed Harry by the lapels. 'Need your tie, old chap.' He zipped off Harry's black tie. Stretching out lengthwise on one seat, he handed the tie to Dane. 'Blindfold me, love, mine eyes dazzle.' Harry crossed his legs and lit a cigarette. 'Winston, darling, you must burn this thing as soon as we reach Phulgarh, or else eternal damnation in a pit of rotting caviar. If this isn't violating the eleventh one —'

'Shut up, Julian. Want to walk to Phulgarh?'

'Aw, sweetheart, don't start on me now. I'm awfully grateful, Winston, really.' Julian lifted the tie over one eye and, leaning, patted Harry's knee. 'The colour scheme's heartrending, that's all.' Covering his eyes again, he leaned back against the cushions and, in a very low voice, began to sing 'Abide with me'.

And this is how the Earl of Ravinspur travelled to Phulgarh.

It was almost dark when they entered Phulgarh the next day. 'We're here,' said Dane, shaking a sleeping Julian. Julian stretched and yawned. Looking out of the window, he saw the river. He rubbed his eyes.

'Hey, just stop this thing. I want to get out.'

'Why?'

'I'll walk. How far's the house?'

'Walk?'

'I am not entering any populated area looking like a member of a medieval tumbler's company.' Julian jumped out of the carriage that had slowed down.

'Ju – wait!'

'Which way?'

'Harry, I'm so sorry —' Dane looked at his friend and tried to smile.

'Get out of here, you bastards.' Harry picked up his tie and wrapped it around his hand.

'Julian, you're obnoxious,' said Dane stepping out.

'I know,' Julian said. Harry's carriage rolled away from them.

'Don't you care about his feelings?'

'Wasn't aware he had any. Never showed any signs.'

'He had that thing – I mean, the carriage – made specially for us.'

'OK, OK, I'll grovel at dinner.'

They walked by the Yamuna. A few children splashed in the water. They walked between cultivated plots, through the crowded bazaar, and reached the temple. 'They're having their daily *puja*,' said Dane.

'God, it's like a country fair.' They walked over crushed garlands and flowers. 'So different, the smell.'

'Incense,' Dane said.

'And flowers and food and people and manure and mud. Is the sky so copper in the evenings?'

'Yes.' They moved through people, cows, dogs. Suddenly a strong gust of wind slapped against their faces. They looked up with all the rest. Dark clouds were moving in swiftly. 'Can't believe this,' Dane said, 'the rains are supposed to be over. Let's walk fast, Ju.' The storm caught them a quarter of a mile from the bungalow.

'It's absolutely fantastic!' Julian yelled with the thunder.

'Let's run.'

'Oh, God.' Julian stood still and raised his face to the whipping rain.

'Are you out of your mind?'

'You bet I am.' A wave of lightning flooded Julian's eyes.

'Let's run, you ass.' Dane grabbed his brother's shoulder. 'Let's run.'

'Look at those clouds – like melting granite.' Julian stumbled as Dane dragged him away.

They ran across the veranda. Ravi Singh and Jugnu stood with the door open. Dane stumbled in dripping mud and water. Harry looked at them smugly.

His shirt clinging to his skin, framed by the night, Julian

stood panting at the door. He swept his wet hair back and wiped his face with his hand. 'How are you, Caroline?'

'Julian.' She came forward and kissed his wet cheek.

'You are as beautiful as ever,' he said, taking her hand.

The fresh damp smell of the night curled around them as they stood on the balcony outside Julian's room after dinner. It had stopped raining. 'Nice balcony.' Julian lit a cigarette. 'Want one?' Dane picked out a cigarette from the proffered silver case.

'Do you like the room?'

'Yes.'

'I'm glad,' muttered Dane.

'I hope things are all right, now,' said Julian with a smile. 'I think I've massaged Harry's ego enough. I do hope he is pacified.'

'He is.'

'Well —' Julian cleared his throat.

'Well what?'

'How've you been, Dane?'

'Fine.'

'You could look at me when I talk to you.'

'You've been away for a long time.'

'So?'

'Mother's worried about you.'

'We are all together now.'

'For how long?'

'I don't know.'

'George Devereux saw you in Paris; you were singing.'

'Was I?'

'That's what he said.'

'Maybe.'

'Ju?' Dane turned and looked at his brother. He reached and gripped Julian's shoulder, his eyes narrowing. As he felt Julian's frail body wince under the hard pressure of his fingers, an odd tenderness coursed through him. He relaxed his hold. 'You must be tired,' said Dane softly. 'Go to bed.'

Julian lay in bed, his hands under his head, and stared at the mosquito net above. Incense, mud, trampled marigolds,

37

copper sky, now, wet, wet, wet, fresh wet white dust, even cows, goats, dogs, and children; then *'saab* this, *saab* that,' Julian, dear, good lord! What the hell is this? Your lordship, said the steward. A light laugh escaped Julian. And what stamp from this different-smelling country? 'Now don't be silly, your lordship,' Julian said out loud. His eyes grew heavy.

What do I say to Julian after so long a time? We've never been all together this way before. You know, Lorna, what I really want to ask him is why he came at all. There was no earthly reason for Julian to come to India. Curiosity can't be reason enough. Has he left behind some awful mess in Paris? I've never known Dane to be so tense. At dinner he hardly ever took his eyes off his plate. If Dane doesn't relax and treat Julian like a normal person Julian's going to shut us out for ever. It's as if Dane is expecting something awful to happen. I want to scream, stop it, Dane! Don't look at Julian that way, with eyes full of fear and distrust. Doesn't matter what's happened before; that was before. Let's forget, start over, start by trusting and reaching out.

Now I have to plan what to say to Julian tomorrow or else I will end up talking about the weather and he about nothing. I don't want to ask him anything. I want him to talk and say whatever he wants. I just want to draw him out covertly with a subtle bait, so that he opens up, lets his guard down and realises that we are not interrogators but friends, family, people who love him.

Let us establish touch.

The early morning sun flooded the bathroom. Dane lay in the tub with his eyes closed as Jugnu shaved him. Julian, with a towel wrapped around his waist, sat on a stool and lathered his face. On a small table in front of him lay a razor, a mirror, a mug of water and shaving soap.

Dane opened his eyes and looked at his brother's profile. 'Why the hell won't you let him shave you?' Dane asked.

'Prefer doing it myself, that's all.' Julian picked up the razor and began to clear his face with long, swift strokes.

Dane bit his lip. What to say to Julian after so many years?

He sits there and shaves my words off. What a silly scene on the balcony last night. Why do I bring up things that are over and lost? Why won't questions go out of my mind? Why ask when Julian never answers?

'Go and get dressed and chat with Mother,' Dane said as Julian left the bathroom.

Standing in front of the dresser in his room, Dane combed his wet hair and frowned at himself in the mirror. On the altar of the old temple ghosts appeared, said Dr Morel. On that altar – that's where they should be, he and Sakhi. They would be . . . lost . . . nothing can help us. But we can be. Nothing can stop us.

Julian bit into a piece of toast spread with honey. Caroline put her empty cup down on the glass-topped table in front of her. It was nice – breakfast out on the veranda. The mornings were pleasantly warm. Conversation had come to a standstill. Weather and health had been exhausted and had produced only nods and grunts. Dane was looking at the food intensely again as if it was going to jump up and bite him.

'Are you two going to the club?' she asked, smiling.

'I think I'm going to take a walk and look around. I'll probably join Dane at the club later.'

'I'm planning to go to Agra soon.'

'I'm sure you'll have a wonderful time.'

'Do you remember the Cartwrights?'

'Vaguely,' mumbled Julian with his mouth full.

'They tried to throw Sarah and you together after you returned from Greece.'

'Oh, yes, I remember. That simpering little bitch.'

'Julian!'

'Sorry. Didn't mean to offend your sensibilities – but that's exactly what she was, and is, I'm sure.'

'Well – anyway, the Cartwrights are in Delhi. Sheila wrote to me a few days ago. They're going to Agra and inquired if I'd like to join them. Sheila might even come to visit. She knows Mrs Bancroft quite well.'

'Julian, you could come and play cricket,' said Dane.

'Cricket, hmm, haven't touched a bat for nearly a decade. I'll join you at the club later. I want to explore a little. Want to take a look at the woods back there. I believe there's a ruin of some sort – a temple or something.'

'Oh – er – the horses —'

'I rather like walking.'

'Whatever you wish.'

'What are you doing today, Caroline?' Julian asked.

'Having lunch with Mrs Bancroft and Dr Morel.'

'I see. There's something I'm a little curious about,' Julian said after a slight pause. 'You said last night that you bought this house from the *nawab*. Will you be selling it back to him when you leave India? Or will this remain as our personal imperial token on this soil?' The sugar cubes landed with a splash into Caroline's coffee from the tongs she held. Dane gaped. 'Never mind,' Julian said with a wave of his hand and went inside.

Jugnu ran through the woods stumbling over twigs, stones, avoiding branches. Reaching the ruins of the temple he ran inside and threw himself on the stone altar. Four pomegranates rolled out of his clothes. He sat up, broke them open and ate two of them slowly. Wiping his mouth and hands, which were sticky and stained purple, he said, 'Shehzadi.' This is where everything would happen, he knew. And he had a story to tell – his story.

Julian stood in the middle of the back yard and looked around. A mango tree – Dane had pointed it out. And banana trees. Servants' quarters. A low brick wall. And beyond, trees and bushes, and tall bamboo groves. He crossed over the low wall elegantly without acquiring any smudges on his cream trousers. It was cooler in here and very green. He breathed in deeply. He liked the smell, the smell of untrampled grass and leaves. With swift strides he moved through the woods. At some points, the sun touched him suddenly, setting his blond hair aflame, and making his olive silk shirt flash.

There was no set path. He had to make his way dodging branches. The grey and brown broken stones of the temple rose from the green. He walked up to the steps of the temple. It wasn't dark inside. The roof was partially shattered. The sun splashed the raised altar; it washed the broken statues, the columns, and the alcove – the empty space – where a god had stood once, stood stone-cold, frozen in some pose of ecstasy now lost. Julian walked into the temple slowly. He stepped up on the altar and entered that sun-flooded emptiness. Pomegranates lay at his feet. Why were they there? He didn't feel the need to ask. They seemed to be part of the altar. He stood there and looked up at the light. It nearly blinded him. And it filled him with an overwhelming warmth. Yet left him craving. He stood there loving the feeling till it frightened him. He leaped off the altar and ran out.

Tired. Nikhil sat down heavily on an overturned basket next to the fruit stall. 'Don't ruin my baskets,' growled the stall owner. Cows and goats nosed around mounds of cabbages, cauliflowers, potatoes, onions, aubergines, tomatoes, lemons. Dogs snarled at each other near meat stalls where chickens were being neatly beheaded and plucked, skinned goats chopped and sliced. Trampled blood, flowers, peels, leaves smeared the white dust.

'I'm tired,' Nikhil said.

'Get up and rearrange the bananas.'

'These ones here are rotting,' said Nikhil after inspecting the bananas.

'Never mind – just place them under the good ones.'

After organising the bananas, Nikhil moved to the grape section and began to fiddle with them, eating them covertly and smiling to himself. He waved away a few flies, then went back to the basket and sat down again. Heera Lal, the stall owner, placed two marigolds at the feet of an elephant-headed deity that squatted on the rattan shelf behind the rows of fruit. Then he folded his hands and touched the edge of the shelf with his forehead.

Nikhil looked over the stalls towards the river. Couldn't see it, but you could hear it. Warmed by the sun, so bright now. Your different light. Where the light of water? What am I doing here in this bazaar? To be at the temple, to look at you and dream.

'*Sahib, dekh sahib.*' Nikhil turned at the sound of whispers all around him.

*   *   *

41

Julian had no idea how long he had been walking. The woods seemed far away now, and the bazaar spread out loud and colourful around him. Fruits and vegetables, bangles, birds, flowers, roasting corn and peanuts, cows, goats, dogs and people jostled one another in his senses. He became aware of the startled glances. Hot and thirsty, he wiped beads of sweat off his forehead and pushed his tousled hair back. He felt something shove him forward; he stumbled sideways out of the way of the force and collided with a fruit stall, overturning rows and rows of apples, grapes, bananas, grapefruits, melons. A lumbering cow pressed him further into the fruits and pushed its way out. Rough and brown hands extracted Julian out of the mess. He dusted himself and removed a few squashed grapes from his behind. He felt silly. Pulling out his wallet he offered the stall owner some money for the damages. The man waved the money aside, picked up a bunch of undamaged grapes and thrust them into Julian's hands and smiled. 'Oh, er, thanks.' He pressed the money into the other man's hand. 'Please.' He turned to go and bumped into a goat. 'What the —' Two hands caught him and prevented him from falling again. Julian turned and looked at his saviour. A pale, thin young man stared at him oddly. Slowly, he released his grip on the earl. 'Thank you,' Julian said, and tried to smile.

He moved to a less crowded region. Clothes hung in these stalls. He went forward and felt the fabric with his fingers. Soft cotton. Long, loose shirts. No cuffs, no collars. Narrow trousers, cut like pyjamas. He looked inquiringly at the boy standing next to the stall. '*Kurta*-pyjama, *saab*,' the boy informed him. Somehow, the outfit struck Julian's fancy. 'The white one,' he pointed. The boy looked him up and down, climbed into the stall, rummaged among the clothes and came out with a set. He held the long shirt up. '*Kurta*,' he said. Julian took it from him and held it against himself. Should fit. The boy held the narrow pants against Julian's waist to check the size.

'Yes, that's all right,' smiled Julian.

'Pyjama,' said the boy.

'How much?' The boy smiled cheekily and put up several fingers.

'Oh, no.' Julian put up half as many. A look of shock spread over the boy's face. Smiling grimly, Julian pressed the money in his palm, took the clothes, rolled them up and walked away. He knew he had overpaid all the same.

He was almost out of the bazaar. Only peanut sellers sat roasting the nuts out here, and old men and young boys sat wrapping spices in large green leaves. He walked past them. They stared at him. Never had a *sahib* walked through the bazaar. They whispered and giggled among themselves. Leaning against a tree, Julian began to eat the grapes. Must get to the club now. He pulled his watch out of his trouser pocket. Twelve-fifteen. Have to find a *garhi*. His eyes searched the area. A group of children attracted his attention. What were they crowding around? He walked into their midst. An old man sat within the ring of small excited forms, playing a flute. The sound touched Julian. Strange, piping melody. Dark fingers moved up and down the body of the flute while the old man blew into it gently, his eyes closed. The flute rested against his lips sideways. Julian watched fascinated. He had never heard a flute produce such sounds. He had never seen a bamboo flute before, pale yellow.

His shoulder against the neem tree, Nikhil held his breath. The old woman roasting corn under the tree looked up and smiled. 'Want one?' she asked, turning the corns over on the charcoal.

'Be quiet,' Nikhil said.

'Listening to the old man play, *chhokré*?'

'No.' Nikhil covered his face.

Dane tried to concentrate on the young man in white in the middle of the cricket pitch. He was fiddling with his gloves and talking to the other batsman. Harry nudged him with his elbow. 'Why don't you want to go to the *kota*? What's the matter? Didn't you like the show?'

'What are these women like?' asked Dane.

'Well, find out for yourself!'

'That's not what I meant. I don't quite understand what's going on. Why do we have to go there? I don't like the way those women look at us.'

'Ah, the lust in their eyes!'

'Hardly. All I saw was disgust.'

43

'What's got into you? Knock a few wickets off after lunch, that'll clear your head.'

'Hear, hear.' Julian stood behind them.

'How long have you been standing there?' Dane snapped.

'Just walked in. I'm awfully hungry; can we have lunch now?'

'Uh, yes. Where've you been, Julian?'

The young men who had been playing all morning entered the pavilion laughing and chatting, with bats under their arms, and wickets and bails. 'Joining us after lunch, Hartley?' inquired one of the men.

'Yes,' said Dane. 'Meet my brother, Rowley. Julian, Peter Rowley. And Cyril Trevors . . .' Dane rattled off names, and the men walked up and shook hands. 'Thomas Sherley.'

'Ah, the earl himself', said Sherley. 'I've heard about your classic cover-drives. I'm a fast spinner.' Julian looked at the young man blankly.

The large circular dining area of the Phulgarh Club had antelope heads on the cream walls, together with sketches of the royal family, and of horses, partridges, mongooses and Lord Curzon at the Durbar. Square tables, seating four, with lime-green tablecloths, took up most of the space. Tall, square, black porcelain vases with tiger-lilies stood at the centre of each table. Bearers moved around with silver and rosewood trays, serving mulligatawny, then curried sole with rice, peas sautéed with onions, and peaches in brandy for dessert. Sherley shook his head at the offered peaches. The bearer walked away.

'You look a little under the weather, Tom,' Trevors said, looking at his friend.

'I'm fine.'

'I'm thinking of going to the *kota* tonight,' Trevors said in a low voice, 'Rowley wants to go. Want to come —'

'Cyril, please, I just don't feel like talking right now —' Sherley looked at his napkin. Trevors, familiar with his friend's moodiness, made a face and turned to his peaches.

Dane, Harry, Julian and Robert Lyndon, the District Magistrate, sat at a table six yards away. Sherley could see Julian's profile. He was laughing – what on earth could that ass,

Lyndon, say to make him laugh? So finely etched the face, and those hands, so —

'*Saab*?' A bearer offered those peaches again.

'No! Don't want!'

'Tom!' Trevors glanced around catching raised eyebrows.

'Heavens!' said the D.M. and blinked twice. Julian turned his head and met the green eyes which refused to look away.

After lunch, they relaxed for half an hour. Then they fixed the wickets and resumed the game. And Julian did get a chance to display his classic cover-drives, his leg-glances, his square-cuts, and pulls and hooks. In fact, he cut, drove, pulled, swept Sherley for twelve fours and hooked Dane for a six. He remained at the crease for two elegant hours till a vicious yorker from Dane uprooted his middle stump. They clapped as he walked away. And Sherley watched Julian smile, pause, whip his cap off and bow. That bow – that old pride that coursed through a cricketer when playing on alien lands; his memories raced back to the green fields of his college where he batted, surrounded by a cheering crowd. So agonising to watch. He had been spurned, Sherley felt. That bow, mocking, to be sure, a sneer for all his balls slammed and swept to the boundary. And later, their eyes had met and understood the weakness of one. Sherley ran back inside, asked for his horse to be brought around and rode back to the Talkot cantonment.

On the veranda after dinner, Dane leaned back and closed his eyes. Julian cutting the air with his bat. His mother chatted on about her day with Mrs Bancroft and Dr Morel. She would be going to Agra soon. The Cartwrights might come to Phulgarh. Everything is going to be all right, now. I'll tell Ju about Sakhi. We'll take him to the *kota*. He likes different things. Well, maybe I won't tell him about Sakhi. No need, really. He felt a little confused, but happy. Cricket always helps. You get together. Funny, all the times they had played together, cricket, tennis, or even fished, hunted, swam, things were fine, Julian laughing, zany and outrageous. But every time he tried to talk to Julian, about love, or just about each other, Julian became cold and remote, impervious. But anyway, cricket had brought them together again, hadn't it, this afternoon? Harry was a bad runner. Move your arse, Winston! he could hear Julian shouting, move your bloody arse. Harry, slightly overweight, puffing up and down the pitch. Dane began to laugh softly.

Julian turned and looked at his brother.

'I was thinking of Harry trying to match your pace and you shouting at him. Poor Harry, you yelling at him, and he's scared of short-pitched balls, too! And I didn't spare him, not once!' Dane laughed. Julian laughed and stood up.

'What was that Harry said about clearing your head?' he asked.

'Don't remember,' said Dane.

Julian stood on the balcony and watched the fireflies. The darkness shot with the fragrance of alien flowers and with the warmth of the grass and earth drew him into its element. The flutetones played again in his mind. Disturbing, somehow. He wanted to block the sound. But something inside him wanted to drown in its waves.

The sounds that came through that slender bamboo flute filled up something. Large empty soundless rooms of a year long, long ago, maybe. Tunes that were never tunes in his head but colours he saw when he closed his eyes. He had never heard such melodies but only felt them as he wandered through long dark hallways way back when . . . That terrible year filled with stories of unicorns and knights and dragons, princesses falling off unicorns. Toes lightly touching the still green lake of Ravinspur. And now, all of a sudden, that almost forgotten unheard sound was a sound and not just colours and something swelling up under your feet, oh, God, a sound, flutetones. Why? To get away from it before it takes over. If it filled that emptiness, then what? Empty altar filled with sunlight. Just standing there and waiting. Pausing under the rich gleam of doorways and looking up.

It hurt, that sound. It forced its way in, into that place which was now a memory. To drag that sound out of his mind somehow.

Soft footsteps made him look down.

A figure moving through the darkness. Dane! Where was he going now? It was nearly midnight. He saw his brother vanish round the side of the house. Smiling, he went back to his room.

What I remember most about that year, Lorna, is Julian wandering from room to room, through corridors. The servants said Master Julian has been doing that for a year now. Nobody knew why. I wonder if you ever saw him do that? The little blond boy would stop suddenly between rooms, at the door, and look up at the woodwork, then almost reluctantly move on. Julian under doorways as if on an altar with an arch overhead. Funny, I write altar. Must be because there are temples all around! But I always felt that Julian was looking for the support of frames the way he would lean his head against a door. Oh, I don't know. Sometimes he seemed to be concentrating on something as he stood at a door, an image, a sound? Only that year. After Dane was born, Dane's cries filled Ravinspur. Yes, we were happy that year.

The ruins of the temple stood before Dane, silent and dark. He went up the broken steps. The altar glowed with moonlight. A full moon was a few days away. He went in and sat down on the edge of the altar. Something was tearing inside him. He lay down and shut his eyes to block the moonlight. His head brushed against something. He turned. Pomegranates. He closed his eyes again placing his face against the pomegranates.

Jugnu moved in softly. He had been waiting a long, long time behind the bushes. He crawled up the side of the steps and peeped in. There he was. She would come, too, surely. Did she love this *saab*, though? No, she never loved anyone. She danced. But there she would be in his arms. Jugnu crawled away from the temple. He felt he had witnessed it all.

Dane and Harry pointed Talkot out to Julian a few days later while riding. 'What's there?' Julian asked.
   'Entertainment,' said Harry. Dane kept quiet. Nights on the altar of an abandoned temple. He was beginning to sense the unreality of the whole situation. What was he moving towards? He couldn't tell Julian. Julian would laugh; wouldn't

listen, wouldn't want to understand. He never listened. Pushing away always. How to make him hear? To grab his shoulders, shake him, force and dislocate this indifference. He looked at his brother holding the horse between his legs, almost one with the animal.

'Good horses,' said Julian as Dane stared at Talkot in the distance. Julian took in the wistfulness in his brother's eyes. To touch him now, just once, a light pat on the hand. Why rekindle trust? Trust didn't exist any more. 'Let's go to the temple in the evening,' suggested Julian. 'I want to see their *puja* again.' And they went to the temple near the bazaar where the people quarrelled and laughed and cried and talked. They heard the bells, felt the heat, breathed in the dust and the incense, trampled over flowers like all the rest. Julian saw the priest throw flowers at the god's feet. An indigo god standing with his ankles crossed, playing a gold flute. Lamps danced around him, held up by demanding hands. There was a strange ecstasy somewhere. The darkness, the light, the slim blue figure, the flute, the bells, the flowers, the prayers, the people, the voices. And there is silence, too, thought Julian. The noise could not reach that blue form out there. The god was lost in the music.

People moved in circles over the polished floor of the club. Julian led his stepmother to the floor. 'Go and dance with one of those poor girls over there.'

'What on earth for? I'm dancing with the most beautiful woman in this room, and I am quite happy,' he said with a wolf-grin. Later, he joined Harry and Dane in the billiard room, and spent half an hour there.

'Stay,' Dane said, as Julian moved towards the door, 'stay for one more game, please.'

'Aw, shut up,' he said, 'it's so godawful boring, ugh, stifling, this place.'

Men came up and shook hands. 'You went to Turkey, I believe,' grunted an old colonel at him. 'Must have felt pretty odd among those savages, eh?'

'Will you be going down to Calcutta to meet Lord Curzon?' The Collector cornered him.

The police superintendent moved in next. 'I heard you've

been going for walks at night. Be careful – these natives can get out of hand sometimes.'

'Lord Ravinspur,' cooed the District Magistrate's wife from the back, 'we should organise a real cricket match soon. We could play against the men at Talkot. And we'd be sure to win with you opening for us!'

'That's him – Ravinspur!' 'Your lordship . . . ' 'Oh, the sixth earl!' Julian felt his white suit freeze around him. He winced and tried to stretch his shoulders. He gulped down two glasses of whisky and slipped out of the club.

Stepping into the night, he loosened his tie and unbuttoned his collar. With long strides he moved towards their bungalow. Pausing for a moment, he lit a cigarette. A comfortable taste between his lips. What would the flute taste like against the mouth? Cigarette between his lips, hands in his pockets, the thin white earl looked up. There was a dazzling moon up there beyond the thick dark leaves of banyan trees. Night ought to be darker, much darker, really. A silly blue-bright moon-dazzle night. He walked rapidly, without a break, till he reached the house. Night stuck in his throat.

Ravi Singh came running to the door and let Julian in. He followed Julian up the stairs and waited while his master ripped his clothes off. Then he put the clothes away and left. Julian opened the french windows and stepped on to the semi-circular balcony. Savage bright was the moon. He could almost feel the light. The silver caressed his body.

The *mali* and Ravi Singh sat in a corner of the lawn. 'Play, play,' said Ravi Singh. 'It soothes the soul.' The *mali* picked up his flute.

Julian tried to shut his ears. That sound again. He wanted to return to his room, close the doors and windows, bury his face in his pillow and fall asleep. But he stood there on the balcony, shaking, his eyes closed tight. Stop it, he wanted to shout. His lips moved soundlessly. Kneeling, he gripped the rails and shook his head slowly, trying to shake the music off. 'Stop it, for godsake, stop it,' he said, opening his eyes. The shock of

49

moonlight made his head reel. He tried to cover his body with his arms, but the moonlight was all over him. He felt washed by flames of light and music. In his veins an intensity imploding; silver-blue cloudbursts blowing up. He found it difficult to breathe. He wanted his heart to pause and start again and beat like before. How did the music enter his pulse and change its rhythm?

Somehow Julian raised himself and stumbled back to his room. The moonlight had entered through the windows and found the bed. He strained against the flutetones that twisted around him. 'Oh, God, stop it, stop it!' He flung himself on his bed. Racked with violent sobs, his slender body convulsed into postures of agony.

Chapter 3

The riot of birds outside woke Julian up. He went to the bathroom and splashed water on his face. Sitting on his bed, a few minutes later, he looked at his feet. He felt tired; his head throbbed.

He took out the clothes he had bought at the bazaar and slipped into them. Loose, white cotton. Rummaging among his footwear, he found a pair of leather-thonged sandals. He went down the stairs as quietly as he could.

Walking through the woods behind the house, Julian looked at the vibrant greenery moist with dew and rubbed his forehead to reduce the throbbing in his head. Why had he come to this country? Because Caroline pleaded? Your father liked India. You've been all over the world, so why not see India? He had never had any preconceptions about this part of the world. He had thought about elephants. Tired of the past. Perhaps that's why he'd come. Tired of its intrusions. And the flute intruded, too. Julian pressed his temples with his fingers and closed his eyes. The god in the temple playing the flute. The woods whistled as the wind moved through the bamboo groves.

Restless, and always running. Stumbling through the green woods of Ravinspur. Rushing through those white gates year after year. For some stillness – like the indigo god frozen with his flute. Like the fabulous storms outside the windows of Ravinspur, a vortex of silence around the flute. Another storm and then there will be calm. Would Ravinspur be quieter than this strange land with its sound? That raging, slicing sound.

Julian paused at the temple gates. The wooden gates were wide open and the courtyard was sprinkled with white dust and pale yellow neem pods. The grey stone temple rose from the centre, square, surrounded by slender carved columns. Julian left his sandals at the gate and went up the steps. A terrace with a low parapet lay before him. He saw the river on the left, a shaft of light under the just-risen sun.

From the dazzling waters, Julian turned his eyes and looked up. The temple was crowned with four intricately carved cones. Under the cones was that dimly lit columned recess with the stone altar and the god in the alcove. So different from the broken, bare temple in the woods. He crossed the terrace and reached the inner recess. Putting an arm around a column, he pressed his cheek against its coolness. It was dark inside, but he could see the dark blue god with his flute. Does he have a name – the fluteplayer?

Another figure entered the inner recess from within the temple carrying a metal plate heaped with flowers. A pale yellow *sari*. She knelt and set the plate on the floor, and began to spread some of the flowers around the statue. Then she sat down and started to make garlands. Julian couldn't take his eyes off her hands, her hands among the flowers, all mixed together, belonging together. One by one she lifted the flowers – gul-mohr, champak, frangipani, jasmine, marigold – and passed a long stringed grass through the heart of each so gently and slowly as if afraid to hurt them. She raised the flowers and held them as if holding water. Her hands and flowers, they touched the turmoil in his heart and caressed it as they caressed each other. He sank down on his knees. He sat there loving the peace for nearly half an hour. Unaware of his presence, she placed the garlands on the plate, rose and left quietly.

White dust blowing in little swirls on the road. The road to the temple, the road from the temple. Far from the temple now. Hands and flowers. The fingers among petals. A flute playing silently. Broken stones in the woods. And the sunlight that filled up the altar seemed to call and want some other's presence.

Green fields and a white road. The bazaar left behind. The temple – can't see it any more. God, it's hot! All that had happened before – a pastiche of arms and legs, floors, wheels, waves, flying wickets and bails. Fights. Somewhere, a guitar, a mandolin, voices. To be away from all that, from all those voices. Say it's not true, Julian. Don't leave – stay, stay, stay. Ravinspur. A lake, four Irish setters, a boat. A funeral. No, two. Death, but no end. Shut it out, all of it. Don't think. God, it's hot.

The river lay in front of him, its body burnished by the sun. He had walked an age. Julian left his sandals on the dry mud of the bank and walked into the water. And the Yamuna received him, opening wide and gentle. He went in deeper and deeper, stretching and rolling on the river's body, drawing the waters around him with long, slow strokes, and lay on her surface, half-submerged. Julian laughed softly and looked up at the sky glazed white with the sun. The river beneath his head laughed with him. The Yamuna shattered around him, flashing up in sparks and breaking on his body. He felt for the hardness underneath and stood up choking, happy, shaking the river from his eyes and hair. Standing waist-deep in the water, he closed his eyes and raised his face to the warmth of the sun. Lifting his hands he swept his wet hair back.

A beautiful, wet, gold god, thought Nikhil standing on the river bank. A god just born of the river, leaving the water now, coming to meet the land.

Under his feet sand and mud shifted as Julian neared the shore. The branches of a tree leaned over the water. He reached out for a branch. Something caught his hand and made him start. A pair of smiling brown eyes. Where had he seen this face before?

'I was at the bazaar the other day when you were knocked down by the cow,' said the apparition, letting go of his hand. 'The goat, do you remember? You would have fallen again.' Julian stepped on to damp grass and slipped into his sandals. 'You'll need dry clothes now. Why didn't you take your clothes off if you were going to swim?'

'I didn't know I was going to swim. I sort of walked into the river. But I feel wonderful now, nice and cool.'

'You're a stranger here.'

'Yes, I arrived last week.'

'You're not working for the Raj?'

'No.'

'I thought as much. You don't look it.'

'I'm Julian, Julian Hartley,' the earl said, laughing, 'I'm sure I don't look a lot of things!'

'I'm Nikhil.'

'What are you doing here?'

'I was at the temple. I saw you there. I followed you.'

'What! Why?'

'I don't know; you seemed different, unreal. When you went into the river I thought you were going to vanish. You seemed to belong to another world.'

'I am from another world,' Julian smiled.

'Yes, indeed you are,' Nikhil said with a laugh, 'are you sure you don't want fresh clothes? I could get you some.'

'Oh, no, I'm fine.'

'We could go to the bazaar and get new ones.'

'No, I'm all right. I don't need clothes, I need food; I'm ravenous.'

'Let's go and eat then. Come on.'

'I don't want to go to the bazaar.'

'I'm not taking you to the bazaar.'

They walked away from the river, away from the bazaar, and reached a shack with a tin roof. An old man sat inside before a huge kettle that spouted steam in the corner of the shack. It sat on a bucket-shaped stove. In front of the old man stood jars of strange candy and biscuits, and fruits in a basket. Outside, four long wooden benches were arranged in rows and on the left of the shack large, flat rocks stretched into a rocky terrain.

'*Naresh chacha*,' called out Nikhil as he walked up to the man, 'we want *chai* and *nashta*.' Julian stood near the rocks and waited. Two men sat on a bench and smoked thin, brown cigarettes. They stared at him briefly. In a few minutes Nikhil returned carrying two clay cups of steaming tea. 'Here, drink this. Not your weak English tea.' He went away again and came back with bananas, apples and some thin brown pancakes.

'What are these?'

'*Roti*,' said Nikhil, 'like bread.' Butter made little pools on them.

'This tea is pretty, er, rich.'

'Yes, it's spiced with basil, ginger and other stuff.' They sat on a rock sipping the hot, sweet tea and eating the fruits and the 'bread'.

Julian tried to veil the curiosity in his eyes as he looked at Nikhil. Fine-boned, very thin. A striking face. 'You're not dark like most other Indians, and how come you speak English so well?'

'I grew up in a *sahib*'s house. I'm a Kashmiri, probably. They are fair-skinned, even blue-eyed sometimes. Aryan descent.'

'What d'you mean, you're a Kashmiri "probably"?'

'Mr Wakeley found me on his doorstep. Mr Wakeley was a schoolteacher in Srinagar. He was nearly forty-five when he got married. They didn't have any children at that time, so they happily took me in.'

'And you were brought up by them?'

'Yes.'

'Why are you here now?'

'Long story, and not a very pleasant one, I'm afraid.'

'You learnt English there?'

'Yes. Shakespeare, Donne, Bacon, Byron.'

'Anything else?' Julian laughed.

'Ah, Vasari, Plutarch, the classics, and of course the Bible.'

'My word, you're a pretty formidable scholar!'

'You must have read all that too, and probably much more,' said Nikhil.

'Well, er, not very much more.'

'Were you at Oxford?'

'No, Cambridge, and at Winchester before that.'

'And after all that?'

'The Continent, and other parts of the world.'

'And now India.' Nikhil smiled and cocked his head to one side.

'Yes, now India.'

'Why are you here?'

'My stepmother and half-brother are here. We're sort of travelling.'

'Checking out one of the imperial strongholds?'

'No. Not really.'

'Then?'

'Just came to see the country.'

'But not the people,' said Nikhil.

'I'm not sure why I have come,' Julian said looking at his tea cup.

'Why did you go to the temple?'

'I guess I just wanted to see.' Julian looked away.

'What?'

'I don't know; the fluteplayer, I think.'

'The fluteplayer?'

'I mean the figure, the god or whatever, the dark blue statue.'

'Krishna.'

'Krishna?'

'That's Krishna – your fluteplayer!'

'I didn't mean to offend you, I'm sorry. I just gave him a sort of a nickname.'

'I'm not offended at all. I rather like the sobriquet, the fluteplayer. He is the fluteplayer. He enthralled people with his music.'

'Is he a god or a saint?'

'Very much a god. A reincarnation.'

'Why is he coloured blue?'

'He was dark I believe, very dark, blue-black.'

'Doesn't anybody go to the temple in the mornings?'

'Sometimes they do.'

'There was a young woman arranging flowers at the temple.'

'Yes, she's always there. Her name is Usha. She's mute. She helps the priest. The priest brought her up.' Nikhil watched Julian tear a piece of the *roti*. 'How old are you?'

'What?'

'How old are you?'

'I, uh, I'm thirty-four – pretty old.'

'You look much younger, really. I'm twenty-four.'

'My brother's twenty-seven.'

'Does he look like you – all gold?'

'All gold! No, my brother's dark, much bigger too.'

'Are you married?'

'No.'

'Do you love anyone – any woman, I mean?'

'No,' said Julian simply. He was a little amazed at the

56

barrage of questions. But he didn't mind. He liked the young man. There was a freshness about him. 'I ought to be going now,' he said. 'It must be nearly midday. I don't want a search party out for me. Here —' Julian reached for his pocket. 'Oh dear.' He wasn't carrying any money. 'I, uh, how much do I owe you for all this food?'

'Nothing.'

'Oh, come on, how much?'

'I didn't pay for anything. I'll be doing some cleaning and odd jobs for the old man. That's the way I usually pay for food.'

'I'm glad I met you,' Julian said, shaking his hand. 'I'd like to see you again some time.'

'Yes, I'd like that too,' said Nikhil.

'Come over —' Julian stopped short. No, he couldn't call him over to the bungalow. Blast! This is silly. They stood staring at each other, wondering where they could meet. Julian explained the location of the bungalow.

'I know where that is,' Nikhil said 'The woods – behind that house.'

'Yes.'

'And there's an old temple in the woods.'

'Yes, I'll see you there,' said Julian, 'tomorrow, at about ten?'

'I'll be there.' Nikhil touched his forehead with two fingers.

'Thank you for everything. I must go now.' Julian walked away rapidly.

This is ridiculous, thought Julian. Fixing a rendezvous. Why couldn't he meet him openly? Why couldn't he call him over to the house? Caroline wouldn't mind. Dane would probably go through the ceiling. This was silly. But he wanted to know about the fluteplayer, Krishna; know more about the flute and the music. Nikhil knows.

Why was Nikhil looking at him that way? He was watched at the temple, and in the river. Julian felt his clothes. They were a little damp still and half-clung to his body. Did they meet by accident?

Never mind. There were other things to deal with right now.

'Where could he be? Where could he have gone?' Dane stopped pacing and sat down on the edge of a sofa.

'He has probably just gone for a walk,' said his mother calmly.

'For a walk? It's eleven-thirty now! And he just left the club rudely last night. What's the matter with him?'

'He seems fine to me.'

'Fine! He's never been fine! He always seems fine because I'm always – oh, damn! You'd think he'd want to spend time with us after coming all the way here. What's he here for? Well, I'm done waiting! I'm finished with taking care of his stuff. What about me, Mama? My life? Cheveley – I want to live there, not at Ravinspur. Don't I matter?'

'Tell him that then. Why rave and rant at me?'

'He's so damned eccentric.'

'So what. Tell him what you feel,' said his mother as she rearranged flowers in a vase.

'He never listens, Mother. How can I make him listen? I don't want to sound like a preacher. Where is he now? Can't sit still for a second. It's only a matter of time before something awful happens and people start talking.'

'Start talking about what?' came Julian's voice like a pistol-shot from the door. Dane turned around.

'Where the hell have you been?'

'Is that any of your damned business?'

'Hope you had a nice walk,' said Caroline as she rose and left the room.

'What's the meaning of these vanishing tricks?'

'I wasn't aware that I had to explain my actions to you or to anybody.'

'We just wondered whether you were dead or alive!'

'Why don't you just drop this watch-dog act of yours.'

'And just wait, wait for his lordship's scandals to drive us out of places? If I had dropped my watch-dog act, Julian, you would be cooling your heels at Reading or Pentonville right now!' Stunned by his own words, Dane sat down heavily on a sofa and buried his face in his hands.

I think Dane behaved like an idiot this morning. But I can understand his outburst. Dane keeps trying to put Julian on an emotional leash.

Well, Lorna, I tried to lighten things up at lunch. Talked

about travelling to Agra and Kashmir with the Cartwrights who are coming to visit. But to no avail.

Somehow they will have to make it up between them – work things out. I feel an outsider. I don't know what to say. I don't have anything to say.

We are creating unreal images in our minds and freezing up. The club atmosphere is sort of like that, too. People are either over-excited or anxious, laughing too much. The men sweat over who's going to bat one-down and who'll be at gully as if they are preparing for Waterloo. The women powder their noses with the fervour of evangelists foaming at the mouth. A button missing from the Collector's cuff is like a train going off the tracks. In this alien land we've lost our equilibrium. We've – no, Lorna, I'm not going to include myself – they, they've come here to change the natural state of things and gone mad in the process. Now there's just the dance of madness. I think Dane's lost control. Julian will, too. Only, he will be king, nay, the god to this madness and change the dance. God, I don't know what I'm talking about. Rambling, rambling. I've got to stop thinking this way. Thoughts I gag all day come back to haunt me at night.

After an uncomfortable dinner, they sat outside on the veranda and stared at the darkness. Dane cleared his throat and forced out a 'sorry'.

'I'm sorry, Ju,' Dane repeated. Julian concentrated on the tip of his cigarette. Dane felt his throat tighten. 'I said I'm sorry.'

'No, you are not.'

'Please, Julian, I didn't mean to, I didn't, I swear. Please, Ju. I'm sorry, I'm sorry – I was – I felt you had left – I mean, gone away again – like before —' Dane tried hard to keep his voice steady.

'All right, all right, stop snivelling. Go to bed, you'll feel better in the morning. Or better still, go wherever you go every night.'

Juian walked through the woods towards the old temple. He smiled to himself as he thought of Dane's discomfort at breakfast. Sleep well? He had thrown the question at his brother mockingly, twice. Reaching the temple, he went up the cracked steps and stepped on to the raised altar. Pearl collar studs caught his eye. As he stooped to pick them up he heard footsteps outside.

'Hello there,' said Nikhil, 'I hope I'm not late.'

Where the hell are my pearl studs? wondered Dane. What in the world did I do with them? He ransacked the drawers, he searched the bed, he questioned Jugnu, he asked his mother. No, the studs were definitely not in the house. Oh, no, Dane groaned to himself. That's where I left them.

Lying there, on that altar, as every night, he had removed his collar. Choking over Julian, dying for Sakhi. How long would he survive this way? Dreaming of her night after night on that altar. The moonlight, the pomegranates; always there, the pomegranates, as if by magic? Damn the studs.

They sat down cross-legged on the altar, facing each other. 'You look uncomfortably sophisticated,' Nikhil said.

'Don't be silly,' laughed Julian.

'Do you know that this was a Krishna temple once?'

'Really?'

'Yes. All those figures on the walls – they depict the life of Krishna.'

'Why isn't there a statue in that alcove there?'

'Don't know. That's really odd, though. It's bad to remove gods from their altars, they say. It's a terrible violation. But so many temples were looted, y'know, by raiders who came across the western borders. They ransacked the temples for gold and jewels, for statues built of gold and silver, eyes of sapphire and emerald. They say altars shouldn't be left empty. And, y'know, they say it's bad to enter temples where there are no gods.'

'What d'you mean?'

'That's what they say. I don't know why. The emptiness, I guess, the void. Wonder what this Krishna looked like – slender, blue, beautiful, lost in his music?'

'Tell me about him.'

'Why do you want to know?'

'Curiosity, I guess.'

'Don't you feel a little odd talking to me? I mean, I'm an Indian and you're not supposed to socialise with the likes of us.'

'I have nothing against foreigners,' said Julian awkwardly. Nikhil shrugged.

'I merely wanted to know whether you regard me as a "native" or as a human being.'

'I'm not sure why you're throwing this at me right now,' said Julian calmly. 'I'd like to get to know you. I'd like us to be friends no matter what social problems lie between us.' Julian reached out and touched his hand. 'Now, I want to know more about my fluteplayer.'

'Your fluteplayer – Krishna – oh, well, I'm a little confused whether he was a reincarnation or the god himself. You see, Vishnu, one of the trinity, was cursed and condemned to be born on earth ten times. Each incarnation of the god would attempt to purge the world of some evil or affliction. Actually, it's not really important to establish whether Krishna was an incarnation or the god himself. In either case, he was playing a certain role. He was part of a certain scheme.' Nikhil stopped and fidgeted with his collar.

'Tell me more.'

'The night Krishna was born, there was a terrible storm. Krishna was like the night – bright, dark, indigo. He grew up in an Edenic pastoral region called Vrindaban, among cowherds. Like all cowherds, he, too, played the flute. But no one played the flute like Krishna. When he played his music, the whole world was enthralled. His flute mesmerised all living creatures —' Heavy footsteps on dry leaves and twigs made them turn.

'What the hell —' Dane stumbled on the steps.

'Hello, Dane. Looking for these?' Julian handed his brother the studs. Dane snatched them from Julian's hands. 'Nikhil, this is my brother, Dane.' Dane took the young Indian's hand gingerly. 'He's telling me a very interesting story.'

'Oh.'

'Well, want to join us?'

'Uh, no, er, I have to go.' Talking to a stranger, a native, listening, so much at ease, sharing what secrets? Why could he not sit that way with him and laugh, and talk?

'He is so different from you,' said Nikhil after Dane left.

61

'Yes, he is. Anyway, please go on.'

'Well, Krishna's music cast a spell on all those that heard it. Men and women loved him. And he loved them back. Sometimes he is confused with the god of love, mainly because of his way of life. He did indeed turn love into a religion! But he was also indifferent in a way. No attachments. No *maya* or *moha* as we say. And then, one day he left. Entering adulthood, he left the garden and the river for the other world where responsibilities lay. His dance in the garden was over.'

'And did he continue to play his flute?'

'As he took his leave of the men and women who loved him, their pain moved him. He knew what he was taking away from them. So he threw his flute into the Yamuna. The river caught the flute and the music. His voice remained for ever with those that adored him. A part of him stayed back in the waters. But that part he left behind. It became the past, separate, different, discontinuous. And he moved into a different world.' Nikhil paused.

'Then?'

'Come, let me tell you the story from the figures on the walls . . .'

The night entered through the open windows, starlit, fragrant, as Julian lay in bed. No, not such calm – not that night. Nikhil's words swept through him like flutetones. The storm, the raging river, a birth; a darkness flooded by the music. A slim blue form lost in ecstasy. An intensity in the centre. Moving still, still moving. Fingers that undid the strings of time. Flutecaress. Be still while the dark fingers play. To drink those flutetones. Julian touched his mouth.

They sat on the sunlit altar and talked. 'I'd like to learn to play the flute,' Julian said.

'And will you stand with your ankles crossed and play upon the souls of others?' Nikhil asked. 'Look at this empty altar! This is where you should stand and play, all lost in your music.' Julian started. 'Krishna fascinates me, y'know,' Nikhil continued. 'You would look perfect with the flute against your mouth.'

'I'm a little too pale, don't you think?' Julian managed a smile.

'The night will wash you blue.'

'The night?'

'Yes!' Nikhil said, his eyes glittering. 'And did you love them back?'

'What?'

'The women who loved you, the men who loved you. Men have loved you, haven't they?'

'I don't know what you're talking about.' Julian looked at him blankly.

'I know how you feel.' Nikhil touched his hand. Julian drew his hand away gently.

'I really don't know what you're talking about.'

'There's something I've wanted to tell you since the day I saw you at the bazaar. I felt you'd understand. A year after they adopted me the Wakeleys had a son. We grew up together. I learned what Phil learned. And soon we realised that there was something else – we felt different. Then we were caught one day, in the attic. I was seventeen. They shipped Phil to England and threw me out. And here I am. Can't change myself.' Nikhil looked into the sunlight for a long time.

Julian wanted to run, but his legs refused to support him. His mouth felt very dry. Nikhil reached out and touched his face.

'Don't!' Something snapped in Julian. 'Don't do that! It's over. All that's over. It does not touch me any more. It has ceased to matter.'

'I won't bother you,' said Nikhil. 'Come to the temple, the other temple, in the mornings. It's peaceful there.'

The news of the day – the talk of the town, Lorna – the *nawab* of Talkot has invited us for a *shikaar*! A leopard hunt. Well, I won't be able to go for this elephant ride, as I'm going off to Agra; Dane and Julian will.

Unbelievable, you know – a black Daimler drew up and a man stepped out; so charming, young and dark-haired, exquisite in a turquoise raw silk *sherwani*, and he handed me a sandalwood scented scroll. Of course, within seconds our servants spread the word like cholera. So, at the club, the Collector kept gasping over his scotch.

A *shikaar*! Next week! My goodness! —

We asked him to come for tea, I said, but his highness wished to postpone it.

Mr Lyndon, the D.M., laughed rather slightingly and said, Of course he'll want to postpone it! The coward. They're very cautious about stepping into our territory. So they prefer to call the shots from within theirs.

Not like us, you mean, Julian said, with our lionhearts we can merrily trample all over theirs.

Under the gaslight of the club dining room their faces looked exceptionally pallid and drawn.

The *nawab* has never invited anyone for a *shikaar* before, and as I understand, we can't hunt in Talkot. It's still officially the *nawab's* territory.

After dinner, Lorna, the room becomes divided into two groups. The younger men from Phulgarh and the Talkot cantonment move towards the french windows, while the officers and the Collector's men have the bearers put a few tables together and sit down to tell the same stories over again. The women withdraw to the blue room as the waiters bring in the cigars and brandy. The blue room is a very convenient room. You can hear everything the men talk about under this guise of privacy.

So, the group near the french windows talked about the *kota* in Talkot. I heard Mr Trevors laughing about the women.

M'lord, Trevors said, it's a fascinating place, the *kota*. It's India's essence, and —

Stinks is what he means, I heard Thomas Sherley snap.

Come, come, Tom. Those women – they're alive, they want you, they want us.

Especially us? Julian asked.

Yes, they prefer *sahibs*.

How d'you know? Do they say that? Have you asked them?

It's understood, m'lord. We have more power here, and they know that. One of 'em even asked me once to get her out of there. Said she'd be my slave for the rest of her life! Believe that! They laughed with Trevors.

Yes, they prefer *sahibs*, they sure do, we can do magic, can't we, and fly them out of there!

Do they have to talk about women this way? Just to impress each other, so that another man will slap his back? What is it they are doing here?

Of course Roanna Lyndon could hardly be quiet after hearing the above. It seems *they* want those women, wouldn't you say? Wonder why? What magic spell have they cast on our men?

Doesn't seem like magic spells to me. All I see are rude assumptions to flatter their egos. Hope Dane doesn't fall prey to these silly notions.

Dane fidgeted all the way home. Julian was very quiet, as he has been lately. He seems calm, but it's more like an iciness. Frozen in motion. Something has got to him. Something has captured his attention. When he is quiet, very quiet, he looks as if he's in a trance.

Jugnu overturned the flute-seller's basket and sat on it. Flutes lay at his feet. Slum kids, servants, women from the construction site. The maidan near the bazaar was the place of most people's afternoon affairs. Some of the women sat around a young bangle-seller and haggled and flirted. Others lay on the dry grass and smoked. The servants were chucking dice as usual. The D.M.'s *khansama* seemed to be winning. The kids had nothing to do, so they picked fights and got into scuffles. This is the time, thought Jugnu. The perfect time. 'Oy,' he yelled. 'There's going to be murder and bloodshed very soon, d'you know? It's Shehzadi – she's got my *saab*!' The men didn't even turn their heads. The children ran towards him. The women turned from the glass bangles.

Jugnu regarded his audience. Women and children. How to make the men pay attention? They always laughed at him, and especially since the day the prostitutes at the bazaar had cracked heartless jokes about his incompetency. Maybe they'll get jealous of his female audience. It didn't matter so much if the women didn't give him any attention. To be admired by other men – that mattered; that was important. After that, the women came automatically. To draw the men with the women and the women with the men.

'So what about your *saab*, *chutiya*?' A woman threw her *biri* at him. Her voice drew all male eyes. She was the she of *The Big Sneeze*. She was the one who couldn't be bought without big money. She was the special she who chose her men and cast them aside at will. Jugnu swallowed.

'On the altar of the old temple in the woods, Shehzadi comes to my *saab*,' he said.

'Really?'

'Yes, I saw him there, them, I mean.'

'And what do they do there, eat pomegranates?'

'Yes, that's exactly what they do.'

'They sit and eat pomegranates all night long?'

'Among other things. She feeds him, he feeds her, the purple juice staining his white shirt, her mouth, her fingers.'

'Won't the prince have her throat slit now!'

'No, he'll fight my *sahib*, and whip her, and shut her up for ever. The *nawab* is involved too. He wants Shehzadi out of the prince's life. That's why he keeps sending Salman away.'

'Yes, yes, we all know that. But Salman is headstrong and disobedient —'

'Right! So the *nawab*'s going to tell Salman about my *sahib*. And then watch what happens! Salman and his bodyguard, Zafar Khan, will get together and try to slaughter everyone. And the *nawab* will try all his little tricks to foil Salman's plans. Oh, we're in for a war! I'm finding out little by little. I'll keep you informed.'

'So your *saab* will be dead in six weeks then.'

'Oh, no, no, no. My *saab*'s stronger than Salman. He'll win.'

'Win what?'

'What d'you mean win what?'

'Acchoo! These *sahibs* make me sneeze,' she laughed and said. 'Acchoo!'

Julian and Nikhil sat on the low parapet of the temple terrace and watched the sunrise on the Yamuna. This temple is different, thought Julian. The one in the woods, with the empty alcove and altar, disturbed him. The emptiness cried to be filled up, and he wanted to fill it up himself. 'It's Diwali today,' said Nikhil.

'What's that?'

'A festival. The festival of lights, you could say. You'll see the sky light up tonight – fireworks, lamps, candles.' Julian rested his unshaved chin in his hand and looked at the day spreading out. No awkwardness between them any more. It slipped away as the past had slipped away.

'I'm tired,' said Julian. 'I've been tired for a long, long time.'

'Then rest.'

'I want release.'

'From what?'

'I don't know. I want to lose myself.'

'You'll have to die then,' laughed Nikhil.

'Maybe,' Julian smiled. 'But I don't want to leave my body. I just want to stand outside the circle.'

'Or in the centre,' said Nikhil.

'Actually, just go away from here, from cities, to some far-off place, dark woods, live there for a while and refocus.'

'Maybe, Julian, maybe there is a place like that. When you go to Calcutta, I'll take you to a tribal village. I've always wanted to go there ever since Will Grey left Srinagar for Bengal. I want to find him again. He used to tell Phil and me fascinating stories.'

'Who's Will Grey?'

'He was a friend of the Wakeleys. He knew about Phil and me but never told anyone. Everyone said Grey *saab* was crazy when he left his apple orchard and took off to live among the Saontals. Maybe he is crazy. But he is fascinating. Would you come with me?'

'Yes, I'd love to.'

He saw her again. She came with flowers and sat and prepared garlands, lit the lamps, spread flowers on the altar. As he walked home past the bazaar he heard the flutetones. He did not wince this time.

I'll be going off to Agra in a week's time. Sheila Cartwright and her husband will be here and then off we go! Maybe Julian and Dane will work things out between them. Between them now there is cricket, riding and the regular club evenings. Last evening I watched them play bridge. They dealt out cards to each other, handed cigarettes to each other, even lighting the cigarettes for the other, but not once did their eyes meet.

Doesn't that happen between lovers sometimes? You know what I mean – when love is intense and frightening, and fear sets in. Do they know what they are doing?

Before dinner we sat on the veranda trying to chat. How was cricket? I asked. We're playing horrid games, said Dane. Julian smiled that smile – do you know that smile, Lorna? That's all there is to do, he said. Look, Caroline, he said in a voice so calm, look at the evening splashing wine-dark across our eyes. Have they both gone mad?

It's Julian's calmness that frightens me – like the calm before a storm. Like a ball of something becoming smaller, tighter, intensely dense, before exploding. He's taut inside, stretched to some kind of a breaking point.

Julian walked his horse to the river. It was one of those stunning afternoons. He knelt and touched the grass. With both hands he felt the ground, the little bumps, ridges, thick grass, stones. Under his fingers he felt something sharp. The point of a buried stone. He tried to dislodge it. It was stuck deep in the soil. Julian began to scrape the soil off around the stone. His fingers dug at the ground with mounting desperation, ripping off grass, weeds. Like a dog tearing at the ground he worked at removing the stone. It was a very large stone it seemed, knotted up, painful and hard. He had to drag it out and look at it, all bloody and torn. If only he could cut it up into little pieces and remove them one by one. The stone came out after a sudden wrench, stained with the blood seeping out from under his nails. He cradled the stone and held it next to his face, sitting so still as if paralysed by its touch. A smell of blood, grass and silt. This was the feeling, the whole feeling, the tearing, the ripping, burning, digging, wrenching, hurt, bleeding, stormy, when the flute played.

Slowly, he raised his face and put the stone down. He looked at his hands. 'Oh, God.' He brushed them against his jodhpurs. 'Oh, God,' he said again. 'What the hell?'

He got up and mounted his horse. 'Come on,' he said and urged the horse to gallop at almost breakneck speed across the wide, flat land next to the river. Faster and faster, and Julian crouched low over the horse's neck.

He dragged the horse to a halt as he neared the house. Ravi

Singh took the reins from him at the gate and led the horse away. Julian pulled out his watch from his jodhpurs. Two-thirty. The Cartwrights were coming for tea at four-thirty. He walked swiftly around the house to the back yard, leaped neatly over the wall and broke into a run as he entered the woods.

Dane paced round the garden impatiently. Julian had vanished again. It was a quarter past four. Tea at four-thirty, Dane, his mother had warned him. The bloody idiot chatting with that Indian chap. Who was he? Skinny, pale. What did these two have in common? Must find Julian. This won't do. He walked to the back. Soon, he was trampling through the woods. Almost panting he reached the old temple. There! Reclined against the steps – thank heav — Dane froze in his tracks.

'It's all behind you, I know,' Nikhil said. Julian lay against the steps of the temple, his knees raised, his fists clenched so tightly that his knuckles went white. Fingers moved through his hair. 'You have such a perfect face. Such perfect bone structure.' Nikhil ran a blade of grass up and down Julian's throat. He was choking. Years fell away from his body. Ten years, maybe more. He couldn't open his eyes. Nikhil leaned over and kissed him on the mouth, lightly, like a breath of air. Something slipped away.

Dane held a branch and looked at Nikhil's calm face. He must drag Julian out or he'd be lost in another nightmare. This was a nightmare. It wasn't real.
　　'Get up, Julian.' Dane couldn't swallow the hoarseness.
　　Quicklime caressed his body. Julian's eyes burned from the heat of the sky. He gasped for air through clenched teeth. Slowly, he spread his fingers out and pressed the soft, warm grass. His face relaxed.
　　'Get up, Julian!'
　　Julian stared into the anger in his brother's eyes. Pain and humiliation rose through Dane in slow waves. The sixth Earl of Ravinspur lay half-sprawled on the ground, his breeches stained.
　　He dragged a stumbling Julian through the woods. Pushing

69

him savagely over the wall and taking hold of his collar, he thrust him towards the back entrance.

'Why through the back . . .' Julian stammered.

'You have to change,' said Dane quietly.

'Why . . . what . . .' Julian looked down, feeling the wetness for the first time. 'Let me go, let me go, Dane.' He was whispering. His voice was slipping away.

'Damn you, Julian!' Dane slammed him against the mango tree. Then, turning on his heel, he walked away without a second glance.

Chapter 4

Lorna,

Choking over tea – could hardly swallow anything. Dane, with clenched fists, as if suffocating in some kind of pain, nausea, maybe.

Sheila – you've met Sheila Cartwright? Sheila, gay, laughing, flirtatious, and Julian, so unreachably charming in his ice-blue suit. The Collector and his wife absolutely stunned by Sheila's outrageous vivacity. Sheila, oh, Sheila's always such a welcome change. But this afternoon, with its dying light, copper spreading around us, copper to indigo, even Sheila's mirth could not blow away this shocking stupor. Dane sat stone-still as if he had a bullet in his head. He stared at Julian with that same look in his eyes: how do I explain this? Years back, at Ravinspur, that awful dinner after the Wilde scandal, and Dane looking at Julian just this way. But why this afternoon? What had happened?

For Julian, Dane didn't exist today. For Julian, only a stage was there, shot with the thrill of words and laughter. Julian was a thousand miles away. His smile hung among us – that's all.

And Sheila said, 'Oh, what a lovely house, Caroline! What a charming veranda! The rajah, did you say? Oh, how perfectly sweet of him – what a darling! Is he attractive? Do you remember, Caroline . . . ? When I first met Ron, twenty-five years ago, what a scandal at first! Ron, you ol' sonofabitch —!' She blew a kiss at her husband. 'And do you remember, that night at Lady Rufford's – when that club on Fitzroy Street was the talk of the town? What a hideous affair. So many of those charming young men had to leave London at the height of the season. What a shame. But remember those pearls I wore that

71

night – the ones with that exquisite grey tint? I lost them at Delhi last week. Isn't that a shame? Delhi's pretty, Caroline, you'll love it. Ron, don't you think Dane's a darling? Just look at him. Dane, stop breaking hearts at once! Oh, Caroline, that charming stepson of yours! He has the most wicked, wicked smile. Oh, you should all come to Boston – oh, those masked balls and swimming pools! Julian would have a wonderful time with that smile of his. Remember that awful dinner at the Featherblows'? Julian got all drenched when that stupid fountain went off suddenly because a footman stepped on something. All wet he was and still so collected and smiling.'

Yes, Lorna, Julian so collected and smiling, whether wet, blue, black or white; even at the *shikaar* next week, he'll be perfectly so.

Maybe we were better off in England. Shouldn't have come to India. No more heartbreaks, please.

Caroline stopped writing and removed a green velvet purse from her dresser drawer and took out a tiny ivory object from it. She stood it on her palm and looked at the miniature temple gateway.

Lorna, she began again, there's never enough love to make up for love that's lost. I have tried, Lord knows, I have tried my best. Charles in India, trying to forget. How to kick loose the past? Charles in Phulgarh – a citadel of flowers, he said. Yes, the flowers are still here. Orange blossom, frangipani, laburnum, gardenia, jacaranda, bougainvillaea and the tiny, white, star-like petals that overwhelm the night.

Dane closed his eyes. The mosquito net around his bed appeared like a veil of mist in the dark. Mist, misty, rain now, wet, the burning would die. He covered his mouth to choke the sobs. No, he had seen nothing. It was a nightmare. Julian was ill, that's all. He must help Julian get better.

At tea, he had sat quietly and smiled at Sheila's stories till Julian appeared. He felt it then – the mangled cucumber sandwich in his left hand. The soggy mess against his palm made his skin crawl. He didn't even realise what he was doing; he just wanted to break, crush, smash. Flicking a napkin off the glass-topped cane table in front he cleared his hand swiftly. Julian standing there with that same face he put on every time he returned to Ravinspur.

In that large sunny room in Ravinspur, filled with Julian's collection of woodblock prints, velvet cloaks, jade ashtrays and all those odd-looking things, Julian stood before the mirror and tried on different expressions. He removed face after face, smiling, sneering, frowning, raising an eyebrow, lighting cigarettes, flicking his hair back, blowing on his fingertips.

'Ah, here you are, Julian.' Julian bending over to kiss Mother and then Sheila.

'Sheila – I never quite managed to fall out of love with you.'

'Don't you dare flirt with me, Julian – I'll spank you thoroughly!'

Julian's white suede shoes. Not a smudge on them. Not even a speck of ash from his ever-ready cigarette.

'So, Sheila, how do you like India?'

'So colourful – absolutely charming, and oh, the silks and corals and pearls!'

Sit there with your scotch and your smile, legs crossed, cigarette between your fingers. Go on, play, Julian, play. I'll take the fall; I'll swallow it all so that you don't choke.

What were you looking at? Where were you? Julian, they were talking to you.

Empty-eyes Julian. Eyes not empty only when you look there. Something fills your hollow eyes from out there. Tell me about it, some day, and I'll cry with you.

'Julian, when are you going to Calcutta? We must be there for the viceregal ball. Oh, don't you smile that way – you love being the centre of attraction!'

'No, I don't. I really don't, Sheila.'

'Oh, methinks m'lord doth protest too much . . .'

You want to be left alone, don't you? Yes, you want to be left well alone. And what will I do? I shouldn't go looking for you. Just wait, just wait patiently. Your brother will do all that he ought to do, do all that he ought to have done; undo all that he shouldn't have done, too?

Here, do it this way, hook the worm on this way . . . Christ what a catch! Eyes laughing, laughing with the warmth of the sky. No, you are not going to drown, I'm holding you up,

don't worry, just try to float this way first. Trust me, Dane.
Nearly twenty years ago. Alone in your room, on stormy
nights, you and your guitar.

Trust me, Dane.

Dane sat up. He couldn't bear the mosquito net. Quietly, he
got out of bed, dressed, and left the house.

On the altar of the ruined temple in the woods Dane lay
almost asleep. His arms crossed around him as if holding him.
Her face rubs against his throat and his arms tighten. The
warm smell of rain on summer dust. He would sleep this way
for ever.

Warm, so warm, and dark. Don't want to think at all. Just
sleep. It's those bells – just rain, rain, rain. Dane slid down and
pressed his cold nose against the altar. Her throat, so warm.
'This is how I like sleeping,' he said. And he heard her say,
'*accha*.'

'And what does Shehzadi get from your blue-eyed *saab, oy,
chhokrē*?'

'I'll tell you if you don't have a sneezing fit again!' Jugnu
tried to grab her hair, but she was quick to roll away. So he lay
back and blinked at the afternoon sun. 'My blue-eyed *saab*
gives her power, power over him.'

'Hah! You mean he never knows what she thinks, so he
assumes everything. That's what they always do.'

'But there's love, and passion, like we'll never know, but
can only imagine.'

'So do you crawl into bed with your *saab* and Shehzadi
every time? Do you become your *saab*?'

Jugnu closed his eyes and made a face. 'Go on, make fun of
me. Only I have the real story. But do you want to know? Do
you believe what I say?'

'You said you wanted to learn to play the flute.'

'Yes, I really do.'

'Will you believe in the flute?'

'What do you mean?'

'Nothing. Come along. I'll take you where you can learn.'

Nikhil and Julian walked out of the woods, went down the
road that led to the bazaar, past the temple. Nikhil touched

Julian's elbow. 'Julian,' he said, 'I'm sorry about that afternoon. I act on impulse too much, get carried away. Don't hold that against me. Never again. I want things to stay this way, like they are now. Your brother, he must be in shock – I mean, I wouldn't be surprised if he were to shoot me! Please let's just forget and —'

'OK, shut up now.'

'Right. Why didn't you tell me you were an earl?'

'What difference would it have made?'

'Don't you like being an earl?'

'It's not a matter of choice.'

'Why did you come to India?'

'To play the flute, of course!'

'You'd better learn to play it damn well then.'

'I will. I do everything "damn well"!' Julian lit a cigarette.

'You've travelled a lot, haven't you?'

'Sort of.'

'What do you want? Besides going away to a far-off place, that is.'

'What I want – I'm not sure what I want. But I know what I don't want. Perhaps I'll find the desired product only through a series of cancellations.'

'I know what I want. I could even spell it out. And I don't have to go anywhere. I have my world in my hands right now.'

'Yours is a pretty small world then,' smiled Julian.

'I love small worlds.'

'Why?'

'Because the gods that dwell in small worlds would be half-human, semi-divine, with hearts and bodies. Yes, I could love their clay feet and bleeding wounds. They would feel my pain, hurt when I hurt.'

'Perhaps.'

'They'd know our weakness because they would be weak. They'd love us badly, but would never fail to bless us. They'd reach out when we reach for them. They'd fail us all the time, and we'd forgive them and continue to pray to them.'

Julian looked at the early afternoon sun and blinked. Forgive gods! Possible perhaps in this green-gold land, with its blue-gold sky. A day-smell of warm earth and grass, bird-sounds, cows, goats, voices, wheels and white dust blowing. They had walked for more than an hour since they left the woods. The old temple in the woods seemed just a place of waiting.

At night, when those flutetones swirled through the darkness, through the heady fragrance of those white star-like flowers, that waiting altar called and the tiredness died, the fatigue collapsed. Something was over. Was it shame, anger? It had slipped away. A starburst, and then swiftly imploding into that lost darkness.

They stood near the maidan next to the bazaar. 'A *sahib* in *kurta*-pyjama' – they stared at him, whispering and giggling. 'A *sahib* – the same *sahib*, again.' They went towards an old man sitting on the fringe of the maidan with a basket of flutes. He sat there smoking a clay pipe.

'Dada, teach him to play – he wants to learn.'

'*Bansuri?*'

'*Jee.*'

'*Baitho, jee.*' He emptied the pipe and tossed it aside. They sat down cross-legged on the thick grass. '*Yeh lo, aisé pukro.*' The old man arranged Julian's fingers on the slim, yellow reed.

A taste, a smell. Julian lowered the flute from his lips and stared at it. Smooth and slender. The old man closed his eyes and played. A lovely, lovely flute. Julian raised it to his mouth again. He felt his pulse change, heartbeats swell into waves, his mind drown. And Nikhil said, 'You're a lost god, torn by sounds that are not sounds, bleeding as you play, bleeding wet, gold and blue.'

After dinner Dane left for a card party at Harry's. Julian declined the invitation. Sitting out on the veranda, he thought of the flute that he had left on his bed. Can't practise it in the house. Weird sounds. They'll wonder what's going on. Against my lips that strangeness. He touched his mouth. The wetness of whisky met his fingers. He wiped his mouth with the back of his hand. Picking up the glass of scotch, he drained it and wiped his mouth again. He reached for the bottle on the table in front of him and raised it to his lips. Four gulps. The whisky ran down his throat. He choked and stood up, coughing. He wiped his mouth and throat with his hand.

Unbuttoning his shirt and picking up a napkin, he stopped the liquid trickling down his chest. He buttoned his shirt and went inside.

Pausing for a moment outside Caroline's door, he pushed his tousled hair back from his forehead, smoothed his shirt at the waist, wiped his hand across his mouth again, then knocked on the door.

'Come in, dear.'

'Are you all packed?'

'Oh, yes. Come in and sit down.' Julian walked in and went towards his stepmother sitting in bed with a book.

'What's the matter?' She laid the book down on the table next to the bed.

'Nothing.' He leaned over and kissed her cheek. Then taking off his shoes, sat down cross-legged on the bed at her feet, and smiled a wide, childish smile, tilting his head to one side. Caroline felt her eyes fill up.

'Julian.' She reached out for his hand. 'Are you all right?'

'Yes, Caroline, I am.'

'Are you sure?'

'Quite.' He is a six-year-old child who is waiting, thought his stepmother. How I love this child. 'I love you. Never doubt that. I know I have been a bad son.'

'No you haven't, Julian. I wish that I could have been more of a friend to you —'

'Don't say that. You have no idea how much – what you mean —' Julian leaned forward. She held him and smoothed his hair.

It was nearly five in the morning when Dane walked up the stairs to his room. What's this he had got himself into? Shake out of it. What was he going to do? He opened his door and stepped into his room.

'Dane.' He turned around startled. Julian was right behind him.

'What is it? Why are you up?'

'I was waiting for you.'

'Why?'

'Can I come in?' Dane moved aside and let his brother in.

77

'Well?' Dane waited. Julian sat down on the bed and lit a cigarette. Dane shrugged and started to take his clothes off. He pulled his shoes and socks off, stepped out of his trousers, took his shirt off, slipped into his pyjamas. He turned around and faced Julian. 'Well?'

'Lie down and relax.' Dane went over to the bed and sat down facing his brother.

'Well?'

'Well what?' Julian laughed.

'What's the matter with you, Julian?'

'Forget that. When will you take me to Talkot?'

Dane looked at the fading night outside his window. 'How about this evening?' he said. 'We'll leave at six-thirty.'

Packed and ready, Caroline waited in the drawing room for the Cartwrights to arrive at any moment. It was eleven o'clock in the morning. She adjusted her white cashmere shawl. She loved shawls. It was a little chilly in the mornings these days, and quite, quite cool at night. She felt Julian's blond head on her shoulder. A six-year-old boy, a thirty-four-year-old man. There is a strange tenderness in Julian which hides. Yes, I have seen the sun in your eyes, dear.

I know how to swim, Mama, I know how to swim! There you stood, Julian, thin and shivering in the sun, your arms grabbing an ecstatic, dark-haired imp, all wet and muddy and looking at me with that smiling assurance that you could take care of him.

Years later, it was Dane who stormed at Charles. Leave Ju alone! He's all right. Leave him alone! It's that club, not Julian. It's not his fault. Charles felt his heart break. He didn't know what to say. And Julian just closed all doors and left.

And there were women. But nothing mattered, somehow. Years later, the sixth earl. In a long, black cloak, Julian, at the funeral. Eyes as empty as the wind. Holding Dane's shoulder throughout the service. Take care of each other.

'Mother!' Dane came running down the stairs. 'I overslept. I'm sorry!' He gave her a hug and kissed her. She smiled at his dishevelled state.

'Get out of your pyjamas before Sheila arrives.'

'I will, I will. I was afraid that you might have left. Where's

Ju? Oh, God, here come the Cartwrights!' Dane moved away from the door as his mother smiled goodbye and stepped into the carriage. 'Don't stay away too long, Mama.' He laughed and waved from behind the door as the carriage disappeared in a cloud of dust.

Julian lay back in the steaming tub with his eyes closed. His damp head rested on the edge. He loved afternoon baths. Dane walked into the bathroom in his pyjamas. He sat down on the edge of the tub and punched Julian on the jaw very lightly. Julian opened his eyes and smiled. Dane punched him again playfully. 'Ju, you're so thin.' Dane looked at his brother's frail body.

'I'm fine.'

'What will you do if anyone ever picks a fight with you?'

'Who would want to pick a fight with an earl?'

'This is not England. What would you do if someone took a swing at you?'

'Why, I'd lay him out flat with my dynamite upper-cut!'

'I'd like to see you do that some day!' Dane said, laughing.

'Maybe you will, some day.'

'You haven't shaved.'

'Not yet.'

'Let me, let me do it!'

'No.'

'Oh, come on, Julian, I'm not going to slit your throat.'

'Your hand might slip!'

'Come on, please!' Dane rushed around getting the shaving stuff together. 'Here, here –' he began to rub the stick of soap on his brother's face, and worked up a lather with the brush. 'Now –' Dane picked up the razor from the table next to the window. He handed Julian a mirror, sat down on the edge of the tub again, tilted Julian's head back further with one hand and raised the glinting steel with a flourish. Julian removed his brother's hand from his forehead, handed the mirror back to him and firmly extracted the razor from Dane's grip.

'You hold the mirror – here, this way.' Dane sighed and watched Julian reveal smooth, tanned skin stroke by swift stroke. Why did he get pushed away? Why did he let himself?

79

Don't get pushed away any more. Scream and fight if need be. No more waiting. Don't care what you're doing with whom, don't care if you laugh at me – I'm not letting you go this time, not letting you turn away any more.

Julian wiped his face. A few bloodspots and flecks of foam, like corals and pearls almost.

'You've cut yourself again!' Dane touched a bloodspot on Julian's throat. 'Here.'

'It's better than having you lacerate my face.'

'Oh, sure.' Dane took a swing at his brother's head. Julian ducked and water splashed all over. 'You're flooding the bathroom!'

'Get out of here you —' Water rose in transparent loose chunks, flame-like in shape, then just breaking at the top and splintering into blue-grey fragments. And Julian was vanishing into that tossing, splashing wall so slowly, so very slowly.

'Jugnu, come and clean up the mess,' Dane yelled, '*burra saab* has gone clean out of his mind.'

Trevors and Sherley sat outside the east barracks of the Talkot cantonment. It was wonderfully sunny. No drill today. They sat with towels wrapped around their waists, waiting for oil massage. Shortly, a boy in his late teens appeared with a bowl of warm oil. He set it down on the long bench on which the two subalterns sat.

'You go first,' said Sherley. 'I'll wait.' The boy started on Cyril Trevors's twenty-five-year-old body. He dipped his hands in the oil, slapped his palms together and began to rub Trevors's back and shoulders.

Sherley stared as if mesmerised. Trevors's bronze torso gleamed with sun and oil. His muscles relaxed under the experienced fingers of the dark, native boy. Sherley's eyes stroked Trevors's reddish-brown hair, strong neck and shoulders, and the contours of his chest. His eyes followed the dark hands all over.

Trevors looked up suddenly and smashed into Sherley's stare. A peculiar sensation coursed through him. He lowered his head and thought about the *naach*-girl he had smuggled into his quarters last night. 'Hey, Tom, that girl was good – the one I had last night. You can have her tonight if you want.'

'You'll get the clap one of these days, Cyril,' snapped Sherley and looked away.

'I think Hartley's coming to the *kota* tonight,' said Trevors.

'I wonder why the earl hasn't been shown the sights as yet,' Sherley said.

'Hey, maybe he'll be here tonight.'

'He's different.'

'What d'you mean?'

'Nothing. Just thinking out loud.' Thomas Sherley bit his lips. The way he moved, the earl, on the cricket field. That face. The way he held the glass to his mouth . . . He hated that man, he decided.

'Damn.' Julian lowered the flute and stared angrily at it. 'I've got to smoke.' He fumbled for his cigarette case in his pocket. The old flute-seller stopped too, put his flute down, and picked up his clay pipe from the dry grass of the maidan.

'*Yeh lo*,' he offered the earl.

'What is it?'

'*Charas*,' Nikhil said. Julian took the pipe from the old man's hands and smelt it.

'What will it do to me?'

After an hour, Julian stood up with red eyes. 'How does his lordship feel?' Nikhil asked.

'He feels fine.' Julian stretched, yawned and picked up his flute. 'Oh, my God! That's much better! That sounded much better!'

'*Shabash beta*,' said the old man. Julian bowed and repeated the performance. Then he threw the flute into the air and caught it.

'I did it! I did it!' He ran about a hundred yards across the maidan and, raising his arm in an arc of movement, delivered an imaginary outswinger with incredible style. He stood at an imaginary crease and hooked and drove invisible balls.

'What a sixer!' yelled Nikhil. 'Have you clean bowled me, my fluteplayer!'

They watched Julian stumbling, falling, running home-wards with the flute in his hand. 'He is not a *sahib*,' said the old man pulling at his *chillum*.

'No, he is not.'

'Not be a *sahib* – but white skin.'

'His skin is not white! Don't you see he has a gold sheen? He has been touched by the sun.'

'*Téra Krishna bana lé inhé*!' The old man laughed and gave Nikhil a light shove. 'Go, go, build a temple for him and fix him on the altar.' Nikhil wrapped his arms around his knees and looked at the basket of flutes.

An impatient Dane stared angrily at the setting sun as he paced the length of the veranda. Julian stumbled up the steps, tried to jump the last two, tripped and fell.

'Good lord, Julian! My God! Are you all right? Where've you been?'

Swearing, Julian scrambled to his feet, pushed his hair back and bared his teeth.

' 'Allo mate! Wher'ya at?'

'What?'

'There's nuffin' to drink in this bloody plice?'

'Julian!' Julian lurched towards his brother and grabbed his collar.

'T'aurais vu ça, mon coco, on était rond comme des queues des pelles, on a remonté le boulevard de Clichy —' He left Dane's shirt and moved backwards. Wagging a finger and giggling somewhat hysterically, he continued, 'on a remonté le boulevard de Clichy, complètement à poil avec les putes et le champagne à l'appui!'

'Julian!'

'Oy! You looks loike you're sick, pet! Eat somefin' that upset you, eh?'

'What on earth . . .'

'Mais tu ne comprends pas . . . , j'ai fumé, et maintenant je rêve éveillé, en plein jour, je vois ton grand nez, tes épaules de boxeur. Ha, Ha, Ha!'

'Ravi Singh! Jugnu!' Dane yelled for the servants and caught hold of his unsteady brother. 'What in the world is the matter with you, Julian?'

'Sod it, chum, Oi'm bloody 'ungry, oi am. Well, don't jus' look at me loike you never seen me, love. Get on with it, mike me some eggs, wouldja?'

Julian drunk in the cellars, imitating Toby the ostler, years and years ago. But he wasn't drunk. Dane shook him lightly. 'Julian.'

'Gaow on, git on with it, mike me some eggs, ducky. And then, and then we could get ourselves a noice bit o'crumpet, we could. Bloody 'ell oi'd dig in the boot for one o'those birds tonight, oi would.' Dane thrust Julian into one of the cane chairs on the veranda and stared at him. Julian spread himself out against the cushions and, holding the flute close to his heart, with half-closed eyes and a dreamy smile, pronounced it to be his only love.

Ravi Singh and Jugnu, who had come running at the sound of *chhoté saab*'s voice, looked at *burra saab*, then at each other. Jugnu looked down at his toes and tried hard not to giggle. After a few minutes, Ravi Singh mustered up enough courage and stepped up to Dane. They talked in whispers for a few minutes. Jugnu disappeared as Dane and Ravi Singh grabbed his lordship under the arms and practically lifted him off his feet.

'What are you doing, darling? Will you let me go – I can still walk.' Julian squirmed and struggled. 'Mother, Mother, they're tiking your dahling boy away!'

Julian stared in horror at his reflection in the cold water of the tub. 'I've already bathed today, thank you.'

'Full fathoms five, now, m'lord,' said Dane, 'and something of you had better fade fast.' The coldness stung Julian like a thousand whiplashes.

'Ohh! Agh! You fahking bahstards!' He coughed, spluttered, choked, lashed out. 'Ah, les enfants de salauds, ah, les fils de putes! Mais, lâchez-moi, bande de cons!' Julian howled and gasped through the next series of immersions. 'You absolute rotters! Let me breathe —' Water splashed up as he was forced in again. 'Dane, you —'

They carried the well-doused, shivering, choking Julian to his room, wrapped up in thick towels. Four pairs of hands rubbed him down roughly. 'Ow, you eunuchs.' Then they slammed him down on the bed on his face. 'Stop it, you sonofabitch.' Ravi Singh flexed his wrists and began his 'revival' massage on his lordship's back while Dane held him down. 'Ow, you swine, you're smashing my ribs. Lemme go at once, awk —' Ravi Singh covered Julian's back with a series of quick hard punches. 'Get this monster off, please my love – agh —' Ravi Singh stopped suddenly and turned Julian over.

'Get up and eat, Julian.' He sat up slowly, making faces. Jugnu entered and thrust a plate of chicken and rice into Julian's hands, and spread a white towel over his lap. Julian set the plate down on his lap and fell on the food with both hands. Dane motioned to Ravi Singh and Jugnu to leave. Julian gulped the food down.

'Now, let's talk about it, Ju.'

'It's over.'

'What is?'

'The food.'

'Just what did you smoke, Julian?'

'May I have some more, please?'

Dane removed the plate from his brother's hands. 'You have had quite enough of everything. Take a nap for half an hour. We have to leave for Talkot in about an hour.' Dane pushed Julian down among the pillows, threw the towel on the floor and pulled the sheets over him. 'Sleep. And, don't smoke hasheesh with the riff-raff.'

'OK,' said Julian with startling meekness and closed his eyes.

Dane sat on the edge of the bed and looked at his brother. Julian gave a soft snore. A couple of stronger snores followed. Dane narrowed his eyes. He pushed Julian's wet hair back from his forehead. The flute lying next to the pillows caught his eye. He examined it carelessly, then put it back next to Julian's head. He stared out of the window at the copper sky for a few minutes, then walked out of the room. Julian opened one eye and followed the retreating back of his brother. Picking up the flute, he held it against his cheek.

Dane sat opposite Julian at dinner at the cantonment. Harry and Trevors were hideously excited about tonight. Dane felt sick. He pushed the meat around on his plate for a few seconds, then looked around. Thomas Sherley was staring at Julian. Julian smiled at Dane and followed his glance.

Sherley had no time to avert his eyes. The earl held his gaze while Sherley blushed and swallowed. Julian turned back to Dane, smiled again and drained his wine. Then he wiped his mouth slowly with the back of his hand. Sherley looked down, his fists clenched.

Sherley stepped out of the *kota* just before the last dance. Dane Hartley was incredibly uncomfortable all evening. And when Sakhi entered to dance, Hartley left. His lordship watched his little brother, too. And, ah, was the li'l brother uncomfortable. Poor ol' li'l brother. Not just poor li'l me. No more. How to clear your head at times like this? Just see black inside your head, no sounds, just a buzz maybe, and black. To get hit and lose it all for a couple of hours.

The men trooped out laughing. As Dane walked out of the *kota* with Harry, Julian casually glanced at Thomas Sherley leaning against the wall. Emerald bright eyes recoiled almost and blinked.

'Hey, Hartley, come on over to the mess. Fletcher's going to sneak some birds in.' Strange, thought Julian, these men have lost their different accents. They were no longer Scottish or Irish or Welsh or anything else. They were just Englishmen; they spoke the same way.

'I say, let's try and steal one of these birds here!'

'The one in green.'

'Nah, nah, the one in blue.'

'Naw —'

Dane wanted to hit Sherley with a passion. The bastard had looked at Julian from time to time with that awful lingering look. And now they were haggling over those women. But she's mine, mine.

'I'm going to lay the one in white and gold,' cut in Sherley. 'I like an easy lay.'

'Aw, come on, Tommy, you know you can't touch her.'

'Want to bet?'

'Come on, Tom.' Trevors laughed at his friend. 'She belongs to the prince.'

'I can buy her off.'

'Let's have a look at those family jewels, Tom.'

85

'How many diamond necklaces do you have in store, eh?'

'Diamonds?' Sherley glanced at Dane. 'Why, I can buy her with' – he ripped his collar studs off – 'just these!' As the men laughed Harry Winston tried to pull his friend away.

'Come on, Dane, let's go. This is silly. Don't make a fool of yourself.'

'Shut up, Harry.'

'Twenty-five pounds if you lay her tonight.'

'Thirty-five – I'll be back in three hours.'

'Three hours! Make it one.'

'Now then, let me have some fun, eh, since others have already had their share,' said Sherley, looking straight at Dane. Dane stepped forward and grabbed Sherley's shirt. Sherley wrenched himself free. The men moved away, puzzled. Dane swung at him, but Sherley was quick to swerve. Dane's knuckles barely grazed his jaw.

'I say, what's going on? What's the fight about?'

'God only knows. Form a ring, fellows.' Dane clipped Sherley this time, straight on the jaw. Sherley stumbled backwards.

'Come on, Tom!'

'I say, this is silly – break it up, break it up.' Harry tried to push his way in.

'Get out of here, Winston.'

Sherley swung a right hook and missed completely as Dane skipped away. Sherley drove his fist at Dane's head; this time his knuckles met Dane's left temple and cut him. Dane staggered backwards, but, regaining his balance, got Sherley full on the nose. Sherley fell against the men who had formed a tight ring. They set him back on his feet and threw him against Dane.

'Come on, Tom, come on.'

Sherley wiped the blood flowing from his nose and barely managed to block Dane's fists with his forearms. They danced around each other, Dane stumbling in anger and frustration as Sherley tried to get him under the ribs constantly. Dane ducked as Sherley suddenly swung at his head. With lightning speed Sherley's left foot shot up and ripped into Dane's crotch. Dane went down on his knees gasping.

'What the hell! That's dirty.'

'Aw, shut up. What rules in a brawl over a slut?'

'I'm glad to hear that, Sherley.' Julian's fist exploded up against Sherley's chin and sent him flying through the crowding men. Sherley fell flat on his back and lay still.

Julian and Harry helped a gasping Dane up and dragged him away from the young subalterns. Angry voices expressed irritation. A fight had fizzled out. Confused and angry, the men began to quarrel. Within minutes, Julian and Harry found themselves in the middle of a brawl. People were all over each other. To make things worse, some Indians, who were leaving the *kota*, jumped into the fray.

'We've got to get out, Harry,' Julian yelled punching the face in front of him. Dane, up on his feet again, threw himself wholeheartedly into the new mess.

'Christ, Ju, where did you learn to slug like that, in Turkey?'

'At Winchester,' replied Julian as he determinedly smashed a nose. 'Dane, let's get out of here.'

'Bloody hell, I'm having fun.'

Sherley opened his eyes slowly and stared at the angry fighting men in horror. He scrambled to his feet and, picking up his coat, looked wildly for a way out. Harry, sitting bruised and dazed in the middle of it all, caught sight of Sherley's escaping figure. He stumbled out of the crowd, ducking and pushing. With a clumsy leap he pounced on an unsteady Sherley and banged his head hard against the iron gates of the *kota*. 'You bloody swine – you started it all.' Sherley slipped once more into oblivion.

'Dane —' Julian grabbed his brother by the arm and pulled him out of the crowd. 'Let's get our horses.' Wiping blood off their faces they ran towards Harry who seemed to be doing a war dance, leaping around and waving his arms.

Dane was deliriously happy. The blood against his mouth was wine. 'There's blood on your mouth, Ju.' He wiped his brother's mouth with his hand. Purple-stainèd mouth.

They fought together. They played cricket together. Dane raised his face and laughed. 'Julian! Yoohoo! Tally ho!' They would hunt together on the *shikaar*. Like men ought to.

Six elephants moved gracefully through brush and red rock-walled passages. Dane and Julian examined the rifles provided by the *nawab*. 'This is not exactly a joy ride,' whispered Julian to Dane who smiled tightly. 'For heaven's sake relax, Dane.' The *nawab* of Talkot, dressed in a light blue raw silk *sherwani*, his hair slicked back with perfumed oil, reclined against the mirror-work cushions of the *howdah*. He held a rose and lapsed into poetry from time to time, addressing Feroze, the attractive young man who sat next to him. Feroze stuffed *paan* into his mouth at short intervals and stared at Julian and Dane.

'Feroze! Ah, Feroze! You alone know what poetry is! You alone know that poetry is grief and grief is poetry.' Feroze wiped invisible tears from his eyes.

'Shayar-e-Hind! Oh, you are the poet of the land,' he sighed, looking at his master's feet.

'Your lordship,' sighed the *nawab*, 'this dear boy is my son's only true friend. Ah, he is true, true. He would die but not betray.' Julian threw an appreciative smile at Feroze.

'Have you any idea where the leopards are, your highness?'

'The leopards? Ah, yes, they will appear suddenly.'

'Really?'

'Yes.'

'Shouldn't we stop and wait somewhere perhaps?'

'Should we? Feroze, what should we do?'

'Whatever you wish, *nawab saab*. I have never seen Salman hunt leopards on elephant-back, so I really don't know what we should do. But we could have some wine. The sun will set soon, and the evenings should be all *sharab* and *shayari*.'

'Yes, yes, wine and poetry!'

'What about the leopard?' Dane inquired politely.

'Oh, the leopard is beautiful. He is a dark wind; he is the cruelty of love.'

'I see.' Julian rubbed his chin.

'My son has killed six leopards.'

'Aha! Why didn't he come with us for this *shikaar*?'

'Alas, he is in Jaipur. He loves Jaipur, the pink city.'

'And how many leopards have you killed before, your highness?'

'Me? No, no, I do not go on *shikaar*. It is all for you, your lordship. I thought maybe it would inspire me. The beauty of *shikaar* . . . Feroze, Feroze, give me Khayyam.'

'I say, Ju, this is silly,' Dane whispered. Julian smiled and turned to the landscape.

Red, brown, grey and dry green. Rocks, plateaus, dark, deep caves. Elephants dazzling with mirror-work fabric and sun. What a clown-show! What were they doing here? Two Anglo-Saxons on parade on an elephant that looked like a Christmas tree. One of the most exciting experiences that India has to offer, the Collector had informed him. People have written books about it. The white hunters . . .

Now, I am a hunter. Julian looked at the rifle on his knees.

The green woods of Ravinspur. You'll never get a bird that way, Dane. My first rabbit! My very first! How do I skin it, Ju? Let's skin it and roast it. Irish setters leaping in excitement. Down, boy. Down, Tag. And Odysseus drove his mighty spear through the boar's heart . . . The hounds ripping the hard flesh of Actaeon . . . Jason and Atlanta and others in Caledonia . . . Cambridge. Starched shirts and Greek. Montmartre and soft velvet jackets, dark cloaks. Wine-stained tables of the Chat Noir. Arms that pulled you down so deftly. It's warm in here, *chéri* . . . there's a moon out there, and maybe a boat . . .

Your lordship! We did not expect you back so soon. The late earl, it was a terrible shock. Her ladyship is in the chapel. A silence, and then: You are not leaving again, are you? You can't do this, Julian! Anger in eyes.

Squeezed into starched collars and neckties. Trapped on elephants and dance floors. What fine elephants, your highness. You look quite ravishing, Helena, Sarah, Hermione, Louise or . . .

Stand with your ankles crossed and play your flute. The altar is empty and the river waits for flutetones. The Yamuna never runs dry, fed by the mountain snows. Meets the Ganga and then flows into the sea. Not one dance after another, but one eternal flow. The flutetones in the waves, moving free; no sound, no silence, only music. Not to be – not to play, but only to play.

Dane glanced at his brother's profile. Julian with his faraway face. What say? What do? Thanks for fighting for me that night, thanks for not asking any questions. Strange, how and when we lose control. Where are these elephants taking us? The pierrot of a *nawab* is dozing, the other clown is fanning him with a rose. How do leopards fit into this scenario?

'*Nawab saab, nawab saab! Bagh! Bagh*!'

'What! Oh! The guns! Your lordship! Feroze, Feroze!'

'My God! What a magnificent creature.'

It stood there, dusty gold with black rosettes, flicking the end of its tail very slowly, a frozen storm in its translucent amber eyes. The rifle lay forgotten on Julian's lap. The leopard stood as silent as the dark shadows of rocks on the altar of the red cliffs with nothing around its sun-touched body but the copper sky. So still.

'*Nawab saab*, you must shoot first.'

'Yes, yes, am I holding the gun properly?'

'Almost.'

'Well, now my beauty – the kiss of death!' The leopard stared coldly at the *nawab*. It flicked its tail twice and, licking its mouth, folded its limbs into a crouching position.

'Just look at that leap.' The rock-faces shuddered into gunshot echoes.

Dane started and caught his breath. It was about to vanish. It had appeared like sudden dust swirls from wheels rushing through wide open gates. It was about to vanish again. Only a trace of dust clouds left as a reminder of its shocking presence.

'Oh – Feroze, help, help, I'm falling!'

'What the hell – grab his arm, Dane. He'll crack his skull if he falls off the elephant.'

'Oh, help, help!'

'*Nawab saab, nawab saab*!' Feroze covered his face and fell on his knees.

'Come on, man, lend a hand, don't just moan.'

'Pull him up, come on.'

'There you are, your highness. You've lost your rose, I'm afraid, and your sleeve is ripped at the shoulder, but you're fine, believe me.'

'Water . . . water . . . my heart . . . oh.'

Dane looked at his brother patting the *nawab*'s arm. Red dust rose around them as the elephants moved in agitation. The leopard vanished with the sun into the darkness of the old red rocks.

A dusty-rose palace in the middle of stagnant green waters.

Talkot spread out around the lake. They moved along marble and sandstone. Rosewood, sandalwood, velvet, crystal, incense, bougainvillaea and attar stroked their senses. After an overwhelming *mughlai* dinner, they sat on a marble terrace overlooking the dark green ripples now flecked with purple and copper of the night.

'*Paan*,' a uniformed servant offered. Dane waved him aside. Julian picked up one of the glossy leaves wrapped in silver paper.

'Interesting taste.'

'Our ancestors thought that *paan* was an aphrodisiac,' smiled the *nawab*. 'But, alas, it isn't.'

Adolescent boys moved around like soft-footed felines, constantly refilling empty wine glasses.

The leopard had vanished so suddenly. Dane kept seeing that leap over and over again. Out of reach, in its own impenetrable world.

'I am so sorry about today. I am so sorry your first *shikaar* was such a disappointment, m'lord. No leopard. I'm heart-broken.'

'Actually, I'm quite glad the leopard got away. It was such a beauty. I came along for the elephant-ride, really,' Julian said with a grin. It had stood so still, the leopard, capturing all movement within its burning eyes, ignoring all sounds.

'Ah, well, let's have some music now. Feroze! The *raga chandrakauns*, a *raga* which prepares one for the pleasures of the night.' Julian stifled a belch and tried to look interested as three musicians appeared and began to play.

'It is being played on the *sarangi*,' informed Feroze. Julian belched again.

'Ooops.' He looked at his brother and realised that Dane was struggling with his digestive system in the same way.

Smiling, the *nawab* turned to Feroze and whispered. Feroze nodded. 'Yes, yes, *nawab saab*, everything is ready,' he replied, rubbing his hands, 'the sandalwood oil, the rosewater, and . . . everything is ready and waiting.'

'Well, now,' announced the *nawab* of Talkot, rising, 'the expression of my gratitude, my reward to you both for saving my life today —'

'Your highness, we —' They looked up puzzled.

'Come now, let me offer you the essence of life.'

Up marble stairs and through long, cool corridors they swept, Julian and Dane fighting to keep the dinner down.

'Here we are. Feroze, have the doors opened.' Two turbaned giants, with scimitars, threw open massive rosewood doors. A fountain leaped in the centre of the enormous room.

'What the —'

'Twenty of the most beautiful creatures – remember, the nights are made for loving.'

'Oh, er, your highness, there's really no need for this.' They stared in horror at the massive divans with brocade spreads, the rose petals floating in the water, the bowls of sandalwood oil, the marble columns, the huge silver mirrors that lined the walls and the ceiling. 'Oh God. This is really —'

'You saved my life, and for that I give you a night to remember.'

'Your highness, please, saving your life was . . . was nothing really.'

'Nothing? You call my life nothing?'

'Oh, no, no, not your life, we mean the act itself was very simple and uh —'

'Come now, enjoy yourself. I insist you indulge in the pleasures that only the East can offer.' Dane and Julian felt themselves pushed gently amidst peals of laughter. 'Oh, I say, listen, for heaven's sake, you don't understand, please.'

'God, I think I have a touch of diarrhoea coming on.'

'Oh, no.' The doors closed behind them.

Young women with dark, flowing hair and kohl-lined eyes, and slender boys, wearing jewelled belts, wrapped around them determinedly. 'Now, then, wait a minute —'

'Perhaps we should have let the *nawab* fall and crack his skull.'

'Ouch! Stop it. Help.'

'Don't you dare.'

'I've just lost my — yikes! Jesus!'

'We've got to get out of here.'

'They're out to strangle me.'

'Don't get backed against the wall.'

'Let go. Ouch.'

'C'mon, you idiot.'

'I c-can't — stop — no-o-o-o! What about crocodiles?'

'A big splash. That's how —'

'You didn't! Twenty gorgeous "creatures" — and you two jumped out of the window?' Laughter and cries of disbelief cut through the darkness.

'The funny thing is,' Julian said, 'the moment we landed in the water we realised something was very wrong. The water smelt awfully soapy and there was a lot of laughter —'

'We fell, y'see,' cut in Dane, 'right before these local women who were doing their regular evening wash! So we thrashed around among dirty laundry and water buffaloes till the wretched women stopped laughing and helped us out of the lake.'

'Why, I would have begged to be locked up in there for a week!' Trevors yelled at Dane. 'Hartley — you gave up the chance of a lifetime!' The men sat on wooden benches outside the officers' mess at Talkot, drinking and rehearsing the *shikaar* and its aftermath over and over again.

Trevors and three other subalterns had ridden to Phulgarh the morning after the brawl to apologise to them. No hard feelings, I hope, m'lord. We all enjoy a good fight once in a while. Do come to the cantonment some time. We are really very ashamed about the whole business. They had shaken hands like true gentlemen and parted. No hard feelings. Nobody was badly hurt, except for Sherley, who had received a nasty blow in the head from somebody.

'Your lordship, you should have persuaded your little brother to stay.'

'Sandalwood oil and rosewater, all those mirrors — how could you have jumped into the lake!'

'We practically left half our clothes behind.'

'Just half your clothes — you're lucky!'

'Oh, some of the women in this country, I tell you, they're vicious. They just sink their teeth right in.'

'Oho, yes, those tribal women.'

'Bloody hell, I'd love to be thrown among twenty of those.'

'Different from our women they are. Sometimes they even stalk you down.'

'I remember, last summer, when we went up to Simla, there was this fruit-seller's daughter . . .'

Julian, with his elbow on the table, his chin resting on his knuckles, watched the young men fling themselves into the past, and into imagined arms of luscious wolverines. 'Oh, to be cornered and torn apart,' sighed a blue-eyed angel with blond curls. 'Oh, to be devoured by twenty Amazons . . .' What did these men really want? Alone and isolated in a strange land, ordered to impose a discipline totally unrelated to the native consciousness, they sought to alleviate their loneliness through physical indulgence, more often imagined than real. The arms that made them comfortable – where were they?

Julian looked at his brother sitting with his chin on the table.

I've lost control somehow, and slipped, thought Dane. And I don't know how to get back on my feet. I came to this country just for fun, and now I feel that I've forgotten how to laugh. Why did this happen? I hate this, but I don't want to get out of it. I have terrible fears during the day, and on nights like this; but when on that altar among pomegranates I can't think or speak. I never wanted this.

'Hey, hey, Fletcher, give us one of your sea shanties!' From somewhere a guitar appeared, and a sandy-haired, green-eyed young giant began to sing.

'Hey, come on, old chap, another one, wha'd'you say?'

'Shut up, you bastards!' snapped a dark-haired young man.

'Why, what's bitten you, Mike?'

'All this silly talk about the women here! All these silly stories about tribal women!' He slammed his mug down. 'Tell them, Dick Farrell, tell them what you told me after you came back from Simla.'

Brown-haired, freckled, Dick Farrell stared at his boots. 'Stop staring at me like I was a two-headed calf or something, bloody hell. You're all wrong – you know it too. I had all these fancies before.' Dick Farrell poured his drink on the ground. 'Now we're going to get all silly and maudlin. Hell, why did you bring this up now, Mike? To be home again. This constant moving from one place to the other – never stops.'

Somebody took the guitar out of Fletcher's hands.

Thomas Sherley tried to shut the music and the voices out. 'O

94

western wind, when wilt thou blow?' He stuffed his head into
the pillow and covered his ears. 'The small rain down can
rain.' His bandaged head throbbed and his throat felt full of
ashes. 'Christ, that my love were in my arms —' They're
having fun as usual. And he's there too. Can't face them any
more. Can't face him any more. 'And I in my bed again.' Why
did I do this? What a frightful mess. Made a fool of myself, I
did. I'm all right. Sherley gripped his head and gasped
painfully. He continued to dig at the pillow with his head. Go
away, go away. I know, you've been there, too, Ravinspur.

Got to drink some water.

If only they'd shut up – all of them out there. No sleep. Ahh,
why is it so hot? Sherley poured the glass of water over his
face. Is it cool outside?

The young soldier strummed on in the darkness. 'That's a very
old song.'

'Yes. I'll sing it again.'

'Orion,' somebody whispered pointing. 'Libra, Scorpio . . .'

'Do you think that a soldier wrote that song?'

'Maybe a sailor did. Maybe . . .'

'It's sort of lonely out here, no matter what.'

'Yes.'

'Sometimes you go and do things you regret later.'

'And nobody understands. Everybody's always too ready to
curse.'

'It isn't always loneliness, though.'

'I know. Do you remember that big scandal ten years ago?
Oscar Wilde and the Marquess of Queensberry's son, and all
about that club on Fitzroy Street?'

Dane jerked his head up.

'Oh, yes, that Oscar Wilde fiasco. Went to prison, didn't he?'

'Not Douglas, though. He left the country.'

'These rich folk, they just go into these things for a lark. Just
to seem different, to draw attention. The others pay the price.'

'Hey, come on, boys, let's get away from all this.' Trevors
thumped on the bench. 'Come on, Fletcher, how about
another one of those —'

'Nah, nah, can't bear the sound of that stuff any more.
Nothing's moving any more. Feel like I'm stuck somewhere.'

'C'mon, let's go get some —'

'Nah. Sick and tired of it all, I am.'

'Why don't you sing, Ju? Haven't heard you sing for years.' Julian looked at his brother, startled. 'Come on, Ju – here, take the guitar.' Julian moved his fingers over the instrument. The strings vibrated against his fingertips. 'Please, Ju.'

'Oh, all right. Er, what should I sing?'

'Anything you want to.'

'Yes, anything you want.' The men turned to him, some shuffling their feet, some filling their glasses.

'Um, there's this lyric by Lord Byron that I like very much. I'm not sure if it was ever set to music. I'll sing it the way I feel it should be sung. It's sort of a "death" lyric.' Julian adjusted the guitar. 'It's called, "So We'll Go No More A-Roving". '

Hiding behind the mess, Sherley sank to his knees and covered his face. Just a little fresh air – that's all I want. They all shook hands and everything is all right again. I'll shake hands too. I'll do anything just to get it over with. This frightful awkwardness. Why can't I get over it? I've tried so hard. Why does the spirit collapse when the body rebels?

'Why did you sing that song, Ju?' The Yamuna flowed quietly, rubbing gently against mud and rocks. The two horses nibbled at the grass. Julian stared at the dark star-flecked waters. Phulgarh slept behind them. 'Ju, why that song?'

'I like it,' said his brother.

'Why?'

'It's about change.'

'Why did you call it a death lyric?'

'I meant a release from the past, that's what it is.'

'Are you sorry about the past?'

'No, not at all.'

'Then why do you want to forget it?'

'Didn't say I want to forget it – simply want to move away from it. The past is not linked to us; it's separate. It's like shedding skin – this shaking out of the past. Want to look at the past with different eyes. Want to make others look at it with different eyes.'

'What do you want, Julian?'

'Don't want to perform.'

'What about —' Dane stopped.

'What about what?'

'What about that club on Fitzroy Street?'

Julian turned his face away. 'It's not what you think, Dane. I got myself into a mess, I know. I got sick and tired of all that, of labels.'

'I never believed anything they said about you.'

'Believe what you want — it doesn't matter now.'

'Ju, this Indian chap —'

'Cut it out, will you.'

'Don't get yourself into another mess.'

'Why don't you just worry about yourself?'

'I — uh — ' Dane slowly pushed his cuticles back with his thumbnail. 'I don't know what to do.'

'So you think you're in love or what?'

'Don't take that tone with me.'

'I see you mooning around, staying out all night. It's difficult not to notice. At the *kota*, you walked out when that famous dancing girl appeared.'

Dane stood up and kicked a pebble into the river. 'This whole thing is impossible, damn it.'

'Then why break your heart over it?'

'I don't want to talk about this.'

'Where the hell do you go every night?'

'Shut up, Julian. You always mock everything I do or feel as if you get some kind of perverse pleasure by making me look ridiculous. That's why you went out of your way to seduce Helena.'

'Blame me for every damn thing that goes wrong, don't you? Isn't that perverse?'

'Why can't I ever depend on you? I stood by you when everyone turned against you?'

'You stood by your imagined concept of "your brother", not by me.'

'And what's wrong with wanting you to be the kind of brother I want? Just think back — how we were, when we were younger — what's wrong with that? What's wrong with loving someone? What the hell is wrong with love?' Dane pulled Julian up on his feet by his lapels. 'You're afraid, Julian, you are just too damned scared. You make me sick!'

'Then just leave me alone, damn you.' Julian shook himself free.

'No, I won't leave you alone. And I'm not going to wait for you at Ravinspur either. You take care of Ravinspur or it can go to the dogs! Constantly waiting, and putting my life on hold while you fly around having fun. Enough! What about me, damn it? I want to do all the silly romantic things I like. I want to live my own life.'

'Well, go ahead, do what you want, leave me alone.'

'Not till I get some answers, Julian. You sit down here and tell me why you left Ravinspur after you returned from Cambridge. Why did you stay away for so long? Was it because of Father?'

'No, it wasn't because of Father.'

'You blamed him for . . . for your mother's death.'

'Initially, yes.'

'You know what happened.'

'Yes — servants' talk.'

'I'm sorry, Ju, I wish you didn't have to find out that way.'

'One night in Dover with some ballet dancer. And she came to know. God! It seemed as if all hell had broken loose that morning in September. And then, they brought her in, late that afternoon. Killed herself to make him suffer. Took the wildest horse out of the stables. Didn't think of me. Revenge was all that was on her mind. And afterwards, he sort of forgot about me, too. Went off to India. Doesn't matter now. I've shut it out. Love doesn't matter any more.'

'Papa never loved me as much as he loved you. He always said you had your mother's eyes.'

Julian stood up and walked towards the river. 'Dane, would you like to take over the title? I'll sign it all over to you.'

'What are you talking about!'

'I feel like staying in India. You'd make a far better earl anyway.'

'You bastard — take my leavings, is it? You damn well take care of what's yours. I have Cheveley and I want to live there free of your responsibilities. And' — he caught Julian's shoulders — 'don't you dare push me away. Love doesn't matter any more — is that so?' He began to shake Julian. Julian tried to break away. They fought each other viciously, Dane trying to pin Julian down, Julian struggling to be free. 'You bastard, squirm all you want – I'm going to make you cry – like I've cried – you're going to cry like you've never cried before – love doesn't matter – cry, you idiot —' Dane slapped him hard across his face. 'Cry – you bastard, you're going to cry – cry – I'll cry with you —'

Unnoticed, the sky had lightened to mauve-grey, then to shimmering opal; and now, the silver waters tossed the sun up among whisper of dawn-hush, bird wings.

Chapter 5

The flute began to respond slowly. Next to the river, Julian sat with the old flute-seller and played while Nikhil watched. Feathery clouds fanned out against the glowing sky of mid-November. The flute was warm with the sun against his mouth.

Nikhil, lying on his back and chewing a *paan* stalk, followed the chiffon clouds. Isn't this what he had longed for? I've found him here, even if I can't touch him. I can look and look all I want. Stand on that empty altar and play. When you leave the garden leave your flute in the river, your voice in the waves. Flutecaressed, I shall drown . . .

Drown. Why do I think of loss, death? Krishna is life, love, fusion, madness . . .

And I'm waiting for that madness. You'll forget what you are. You'll forget your head.

'How's your head, Tom?' Cyril Trevors touched his friend's bandaged head.

'Better,' mumbled Sherley. Trevors sat down next to him on the bench outside the mess.

'You ought to go and apologise, Tom. Shake hands and forget about it.'

'I made a fool of myself, Cyril.'

'You were drunk, that's all; they'll understand. Buck up, Tom,' Trevors grinned. 'I've never seen you get knocked out before.'

'He took me by surprise.'

'Did you hear us that evening, Tom? We had a smashing time. But then we got a little homesick, all of us – ah, but it was fun. Could you hear us from the barracks?'

'Yes.'

100

'Even his lordship picked up the guitar and sang, you know.'

'Yes, I know.'

'Go and shake hands with them, Tom. I'll ride to Phulgarh with you, if you like.'

Shake hands. How can I escape you, Ravinspur? I hate you because you make me dream.

'Come on, Tom, let's go.'

'Yes, uh, the sun feels good.'

'Yes, it's a wonderful day.' Trevors looked at his friend, puzzled. 'Are you feeling all right, Tom?'

'Yes, let's go.' How to shake hands with him? I'll just close my eyes, Ravinspur.

'Could we ride faster, Cyril?' Sherley dug his heels into his horse's sides. They had shaken hands. Hands touching cold and stiff; forcing themselves to smile at one another. And he came forward, too, flute in hand. Hope your cut heals fast, Sherley. Cricket tomorrow, m'lord? 'Ride faster, Cyril.'

'Why, what's wrong?'

'Nothing – just want to feel the wind against my face.' Sherley tore his bandage off as the horses broke into a fast canter.

'Tom, what are you doing?' Sherley's forehead bled afresh as his fingers ripped the lint off. 'Tom!'

'Leave me alone, for godsake.' The wind moved the blood away from his eyes and into his dark hair. Trevors watched his friend gallop off the dusty road and across the grassy stretch of land that sloped towards the wheat fields.

'Tom, where are you going?'

So much better this pain. Sherley crouched over his horse's neck. This blood tastes good and salty. This pain saves me.

'Sherley!' Trevors tried hard to catch up with his friend. 'Tom, stop.' At last the reins were within his grasp. Trevors caught the reins and dragged the other horse to a halt. Sherley rolled off the saddle and fell on the grass without a sound. His blood-soaked hair and face began staining the bright sun-lit grass.

Julian walked through the woods as the dawn seeped through

the dark leaves, through clusters of frangipani and bamboo groves. The grass and fallen leaves were wet with dew. He passed the ruins and reached the white road that led to the Krishna temple.

Leaving his shoes at the gate, he went up the steps slowly and stretched out on the wide terrace before the inner recess. The stone was cold and refreshing against his body. Above, just sprays of pastel clouds and a limitless pearliness. There was nothing else. He was lost in the opalescent nothingness, lost, lost and free.

Leaning against a column, he watched her arrange flowers at the altar. He wanted to touch those petals. He wanted to lift them up and place them on the altar. A pair of slender blue feet covered with petals. As she left, he moved towards the altar lit with lamps and incense.

'Wait.' Julian turned around, startled. 'You can't enter – you have to bathe first.' Nikhil stood there with flowers in his hands. He placed the flowers on the altar and smiled. 'Come with me.'

Nikhil drew a bucket of water up the well in the temple courtyard. Julian raised the bucket over his head and let the water cascade down his body. The first rays of the sun caught him shivering.

Kneeling on the altar with flowers in his hands, Julian looked at his fluteplayer.

'He will not satisfy your hunger,' whispered Nikhil, 'thirst if you yearn for release. When your soul thirsts, he will respond. Now, place the flowers at his feet. This is sandalwood paste – it feels cool and fresh on your forehead. Light the incense. You will fly when the flute sings.'

Back from Agra and into Meena's caring hands again! This woman has magic fingers, Lorna. My headaches, backaches, calluses disappear at the touch of her fingers! While massaging my feet last night, she told me tales of wonder. *Saab* plays the flute, *memsaab*, she said. Julian! *Jee, memsaab, saab* plays like Krishna. A god! So Julian plays the flute near the bazaar. He's picked up an Indian friend called Nikhil, Meena tells me. The fellow is an *'awara,'* a loner, one without any ties of family or friends. At the bazaar, they talk about Julian: how can a *sahib* play the flute? Why does a *sahib* play the flute? Is he a real *sahib*? They say his skin is golden and not white! Meena says all the servants know, so all the *sahibs* will know about his lordship's fluteplaying! I don't find that so scandalous, but I'm sure Dane will, especially since Julian's mixing with the riff-raff. So much more interesting than the stuffed shirts at the club.

Anyway, if the flute makes the earl happy, then let him play the flute. But I'm curious to meet Julian's friend; I don't think I'll get the chance.

Meena tells me there are other stories. Jugnu, the boy who takes care of Dane's things, spreads tales about him. But Meena wouldn't tell me what he said. She said, *chhoté saab* is young and headstrong. Couldn't get another word out of her.

Julian's playing the flute in this citadel of flowers. And what is Dane doing in this foreign land?

Dane sat on the altar with his chin resting on his knees, his hands clasping his ankles. His dinner jacket, collar and tie lay on the blanket that he had spread on the cold stone. To lie here and think of her. To think of her and block all thoughts of Julian. Had he hurt Julian that night? Did he hit him too hard? Julian crying in anger, not really crying. Julian would never bring it up, never mention the fight, like he never reopened anything, any fight that had ever taken place between them. Clam up and bury it. That was Julian.

God, what was he doing here? He should just go back to England; leave without looking back. Or he should blow his brains out. He must do something.

Pomegranates. Striking one against the floor, he cracked it open. In the faint moonlight, the fruit glistened like wine-soaked pearls. As he dug the pips out with his fingers and ate, the purple juice ran down his throat. Laughing and feeding each other, and dreaming. 'Dane,' she repeats over and over again. He felt ridiculously happy. His white shirt was spotted with the purple juice, his mouth was all sticky and he loved it. 'Purple-stained mouth,' he murmured. Sticky hands against the mouth. 'Sakhi,' he said, 'Sakhi, you're mine.'

*　　*　　*

'My *saab* makes her dream,' said Jugnu. 'He makes her feel free. She's tired of bonds and wants to escape. She'll be as free as your hair between my fingers and —'

'Oy, keep your hands off me, *chutiya*! Think you can seduce me with these silly stories? Let's see your money first.'

'Ah, her hair is like dark rain clouds, her eyes like quicksand. Salman's heard about her infidelity and is galloping hard through the desert on his black mare, Dilruba. He is coming to take back what belongs to him. Won't you even let me hold your hand?'

'Acchoo!'

She offered him the roasted corn cob flavoured with lemon juice and rock salt that she was chewing on. He took a bite. 'Acchoo!' She sneezed again. 'Ram, Ram! Your *sahibs*! You smell of them nowadays.'

'She belongs to him now,' he said. 'He even pulls her hair like this.'

'Aoooh! *Chutiya*, take that.' Her knuckles caught the side of his mouth. Within seconds Jugnu tasted blood.

'She's owned by two men – that's what she deserves.'

'Nobody owns her. She's just your fucking fantasy. And – don't play games with me. I can buy you, sell you and buy you back again.' She tossed the gnawed corn cob away.

'Your playing has improved,' said Nikhil. He sat hugging his knees and staring at Julian's blond head against the grass. His personal god at his feet. What more? The river rushed by them. Julian played intermittently, producing half-tunes and whistling sounds.

'Tell me more about Krishna,' said Julian.

'What do you want to know?'

'What was he like?'

'He was slender, dark and beautiful. At least that's how I picture him. He was aware of his effect on living creatures; he responded to the love offered to him without actually surrendering himself. They came to him for advice, for protection, for love, for friendship, for just a touch which could redeem the dream. And he let his music soothe all torments, yet create a terrible thirst.'

'What about the storm?'

'That was the night of his birth. In a prison in Mathura, a woman lay in a trance. A man cradled the baby in his arms and crept out. The guards had collapsed senseless; it was no prison then; the heavy, barred doors swung open as the thunder silenced the world, as the lightning split the darkness. The river had flooded the city, but she swept aside to make way for the man who held the baby. To Vrindaban they went, to the garden where the baby had to be abandoned, in a way.

'He grew up on his own, and learned to play for others but not with others. Of course, this is how I perceive Krishna: alone and indifferent, adored but not loved.'

'The garden?'

'Yes, the garden where you play. Alone, Krishna played in the garden, surrounded but not touched by others. Men and women fell at his feet when he played the flute. But he stood apart from them with his music. He was not one of them. He played a different music, he created the music —'

Very slowly, Julian began to play more consistent flowing tunes.

'Krishna played to the cows while they grazed. Look, do you see those cows there? They are grazing, but they raise their heads as they hear your flute; they recognise the flute. The flute makes us dream.

'The women adored Krishna and he laughed at them. He played to them, the women and the children, and they laughed, surprised and excited —'

Julian stepped into the water slowly. In the river you forgot everything. The women, who were settling down to do their evening wash, pushed their mounds of laundry aside and looked up. The children, rubbing mud on each other, turned around. Julian held out his hands. 'Sahib! Sahib!' They ran to him. He touched wet, muddy hands, tiny hands that rubbed the slippery mud all over him.

Hands pulled him into the Yamuna. The children flickered like tadpoles among the sun-splashed waters. They pulled his hair, his legs, his arms, his clothes. Laughing forms snuggled against him, felt his golden hair to see if it was real. 'Sona, sona!' Wet and muddy, he played his flutetones for them. Women tore bunches of flowers and threw them at him.

He pulled the waves around him and moved away from laughter and voices and hands and flowers. The music in the water, the waves whispered with sunlight, a storm against his ears. Silver flames swept his skin. Flutecaress. Then hands sneaked up around him and pulled him back to the bank, to flowers and voices and laughter.

'The cowherds with their cows, the women, the children, all went home to light the lamps, and to sleep and dream as the sun went down among flutetones. Come, Julian —'

Vermilion gul-mohrs in his hands, Julian smiled. 'How did he wear them?'

'Like this.' Nikhil wrapped a blue scarf around his head and tucked in the flowers.

'Now what?'

'Now play! Cross your ankles and play for the cows.'

'I play for myself,' said Julian quietly and began to play.

And Nikhil said, 'The flute sang of the river – of the river's love that flowed wild. It celebrated the wind, for the wind was wilder than the waters. In windtones there were flowers and grass, shades of sky, a golden twilight – the cowdust hour, meandering paths through sunlit forests. On moonlit nights, the flute touched leaping fishes, silver-scaled, tinged with lotus-bloom, swinging out of the river on the crests of waves. On evenings such as this, the flutetones undid carefully coiled hair and tumbled it over sandalwood shoulders in heavy, dark waves.'

To bury his face in her long dark hair and laugh. Pome-granates!

Dane, she'd say, Dane. Dane.

Julian, you said, don't think too much. Never to wake from this dream. It's slipping away. I'll wake up suddenly and find myself in Ravinspur. I can't get beyond this.

One, two, three, four, five, six long steps, feet rising up, body moving slow at first, then sudden speed, and an arc of dream movement, the arm rising. The red ball flying from his fingers towards that blond head without touching the pitch. Lying on a wooden bench outside the barracks and relaxing under adolescent hands that massaged expertly, Sherley closed his eyes and returned to the cricket field. Spinner, they thought he was, an off spinner, good leg spins once in a while, never too fast, but could make that red ball leap and curve viciously. Hah! A fast bowler is what he had always wanted to be. He could be if he wanted to. Trevors at first slip had sucked in his breath in shock. Sherley bowling fast! Not just fast, dangerously fast, the ball coming straight and hard at his lordship's head, ribs. And his lordship ducking, swerving to avoid the blows. Body-line bowling, they whispered. So fucking what? Play, if you can. Hit me back, come on. Hit that ball back at me. God! If I could have only cracked that fair head of yours, Ravinspur. The blood on your face, among your hair, staining your white shirt, running down your smooth chest . . . Ah, I'd wipe the wetness with my hands and lick the salt off my fingertips.

'Hey, Tom.' Trevors walked towards his friend, his uniform well-starched and ironed. 'Hey, Tom, don't do that to his lordship again. It wasn't fair really. It did seem like you were aiming at his person and not at the stumps.'

'Christ, leave me alone, will you! Can't a man bowl fast sometimes?'

'Just a suggestion; there's no need to shout.'

'Cyril —'

'Yes?'

'I'm thinking of asking for a transfer.'

'Oh.'

'Would you miss me, Cyril, if I went away?' Cyril Trevors felt a trifle staggered at Sherley's inquiring gaze.

'Miss you — what d'you mean?'

'I really like you, Cyril. You're probably the only friend I've ever had. Men don't take to me easily.'

'But I'm sure women do, Lucifer!' Trevors laughed.

'I'll miss you, Cyril. You've always been kind to me.'

'Oh, shut up, Tom. Go get a transfer and get lost.'

'I've got to get myself a canary, dahling. I've just fallen madly in love with a canary.'

'Go to hell.'

'I've been there, too.'

'Get up and get dressed, Tom.'

'Get this boy off my arse, then.' Trevors motioned at

Sherley's masseur to leave. The boy picked up the bowl of oil, smiled faintly and walked away. 'That boy knows his job all right. My body's never felt better.'

'Well, get up now. Don't let the O.C. catch you this way.'

'With the boy astride my arse, you mean.'

'You're in a damned strange mood, old chap.' Trevors looked at Sherley, puzzled.

'You bet I am, Cyril,' grinned Sherley and got up. 'I had better go in and wash and shave' – he turned and looked at his friend – 'and writhe in my own desperate hell.' Trevors watched Thomas Sherley's strong, young body disappear into the dark interior of the east barracks.

Cows, mud, water, children, hands, flowers, flute, flutetones, storm, green fields, 'play, Julian, play,' laughter, voices, an empty altar – they tossed and turned in Julian's mind. What had happened? He couldn't quite sequence the events. Dark soft mud, splashing water and an entering into some wondrous cavern of thoughtlessness. Writhing and twisting around him the river and the flutetones. Dane's fists vanished, the sting of slaps, the pain of knuckle against mouth, nose. He sat awkwardly on the railing of the veranda and stared at the magenta shock of bougainvillaea against the white wall. He got up and sank into a cane chair. The sun hit his eyes too suddenly and made them water. Krishna was Krishna. He played to the cows, danced on the waves, wore vermilion flowers in his hair; he was outside the circles, at the centre of the circle. He had the power. Julian looked down at his hands and his forearms. Why was he this colour? Why couldn't he be dark, just dark? Was it silly to play the flute among the cows? The children had loved rubbing mud all over him. They had thrown flowers at him. He had played for them. The river had wrapped around him. I am not me any more; I am an other; I wanted to be an other. They don't know who I am; I was just the fluteplayer. Just another storm, just another storm is all I want – a storm like the one that caught me on the first night.

'Julian, have you been sitting here all afternoon?' Caroline touched her stepson's shoulder.

'What – oh – yes, sort of.'

'Is that a flute of some sort?'

'Yes.' Julian picked up the flute from the table. 'I've learned to play it. Would you care to listen, Caroline?'

Julian played the flute with his eyes closed, lost, almost in a trance. He looked so strange, Lorna, and alien in spite of his dark blue silk shirt and pleated grey trousers. The yellow twilight, deepening to copper, tinged Julian's skin with a golden glow. The fine bones of his face seemed sculptured to perfection. Even the servants left their chores and crept towards the music.

When Julian lowered the flute, the servants ran back into the house as if shackles had been removed from their feet. I heard Ravi Singh murmur, *Madan-Mohan, Madan-Mohan,* in a shaking voice as he walked away.

Julian plays the flute like the past vanishing into nothingness. I dreamt of my first year at Ravinspur while he played. But now as I write I'm finding it difficult to recapture that year I saw unroll before my eyes this evening. I wanted to tell you about that year – I feel I should; I owe it all to you, all my happiness. Such irony! So let me tell you in a different way than I have previously. About Charles and our love. He never lost his guilt, but he was able to love again. What we had was too much a romance to be real, but it was a real romance. We loved with a desperation. We loved to rest our hurts, to fight our loneliness. I can't say it any other way. How can I tell of loving? I can only tell of the taste and feel of love, the looks and touches, the constant awareness of and wanting the other's presence.

Julian and his flute – what of that?

And his Indian friend? I guess Julian's touching their lives in a way the rest of us can't or won't or haven't. I wonder what he knows about their lives, their days and nights? What change will this new music bring to his life? What will he learn from their hopes and desires?

In a shack a few miles from the bazaar, a woman patted four dark heads and hummed tunes. She pulled a frayed and torn blanket over the tiny bodies and looked at them intently. Finally, convinced that the children were truly asleep, she

109

stood up and walked to the other end of the dingy shack where Nikhil sat cross-legged. She served him some food on an aluminium plate from a pot steaming on a bucket-shaped stove. The faint light from the lantern hanging on the unsteady wall brought out the hollows in their faces.

'It's good – the *khichri*,' mumbled Nikhil with his mouth full.

'Want more?'

'No.' Using his fingers deftly, Nikhil conveyed the yellow slush to his mouth. '*Achar hai*?' he inquired.

She removed a chunk of pickled lemon from a jar, dropped it on his plate and licked her fingers. 'Repair the roof tomorrow, Nikhil.'

'*Zaroor*. But you know that the rains are over.'

'Do it all the same.'

'I will.'

She looked at the young man's frail body as he ate silently. 'Stay with me,' she said, reaching and touching his hair, neck, shoulders. Nikhil stood up and carried his plate and glass to a corner where dirty dishes were heaped. He rinsed his fingers in the glass of water and then wiped his mouth.

'When is your *aadmi* coming back?' he asked and moved towards the sack that functioned as a door.

'He is not coming back.'

'Find someone else.'

'You stay. I need somebody to help me.'

'I'll help you, Tulsi, but I won't stay with you.'

'Just stay tonight, then.'

'No.'

'Just sleep here.'

'OK,' sighed Nikhil. 'I'll sleep right here; you sleep with the children.'

He watched her fall asleep with the children snuggling against her for warmth. She had been feeding him for months, now, and he had done odd jobs for her, looked after her children while she worked. He had fixed the roof twice already and it was falling apart again. I'll get hold of a tin sheet tomorrow. That'll hold together. The walls need more mud and bricks. I'll steal some from the construction site. Well, she could steal it herself, after all she works there all day long, carrying piles of bricks on her head. It's so ugly, that place. Why do they need another courthouse? They had removed all the grass and trees. The junior engineer was giving her a hard time, she said the other day. Maybe she shouldn't work there. If only some man would come and move in with her . . .

Nikhil pulled the thin blanket up to his chin and closed his eyes. I wonder what he is doing now. Can't touch him. What have I done to him? Don't think, don't think. This is the only way I can hold him. He wanted to be different, to be an other; playing the flute he is an other.

Flute in his hand, Julian stepped into the old temple, into that sunlit altar. He stood in the blaze of light and looked out at the dark woods that surrounded the temple. There was a different light here. It created that peculiar yearning. The emptiness yearned, it seemed, and transfused the thirst into him. He had longed to stand here for days, but a strange fear had kept him from this temple. The other temple was safer. No emptiness there. The fluteplayer reigned on that altar. Here, the bare altar just waited.

But it was not empty any more. He stood there and filled it up. It called him, it demanded his presence, he felt. He feared its call, but he prayed for it all the same. Call me, call once again for me, he had whispered over and over again, night after night.

The altar cried for its vanished fluteplayer – what else? And here he was, flute in hand, waiting to play. That empty alcove there, that's where Krishna had been. Julian positioned himself in that alcove, crossed his ankles and began to play very, very softly. The flutetones encased him; the music surged up around him like rising waters. He felt nailed by his flutetones, inescapably transfixed against the stone, unable to move, and able only to play. He lowered his flute slowly and leaned his head against the alcove wall. Spreading his arms, he spanned the alcove space. The stone wall was cool against the backs of his hands. Carved in stone, Krishna had stood here and played in that pose of intense and vulnerable sensuality.

The flute slipped from his fingers and rolled over the altar. The sharp noise made Julian open his eyes. The warmth of the mid-afternoon sun flooded him. Something had entered him, he felt; he had received the music perhaps.

'Badri Lal, Badri Lal!' Nikhil ran towards the old flute-seller who was panting and running around the maidan after the children who had snatched his flutes. 'Badri Lal!' Nikhil caught the old man's elbow. 'Stop. Listen to me.'

'They've taken all my flutes!'

'Never mind.'

'Never mind! I made them myself! They are my life.'

'You'll forget about your flutes when you hear the *sahib* play. Come with me to the river and listen to him play.'

'We'll come and listen to *saab* play! We'll play flutes, all of us! *Krishna-leela, Krishna-leela!*' The children surrounded Nikhil. Badri Lal snatched his flutes from the children.

'Take that, you little monkey! Take that! These little —'

'Stop it, you old clown. Come with me to the river all of you, and bring those cows, too.' Nikhil pulled Badri Lal along and the children rounded up the three cows and followed.

At the river women oiled their hair, washed clothes, bathed, filled pitchers. The children helped by scrubbing the clothes with chunks of large yellow soap, rinsing out pitchers, and even holding bottles of oil and waiting on the women. Buffaloes floated unconcerned. Cows sat chewing cud and licking their calves from time to time. Some nibbled the warm, moist grass. Badri Lal stuffed his *chillum* and prepared to smoke. 'You won't need that,' said Nikhil. 'When you hear his flute, you won't want that.'

Julian climbed up on a flat rock near the bank and looked at the mêlée. Nikhil ran up to him. 'They're waiting for you. Won't you play for them?' Julian smiled and sat down on the flat surface of the boulder.

'Look, look,' the children whispered, '*saab* is playing the flute!'

'How did he learn to play like that?' muttered Badri Lal. 'It takes time to play that way.'

Nikhil rested his head against the rock on which Julian sat cross-legged. 'They are lost in your music,' he said. 'You have the magic.'

And was it really happening – the magic? Julian wondered. Are they really enchanted by the flute? Or is it just he who dreams, who feels the ecstasy? He, lost, playing, playing, playing. But it's a different music; it was his personalised myth; he had created his own myth and entered its world. They were staring at him in wonder. There was a magic somewhere.

'Look, the *saab* with eyes like the rain-washed sky and hair like warm sugar-cane juice plays the flute.'

'Why does a *sahib* play the *bansuri*?' The women whispered and the children giggled. '*Pagal hai, yeh sahib pagal hai*. A crazy, white man with a flute, eyes closed, sitting on a rock. He's crazy, crazy as the wind,' they laughed. 'But he is beautiful. He is beautiful and mad.'

Is it he or the flute that plays? thought Badri Lal, taking a long drag from his *chillum*.

Jugnu watched his *burra saab* play. How could this happen? How could he enchant all with his flute? They think he has some magic. *Saabs* can't play our flutes. You have to lose yourself to play the flute that way. You have to have that madness of Krishna that draws men and women alike. *Saabs* always so controlled. *Saabs* never lose their minds. Who knows, maybe *saabs* really have some magic we don't know of like the men who hang by their tongues at fairs.

They say he plays like Krishna. That dolt, Ravi Singh, feels *saab* is an avatar. Hah! The only avatar left to come is Kalki not Krishna. And if Kalki should play the flute then we'll all drown in the river with him. Look at them watching this *tamasha* open-mouthed, amazed by a *sahib*'s madness. Does he believe in the flute, in its power to enthrall the world? Will there be terrible unrest and madness now that Kalki plays the flute?

The tea cup slipped and fell and broke. 'Blast!' Dane muttered. Dane overturned the pot of honey shortly afterwards and swore again. He dropped the butter-knife twice and then his toast.

'What's the matter, love – developing palsy?'

'Shut up, Ju.'

113

'Are you feeling all right, dear?'

'Yes, Mother.'

'There's no need to snap at us,' said Julian sharply.

'You look upset, Dane. Is everything all right?'

'Everything's fine. I'm fine. I just want a little peace and quiet in the morning.'

'Banging and smashing things at breakfast is hardly the way to ensure peace and quiet.'

'Cut it out, will you!'

'Don't you yell at me, Dane.'

'Oh, I might as well tell you now,' cut in Caroline hurriedly, anticipating a fight, 'the servants are all taking off on Tuesday. There's a fair or a bazaar of some sort in Talkot next week and they all want leave. The *khansama* is not going, though. So he'll take care of things. I'll be spending Tuesday with Mrs Bancroft and others. The D.M.'s wife has organised a picnic, I believe.'

They turned and looked at her, not quite knowing what to do with this piece of information at the moment. 'There's a fair in Talkot on Tuesday and all the servants are going there,' repeated Dane.

'Yes, dear, Mrs Bancroft said it's quite a big event for the Indians.'

'I see.' Dane stared at his plate for a few seconds. A big event for all the Indians. All the Indians. 'Thank you, Mama, I love you.' He got up and kissed her. Caroline wiped the bread-crumbs off her cheek and watched her son run down the drive.

'I think you've just showed him the way to get into trouble,' murmured Julian and poured himself a cup of coffee.

Jugnu raised the binoculars to his eyes and took a sweeping look at the Talkot fair spread out below. The Ferris wheel had stopped for a few minutes and Jugnu's seat was the highest point right now. He had stolen the binoculars from the Collector's *khansama*, and with them he could scan every little detail of the fair – who was there, who was arriving, who was leaving ... There were men hanging by their tongues, men lying on beds of nails, magicians tossing skulls and bones, boys writhing and contorting their skinny bodies to drumbeats, snakes coiling around their owners, women appearing as mermaids in dark tents, two-headed animals. Then there were monkeys dancing, men, women, and children on tightropes, and of course roasting corn and peanuts, candies wrapped in dirty paper, potatoes in spicy tamarind juice and yogurt. Crude, wooden merry-go-rounds, bangles, toys, birds chirping and singing in cages – all spread out noisy and colourful. He saw some of the soldiers from the cantonment ride in.

Trevors *saab*, yes, he was at the club frequently, and ah, Sherley *saab*. All the shoeshine boys said he was short-tempered and moody. And two other soldiers. All here to look at the hanging man and pick up whores. Swearing, to be sure, as cows and goats bump into their horses. And, my God! The women were trying to pull them down from their horses! Whee! The giant wheel swung into motion.

The fair danced up and down so close to his eyes.

'Dane *saab*!'

He couldn't believe it – his *chhoté saab* rode in with Winston *saab*.

And, unbelievable! Julian *saab* was dismounting outside the fair grounds, tying his horse to a tree, now walking in with Nikhil! There, they've found each other. Shaking hands with the soldiers. *Chhoté saab* doesn't seem too happy. Turns away. Why? *Arré, kya kismet hai* – those women are pulling at them! Ah, what's going on there? Sherley *saab* is looking at *burra saab* intently. Nikhil is looking at Sherley *saab* intently now. Sherley *saab* is loosening his collar. The fight at the *kota* – maybe they're still angry at each other. Wonder what's going on between *burra saab* and Nikhil? Why did Sherley *saab* and Nikhil look at each other that way?

What now? *Chhoté saab* seems to be angry with *burra saab*. *Kamal hai!* I must be dreaming – Shehzadi! Shehzadi – Sakhi – the prince's *mehbooba* has arrived! Such excitement – everyone wants to pay homage to her. Throwing flowers at her feet. Those bangle-sellers, they're offering her bangles.

Putting two fingers in his mouth, Jugnu whistled as loudly as he could.

Oh, God! Her face is my curse. Oh, Shehzadi, oh! *Hé Ram,*. people are moving aside and making way for her. Ah! look at the men sighing after her. Ah, Shehzadi's going towards the bangle-sellers. The young one – the lucky *chutiya* – she touched his head. It's all *kismet*. Puny bangle-sellers like that *chhokra* receive caresses, while a *jalta hua jawan* like me rots up here.

Kya?! I can't believe my eyes. Who is that riding in on that white stallion? It's the one and only Zafar Khan, the prince's bodyguard! What a moustache, what clothes! Oh, the women are clutching at his legs. Rot, rot up here, Jugnu, you *ulloo ka pattha*. Why didn't you get off this contraption when it stopped? *Oy sala!* Zafar Khan is giving her something – Oh, God, I can't believe this either! *Chhoté saab* has jumped off his horse and is running towards Shehzadi. *Sala!* Will Zafar Khan chop his head off with that great sword of his?

Chhoté saab has grabbed Sakhi by the shoulders! Ohh! This is passion, *muhabbat, ishq!* Now his head will be cut off. He'll die for love. Shehzadi has slapped him, a stunning blow. Dane *saab* reels backwards. Julian *saab* and Winston *saab* catch him, drag him out. They are mounting their horses.

And down below, commotion, *hangama!* A *sahib* slapped by a *nachnewali* in public! If only I could be down there and not up here!

Two miles from the fair, they reined and dismounted. 'Stop sobbing in this imbecile way at once!' shouted Julian. 'You brainless idiot! It's going to be the talk of the town now.'

'She slapped me – oh, I —'

'Stop this snivelling. Shut up right now.'

'Dane, you really shouldn't have – you can't do things like this.' Harry sighed. 'Getting slapped in public by one of 'em, by the prince's mistress – God knows what stories will spread – oh, God! People will wonder why . . . A *sahib* getting slapped in public by a native woman – it's a matter of *izzat*, y'know. You'll never be able to show your face at the club after this.'

'Rubbish, Winston. Let's just go home.' Julian mounted and shook his reins.

'How could she slap me, Ju —' Dane's voice broke.

A resounding slap from Julian's right hand set Dane's mare galloping into the sunset.

Slowly, the four subalterns rode out of the Talkot fair. There was excitement back there. People couldn't stop talking. 'What was that all about?' asked Trevors.

'Lost his head – too much to drink, perhaps?' Dick Farrell suggested.

'Didn't seem drunk when we shook hands,' Rowley said.

'Lost his head – must be this country,' Trevors said with a laugh. 'What d'you say, Tom?'

Sherley shrugged and moved his horse ahead of them. 'In one of his damn moods again,' Trevors said.

Sherley tossed his hair away from his eyes. Who was that native with Ravinspur? Why did he stare at him that way? As if he was touching him almost. No! Who was that bastard?

Ravinspur had looked at him, too, with that spurning look. Above all that, does he think he is? Not that skinny native, he isn't, not if he looks that way. Losing his head – did he now – did Hartley? Losing one's head. Done that, too. Ah, Ravinspur – no, I'll never touch you.

People yelling and screaming back there over a *sahib* losing his head. But this twisting deep inside – how to lose that? Just to get away from it all.

I don't know what's going on any more. Julian seems so nonchalant it's amazing. And something has certainly happened to Dane. He broods night and day. Lorna, if only we could escape the madness that surrounds us. I keep thinking of this cloudiness as madness. Don't know why. Inside our heads is everything still the same? At the club last evening, the Superintendent of Police, Mr MacLeish, hit Mr Lyndon, the District Magistrate. Roanna Lyndon clutched a bearer and fainted. Wiping his bloody nose, Mr Lyndon gasped from the floor, 'Roanna, for heaven's sake, not the bearer!' They were arguing about temple art. Dr Morel said it was just one of those days – too much stuff in their heads. But what's inside Dane's head now? I asked him what was wrong. He said he had a headache. His marathon sulk has given *me* such a splitting headache that right now I'd believe anything about heads!

What's wrong with you, Dane? His mother's voice irritated him. Julian and Harry had slapped his back about two hundred times and said, buck up, now, come on, or something equally idiotic. And of course their mocking laughter.

Everything had gone wrong. How could this have happened? Slapped, spurned. Impossible. She wanted him, he loved her. She had looked at him so many times while she danced, he was sure. She always looked at him, didn't she? He wanted to take her away from there and run off to the mountains or something. He was going to carry her away. He had planned to rescue her at the fair, just go off with her like that doctor in Dr Morel's story.

Silly dreams. So real. Not dreams.

'Julian,' Nikhil said, 'come have dinner with me.'

'Gladly,' he said, 'Dane's sulk is fogging up the house.'

Reaching Tulsi's shack, 'Wait,' Nikhil said, 'let me tell her you're with me, or she might panic. She doesn't like *sahibs*.'

'Why did you bring me here then?'

'She cooks well. Look at those two girls playing hopscotch, they're Tulsi's daughters. The older one's six, the other, four. And that one, there, with the marbles, she's three. Tulsi has a son, too, a year old, sick all the time. He'll probably die pretty soon.'

'Nikhil!'

'Wait here. Let me call her.'

Nikhil went inside the shack. Julian stood outside and looked at the two girls, slim and brown, their shoulder-length hair streaked with mud. They gave him covert glances. 'Hello,' he smiled and went towards them. Holding hands, they drew back. He sat down and, tilting his head to one side, smiled widely again and stretched out his arms. They crept towards him slowly, and gingerly touched his fingertips. Growing bolder, they fingered the sleeves of his cotton *kurta*. Then, within seconds, they were feeling his hair and face and smiling shyly.

The girl playing with marbles ran inside after Nikhil.

'I don't want *sahibs* here,' Tulsi said.

'He's different. He's going to eat with us. He's nice, not like the *saabs* at the construction site. Come outside.'

'No.'

'He plays the *bansuri*. He'll play for you.'

He pulled her outside. 'Julian, this is Tulsi.' Julian saw an under-nourished woman of about thirty with frightened dark eyes and a tired face. The girl hiding behind her looked at her sisters messing the *sahib*'s hair and climbing on his back. Slowly, she moved closer and touched Julian's hand. Julian laughed and, picking up the child, stood up. The other two snuggled against him happily. They had never known a man to smell so clean and fresh. They held his hands and sniffed and sniffed. Julian was relieved that they did not have runny noses. Tulsi stared in horror at her daughters' forwardness.

They sat outside with steaming *khichri* on aluminium plates. Tulsi went inside to quiet the wailing baby. Nikhil looked at Julian and suppressed a smile. 'Eat,' he said and neatly scooped the buttery lentil and rice mixture into his mouth with his fingers. Julian watched Nikhil's action. He tasted the stuff with his fingers first.

'It's delicious.'

'Yes, it is. She's a good cook.'

'Um, I'm not quite sure how to do this.'

'Do what?'

'I mean, I've never used my fingers.'

'Oh.' Nikhil began to laugh. 'Watch me and learn.' Carefully, Julian worked his way through the food.

He ate as elegantly as he possibly could. Tulsi came and served them vegetables: cauliflowers and potatoes cooked together. 'This is really good,' said Julian. '*Shukriya*.' Tulsi smiled shyly and went inside again.

'She's a little suspicious of the *sahibs*. The junior engineer at the construction site is bothering her. She has run into some awkward situations before.'

'I'm sorry that we're such a nuisance.'

'Don't include yourself, Julian. You are not one of them.'

'Yes, I am, in certain ways, and I can never escape that.'

They washed their hands and settled down outside. Tulsi sat on the doorstep, cradling the sickly, one-year-old boy, while her daughters jumped all over Nikhil, tickling him and pulling his hair. Julian lit a cigarette and looked at the fireflies.

'Ask him to play,' Tulsi whispered to Nikhil.

'Let him finish his cigarette — I'll ask him afterwards.'

But they didn't have to ask. Stubbing his cigarette on the ground, Julian picked up his flute. He felt the river against his ears, the moonlight on his face, and in the darkness there was wild gardenia and musky incense.

The children listened, hands clasped. Tulsi moved towards the slender form and, bending down, gently touched his feet with her hands. Julian opened his eyes at the light touch and lowered the flute. She had touched his feet the way the woman at the temple touched that fluteplayer's feet every morning.

'Let's go to Talkot,' Julian said to Nikhil sitting on the temple steps as they watched the sun come up and flood the river with silver and gold.

'Talkot?'

'Yes, I want to see that other temple.'

'That's a Shiv temple.'

'I want to see it. I want to get out of Phulgarh. I'm tired of Dane's epic sulk. It's been days. Get over it. No – he must sit on the veranda and look pathetic and ask for pomegranates. Anyway, I just wanted to see a different temple.'

'Julian.' Nikhil stopped him at the steps of the Talkot Shiv temple. 'I'll wait here on the maidan and enjoy the sun. Don't eat or drink anything they give you inside.'

After inspecting the phallic symbol inside the dark interior of the temple, Julian stepped out with a clay cup full of milky fluid. 'Don't drink that,' cried Nikhil wildly.

'Why not?'

'It's *bhang*!'

'It smells all right, and' – Julian took a sip – 'it tastes fine.'

'You'll go crazy!'

'That's all right.'

In half an hour, Julian was rolling on the grass among cows and children, laughing hysterically and singing nursery rhymes. Nikhil buried his face in his hands and sat down. God, how long will the *nasha* last? One cup – well, maybe not more than two hours.

Ravinspur? Sherley drew in his breath sharply and brought

his horse to a halt. He had left the cantonment for an hour's ride. 'Hey, *idhar ào*!' He called one of the children running around. Three of them ran up to him.

'*Jee saab?*'

'What's the matter with the *saab*? *Kya ho gaya saab ko?*'

'*Nasha, saab, nasha. Bhang, bhang!*'

'I see.'

Julian stretched and rolled on the grass. He flung off his shirt and clutched his head and roared with laughter. Sherley gripped the pommel hard, his knuckles turning white. That complete physical abandon, vulnerable and intense, between the warmth of grass and sky, made Sherley's mouth go very, very dry.

Nikhil raised his head at the sound of hooves and accented Hindi. That soldier again! Eyes, the colour of neem leaf. That strong, tanned throat rising from the open-necked khaki shirt. He saw the soldier's eyes follow the lines of Julian's body against the grass.

Nikhil ran to Julian and grabbed his hand. 'You should go back to Phulgarh now.'

'Oh, yes, yes, right away, tally ho! Here I come.' Flinging an arm around Nikhil, he let himself be propelled towards his horse.

As Julian rode away, Nikhil turned and met Sherley's eyes. Sherley walked his horse towards him. 'Hey, *saab ka nauker hai?*'

'We're friends,' answered Nikhil in clipped tones.

'Know the language, eh? I guess it makes things easier, what?' Sherley looked him up and down. 'What does he see in you, you pathetic little native?'

'I don't think you know Julian,' said Nikhil.

' "Julian," eh? "M'lord" is what I call him.' Sherley spat on the ground. 'And that's how I feel about his high and mighty.'

'Is that why you can't take your eyes off him?'

Sherley's crop whipped the air. Nikhil ducked in time and jumped away. 'Don't you dare touch me, soldier.'

'The name's Thomas Sherley.' With a sudden movement he leaned and caught Nikhil's hair. 'Come over to the cantonment some time.' He dug his heels into his horse's sides and rode off. Nikhil felt his body burn.

Sitting on the river bank, Julian closed his eyes and smiled. Dane brooding on the veranda. Go on, go play cricket, darling, and get drunk religiously every night. You'll feel much better. Go and ride with Harry. How about bridge? Billiards? Only Julian's nimble footwork had kept him from receiving a black eye, a broken nose, a dislocated jaw and a crushed sternum. He chatted with Caroline to keep her mind off Dane. The fair incident hadn't yet received any publicity. Everything was splendid, he told Caroline.

So now he played his music and forgot about his brother. Nikhil wasn't here today. So what? The magic was here, with him, in his music. It enthralled the world.

The children laughed and turned away to play marbles and chase butterflies; the women, washing clothes, concentrated on stains and spots. 'The crazy *sahib* – let him play. He's always here at sunset.' They forgot about him on this sunny November afternoon. He was there every day, and he never did anything different. He was just the *sahib* who played the flute. Where were the magic and the madness?

The storm pounded against the darkness with sharp slaps of lightning and slow thunder. Holding the flute against his heart, Julian sat and looked at the storm from his balcony. They hadn't raised their heads, the cows; and the children hadn't rushed to him in wide-eyed adoration. The women hadn't even turned around. But the flutetones had soared up among the copper-tinged clouds. What about the magic? Nikhil said the flute had the magic. He had the power. So why didn't they turn to look at him, wonder at him when he played to them? Lies, then, all he had heard, all he had seen?

The wind nearly swept the trees to the ground. And then came the rain and made him gasp with the shock of its slap. Cold and stinging, the rain forced him down on the floor, tearing at his throat and face, whipping his body. He lay there, shaking, unable to resist or accept.

Dane ran through the woods soaked to the skin. She'd be there tonight, too, the way she was always there, in his mind.

There would be rain on their bodies and they would love with every flash of lightning. They wouldn't even hear the thunder.

'I don't have the power any more,' Julian whispered. 'I have lost the power. Why didn't my flute call them?' He needed to stand on that altar, he felt, he had to stand on that altar and breathe afresh whatever filled that emptiness. He had to get there somehow. It was calling him through the storm. If only it would stop calling! Why hadn't they come to him when he played? Had he been dreaming all this time and listening to lies?

Flute in his hand, he ran through the woods in the rain. 'Give me back my power!' He had been the other, the other him, one body, one soul, flutedark, flutewild, ah, flute-caress —

Entering the woods Nikhil crouched under branches. The temple would provide shelter from the storm. He bit his lips as Tulsi's worried face flashed in his mind. Tulsi waiting up to keep the food warm. *Ganja* had knocked him out for nearly five hours. He ran as fast as he could towards the old temple.

Strangled cries and running, stumbling footsteps stopped his heart. He hid behind a tree and waited.

Dane lay on the rough blanket that covered the dusty floor and listened to the storm outside. Why was he such a fool at times? Julian's so calm and rational. Flashes of lightning lit up the altar frequently and exposed the empty alcove. Wonder what was there in that alcove? A statue probably. A god of some kind. Maybe a god like the one in the other temple – the blue god with the flute.

Julian playing that flute of his on the veranda that evening. The servants staring at him as if he were — On stormy nights at Ravinspur, he would sing to the wildness outside, guitar on his knees. When they had gone to the other temple, Ju stared at the statue on the altar in an odd way.

Why would he choose to learn the flute of all things? Wonder if that Nikhil introduced him to the flute? That chap — Never mind. Why does he look at Julian that way, as if he sees something else?

Footsteps splashing through wet grass and mud made Dane sit up. He got up quickly and hid behind a broad column, holding his breath. In a flash of lightning, he saw his brother stumble into the temple, clutching a flute. Julian slipped and fell on the wet altar.

'Julian!' Dane whispered. 'What's happened to you?' Then he saw Nikhil rush in and run towards his brother.

Nikhil was just about to touch Julian's limp and wet body when a pair of strong hands grabbed Julian's shoulders and pulled him away from him. 'I'll take care of him,' Dane said and picked Julian up.

With his brother in his arms, he stood on the altar getting wetter and colder as waves of rain came in through the shattered roof. 'He lied, he lied!' Julian struggled to break Dane's hold. 'There's no power – give me back the power – not a dream, not a dream – it was real – when I played, it happened – give me back the power –' Dane held him tight and walked out into the storm.

Outside, Nikhil threw himself on the wet, muddy ground under the banyan tree. What had he done? All for love? What had he turned him into? Convulsing into a foetal crouch, Nikhil tried to control his sobs. The hysterical, cracked voice cut into him again and again. 'Give me back the power! You lied, you lied!'

Dane, terrified at his brother's delirium, held him and tried to quiet him in vain. 'Julian, Julian, please stop. God, what's the matter? Who's done this to you?' He shook Julian over and over again as he stumbled through the woods, carrying him. 'I'll take care of you. Just be quiet. Julian, it's me, Dane. Look at me, Julian, Julian, it's me, Dane.'

'Dane —' came his brother's voice after a long, long time. They were almost home.

'Ju, it's me,' he whispered and held Julian's head against his neck. 'Ju —'

'Dane,' he said, barely audible, 'Dane, take me home.'

'You are home, Ju, I've brought you home. You'll be all warm and dry again.'

'Dane – I died, Dane, I died —' Julian's voice broke and he cried against the warmth of his brother's throat.

'It's all right, Ju, everything's all right.' Dane held the frail body and kissed his brother's forehead. 'We're home.'

Morning spreads out grey and dull; it drizzles copiously. Julian tosses and turns on his bed, his body burning with fever. His delirious state alarms us, although Dr Morel tries to calm us down. Lorna, he's been wonderful. 'He's not going to die, is he?' I've asked for the hundredth time, I'm sure.

'Oh, no, no, he is hardly anywhere near death. Caught a chill, that's all.'

Dane tried to explain to me what had happened.

What were you doing at the temple? I asked.

'Oh, I, er, I wasn't there, er, I followed Ju, er, as he ran out of the house, I mean —'

And Julian – is he lost in some nightmare? He keeps crying in a broken, harsh voice, 'He lied, he lied! Why didn't it happen? I've got to reach that – I've got to keep running till I reach – let me go – don't stop me – I've got to get it back!'

I don't understand what the matter is.

'Nothing really serious. He'll be fine in a couple of days. Don't worry,' Dr Morel has said a thousand times.

'It's the flute, Mother!' said Dane. 'Yes, it's done something to him.'

What can a flute do? Julian's terribly disturbed.

'Is he very emotional?' Dr Morel inquired.

'Emotional! He's a reg'lar cold fish!' Dane said.

Julian is not a cold fish. He's just very reserved, that's all.

'The flute can be disturbng, sometimes,' Dr Morel said. 'Just one thing, your ladyship,' he added later, 'when I was with his lordship, giving him another dose of the medicine, he said something a little odd, something about his head. You see, I said to him you'll feel better in a few days. This country has a way of clearing your head. He laughed and repeated, clearing your head! There are things inside my head that I don't dare face. But you will face them some day, I said. And don't worry, your ladyship, he will straighten things out by himself.'

Caroline sat down on the edge of Julian's bed. 'Julian, can't you talk to me?'

'I'm not sure what to say, Caroline.'

125

She ran her fingers through his hair. 'Maybe you should go back to Ravinspur.'

'No, I've got to stay here and work things out. I've got to come to terms with it. I can't give up now.'

'When will you return to Ravinspur, Julian?' He turned his face away. 'You can't run away from what you are, dear.' She took his hand and felt his fingers tighten around hers. 'You are the Earl of Ravinspur, Julian. You are not just Julian.'

'Yes, I know that I am trapped for ever.'

'It's not a trap, it's a place, it's a niche. It is you who control it. Why must you feel that it controls you?'

'Because it does. Wherever I go it chases me.'

'Why run from it – turn around and step on it.'

' "Step on it" – ah, yes.' Stepping upon altars, stepping into alcoves, into flute-darkness. 'I need some space, Caroline, space to breathe.'

'Running only makes you breathless, don't you know that by now?'

'Yes, but it keeps you in motion.'

'Julian, you can't run away from everything for ever —'

'Running away? Who's talking about running away?' His voice rose. He snatched his hand away. 'Can't you understand that I'm not running away any more? I'm running to – I'm running towards – oh, and I felt I was almost there!' He turned over and buried his face in his pillow. 'I'm not running away,' came his muffled voice. 'Damn it, I'm running right into it!'

Chapter 6

'Listen,' Jugnu said to the women, 'over wide, rocky surfaces and dry plains, a black Arab mare gallops hard with a body crouching over her neck. White dust rises in towering swirls and sprays the sunset. Urged by the pressure of heels, the mare climbs up a plateau. *"Ruk ja, Dilruba,"* whispers the face next to her ear, *"ruk ja, pyari."* The mare halts on the top of the plateau and snorts. The figure on her back straightens and throws off the thick, white cashmere blanket covering his shoulders. He wears a mud-stained, white silk *kurta*. He flexes his shoulders and looks at the misty-rose palace in the distance. The sun sets and the sky fades to dusty copper.

' "Ah, Talkot," he says softly. His dark eyes narrow as he follows the outline of the palace. Lifting his hand from his mare's neck, he feels the stubble on his otherwise clean-shaven face. His face – pale and finely etched like the faces that only centuries of blue blood create. His jet-black wavy, hair, tousled from the long ride, paints shadows under his sculptured cheekbones, shadows which also bring out the – the —'

'The what, *chutiya*?'

Jugnu scratched his head. 'His mouth is firm but weak at the same time, because he is weak with love. And arrogant, too.

'Running his fingers through his Arab mare's mane, "It's not true, I don't believe it," says Salman, the prince of Talkot. "She is mine and always will be." ' Jugnu paused. She, She hadn't sneezed as yet. My God! Maybe She was entranced. 'At the palace – *bahut hangama. Chhoté nawab* has arrived. Angry and almost in tears —'

'In tears! The prince?'

'Yes. In his marble room he chews the end of a cushion and

127

asks Zafar Khan about the *sahib*. He knows what happened at
the fair, about the lovers' quarrel, from Zafar Khan. Zafar sent
a note with a carrier pigeon to the prince in Jaipur telling him
about Sakhi's infidelity. Find out, Zafar, he says, at once, and
now go bring her here. Then the *nawab* enters and orders
Zafar Khan out. Feroze comes with him and brings new
clothes for the prince. Salman stamps and screams and orders
everyone out. The *nawab* tells him to forget this worthless
nachnewali. But my honour has been touched, says Salman, I
cannot ignore infidelity. They have no right to meddle with
our women. Maybe it is our women who meddle with them,
says the *nawab*. Maybe white skin is more attractive. But my
honour has been touched! The *nawab* commands, Salman,
you should consider yourself above petty revenge. Honour is
no paltry thing, says the prince looking at the moon.'

'Where did the moon come from?'

'Shut up and listen. The *nawab* raises an eyebrow, your
honour? Yes, Father, my honour. Only fools, says the *nawab*,
would place their honour in a woman's hands. *Inshallah*, they
should suffer for such carelessness and stupidity. But Salman
wants revenge. Sakhi will have to dance on broken glass to
prove her fidelity.'

'Hah! What now?'

'One kiss, *pyare*?!'

'Get away, *badmaash kahin ka*! Go do your chores in your
sahib's house. Aachhoo!'

Tulsi balanced the bricks on her head, and smiled weakly at
the old woman who steadied her. 'That's the last lot,'
muttered the woman.

'Thank God.'

'Feeling dizzy?'

'A little. Haven't eaten all day.'

'Well, sit down for a while.' Tulsi sat down next to the pile
of bricks and accepted the offered *biri*. She stood up in a few
minutes. Holding the plate-like basket, piled with bricks, on
her head, she walked towards the men erecting a wall.

When the men and women sat down with their lunch she
had moved away. The three *sahibs* had yelled at the peon for
arriving late with their packed lunches. Then they had swept

the papers off that table near the storage shack and sat down on those wooden chairs. Spreading those clean white napkins over their laps, so neatly and carefully, they ate off white china plates, the steaming meat and vegetables, and soft, white bread.

The two engineers and the contractor moved around the construction looking for flaws in the cement-work. The men worked ceaselessly, taking only an hour off to stretch their bodies on the dry, shadeless ground.

Tulsi paused and adjusted the basket on her head. The place looked so odd to her. A half-built wall and the fresh-laid foundation. Why were they building another courthouse? They had cut all the trees, except a banana tree, and that one would never bear fruit. She lowered the bricks from her head.

Nikhil jumped off the *tonga* and thanked the *tongawallah*. 'It's a long ride to Phulgarh from Talkot,' said the *tongawallah*.

'Yes, I know.'

'Well, then, how about handing me some money, *chhokre*?'

'Money? Why, I rubbed down your horse, fed him, cleaned your *tonga* and even took your horse to the blacksmith for shoeing!'

'*Badmaash kahin ka.*'

'*Shukriya,*' said Nikhil, 'I'll walk from here.' The *tongawallah* drove straight into the congested bazaar with people screaming and swearing at him.

Nikhil rubbed his eyes. He was supposed to meet Tulsi at the site at sunset. He kicked the pebbles on the road. What was he to do now? Everything seemed out of control. Nothing made any sense. Julian hated him he was sure. Had he lied? Julian was his dream. He had not lied. But he had made Julian play for others. He should have kept Julian for himself. They laughed at him; they did not turn to look at him. Julian had ceased to be new to them. What in the world can I do? Nikhil blinked and rubbed his eyes. There was nothing to care about any more with Julian lost.

One of the men came up and took the bricks from Tulsi. She wiped her forehead with her hand and turned to go.

'Tulsi —' A male voice arrested her. 'Tulsi.' She turned around and faced the brown-haired, grey-eyed man of about thirty-five, dressed in khaki. He sat on the edge of the long wall and stared at his nails.

'*Jee, saab?*' His clothes always amazed her. Never a smudge on his starched, ironed clothes, even after a long day of heat and dust. His shirt never stuck to his back with sweat. Didn't they sweat, these *sahibs*? White skin is always clean, Kiran, the prostitute at the bazaar, had told her once. *Sahibs* are careful about dirt.

'I don't need you here from tomorrow,' he said in curt broken Hindi.

'*Saab* —' She bowed her head and walked away. Squinting in the glare of the sunset, he looked at her.

'OK, OK, *bus karo, ghar jao,* no more work today,' she heard him bark at the men and clap his hands.

Behind the half-constructed wall, Tulsi stood and stared at the darkening sky. The men had left. Nikhil had said that he would come to the construction site to take her home.

'Tulsi.' The shock of that husky voice nearly made her collapse. Percy Holloway, the junior engineer from Delhi, casually leaned against the wall, holding a sack of rice. 'This could prove to be useful, y'know,' he said in English.

'*Saab* —'

'*Chawal.*' He dropped the sack at her feet.

'*Nahin, saab.*' Tulsi moved backwards.

'Oh, come on now.' He grabbed her arm. She tried very hard to scream.

'Just what do you think you are doing?' The cold voice startled Holloway. He left Tulsi's arm and turned.

'Tulsi – come, let's go home.'

'Why, you little —'

Tulsi covered her face in horror and ran as Holloway flung himself on Nikhil.

She ran to Nikhil as he stumbled into the shack hours later, his face bloody, his clothes torn. 'Go and tell the *sahibs* at the bungalow —' he said, and then passed out in her arms.

Julian curled up in the cane chair on the veranda and closed his eyes. The afternoon was cool and breezy. There was an incredibly wonderful emptiness inside him. Waves bounced under him, around him, ever so gently, and made his body lighter and lighter until it became a part of the waves. He was the sky in the river, blue, silver-blue, white, sun-white, sun-gold. Deep, deep among windwaves, sinking, sinking . . .

Dane came out on the veranda and looked at his brother sleeping peacefully. Lying there, curled up, hands between his knees, his face against the cushions, he had such a pixie look about him. A violet silk shirt. The colours that Ju chose! Dane picked up Julian's pearl-grey jacket and covered him with it. Then he pulled up a chair and sat down and scrutinised his brother's face. No, it wasn't really a cold face. Not now, anyway. How come he never fell in love? There had been so many women in his life. What did women see in him? Harry said that it was the indifference in his eyes; he said that Julian's face frightened him at times. Strange, Helena had said the same thing. Julian scares me, Dane, she had told him one night. And a few days later, she had left him. What was so terrifying in his face? There is such lostness in his face right now.

Julian opened his eyes slowly and turned. Dane sat there, his face cupped in his hands, an odd little smile on his lips. The sun brought out red lights in his dark hair. Too much impulse and stubbornness in that nose and chin, thought Julian. Yes, Dane was incredibly good-looking. No woman had ever rejected Dane except Helena. But then, Helena was after a title, not a man; and Dane was not the Earl of Ravinspur. She was all wrong for him anyway. It's a wonder, really, that he doesn't hate me in spite of everything . . .

'Something the matter with my face?' Julian asked and yawned.

'Is something the matter with mine?' Dane flung back at him.

'Why the hell were you staring at me?'

'Why the hell were you staring at me?'

'I was just trying to stare you down!'

'I'll bet. What were you thinking, anyway?'

'I wasn't thinking.'

'Well, I was,' said Dane. 'I was wondering why you scare people.'

'What?'

'I was trying to find what is it in your face that is so frightening.'

'Why, I have the most harmless face in the world. You're the one in the family who was blessed with the Byronic element.'

'Indeed. Helena felt otherwise.'

'Helena was a scheming little bitch.'

'Shut up, Ju.'

'Dane, I did not seduce her, as you would like to think. In fact, I wasn't really interested.'

Dane looked away and smiled drily. 'Ju, we all know what happened, and I don't really care any more, so let's just drop it.' Julian sat up, put his jacket on and adjusted his collar.

'I'm going for a walk,' he said, 'want to come along?' Before Dane could answer, Harry's voice hailed them.

'Dane, you're not going to believe this! It's just awful! It's all over town!'

'What is?'

'Everybody knows about it now!'

'Knows about what?' Dane stood up, alarmed.

'What else?'

'Oh, God.'

'I just met the Collector; he said that they are desperately trying to hush the matter up. He specifically told the D.M. to tell everybody —'

'Rather an odd way of keeping a secret.' Julian shrugged. 'They'll get over it. Gives 'em something to talk about.'

'But what a scandal! Good grief! What about Dane? It's a matter of *izzat* – getting slapped!' Harry's voice hit a hysterical pitch.

'What are you getting so worked up about? Just a slap. I've survived worse. Forget it.'

'But – but —' Movement among the bushes made Harry turn. 'What's that thing there?' Harry leaned over the veranda rails.

'Tulsi!' Julian ran down the steps.

She stood there shaking and stammering. '*Saab – Saab –* Nikhil —' She stopped and covered her mouth.

'What is it?'

'*Saab —*' she started again and stopped.

'Tulsi, where's Nikhil?' Julian asked.

'*Saab, woh – usko –* engineer *saab né —*' She turned and ran.

*   *   *

132

Julian and Dane pushed their way through the bazaar, through the Indian section of the town, and finally arrived at Tulsi's shack. 'Go and play with those children,' said Julian and went inside.

He was shocked at Nikhil's state. 'Let me take you to the hospital, you need medical attention.'

'I'll be all right.'

'That man ought to get ten years for this!'

'You don't understand, Julian, he's a *sahib*.'

'What about her? What is she going to do?'

'Don't worry, Julian, I'll find work. I was going to talk to Dr Morel and ask him if he needs extra help at the hospital.'

'That's a good idea,' said Julian. 'I'll speak to him myself.'

The three girls, busy making a mud obelisk of some sort, stopped and stared at Dane. He looked different from the *sahib* who had played with them before. This *saab* didn't smile or come towards them. Dane shuffled uncomfortably under the wide-eyed scrutiny.

'Let's go.' Julian stepped out of the shack and touched his brother's elbow.

'They are staring at me funnily.'

'Never mind. We have to take Nikhil to the hospital.'

Standing at the far end of the lawn after dinner, Julian rubbed his eyes. He had done what could be done with Nikhil. He had taken him to the hospital and Dr Morel had done the needful. He would be fine; in ten days the stitches would come off; no bones broken. Percy Holloway would go scot free. They would just have to forget.

'Let's go to the club.' Dane came up and caught his arm.

'Billiards,' Harry said.

'Not tonight,' said Julian.

From the veranda, Caroline and Dr Morel looked at the three figures in the distance. 'I wonder what they are talking about? They have both been very preoccupied lately.'

'Why are you so worried about two grown men?' inquired Dr Morel.

'Because they – because they – because I want them to be happy.'

133

'Maybe they are happy.'

'No – there's too much – oh, I don't know!'

'Will you tell me something honestly? Why did you really come to India?'

'My late husband loved India and that's why I wanted to see the country for myself.'

'Now, now, your ladyship, is that really the whole truth? Wasn't it your main intention to make Dane and Julian face each other? And you certainly have succeeded in doing so.'

'I also wanted Julian to come to terms with his responsibilities. I want him to feel that he has not been trapped into certain situations. He has got to realise that you can't run away from what is essentially a part of yourself.'

'Perhaps he does realise that deep inside. Don't you see that although the flute disturbs him he continues to play it?'

'Dane said that the flute controls him. That frightens me. What does that mean?'

'Well, we could sit here and philosophise for ever, analyse to our hearts' content, label his lordship until he is a perfect specimen and arrive at some really pat and smug conclusions about the state of his mind, about his *idée fixe*, and so on and so forth. That would satisfy our souls, I'm sure. We would have in our hands a character who has been clearly defined and turned into a type. Can you tell me why we must do this? Why can't we accept the Earl of Ravinspur with all his oddities and self-contradictory elements and just say "what the hell, he's a fine fellow, and I like him"? And like him I do! Do you know that he came to the hospital this afternoon and practically implored me to give some Indian chappie, who looked like he'd been badly beaten up, a job at the hospital?'

'Well, I do love him very much. But I want him to be happy, I want to help him just like he helps other people.'

'Caroline!' Dr Morel sighed with exasperation. 'If your stepson needs your help, I assure you, he will take it by force!'

'Howard,' said Caroline, 'don't you ever call me "your ladyship" again!'

Nikhil tidied up Dr Morel's consultation room at the hospital. He liked working here, and he liked Dr Morel. He sat at the table and took down people's complaints and passed them on to the doctor in the next room. Then, as Dr Bose, the Bengali doctor who assisted Dr Morel, came and called out names Nikhil escorted the patient to the examination room. Of course his responsibilities did not end there. He also had to make up little packages of medications for the patients, according to their prescriptions, and re-explain dosage and other instructions. His own bruises had practically disappeared and the stitches on his forehead were due to come off in a few days. Julian had brought him to the hospital almost by force, helped partially by Dane. And now, here he was dusting furniture, watering plants and rearranging chairs and papers.

Julian hadn't even mentioned the flute or the temple. Nikhil hadn't had the courage to do so either. We've reached an impasse, thought Nikhil as he watered the tiger-lilies outside Dr Morel's consultation room. I've got to break through it, somehow. I've got to get you back. All my life I've searched for a certain face, for a pair of eyes, and the moment I saw you, my dream became defined. I cannot stand by now and watch the trashing of that dream. You have made me dream too much. I can't let go now.

'You're flooding the place, son.'

Nikhil started and set the sprinkler down. 'I'm sorry, so sorry, I'll mop it up immediately.' Dr Morel watched him clean up the mess, all flustered and confused.

'How does your head feel now? I'll cut the stitches in two days.'

'I'm fine. I really am very grateful for everything you've done for me.'

'You should be thanking his lordship really.'

'Yes, I am very thankful to him. He, uh, he —'

'He is a remarkable person.'

'Yes.'

'How long have you known him?'

'I met him, I think, a couple of weeks after he came here.'

'I see.'

'He's been very nice to me.'

'I hear that he has taken a fancy to playing the flute.'

'He plays like a master.'

'Did you introduce him to the flute?'

'I? Oh, no, uh, he, uh, went to the Krishna temple near the

135

bazaar one day, and saw the idol with the flute, and later he heard someone playing the flute somewhere, and liked the sound, I guess, and uh, got himself a flute, and —'

'And he told you all this.'

'Yes – no – he asked me about Krishna, about the flute – I —'

Nikhil stammered and fidgeted under the scrutiny of the old eyes.

'I'm not sure why you are getting so upset,' said the doctor calmly.

'I'm not getting upset! I really don't know – I have no idea – Julian – uh —'

' "Julian"? You call his lordship "Julian"?'

'He asked me to – he is not like others. I had better go now.'

'Son,' Dr Morel reached and held Nikhil's shoulder, 'son, we all have our dreams, but we should not impose them on the dreams and weaknesses of others.'

The sun's last warm blaze dazzled Nikhil's eyes and made them water as he moved away from the doctor and turned to go.

'It's getting pretty late, I'd better go now.' Harry Winston shifted uneasily in a chair on the veranda. Four hours of poker had given him a backache.

'One more time,' said Julian. 'Wake up, Dane.' He shook his brother who was curled up in a cane chair, fast asleep.

'Er, Julian, it's two in the morning.'

'Sit down, Winston. You can't leave just because you're losing.'

'Oh, go home, Harry.' Dane yawned.

'Dane, this is no way to —'

'Ju – go to bed.'

'Good night.'

'Winston!'

'Ju —'

Dane fell asleep with his clothes on. Back in his room, Julian paced for a few minutes, then sat down on the edge of the bed, looking down at his feet, his hands between his knees. Anything to keep his mind off the flute. Poker. That kept his mind occupied. He had escorted Caroline to the club in the evenings and played billiards for hours, till his eyes hurt with the strain and his back ached. He had discussed the Bengal situation with the D.M. and the Collector, but had refused to make any statements about Lord Curzon's policies. A trip to Calcutta for the viceregal ball sounds charming. Yes, of course, Caroline. A cricket match at Talkot soon? Would be delighted to lead the Phulgarh team. And Julian had busied himself selecting a strong eleven.

Jugnu lit a *biri* and looked at her. She was smoking *ganja* like he smoked *biris*. He reached out towards the *chula*. The coals were red with tiny blue flames around them. Late at night people always gathered around the flute-seller's stove to drink and chat. The flute-seller, Badri Lal, began to play softly. Jugnu moved closer to her.

'Listen, the *rakhail* has forgotten her place, *pyaré*. She refused to go to the palace, d'you know? Salman is restless and mad with anger and passion. But he cannot go to the *kota* and drag her out by her hair, because a prince can't go to the *kota*. He tries to preoccupy himself by doing other things the *nawab* wants him to do. But then he buries his face in his Dilruba's lustrous mane. She is mine, mine, he whispers. How can she betray me? Dilruba, you're mine, forever mine. The mare stiffens and snorts. She understands. But do you?'

'Acchoo! Get lost.'

'Salman will kill her surely. The mare's mane is black and soft and caressing.'

God! It's so dark in here. Julian lit a match and stared at the flame. As he raised his head, the flute lying on the writing desk near the window caught his eye. Sitting at the desk, he lit match after match and stared at the flute. With each flash of fire it shone gold and then vanished into the darkness. Julian lit the candle on the desk and set the match-box down. He kept his hands tightly clasped between his knees while he looked at the flute. He would never touch it again. It had failed him. Could never forgive. The faint bamboo odour entered his senses and drew him closer. His mouth almost touched the flute. Did it still taste the same? Not again. Not ever. He rested his forehead on the edge of the desk. His hair, which had grown long, brushed against the flute. It was terrible to be alone; to be alone with the flute. It was unbearable, the room. He raised his head and looked at the flute again. Will it ever be the same? Would he ever be free of it? His face was taut with pain. Clenching his fists as hard as he could, he shook his head twice as if to shake off a tightness. His body convulsed uncontrollably, and his face came down and rested against the flute.

'Salman lies still among velvet cushions and silk spreads. I see his thoughts like I see those burning coals out there. In the darkness behind his closed eyes he remembers . . . Shehzadi, on the boat, dreaming of endless night, hating the dawn . . . On the marble terrace, the *raga chandrakauns* on the *sarangi* . . . Near the lake, some evening, tossing silver at a young boy with an unceasing flute . . . ? Anything you want, Shehzadi, pearls, rubies, diamonds, the prince's heart . . . Just freedom, she had said. Love is a hunter, a captor, he had laughed, and I am bleeding to death – how then can you be free, Shehzadi? Don't you dare sneeze, you bitch. Those coals they always give more warmth and affection than you do.'

'Then take your stink there, *chutiya*.'

Dane rolled over in his sleep and reached for the extra pillow. His hand went over something slender, warm and breathing, and he woke with a start. 'What the —!' He put his hand over his mouth to stifle the scream of surprise. 'Ju, what are you doing in my bed?'

'Let me sleep, damn you,' Julian slurred sleepily.

'What're you doing here? Are you all right? Julian!' He shook his brother till Julian opened his eyes, angry and irritated.

'Damn you, will you let me sleep!'

'Damn you, why are you here?'

'My bed felt damned uncomfortable, that's why,' snapped Julian.

'Why, what's wrong with it?' Were they going to fight again after all these years over uncomfortable beds, smoking fireplaces, draughty windows . . . ? Julian sneaking into Dane's bed, Dane crawling into Julian's – they did that so often, then.

'Do I have to answer these imbecile questions now?' Julian

138

rolled his eyes and turned on his side to go back to sleep.

'How come you're still dressed?'

'Oh God.'

'I don't like sharing my bed, I like sleeping alone.'

'Really?'

'What the hell's the matter with your bed?'

'Oh, for heaven's sake!'

'I need the pillow you're sleeping on.'

'Just hold me, darling, and go back to sleep. My body's far more exciting than this pillow of yours.'

'Get out of here, you —' Dane sent Julian flying out of the bed with a kick.

'You bastard.'

'Get out of here.'

'I'm going to teach you the lesson of your life.' Julian flung himself on his brother.

In the course of the ensuing mad scuffle, the sturdy teak bed groaned, creaked, rocked and ultimately gave way with a resounding crash, raising the countess and the servants. They found the two brothers pulverising each other in the middle of the caved-in bed.

Thomas Sherley wiped his just-shaved face and stared at his reflection in the small mirror on the table. He saw his cricket whites, crumpled and torn on the bed, in the mirror beyond his face, and bit his lips. Dropped from the team for the upcoming match. They were giving Barnett a chance. He's a good spinner, too. And of course he's the O.C.'s nephew. A smile and a pat on the shoulder from Woodburn, their captain. And Sherley had blinked and swallowed twice. Don't take it too hard, old chap. Trevors had patted his shoulder, too, last night. Have to give everybody a chance. Oh, come on, Cyril, I know why they've dropped me. They're afraid that I'll crack his lordship's skull. Late last night in his room, Sherley had ripped his cricket whites to shreds in rage.

'What shall I do now?' Sherley asked the mirror. 'Should I shake Rodney Barnett's hand and congratulate him at breakfast, or should I drop my scrambled eggs on his lap? I could even drown him in his coffee cup.'

He fingered his cotton undershirt at the throat and smiled

wickedly at his reflection suddenly. Ah, Ravinspur, I shall watch you play to my heart's content. I'll watch you move, run, stretch, maybe even trip and fall. I'll watch you get out – caught at first slip, I hope. Or better still, let it be hit-wicket; tread on your stumps. Great! Sherley threw his head back and laughed. That's the way it should be! Ravinspur, Ravinspur, twist your ankle, do, and Jesus Christ, I'll carry you back to the pavilion. Woodburn has dropped me from the team all right, but he's put me in charge of first aid!

I went to the Phulgarh hospital yesterday to visit Dr Morel. Pretty red brick, bougainvillaea, not many major cases, never more than five or six surgical cases a month. A small hospital, but not crowded, neat and clean. And, Lorna, Howard introduced me to someone.

Dr Aloke Bose – the Bengali doctor. I'd say he's in his early thirties. Invited them both to tea. Howard said he writes poetry. All Bengalis write poetry! Maybe Julian and Dane will like this young man.

Then, as I was leaving, Howard said something odd. He said Nikhil hero-worships Julian. Why did he say that? Julian shouldn't like that; he doesn't like living up to other people's expectations. On the contrary, said Howard, your stepson enjoys the adoration. Doesn't make sense. What about the flute? I asked. Same thing, he said. We must all have our little fantasies, dreams, I mean, your ladyship. Please will you ask your *khansama* to bake the most disgustingly rich German chocolate cake for tomorrow?

Caroline sipped her tea and listened to Dr Morel relate the history of Talkot to Dane. Julian seemed immersed in what appeared to be a rather absorbing conversation with the young Bengali doctor.

'The present *nawab* of Talkot,' Dr Morel cleared his throat, 'he is —'

'Do you know anything about his son?' cut in Dane.

'So you were in England for a few years —'

'Yes, for my medical degree.'

Dr Aloke Bose had been born and brought up in south

Calcutta, Julian came to know. After he returned from England, he had worked in Delhi for three years before coming to Phulgarh. He told Julian about Calcutta, about the Bengalis, about Tagore, the great poet of the day, Lord Curzon's attempt to divide Bengal, the terrorist movement that was trying to counter Curzon's policies, and the big annual festival of the Bengalis – Durga *puja*.

'*Puja*?'

'Yes, that means —'

'I know. I visited the Krishna temple here.'

'Krishna is different; Durga is the —'

'Krishna played the flute, didn't he? And the flute charmed the listeners.'

'Er, yes, according to myth, Krishna grew up among cowherds and —'

'How do Indians feel about the flute?'

'Indians, um, I don't know about Indians, but Bengalis attach a lot of romantic nonsense to the flute.'

'Like what?'

'Well, uh, beautiful women, in fairytales that is, are always falling hopelessly in love with strangers playing flutes on moonlit nights, and stuff like that. There are all these stories about how the music of the flute reaches the soul, and once it enters the soul, you can't get it out of your system. The flute, they say, evokes a sort of terrible ecstasy that quite obsesses the listener. It's a bag of moonshine really!'

Julian looked at his hands. 'And what about the person who plays the flute?'

'You mean Krishna?'

'The other ones as well – in the fairytales, like you were saying —'

'In the fairytales, the fluteplayer is usually a stranger who arrives from a distant land; he is portrayed as possessing an almost ethereal, androgynous beauty, cold and indifferent, lost in his music on a moonlit night, and that's when people hear his music and catch a glimpse of him, and completely lose their heads.'

Dane looked at his brother and wondered what had brought that strange light into his eyes. What are they talking about? If

141

only I could hold his attention that way. His hair is long again – just the way it was when he came back from Alexandria. I wonder what Ju is going through. What does he find in the flute? I wish I could pray without feeling embarrassed, then I would pray that you become you again, the you that I want to see in Ravinspur.

In the hazy yellow of the gas lamps, Julian's face looked smooth and polished. Dane looked away, feeling awkward suddenly.

'Dane! I thought you were interested in the history of Talkot.'

'What happened to Krishna?' Julian asked.

'He left Vrindaban, the place where he grew up, and went to Mathura. He was the king of Mathura.'

'I see.'

'Then he entered the political world and became —'

'Did he like being a political figure?'

'I don't know,' laughed Aloke Bose. 'He was even involved in a great battle; he was the charioteer of Arjuna, a great warrior.'

'Fluteplayer and charioteer.'

'Yes, he guided and taught and advised, he was —'

'What happened after all that?'

'He died.'

'Died? But he was a god!'

'Well, he didn't die in our sense of the word; he went back to the world he came from.'

'How did he "die"?'

'As far as I know, Krishna was resting under a tree in a forest when some hunter shot at his feet with a poisoned arrow by mistake.'

'A god died when someone hurt his feet – that's odd.'

'Well,' laughed the doctor again, 'myth is odd.'

'Did he forget the flute after he, er, left the, er, garden?'

'Oh, no, the flute was always with him.'

'Even on the battlefield?'

'The flute was part of him. I mean, Indians can't imagine Krishna without his flute, whether he is portrayed as cowherd, lover, king, ambassador, charioteer, teacher or whatever. The flute blends with all his roles.'

'I believe that Krishna is reincarnated in every age or something like that?'

'Yes, but there's only this age, or *yug*, as we call it, left! This is supposedly the last age before the world's destroyed and recreated, and this is the *kalyug*, or the corrupt age. And y'know, we have a joke about this Krishna business. People who are a little too charming are called Krishnas of Kalyug, corrupt Krishnas! The last avatar is supposed to be Kalki who will destroy everything. The flute in the hands of Kalki will be a power-hungry flute!'

'Do you worship Krishna, Dr Bose?'

'Worship Krishna? Oh, no, no! All this has nothing to do with some silly religion! It's all myth – perhaps our mono-myth.'

In the middle of a green field, two men watched the tossed coin fly up and spin and glint in the sunlight. 'Oh!' whispered the ladies of Phulgarh, some sitting inside the Talkot cricket pavilion, some standing at the edge of the oval field. 'Oh, I wonder who will win the toss?'

'Oh, I hope the earl wins the toss!' squealed Mrs Lyndon. 'I'm simply dying to see him bat!'

'Sorry, Roanna,' came the Collector's voice from behind, 'Lesley Woodburn just picked up the coin and he will certainly choose to bat.'

All the spectators at the Talkot cricket grounds burst into applause as the Phulgarh team came out to field headed by Julian. The much anticipated cricket match between the men of Talkot and Phulgarh was about to begin in a few minutes. The Collector and the officers of the Talkot cantonment had conferred for two weeks and made all the arrangements for a few days of sun, cricket and entertainment. Nobody could complain about the living arrangements. True, army barracks are not proper accommodations for *memsaabs*, but with the addition of potted plants sprinkled all over the place, bright curtains, flowers, cane furniture, plenty of mirrors, hot water, candlelit dinners and handsome young men in uniform things were satisfactory.

Nikhil stood with the Indian crowd on the other side of the

grounds and watched Julian set up the field, choose his bowlers, and take his position. He saw Julian in control of the game, moving his fielders around, conferring with bowlers, preventing boundaries, effecting maiden overs.

Sitting on a bench with first-aid kits and three other assistants, Sherley bent over and covered his face. Woodburn was about to be caught at second slip. Julian's body leaped and arched backwards in mid-air, and his hands closed around the ball; a body in full control of itself, it seemed, as it spun around in the air and rolled on the warm grass. 'Classic, classic.' 'Almost inimitable.' 'Breathtaking.' Voices tightened around Sherley's temples.

'I'm going to walk around a bit,' Sherley said to the three young men. He stood up and stretched.

The shadows were growing longer and longer on the grass, and it was evident that shortly the players would begin to complain about the light. The Talkot team was all out for 203 an hour after tea. Sherley watched the District Magistrate of Phulgarh play some very conservative strokes in an over, and turned away bored. The Earl of Ravinspur was not on the field any more.

He wandered towards the other side of the grounds and looked at the Indians leaning over the fence. 'What a bunch of apes,' he said to himself. 'Why the hell are they staring at me, the bastards?' Sherley felt like a pinned butterfly under their sharp, dark eyes. He turned away and looked back at the first-aid boys in the distance. The Earl of Ravinspur was sitting on the bench and having his elbow attended to. Sherley couldn't check the intense rage that swept through him. He vaulted over the low fence and landed on somebody's foot. 'Get the hell out of my way!' He kicked and pushed his way through the gaping crowd and headed for the barracks.

Nikhil walked cautiously towards the barracks. Nobody was allowed in here, he knew, and he might get into trouble if he was caught trespassing. But he just wanted to take a look around; he had never been inside a military cantonment before. He could see some people bustling around the mess in the distance. Probably getting things ready for dinner. Julian

144

will be all dressed up for dinner. I could hide out here somewhere, and later tonight peep into the mess and see what Julian looks like in his other clothes. Wish I got to talk to Julian more often. Has he thrown away the flute, or does he still play it once in a while?

'What the hell are you doing here, you —' A hand seized Nikhil's shoulder and propelled him around. 'Why, it's his lordship's skinny little sugarboy!' Sherley gripped Nikhil's hair and pulled his head back.

Nikhil tried to wrench himself free. Sherley dragged him into the nearest barrack and shut the door. Nikhil tried to turn away from those green eyes. Sherley ran his forefinger down Nikhil's throat.

'You poor thing,' he said, 'you pathetic little creature, you're simply starving.'

Dane sat inside the pavilion and strapped his pads on to his legs. Julian had asked Dane to bat one-down in case one of the opening batsmen were to get out before end of play that day. It was so boring sitting here and waiting. He picked up his bat and gloves and walked outside. The Phulgarh team was out there watching the D.M. and the Collector's nephew tackle the new ball. Dane strolled past the first-aid boys and towards the white fence. The shock of dark faces watching the game made him smile. There had been many, many fences that he had hung over and watched Julian on a green field, cutting through the air with his bat. Those powerful crossbat strokes. And Helena saw him play, too – that was the first time she saw Julian. He had walked by them with a mocking smile in his eyes after the game.

He had stood with his hand on Dane's shoulder for a few minutes and watched the game. That wonderful feeling – his hand on my shoulder. During Papa's funeral, he stood next to me holding my shoulder in the rain. And then he left again. Where shall he go after India? I've got to take him back to Ravinspur, somehow. I've got to make him stay.

They all stood in the billiard room, after dinner, watching Julian and Major Briggs send the balls spinning across the green felt. Julian chalked his cue and prepared for the next shot. They could hear the women laughing in the next room.

Under the gaslight that hung over the billiard table, Julian's hair looked almost silver-blond and his eyes shone a crystal, transparent blue. Dane regarded the intent faces that were waiting for the balls to go spinning again. Why he turned and looked at Sherley at the far end of the room he didn't know. But Sherley's expression startled him. There was something in those green eyes that frightened Dane.

Sherley looked down at once. He took a deep breath and smiled.

Nikhil slipped into Tulsi's shack as noiselessly as he could, without stumbling in the dark.

'Who's there?' Tulsi stirred in her sleep.

'Just me. Go back to sleep.'

'Is something wrong?'

'I just want to sleep.'

He curled up in the frayed blanket and closed his eyes. He saw blazing green inside his head. It burned and burned and made his mouth dry and bitter. I can never face Julian again. I have sinned, betrayed; I have defiled myself.

Dane lay on the bed in the transformed barrack and stared at the corrugated ceiling. He had left the billiard room a little before midnight. He couldn't bear to look at Sherley. He would have to tell Ju about Sherley. But what would he say? What kind of trouble were they in for now? He must watch out for Ju.

He turned on his side and stroked the bed. They were so close tonight. She was so very close. He should go into the *kota*, quietly, up to her room, clear things up. How could she have slapped him? She always looked at him when she danced. She wanted what he wanted, he was sure. He wanted to save her from the prince, from that place. There was still time to do something, to make things right. But he was stuck here and could do nothing. Why? Why not – no, Julian would kill him. One act of daring – just once – why not – right this minute when nobody was around . . .

Dane flattened himself against the side of the *kota*. Jumping

146

over the wall had been easy. He had dashed across the courtyard in his socks. This is terribly rash and thoughtless. If anything goes wrong it'll be my fault. I'll kill myself. He stood between two large frieze windows. Julian will kill me, surely. When will I ever be calm and rational? Dane crawled under the windows of the first floor and reached the side door.

It was very dark. He seemed to be in a long corridor. He could hear faint voices, hushed laughter, cursing. Where now? He stepped forward and howled in pain. Sharp fragments of glass cut into his feet through his socks.

Doors opened; men and women rushed out; people started screaming and yelling; Dane stood rooted to the spot, holding his bleeding foot in his hand. Light fell on his face. 'A *sahib*,' he heard, and then a very English voice said, 'Good morning, m'lord.' Dane stared at Thomas Sherley who held a lamp before his face.

Julian ran out of the barracks and caught hold of Harry who was lighting a cigarette. 'Where's Dane?'

'What?' Harry dropped his cigarettes. 'What d'you mean?'

'Dane's not here.'

'I, er, saw him leave pretty early.'

'The bloody idiot! The blasted, reckless idiot!'

Dane stumbled into the barracks at about five in the morning and collapsed on the bed. Julian and Harry pounced on him. 'Where the hell have you been?'

Dane rolled on the bed gasping, and finally broke into loud hysterical sobs. They tried to quiet him by stuffing his face into the pillows, shaking him, swearing at him, even punching him in the middle. But in vain.

'What's the matter with him? Christ! What's the matter with him?' Harry shook with fright. 'Where are his shoes? His feet are bleeding!' Julian gripped Dane's collar, raised his head and stared into his delirious eyes.

'I will kill you after breakfast,' said Julian and knocked his brother out cold with the hardest punch he had delivered on anybody's jaw.

'Ouch,' said Harry Winston and winced.

Of course, there's something else going on besides the cricket

147

match, Lorna! Dane seems somewhat chastened; he's limping, too. And Julian and Harry seem to be watching over him. I'm sure something hideous has happened; I overheard something about someone getting slapped. They were whispering in the card room but shut up when they saw me. A minor catastrophe, I'm sure! I feel curiously relieved, however, not worried at all for a change – when I see Julian watching the game with his hand on Dane's shoulder. They'll take care of each other.

Looking at Julian sweep a ball to the boundary and complete his century, Dane felt overwhelmingly elated in spite of the yelling and cursing he was receiving. That was his brother over there, leading them to victory. The Phulgarh team won by six wickets, and the match was over soon after tea. Then the most incredible thing happened. As Julian flicked his cap off and bowed, and they all ran around shaking hands, the Indian crowd leaped over the fence and swarmed into the field. They raised Julian up on their shoulders and danced all over the field. The police rushed in and tried to rescue the earl and settle the commotion. People watched aghast. The 'natives' were soon beaten off the grounds, and nobody was seriously hurt; only the Earl of Ravinspur had twisted his ankle jumping off somebody's shoulders.

Sherley froze on the bench as the first-aid boys rushed towards Julian who was hobbling across the field. Go on, a voice said inside him, go on, this is your only chance. Weren't you waiting for just this? But he just sat there on the bench unable to move an inch. He saw them bandage his ankle and help him back to the pavilion. Sherley felt a guitar vibrate. It was dark, very, very dark. He couldn't see clearly.

'I really don't want to watch this, Harry,' said Dane as they stood among the crowd in the maidan outside the cantonment and watched the cockfight.

'Neither do I, really. These army blokes always get excited over these awfully bloody sports. We'll be invited to see bear-baiting next, I'm sure.' The men shouted, cheered, betted as the two cocks, with knives tied to their legs, flew at each other. 'The prince has a wager on one of the birds,' they heard someone say.

Julian stood away from the soldiers and his brother. He had seen cockfights before; he found them interesting, but painful to watch. The strong golden twilight drew his eyes away from the ring. Four days of cricket, and winning finally. There was music in each swift stroke of the bat, as the ball cut through the air and sent the bails flying. The body moved in rhythm with the game. The music was in the sunlight, in the grass under his feet, in the dust that rose from the ground. The storm was all around him, imploding in him.

A sudden hard pressure and vigorous movement against his right shoulder almost knocked Julian off his feet. He steadied himself and turned. The most beautiful black mare was rubbing her forehead against his shoulder. 'Well, hello there, gorgeous.' He scratched her forehead and, without glancing at the rider, moved away.

Julian squeezed himself next to his brother. 'Let's go, Ju,' said Dane, 'it's awful.'

'We are leaving tonight, Dane.'

'But —'

'Dane,' Harry touched his elbow, 'let's get out of here right now.'

'Why, what's the matter?'

'He's here – the prince – and that bodyguard of his. They're looking at you.'

Dane looked straight into the pair of dark eyes and held their gaze over the fight, the blood-stained dust, the crowd. He saw a fine-boned, passionate face and a lovely black mare.

Pulling the satin quilt up to his chin, Dane closed his eyes. They were home again – back in Phulgarh. Rushing through the darkness on two *tongas*, making excuses to Mama, leaving her there. God, what had he done? And Sherley, had he followed him? He had never seen Julian so angry before. Even Harry was disgusted with him now. Dane felt terribly alone. If only he could crawl into Julian's bed . . . There were times when Julian had taken his hand and pulled him along. Forget that, Dane. Let's look at something new.

Want to see London, Dane? At sixteen, walking through Soho, stuck to your side, Ju, as if we were joined at the hip. Scared and fascinated, couldn't see things fast enough. Too much rushed by. Read these. A pile of books, you just threw them on my bed one night. And then you went away. You're the only one I've ever believed in, Ju. This is the first time we've played cricket together. But what now? I've ruined everything.

'Believe me,' Jugnu said, 'now it's only a matter of days. The prince has seen my *saab*'s indigo eyes and defiant mouth and is planning carefully. Besides, my *chhoté saab* was seen at the *kota* late at night, bare feet, cut his feet on broken glass. And Salman knows. The *nawab* has been informed about their meeting at the cockfight, and he is planning, too. He sent for his ferret, Imran Firdausi, and asked him to find out when and where Sakhi meets the *sahib*. And then he will show Salman that it's all the woman's fault, not my *saab*'s. The *nawab* doesn't want any trouble with the *sahibs*. He'd rather have the *nachnewali* killed and out of his son's life. He's planning to send Salman away to Akhner for Prince Zaheer's coronation, and he's also arranging a marriage for the prince with Princess Roshenara. But the prince refuses to marry. Ah, but soon bloodshed and murder and – and – loneliness.' Jugnu stopped and turned his face away.

'Come, come sit next to me, Jugnu, and tell me more. I'll never sneeze again.'

'*Accha*, why not? And why should I tell you my story, what do you give?'

'My time and patience, *pyaré*. Come tell me more.'

'Your hair's not as soft as I thought. Well, anyway, through Imran Firdausi, the *nawab* knows that Sakhi meets my *saab* in that old temple in the woods. Firdausi found evidence – pomegranates. They will meet again under the full moon.'

'How do you know they'll meet under the full moon?'

'Lovers always meet on full moon nights. It's the time of forbidden love. Everybody knows.'

'So what will happen?'

'The *nawab* told Firdausi to keep his mouth shut. The prince mustn't know. He might kill them both in anger and jealousy, and then the *sahibs* might destroy Talkot. But the *nawab* didn't pay Firdausi. So the scum went straight to the prince and told him everything for a ruby ring.'

'Then the prince will ride to the temple the night of the full moon and kill your *sahib* and his *aurat!* I don't believe a word of this.'

'Would you like to come with me to the temple that night and see for yourself?'

'You buy me twenty glass bangles if nothing happens.'

'And what if something does?'

'A – a – acchoo! I'll think of something.'

The flute was cool against his fingers. Night after night, Julian had looked away from it, afraid and confused, hating its presence. Being alone with it was unbearable. But now, the flute rested on his palm, pale gold, light, airy light, a soft, still wave. It would play what he wanted to play.

On full moon nights, alone, in abandoned places, the fluteplayer would stand and play and enthrall the world. Splendidly dangerous and wonderfully safe. A stage-set. Julian turned away, smiling. To play on unconcerned, without thought. The flute caught the sunlight and gleamed in Julian's hand.

'Come,' Jugnu said and pulled her into the woods.

'Not so fast. Wait, my *sari*'s caught. Oh, thorns!'

The wind tore through the trees and whipped against them. Faint moonlight helped them follow the narrow path. They ducked under branches. It was getting stormy, but there were very few clouds. 'Why is it so stormy on a full moon night? No clouds but just this strong wind?' A strange, piping sound came from somewhere. The sound became clearer as they neared the temple. Then they heard it, and along with it another sound: pounding hooves. Jugnu tried to swallow his heart down. What was happening? 'We have to hide,' he said hoarsely. 'I don't understand. Come behind these pillars.' His pulse racing, he held his breath and listened. High, piping . . . It was as if a dam burst in his head.

Thundering hooves drowned the piping melody. A black mare raced up the stone steps, across the stone floor and,

151

neighing with fright, reared up in front of the altar. The rider tried in vain to calm the trembling mare.

Bathed by the silver-blue glitter of moonlight, darkened blue by the night, a rich blue shawl carelessly flung over his shoulders, sat a slender being, cross-legged, on the altar. Fragrant smoke of several incense sticks swirled around him. He sat amidst flower petals, thickly strewn; petals were in his silvery-gold hair, on his shoulders, over the shawl. A gul-mohr blossom nestled behind his ear. A flute against his mouth, his eyes closed, he played on oblivious to the pounding hooves, the animal cry of fear.

The rider drew a jewelled dagger from his waist and stared at the ethereal fluteplayer. Several minutes passed; he played on unmoved, an unbroken, exquisite cadence. Then, as if waking from a dream, the being opened his glittering eyes. 'What seekest thou, wanderer?' His soft, deep voice echoed in the temple.

'I am Salman, the prince of Talkot.' The rider gritted his teeth to stop his voice from shaking. The being looked at him serenely, without interest or curiosity.

'Hast thou found thy answer, fair prince?'

'Who are you?'

'I am a fluteplayer on an empty altar playing through endless night.'

'Are you here every night?'

'I have not ever known day.'

'I am sorry to have disturbed you, *yogi*. I am sorry to have broken into your – your – repose,' the rider said, sheathing his dagger. Very slowly he walked the mare out of the temple.

'Good night, sweet prince,' the fluteplayer's voice rang behind him.

'Dane!' The countess walked into her son's room without knocking. She had just returned from the tea at the club.

'Mama!' Dane had just stepped out of his riding breeches. She ignored his semi-nude state and threw her hat and bag on the bed.

'Sit down!'

'What's the matter?'

'I can't believe what Dr Morel just told me, and I'm glad he warned me —'

'What did he say?'

'Dane, you are the most reckless, thoughtless, brainless, foolish —'

'Is something wrong?' Julian walked in.

'This sort of indiscretion —'

'Caroline, what's wrong?'

'If you must have an affair does it have to be with the prince's mistress? Then a public fiasco – a fight in the middle of a fair – servants talking – you were seen sneaking out of that place in Talkot —'

'What?'

'It's all over Phulgarh. What I'd like to know is how Roanna Lyndon found out about it before I did! Why am I the last to find out? It appears people have been talking for quite some time.'

'Er, Caroline —'

'A mess like this! I don't care what the English population thinks, but the *nawab* and his son will be out for blood! Dane, how could you have got yourself into a mess like this?'

'Mother, you don't understand – it's not true!' Dane buried his face in his hands.

'Not true? Why is everybody talking —'

'Servants, Mama, oh, I don't know what to do!'

'Caroline —' Julian scratched his head. 'I think it's time for us to leave for Calcutta.'

Dane tossed and turned in his bed as the storm outside nearly uprooted trees. Three or four weeks in Calcutta. Unbearable! How on earth did Roanna Lyndon find out . . . ? Three weeks in Calcutta! And we leave tomorrow afternoon. I'm so glad Harry's coming with us. Good old Harry. He's worried sick about all this. How cool and collected Julian's been. What am I going to do? I'll be so far from all this, so far from reality almost.

Another sound penetrated his consciousness through the raging storm. What was that? Whistling? No — Dane got out of bed. Was a window open somewhere? He stood outside his room and listened. Where was that sound coming from? The notes grew stronger as he neared Julian's room. The heavy, wooden door was closed, but wild, ecstatic tones filtered through faintly. He opened the door slowly.

Ravi Singh loved watching storms, especially such terrible ones. He thought of the birth of Krishna – that wild, stormy night when the Yamuna was ripped apart. He sat near the french windows in the dining room and sighed. His *saab* playing the flute in the maidan, on the veranda. 'Gopal, Gopal, Madan-Mohan, Govinda, Govinda, Bansidhar, Narayan, Narayan, Krishna, Sri Krishna,' he whispered, 'no, it can't be. I'm dreaming. It's just the storm. No,' he laughed, 'I'm dreaming. Am I dreaming? Why aren't they fading, the notes? Where? Where are you?'

In a flash of silver lightning they saw him. The french windows leading to the balcony were wide open. The rain fell in waves behind him. Lightning came again and again and sheathed him in blue flames. Stripped to the waist, he stood there, ankles crossed in the eternal pose, flute against his mouth, playing, his eyes half-closed as if in a trance. His silk pyjamas, drenched by the rain, clung to his legs. There was indescribable, ecstatic peace on his face and breathtaking beauty of complete fusion of thought and action.

'Julian! Have you gone stark, staring mad?' Dane tried to grip the wall.

'Oh, lord, oh, lord, have I been blind, oh, lord!' Ravi Singh went down on his knees at the door of his master's room, his hands clasped. 'How could I have not known, oh, lord? Forgive me my sins, oh, lord, for I have always believed that you would return one more time.'

'Julian —' Dane choked.

He lowered his flute and looked at them. 'Go back to sleep, Dane.' Swiftly he crossed the room and closed the door.

PART TWO

Altars

Chapter 7

Lorna,

We rushed by green fields of sugar-cane, clusters of banana trees, buffaloes floating in canals, children throwing stones at the train. And when the train had stopped briefly, in the middle of nowhere almost, on a bridge across a canal, Julian turned from the window, saying that he wanted to plunge into the water with the native children.

Sitting in the plush hotel room and staring out of the window at Chowringhee Street, I breathe in the evening air of Calcutta, the capital of the British Raj. We're centre stage now. Unreal city, said Julian. Should I say that, too? While Sheila exclaims about the silks and the viceregal ball, about all those that are here this year from London, Julian points out this city to me. Yes, he has been talking to me a lot, spending time with me, and Dane.

Unreal city, he said, on the banks of a muddy river where the Englishmen had built homes, homes like the ones they knew in England. But the life that the city throbs with is an alien life. Sunset over muddy waters, brown bodies of children racing after *sahibs* on horseback, crowds gathering around old men with dancing monkeys, women walking away from the river with pitchers at their waists, their long black hair swinging in the breeze, cows and goats blocking carriages in the streets. This is what we see. But look there – at the shoeshine boys on the pavement, grabbing at legs passing by, trying to coax the *sahibs* to step on those wooden platforms for the 'best shoeshine job in the Raj'. There are two different worlds out there and the only link between them is service.

Unreal city, living, urgently living with its hazy yellow gas-light under a dusty purple sky. And Phulgarh, always a little sleepy. Such a shock of life here; wherever you went, always that faint odour of blood and mud mingled with the moist river breeze.

Sheila drags us everywhere. The New Market, the Strand, the racecourse, polo, the Eden Gardens, Belvedere . . . Not a moment's quiet. All week long – tea-parties, luncheons, dances, shopping. Constant talk of terrorism at teas and dinners; at cricket matches one hears the word 'expansion' a great deal. Although the men are very gung ho about 'improving the whole system', more railways, and shipping natives here and there for construction, there seems to be a strange feeling of discontent in the air. When you walk down the streets the Indians don't smile at you. They might do a *namaste*, but it's a mechanical gesture. In Phulgarh, they never seemed hostile. This is the city of Kali, Lord Rutham said at dinner last night. (He remembers you with such fondness.) Kali, the bloodthirsty goddess who demands sacrifices. They sacrifice goats, buffaloes and even, in secret, girls and boys. There are temples in the city itself where they kill animals during ceremonies. I can't figure out where Charles got all those happy stories; all I keep hearing are these horrifying things, not stories, but real things. The dreadful indigo business – totally hushed up now. Natives slaughtered, Englishmen killed. Now the terrorism. And all that the men have to say is that, oh, we'll finish 'em off, oh, we'll take care of it. The restless air of Calcutta sends chills down my spine. Don't they feel it, too?

Julian has been all over the city, even to its northern parts, with Nikhil. He travelled with us because Julian wanted him to come, but of course due to the rules Nikhil had to sit in a different compartment.

Nikhil takes him to odd places. Julian tells me of fresh coconut water, children fighting under the gushing water of water pumps, bazaars with overwhelming smells of slaughtered goats, fish, sandalwood, wood fires. This is how we like to see this place, he said. Dirty vignettes full of noise, smell, and colour. Well, how do you see? I asked, a little peeved. He laughs. Have you seen corpses set aflame on pyres of sandalwood, flowers and incense? Sitting on the river bank, on a moonless night, knots of flames behind us, and just our voices, Caroline, Nikhil's and mine, the cry of foxes and the faint 'om–om–om' of chants.

The night was too silent around them, and too stifling. The pyres were burning and burning, endlessly it seemed, scattered but linked at the same time in a strange way. The past was being incinerated slowly, but surely. The ashes were gathered up and thrown into the river.

A very muddy river, called the Hooghly.

The viceregal ball was comforting in an odd way. Belvedere is gorgeous. We were back among familiar tinsel. There wasn't much thinking to do; you just had to talk and smile charmingly. You braced yourself up in these clothes and relaxed with a vengeance. Oh, Lorna, it was so easy to move in rhythm there. As I danced with Julian he said the oddest things with a hideous smile. Don't smile that way, I told him. That's not you. What's me? he asked. Dear Caroline, in these clothes, speaking this language, amidst this glitter, I could be anything – Prince Charming, fairy godfather, Tom Thumb, St George, Merlin, Don Juan . . . even Krishna. The lights are so bright that the darkness out there draws me. What do you mean? He just shook his head and said, I'll be going away for a few days. You and Dane and Harry and Sheila – go off to Puri. I'll meet you back here in a few weeks.

Dane has been nagging Julian about coming to Puri with us. He tailed Julian all over Eden Gardens, all around that quaint Burmese Pagoda. But who can change Julian's mind?

He doesn't know where he's going. He'll find out, he said. Walking along the Strand I kept thinking why I worry so much. I worry because I love him and don't want to nag. He is a child still when the wind is in his hair and his eyes are not facing other eyes. Will this be his last run?

And what about Dane? I never had to worry about him because he was – is – always there, always reaching out. Howard laughs at me. Two grown men; shouldn't worry about them. They can take charge of their lives. Have to let them be what they want to be. But it is so difficult to let go. Especially now, knowing that I'm really alone, without Charles. Somehow, I, too, dread going back to Ravinspur. The last two years – there was no time to think. Settling things. But now, all that's taken care of; what if time drags when I'm back at Ravinspur?

Take my mind off that.

Lorna, I saw a yellow-brown sunset, with a flash of orange here and there. Peanut-sellers, shoeshine boys, fishing boats, steamers, ships in the distance.

At the ball, all they talked about was the cricket match and the partition of Bengal.

Julian said, walking through narrow streets we saw a group of boys. They screamed at us and threw stones. They want us out, Caroline. We want to divide their state for political purposes. We'll be tearing their lives apart.

If you were here, you too would sense this restlessness.

Talking about restlessness – Julian scares me now. Oh, among people he's the perfect earl. But his eyes are searching desperately now. He's going away with Nikhil – I don't understand their friendship. It's real and unreal, like adoration. Don't want to know, really. All I know is that he's going away again. To visit someone called Will Grey who lives in a tribal village. I don't know if Calcutta is getting on his nerves. I don't know what it is, but sometimes there's a tidal wave in his eyes that's about to crash on the shore.

Waves glistening with phosphorus are crashing on the sands of Puri. Sands so silver in the moonlight. And, Lorna, dolphins, leaping from waves, dolphins shimmering green with phosphorus. At sunset, men in long narrow boats drag in large nets of fish, pearly and opalescent in the last rays. I can see Dane on the beach from my window. He's taken off his shoes and stands ankle-deep in the waves.

I can see Calcutta flash – Fort William, Park Street with its shops and lights and beggars. And Alipore – Warren Hastings and Philip Francis raising their pistols at four in the morning. Those big, beautiful houses with their disciplined greenery, and Julian pointed out small dark heads peeping over the walls of Belvedere, wondering what went on within those walled-in Anglo-Saxon lives. The first thing we built were walls; then the homes. What would happen if the walls fell one day and life stormed in?

I think we have moved away from a lot of things. A lot of things are over. I feel I've told you almost all that was in my heart. Sort of wanted to store the past for ever, cling to it and possess it like a thing. This diary, too, is like that to me. I've entered it; now I can't give it up. I have to somehow.

This going away again – what will he find? Perhaps he will come back secure.

The red dust smothered the road travelled in rose-mist. The coconut palms were dark in the distance and the green of the banana trees was growing softer and softer. Julian's body lurched with each bump of the bullock cart. He sat with his chin on his knees and looked at the road stretching into the flushed horizon. Why couldn't he shake the past off his heels? Whatever is over should be really over. It should fade like the flowers that dropped from Krishna's head as he left the garden. The past is so empty. No remorse or regret, only emptiness. Large empty rooms of Ravinspur, echoing, echoing. One long empty year. Beautiful rooms, all covered with sheets and sheets of fabric. Rooms that seemed to ring with laughter. The echoes!

It's been so long. So long and so far from those green woods.

Nikhil sat with his eyes half-closed. Often, the bulls butted their way through cows, goats, dogs and children. Julian so close again, and in these loose, familiar clothes. Back in Calcutta, Julian so intimidating suddenly in his fancy clothes. When he looked like that he was someone else, not his Julian with the flute.

Had he been dreaming all this while that this slouching form was his Julian? He wore those clothes with such ease. And his face changes when he wears those clothes. He looks at something beyond me, beyond this world almost. If only I could fill up that emptiness. What have I done to myself? All I want is to be left alone to dream.

The man handling the cart whistled and hooted. A thick brown shawl covered his shoulders and a strip of red cloth was tied around his head. Julian turned his head and looked behind. The red earth of Bengal, the rich red earth where they grow rice. Only the road ahead was visible. He could see huts in the distance, across the mustard fields, mud huts with thatched roofs; and herdsmen, far away, rounding up their cows and goats, slapping them homeward. The bird-calls were growing fainter and fainter; the lazy hum of crickets settled into the darkening gold of the mustard fields. A rose-gold ether. At the cowdust hour the flute drew them home.

He is far away again, thought Nikhil. He looked at Julian's feet in leather sandals. Just as we touch the feet of our gods, the evening touches this red dust.

Julian wanted to reach for his cigarettes, but his arms remained wrapped around his knees. The dark flush of the evening swept through him and caught in his throat.

The narrow road meandered past dark waters and looming black palms rising in arcs, dimly lit huts, cows and dogs with glinting eyes.

'The earth draws the evening over her face, like a bride draws the veil,' Nikhil said. 'That's how our poets say it.'

'Do you think we'll reach it tonight?' Julian asked.

'Yes, we will.'

'I've had seven very interesting days on the road. Never knew any place like this existed.'

'But you've seen other countries.'

'Yes, but this is different.'

'Is it awful travelling this way? Sleeping in old *dak* bungalows, and I know bullock carts aren't very comfortable.'

'I love it.' He looked at the gauzy darkness. 'I remember Alexandria with its summer breeze sticky with limedust. A taste of ashes. And this red dust, as if a pomegranate had turned into a cloud.'

'Look!' Nikhil touched his arm. 'Look there!'

'What are those flashes?'

'Will o'the wisps.'

The palm trees were lined with silver now and the broad leaves of the banana trees glistened silver-green. The road was no longer red. Silver-blue dust swirled up from the hooves and wheels.

'Y'know, about will o'the wisps, they steal your soul away. Sometimes, travellers who lose their way follow those flashes of light, and nobody ever finds them again. They are lost for ever.'

'Tell me about Will Grey.'

'We're almost there.'

The cart stopped suddenly. 'What's wrong?' asked Julian.

'We have to change carts. These bulls are tired.'

'But where are we?'

'We're almost there.'

There was a shack on the side of the road. A man sat inside preparing tea. Their cart driver unhitched the bulls and went inside the shack to warm his hands.

'Want some tea?' Nikhil inquired.

'No, thanks. But I've got to, er, I think I'll go there.' Julian vanished temporarily into the darkness.

They climbed back into the cart as soon as the driver whistled. Julian looked at his watch. 'It's nearly midnight.'

'Go to sleep.'

'Too many mosquitoes.'

'I hope you survive this adventure, Julian,' laughed Nikhil. And the mosquitoes laughed too, it seemed, their crazy buzzing laughter.

The night deepened suddenly. There were trees all around them. 'Will Grey's bungalow is on the other side of the woods,' Nikhil said. 'It's not quite the *sahib*'s bungalow, but it's habitable. And there's always lots of food.' His fellow traveller's response startled him a little. He had never heard Julian snore before.

An hour later the cart jolted to a stop. 'Julian,' whispered Nikhil, 'Julian, we're here.' He touched Julian's hair lightly. So soft.

After paying the man, Julian ran his fingers through his hair and straightened his clothes. It was too dark to notice all the ravages of time and negligence. But he could see that the veranda was practically falling apart. The interior was lit by one lantern that stood on the floor of the stark and bare drawing room.

'Let's go in,' said Nikhil.

'Are you sure?'

'Of course.'

'Where's Mr Grey?'

A young woman in a *sari* came out of the house carrying a lantern and motioned them to follow her. She led them to a large room and placed the lantern on the only table there.

163

There was a narrow bed with a thin mattress and a mosquito net. Nikhil sniffed the sheets and the pillow. 'Clean. He got my message.' Julian touched the surface of the table. No dust. He set his cloth bag down. 'Are you hungry?'

'I'm too tired.'

'Good night then. Sleep well.'

Julian crawled into bed and tucked the ends of the mosquito net under the mattress as he had seen the servants do in Phulgarh.

The growing warmth woke Julian up. It was as if the mustard fields had swept into the room. There were bamboo groves outside his window. Sparrows caused a riot. He threw the blankets off.

The cement floor was covered with grass mats. The walls were whitewashed and the ceiling had wooden beams running across it. A clay pitcher of water stood on the table. A hibiscus bush leaned against the window, glowing with large crimson flowers. Goats ran around; dogs barked; voices of women singing filled the air sporadically. And there was sudden laughter among the branches of the huge mango tree. Laughter in those rooms at Ravinspur. The echo! Among the leaves there were laughing dark faces and excited hands clutching branches and reaching for the sky. They had appeared with the warmth and the sunshine, the children. He wanted to join the world outside. It was so shockingly alive.

Two buckets of water stood on the cement floor of the bathroom; an aluminium pitcher filled with cold water, a stone basin, a table, a stool and – incredible – a shining razor, soap, shaving brush, clean towels, two tin mugs. Also, a gecko on the wall. He filled the basin with water and splashed his face.

As he re-entered the room wearing a towel, he noticed a small wicker basket of fruits on the table. When did that appear? Pears, apples, bananas, grapes. He put on fresh clothes and picked up a bunch of grapes.

The veranda had no railings and it was not white any more. The crumbling plaster was covered with a creeper with tiny mauve flowers. Mango, banana, peepul trees, bamboo groves

164

and coconut palms surrounded the house. And there was sunlight, stunning bright. Julian caught small dark bodies flashing in and out of the greenery, occasional laughter and strains of song again. Wonder where Nikhil is?

'So, his lordship likes to dress native?'

Julian turned around. A tall man stood leaning against the door. He wore a long white sheet wrapped around his waist, and a shawl over his shoulders. He was big-boned, but thin to the point of being cadaverous. Years in the tropics had turned his skin from pinko-grey to cinnamon and his hair to silky flax. His clean-shaven, age-lined, hollow-cheeked face was still attractive. His hands moved through his hair constantly. 'Good morning,' he smiled and delivered an actor's bow. 'How does the Earl of Ravinspur after a week in a bullock cart?'

'Very well, thank you.'

'William Tyler Grey.' He stretched out his hand.

They walked through the wood, Will Grey pointing out and identifying the different trees, creepers, flowers and birds. 'Peepul, banyan, bakul, champak . . . Here, smell this, and this, and this . . .' Flowers were thrust under Julian's nose. 'Do you hear that? No, no, the fainter cry . . .' Children appeared out of the greenery in sudden bursts. *Eeeh*!' '*Grey shayeb*!' Tiny hands tugged at Will Grey's clothes. 'The little bastards!' laughed Grey, 'always tugging at my clothes, the tadpoles, trying to see what colour my balls are! Here – Hartley, hold these' – he dropped the bunch of hibiscus blossoms in Julian's hands – 'while I adjust my clothes.'

'Let's go to the village,' Grey said after trying to catch a parrot in vain for nearly half an hour. 'These birds are too damn pricey.' He clambered down the banyan tree. 'Damn that bird. I've been trying to get her for one whole week now.' He dusted himself and refastened the sheet around his waist. 'Well, let's see . . . you look terribly bland, Hartley.' He stuck large hibiscus blossoms behind Julian's ears, tore a long section of a flowered creeper and wrapped it around Julian's shoulders. 'Now, that's much better.' Then he adorned himself in the same way.

The red clay again as they entered the village. A path ran along the banks of a shallow pond where buffaloes floated and children played hopscotch. Mud huts with thatched roofs. Mud walls with white and orange hieroglyphics. Women filled clay pitchers at the well; men spread manure over vegetable beds; old women sat weaving baskets and some prepared dung cakes for fuel and slapped them on the walls of the huts to dry in the sun. Some children fought over coconut husks, and occasionally harassed the cows and the goats and the dogs. They all stopped as Grey walked in with Julian.

Children threw themselves at Grey, trying to climb all over him. Some of the children were light-skinned and brown-haired. He grabbed the women and kissed them before they could duck and run. Julian watched in silence. 'The little bastards – going for my balls again!'

'Julian!' Nikhil came running up to him.

'What are you doing here?'

'Sleep well?'

'Yes, but —'

'Here, I have something for you.' He thrust a flute into Julian's hands. 'I had it made this morning. Wanted to give you something, sort of.'

'It's lovely. Smells very fresh.'

'Yes, it's new bamboo. It's a wee bit more sophisticated too.'

'Thank you.'

'Why are you wearing hibiscus?'

'Your Grey *saab* insisted.'

'Don't wear hibiscus. Only gul-mohr. How dare he —' Nikhil pushed himself through the crowd of women and children. 'Grey *saab*, don't you make him wear hibiscus.'

'Why, it's the skinny little sonofabitch from Srinagar!' Nikhil ducked as Grey tried to box his ears. 'How are the Wakeleys?'

'I have no idea.'

'So what's wrong with hibiscus?'

'He wears gul-mohr.'

'He'll wear what I wear.'

'No, he will not.'

'Hey, wha'd'you say, your lordship, hibiscus or gul-mohr?'

But there was no response. His lordship was nowhere to be seen.

Julian removed the flowers and threw them on the ground,

and tore the creeper from his shoulders. Gripping the flute, he walked rapidly towards the bungalow through the woods. They were so taken up with Grey, the children, the women, the whole damned village. He had lived there for nearly seven years, but still the fascination hadn't worn off. Why? What was there in Will Grey, that clown? He was crackers, absolutely bananas, head empty as a coconut shell, cooing with birds, climbing trees, sticking flowers in his hair, perverting children —! They clung to him, nestled against him, worshipped him almost. As if a god in his garden he — What was so thrilling about him?

I should go back. Go back to Ravinspur. This is crazy.

Splatch. 'Oh, damn!' Grey's elusive green parrot flew off the banyan tree screeching in satisfaction.

Day after day Julian watched Grey's rituals. In the mornings, he would go to the village and let the children fall upon him; in the afternoons, three or four women would come to the bungalow with food. Before eating, Grey would stretch out in the sun and receive an oil massage from the women. Then he would go for his cold bath, after which the women would dry him with rough towels. And then, clad in his sheet of cloth, which he called a '*lungi*', and a shawl, he would sit down cross-legged on a grass mat on the veranda and eat with his fingers. They all ate with their fingers off banana leaves. After his afternoon siesta, Grey *saab* would rouse himself, yawn loudly, and yell, '*Bhola.*' A boy would come running with a flask of honey wine. That took care of Grey's evening and night. Often, he kicked women out of bed in the mornings. But still they returned at night.

While Julian watched amazed, not understanding Grey's charm, someone else observed the daily rituals, too. She was Tara, the woman Julian had seen on his first night at Grey's. Tara took care of the house. She moved around silently, and when Grey stretched out for his massage, she stood near the bamboo groves and watched with half-closed eyes.

Nikhil made garlands every day for Grey who wore them round his neck. One day, Grey threw a garland at Julian. 'Hartley, you wear one too.' Julian put it on. 'Hey, what's with the flute? Do you play or what?'

167

'He plays like Krishna,' Nikhil said.

'Play then, damn it.'

Julian laughed and played for a few minutes. 'That's pretty good. Goddamnit, that's bloody good! Here, have a swig.' After two quick gulps Julian felt as if his chest was on fire. 'I say, Hartley,' slurred Grey, 'ever made a swing?'

'A what?' Julian coughed and slapped his chest.

'A swing – damn it – the thing kids go to and fro on – two ropes and a board.'

'No, never made one.'

'Help me string one from that mango tree over there.'

'Now?'

'No – tomorrow, tomorrow. Too tired tonight, and too goddamn bloody drunk. Sod it, the bloody petty pace – nah, the creeping creeping – what I mean is – the last asinine syllable – d'you get it? There's so much to tell, but sounds like an idiot's doing the telling, right? A rite of passage – this passage to India, for us. Not even the pity of it – damn it, never, never, never, never, never. Cover your face when you play that damn pipe of yours, cover your face —' Grey stopped short and stood up. 'Ah, could *coitus quietus* bring, ah. Goodnight, sweet prince, sigh no more – undone endlessly, endlessly . . .' His voice trailed off as he went inside.

'That was some tirade,' said Nikhil.

'What on earth was that all about?'

'Ask him tomorrow.'

Julian climbed up the mango tree holding the end of the thick rope between his teeth. He twisted it around the branch they had decided on and let the rope down to Grey. On the ground once again, he whistled with relief.

'Go up again,' said Grey, 'here's the other rope.'

'Thought we were going to take turns.'

'You need more practice.'

'Doing what?'

'Climbing trees.'

'It is not required in my station in life to climb trees.'

'Right now it is. Go on.'

Julian tried to stare Grey down, but it didn't work. The children were so excited about the swing that Julian didn't feel like getting into an argument. So, up he climbed again with another rope between his teeth.

The swing fixed, Julian sat down on a fallen tree trunk and lit a cigarette. 'May I have one?' asked Grey. 'Haven't smoked a cigarette for years.'

'Hope the ropes don't break,' Julian said as Grey, cigarette in his mouth, joined the six kids on the swing. With two girls on his lap, one boy on his shoulder, one climbing up the ropes, another boy on the branch from which the swing was suspended, Grey closed his eyes and moved the swing gently.

'Why d'you play the flute?' Grey asked from the swing.

'I like it.'

'Why?'

'Like the sound.'

'That stringy, coiling sound?'

'What do you mean?'

'The strings, m'lord, are false.'

'Why so much Shakespeare since last night?'

'What do you mean, your lordship?'

'Were you an actor?'

'Didn't that scrawny sonofabitch tell you?'

'No. Just said something about your apple orchard, or was it cherry?'

'Very funny. Apple, it was. That was Srinagar. The actor lived a long time ago.'

'Why are you here, Grey?'

'I hate that unreal world out there. This here is real, see, this rich red earth. Never mind – time to get drunk now. *Bhola!*'

Julian coughed over the honey wine a few times and handed the flask back to Grey. 'Think you're a god, Grey?'

'No, blast you, you think you are, that's the problem.'

'I merely play, that's all.'

'I play, too,' said Grey, smiling coyly.

'Who? Oberon? Prospero?'

'Never! Played Orlando, Feste, Lucio, Bosola, Flamineo, Faustus, even Lear for a night. I was at Edinburgh, mind you. Read all that was there to read. Then my father died, and my mother ran off with a sailor. And I got interested in Shakespeare. So I joined a travelling theatre company. And then I heard about indigo.' Grey paused.

'Then?'

'Why the hell should I tell you anything?'

' 'Cause I have a pretty face.'

'Fuck you.'

'Go on, so what happened after that?'

'Sailed to India. An indigo planter just when the dye was not required any more. Ah, you should have seen what the planters did to the natives. We needed the dye, y'see. And this rich red soil was purr-fect for the blue poison. So we stopped the natives from growing rice and whatever was edible and made sure they planted indigo. Suddenly we didn't need the stuff any more, we decided. But we forgot to tell them for a few years, I think. When it was time to collect the taxes, the natives couldn't sell the indigo, 'cause we didn't want it. The land had become so infertile due to indigo planting that the peasants weren't even able to raise enough crop. This was decades ago, by the way. I arrived when it was practically all over. And it was all over very soon. Pass the bottle. What's the point of telling you this? Why d'you wanna know, eh? Wha'd'you care, you patrician sonofabitch? Wha'd'you wanna know anyway? 'Bout me? Wanna know about me?'

'Yes, I do,' Julian said.

'The natives couldn't take it any more, so they chopped off a few white heads, burned plantations. And the Raj took care of the trouble in its own sweet way.

'Went to Kashmir then. The paradise on earth – the Mogul emperors called it. Srinagar. Bought me an apple orchard. May I have another cigarette? Thanks. Well, that didn't work either. So I came back here, where indigo had burnt the land blue and barren.'

'Blue's not barren,' Nikhil said.

'Indigo was.'

'You like it here, don't you?' Julian asked.

'I love it here. They give and they give, and all they want is a smile, a touch.'

'And what do we give them?'

'What do we give them? Why, the Raj gave them indigo, blue eyes and men who want to rule the world. They've burned the indigo, turned away from blue eyes, but the men, the men caught them and broke them. God, am I happy the

170

earth is still red here. At least they eat well here, and they smile, too.'

The bamboo groves clattered softly in the wind. With slow steps, Julian walked towards the bungalow. Grey was among the Saontals again getting his morning dose of adoration. The flute in his hand turned gold, then green, gold, green, gold, as the sun found it through the thick leaves overhead. Why didn't they notice him when he stood there with the flute? He had smiled too. But —

Nikhil sat on the veranda making garlands of frangipani, gul-mohr, jasmine and hibiscus. 'So they didn't notice you,' he said without looking up. Julian sat down on the steps. 'Here —' Nikhil threw a garland around Julian's neck. 'Now, go play to them.'

'I feel silly.'

'Go play for yourself. Ignore them.' He must play for them, upon their hearts, in the garden, must be worshipped, adored so that he can believe again. He in his garden, adored, always out of reach, on an altar of flowers, lost in his music, only mine when he plays.

And so he went and leaned against the gul-mohr tree near the pond and, crossing his ankles, began to play. Liquid sounds swept his heart to a riverside. Flutegreen now, flutegold, flutewaves, flutetones —

Then the children found him. He sank cross-legged on the grass. They sniffed his hair, his skin, his clothes. The women left Will Grey with slow hesitant steps. Like a warm rice field in summer, his hair; his skin like the cowdust hour; his face, neither man's nor woman's.

Men stopped tending vegetable beds and turned. Old women forgot to put the *paan* leaf in their mouths. Perhaps even the cows raised their heads.

'What's the meaning of this?' muttered Will Grey and sucked his forefinger. 'He has no business being here and doing that to them, us. Go back to where the rest of your blood is – on the beach, no doubt, among shrimp and sunset.'

Dane removed his shoes and walked barefoot on the sand. It

171

was impossible to sit on the terrace and just listen to people talk about 'quaint bazaars,' 'delicious shrimps', 'gorgeous weather'. Didn't they notice anything else? In the afternoons, those wiry, dark men in their narrow boats leaping over waves, searching the fish-crowded waters, salt-crust on their bodies, nets in their hands. And as they pulled those pea-pod boats on to shore, they sang, their voices rising with each heave of their muscles. Then they spread open the large nets, and the fish glistened pink, silver, blue, purple in the sunset.

The sea was so dark now, even though the waves shimmered green and the half moon shone white. It shone silver on that altar. He dug a little hole with his toes. Wonder what she's doing now? Sleeping, maybe? Thinking of me? Does she think of me? What does she eat? Pomegranates?

Wish I could run back to Phulgarh tonight. Why can't I leave like Ju does? What would Julian do now? Would he have . . .? Wish I could ask him.

He felt the waves slide over his feet and the sand slither away as the water fell back. There aren't even any choices any more. Decisions are made long before choices even become clear.

All through those cold nights in the temple I waited for nothing. If only I could just forget everything else, not think at all, be mad, mad, mad, and angry, run, hide maybe.

Dane dug his fists into his pockets and walked back to the hotel.

Julian, what would you have done?

'Hide!' yelled Nikhil running towards them. Will Grey dropped his cigarette on the veranda and stood up. 'Hide!' panted Nikhil, 'they think he's here somewhere.'

'Let's go.' Grey hoisted Julian up.

'Why? Where?'

'Will explain later. Come on, run.'

Ten minutes later, they stood inside a circle of banyan and peepul trees. They collapsed on the ground panting. Under them were only flowers, tiny, white flowers, heady and sweet with trampling.

'What are we hiding from?' asked Julian.

'This is the thickest part of the woods,' said Grey.

172

'What are we hiding from, damn it?'

'From the police,' said Nikhil.

'Why, what have we done?'

'It's not us.'

'Then what?'

'They're after a terrorist who hides out in the village occasionally.'

'What's that got to do with us?'

'I'm supposed to detain him and turn him in if he comes here,' Grey said.

Six broken, bleeding, limp bodies lay near the pond. Grey, Nikhil, Julian and the women washed cuts, bandaged heads, soothed wailing children. 'This one's a lost cause,' muttered Grey. He rolled a twisted body down the sloping bank of the pond.

'What are you doing?' Julian raced after the rolling body and grabbed it just before it hit the water. The boy was nearly faceless. His sternum was crushed and blood still trickled from his ears. He picked the boy up gingerly and carried him back.

'They proved their point on that one, lovey,' laughed Grey. Julian placed the boy on the grass quietly.

As he bent over the water an hour later to wash his hands, he caught his reflection in the pond. Funny, as if a hibiscus bush had exploded against his chest.

'Why do they beat up these miserable wretches? Because they hide the terrorists.'

'What the hell is going on and why are you involved in this?'

Grey looked at Julian's angry face and smiled. 'Once upon a time there was a very angry boy,' he said.

'How about a straight answer for a change?'

'Tell him, Grey *saab*, he should know.'

'Come, come with me, Hartley. I'll deliver the goods. This is what happened: Lord Curzon wishes to divide Bengal in two — east and west Bengal — for purposes of administration. People's families and property will get divided, just like that. You can't possibly understand the emotions. These are Bengalis. Therefore, the anger and the violence. They want to get rid of us, that's all. But we don't want to go. We're having a splendid time out here!'

'What about this terrorist?'

'They all need hideouts, and this particular one chose this particular spot.'

'Why are you supposed to turn him in?'

'Why d'you think? Just a matter of skin, Hartley.'

'Where is this terrorist now?'

'Somewhere here. He'll appear one o' these nights and sing.'

And appear he did, Gautam Sen, the terrorist, thin, pale, hungry, and laughed at Grey with stormy eyes. Here he was, Gautam Sen, sprawling on the veranda steps and singing. Grey choked on the honey wine twice and slapped his chest. Nikhil peeled the petals off a hibiscus and stared intently at the large, yellow stamens. Why do I bite my thumb so often these days? thought Julian.

'Do you want to know what I'm singing of?' The terrorist turned to Julian. 'I'm singing of the moon. Its laughter crashes through the dam of night and overflows.' He scratched his head. 'I killed a British civilian three days ago. He was red-faced.'

'I don't think you should use this village as a hideout,' Grey said. 'They killed a boy yesterday and beat up five men.'

'You don't understand anything. You're white.'

'I don't think the Saontals should suffer because of you.'

'They're loyal.'

'I'll turn you in if you come here again.'

'Really? I'll just have to shoot you then. And maybe him too.'

'Just like that, eh?'

'Just like that – bang, bang.'

'When will you grow up?'

'I'm twenty-two, y'know. If I hadn't dropped out of college —' Julian looked at him smile at the moon with his hands behind his head. 'I hate you all,' said Gautam Sen. 'You have no right to be here and you know it! Get out of our country. How dare Lord Curzon even think of splitting our state in two just for the sake of convenience.'

'I agree with Grey,' Julian said, 'I don't think you should impose yourself on these people. Find some other place to hide.'

'These Saontals love me. I sing for them. They feed me, take care of me when I need taking care of. You – you forced indigo on our people and lured them with false hopes. These people, they supported the indigo planters, gave them their all, and the planters abused them, destroyed them. You have no right to be here. You threaten their security.'

'Don't keep harping on the indigo,' Grey snapped, 'that was decades ago. Concentrate on the present grievance.'

'Let's just concentrate on the moonlight,' said Julian. 'It looks pretty serious, y'know.'

'Yes,' slurred Grey, 'the full moon, ah, in a few days. They're waiting for it. There'll be a bloody wedding and they'll dance out their bruises.'

'You look like a Buddhist.' Gautam looked straight at Julian without squinting, although the morning sun was very bright. Julian lowered his aluminium mug of tea and looked at the garlands heaped on the veranda.

'What does a Buddhist look like?' he asked.

'Like you, except that they shave their heads. I wonder what you would look like with your head shaved.' Gautam cocked his head to one side. 'They have faces that seem to have suffered and turned into masks.'

Julian blew into the mug to cool the tea.

'You frown very intensely like most Buddhist monks.'

The tea was still very hot; Julian blew over its surface again.

'How come you don't look like other Englishmen?'

'I don't know.'

'Something in your face is very un-English.'

'Good tea,' said Julian.

'Do you go to church?'

'No.'

'But aren't you supposed to?'

Julian shrugged and took another sip.

'You're Christian, right?'

'I guess so. There's Jewish blood somewhere in the family too.'

'Your mother?'

175

'Oh, no. My great-great-grandmother, I think.'

'You play the flute well.'

'Thank you.'

'Yesterday, in the afternoon, when you were playing the flute, and the children were at your feet, and the women too, the scene looked almost mythical. Only it's difficult for me to picture a blond Krishna!'

Julian choked.

'Are you all right?'

'Yes, yes, um, yes.'

'They're in love with you, all of them. They talk about you all the time. Last night the women were talking of making garlands for you. Would you like that? Would you like to be worshipped and adored as the Krishna of *kalyug*?'

Holding the warm mug in his hands, Julian stared at the tea. 'What was Buddha like?' he asked after a long pause.

'Buddha? He was an avatar of Krishna, or Vishnu, I should say. He was born a prince. His father was told that the prince, Siddhartha, would leave the kingdom and become a monk. So they tried to keep him unexposed to the miseries of the world by sort of imprisoning him in a beautiful garden, a – a – terrestrial paradise. But it didn't work. One chariot-ride through the city and the prince was lost. He went off one night to get enlightened and deal with the sufferings of this world.'

'And he achieved nirvana?'

'Right – so you know the story.'

'His life was different from Krishna's.'

'Oh, yes, of course. Krishna was such a decadent!'

Julian's knee smarted under the spilled hot tea and he sucked in his breath in pain.

'Krishna's adolescence was one long sexual experimentation. After that, he entered the political scene and helped one warring faction win a battle. A shrewd politician, that's how I see him.'

Julian set the mug down on the floor. 'I don't think Krishna was all that bad.'

'He had no feelings.'

'How do you know?'

'He never fell in love. He left the woman who loved him.'

'All that's really irrelevant.'

'Oh? What's relevant? Are gods supposed to be cold, arrogant sons of bitches?'

'I think Krishna's music was emotive and important. It gave people something to dream about.'

'His flute turned people mad. They craved for the music as if it was some kind of a drug they had got addicted to.'

'You've got this all wrong, Gautam.'

'Well, go ahead, tell me what is right.'

The tea was cold and tasteless.

Krishna played for them because they craved him, thought Julian as he sat among the children under the gul-mohr tree and played. Like mountain streams and fish leaping from waves was the music; like laughter of moonlight and children among bamboo groves.

As the women moved towards the fluteplayer, Grey got up and left.

What was once a well-furnished Victorian drawing room was now stark and dimly lit by two lanterns set six feet apart on the floor. The terrorist had left. The three of them sat on grass mats and ate off banana leaves. Rice, dal, cabbage and peas, and fish. Julian picked at the fishbones with his fingers. He always ended up using both hands while eating fish. Too many bones. Why the hell did they eat fish that had so many bones? Tara came and refilled their glasses with water. They never spoke to each other – Grey and Tara. Grey mumbled a few words at her sometimes, and she either nodded or made monosyllabic sounds. Grey's shoulders stiffened in her presence, and he constantly adjusted his clothes. Didn't she notice Grey's discomfort? Julian wondered. When the village women massaged Grey's thin body, she just stood and watched, day after day, as still as the dark banyan trees, but she carried the bamboo groves in her eyes.

'You are stealing my cattle, damn you!' Grey stood up and licked his fingers clean. 'Day after day, you and your bloody flute. Leave them alone. They're mine.'

'We are leaving in a few days, after the full moon,' said Nikhil.

'I forbid you to play your flute.'

Julian picked at the few stray peas on his banana leaf.

'You will not play in the village.'

'I'll play where I damn well please.' Julian stood up.

'You can't take what's mine.'

'They're not your property; they are people.'

'My people.'

'Yes, your majesty,' said Julian with a bow.

'What do you want, Hartley?' Grey caught Julian's arm. 'Take over and usurp the throne? Will you? Will you live like me – can you, you poor little patrician? Can you live here for ever and forget about your people, make these your people? You'll have to give up everything to be king here. No, you don't want to be here for ever. This is just a phase, a whim, a power game for you, between you and me, to see who'll win. Don't you see, you fool, there's nothing to win! It's giving, just giving. You just want the thrill of adoration, to unsettle our lives for a brief moment and then leave all smug after this satisfying game. Do I despise this game. My lord, this is not you. He – that bastard from Srinagar — has turned you into this. Look at yourself – what are you: a trapped god or a free man?' Grey let go of Julian's arm. Julian left the room slowly.

'He can't do this,' Grey said to Nikhil.

'We'll be gone in a few days.'

'He's stealing their souls.'

'The flute has stolen his.'

'You've destroyed him, you bastard.'

'Plays well, though, doesn't he?'

'Yes, he plays, all right. Yes, he plays and he plays, he like Krishna, and you, you scheming bastard, you play his Kalki. Not god, neither you nor him, but demons that tear the soul.'

About a thousand steps, it seemed. Wide, almost a mile wide? Moonlight over marble steps leading up, up . . . That was his shadow on the steps. Julian started. A long cloak swishing below his knees, a top hat, a gold-topped cane. Gleaming black shoes – pat, pat, pat, pat. Doors – doors like the jaws of a whale. Ivory doors? My word – what a floor! Black and white, black and white. Columns too. Scores of 'em. The light – ah, chandeliers? No . . . just the moonlight? I? An Inverness cape? Can't believe this – that was ten years ago. Black top hat, tails and close-fitting trousers. A red waistcoat with tiny gold leaves, a white shirt and a red bow tie. Rouge; sparkling silver powder against his temples.

With white-gloved hands, my lord of Ravinspur swept the cape off his shoulders. It fell at his feet. He tossed his hat off and moved forward rapidly to the middle of the enormous floor. Spreading his arms out elegantly, he twirled once. A hundred forms twirled with him. Mirrors. Mirrors all around. No walls. He felt something under his feet. Petals – myriad petals, all over the black and white floor. And he was dancing, dancing suddenly. He had to dance. He must dance here. Watching himself he danced, his body moving in sensuous rhythm to a faraway, high piping melody. They had been waiting for this, he felt. They, they. He danced among his reflections, in sweeping circles, like widening ripples in a pool.

He sent the cane flying. With the tips of his fingers he removed his gloves. His coat slid off his body. Then his fingers found his tie, and the buttons of his waistcoat and shirt. 'Forgive me, oh, lord, forgive me,' he said, 'for I adore thee. Forgive me.' He stepped out of his trousers and slipped off his shoes. 'I adore thee, oh, lord, forgive me, I adore thee.'

Where was the music? He danced towards the sound and it moved away every time. Fainter, fainter, then cutting through the dark in a sudden wave. On the right – no, on the left? Before? Behind? Where situated that power? Moving still, still moving. Stop somewhere! At some point! He wanted to stop and listen and find the point. But his feet moved free of him, his body swayed without him.

Aching, aching, aching. He would crumble but his feet would dance on searching for the music. He whirled across the petal-covered floor, round and round and round. Long-drawn notes, twisting, pulling. No more. No more. Feet must surely bleed, and body break. 'Oh, lord, forgive me, I can no more.' Unceasing, controlled frenzy of notes. And then he tripped and broke to his knees.

Waist-deep in flower petals. He splashed himself with petals, lifting them with his hands as if holding water. They were soft against his burning face. Raising his face to the night he threw the petals high into the air, laughing, crying, laughing. He felt his hundred selves throw petals upwards, laughing, crying, laughing.

A stormy river of petals swept around him, over him. Lightning came petal soft, and like the hush of falling petals the thunder. They wanted him, they loved him. Must dance, must, must. But he couldn't rise. The petals were too thick and heavy. His knees buckled again and again. 'Lord, help me, help me, oh, lord . . .'

A sharp cold wind twisted around his frail body. Where was the warm river of petals? They were looking at him, at his nakedness, the hard mirror eyes. He bent over and tried to cover himself, hugging himself, his head touching his knees. They crouched with him. 'Don't do this to me, please, don't do this.' What music had he danced to that had abandoned him? Whose music? It was cutting cold, the wind. It rattled against his ears, a dry, white rattle. The moonlight was a shaft of ice.

'Warm rain rain again, warm rain rain,' he pleaded. 'Warm rain, please, warm rain, warm rain rain . . .'

Grey rubbed his eyes and buried his face in his pillow. An odd moaning from the next room made him uncomfortable. 'What the hell is that? Has he got malaria or what?' Cursing, he rolled out of bed, struggling through the mosquito net, and reached for his shawl on the chair. 'Blast. Hope I have quinine.'

'Hartley, Hartley —'
'Warm rain, please, warm rain rain, please —' The wind was so rough. It rocked him vigorously.
'Hartley! Wake up, damn it!'
'Warm rain rain, oh, please, warm —'
'Wake up, blast you.'
'Warm – what – oh – warm – rain – I – I —'
His body was cold and clammy, his clothes soaked with sweat. Cradling his knees, he sat on his bed, whimpering.
'Are you all right?'
'Grey —'
'Son, are you all right?'
'Yes. Thank you.' Julian took the towel from Grey and wiped his wet face. Grey stroked his damp hair.

'How 'bout some hot milk with honey?'

'That'd be nice, thanks.'

'Go back to sleep for a couple of hours after the milk; you'll feel much better. You don't have malaria, don't worry.'

Sitting on a fallen tree trunk, Julian watched Grey get his daily rub-down. The children had cornered a goat and were desperately trying to ride it. But the goat was viciously determined not to be mastered. Butted rudely by it, the children yelped and collapsed on the ground. The three girls on the swing laughed at the light-skinned, brown-haired boy who, after several falls, managed to get on the goat's back. An unrestrained cry of triumph and, the following second, a humiliated heap on the red clay. Julian found himself joining in their mirth. The boy, whose name was Benu, screamed in anger and chased the laughing girls. Unable to catch his mocking rivals, he turned towards Julian who suppressed his amusement at once. Benu marched up to him and faced him, legs apart, fists behind his back. The half-breed boy's defiant little face startled him. Julian held his ears apologetically and smiled. Benu's face relaxed, and he reached and touched Julian's hair. '*Alo*,' he said, '*alo*.' That means 'light', Julian recognised. Then, Benu stretched out his bare arm and, pushing Julian's sleeve up, laid his arm next to Julian's. He touched the inside of Julian's forearm and his own and frowned. Julian was a toasted golden-brown, and Benu was the same, except that there were freckles on his arm and his little face.

Nikhil, watching this little scene, felt oddly uncomfortable. 'Benu,' he called, 'Benu, what are you doing?'

'He's like me,' the boy said. 'Why do you say he's a god?'

'Don't touch him,' said Nikhil.

Unable to follow the dialect, Julian ruffled the boy's hair and gave him a hug. Benu put his arms around Julian's neck and buried his head in the hollow of his throat. Julian drew in warm red mud in his hair and sun-baked skin.

He did not want to go down to the village with Grey and Nikhil to watch the wedding preparations. It'll be fun, do come along, Nikhil had urged. They have this bathing ritual –

you'll love it. But his head ached and mouth tasted queer, so he just sat in the sun and watched the children play hopscotch and Benu on the swing. He wanted that boy's arms around his neck again, and his freckled face against his throat.

'Benu, come here,' he called. The boy jumped off the swing and ran to him. Julian did not quite know what to do then. He ruffled his hair again, and lightly touched his forehead with his fist. Benu's tough little fist shot out at once and slammed against Julian's jaw. 'Ouch! So – you want to box, eh?' They were laughing and hitting out after that, Benu dancing in glee, ducking; Julian, sitting on the tree trunk, swerving to avoid hits on his nose and mouth, but occasionally letting the child punch him on the jaw and in the middle. 'Pretty good! Hey, nice, nice. Ouch. Careful now. Ouch . . .'

Dragging him by the hand, Benu took Julian down to the village. All the huts were decorated with coconuts, mango leaves and trimmed banana trees. Although people were bustling around with pitchers of milk, baskets of fruits, vegetables, freshly slaughtered goats, there seemed to be a wonderful laziness in the air. Grey sat on a wooden board, smoking *ganja*, while the women rubbed some kind of beige paste on his body. Nikhil sat with a bucket of dark blue powder and sifted through it. 'Who's getting married?' laughed Julian.

'Julian – look at this! Come here.'

'What's this powder?'

'Indigo.'

'As smooth and bright as a peacock's throat,' said Grey.

'Isn't it gorgeous?'

Before Julian could answer women and children ran to him and dragged him down on another wooden board. They whisked off his *kurta* and began to rub that paste on his body. 'Sandalwood and turmeric,' said Grey. 'Smells as light and heady as the moonlight.' Julian squeezed his eyes shut and grimaced as the two girls rubbed the paste on his face.

'Why are they doing this?'

'Purification,' said Nikhil.

'Getting me ready for the kill.'

'No; for the dance.'

They poured hot water over him and washed the dried paste off. Hot water! What a luxury after all these days of cold baths.

Benu flung himself on Julian with each splash of hot water, laughing and squealing.

Dry and warm, Julian lay on the grass. Benu sat on his chest and sprinkled flower petals on him from a basket. Nikhil chewed his fingernails and watched in silence. Tara, filling her pitcher at the well, turned and looked at the two men. She watched Grey scoop rice, milk and chopped bananas into his mouth from a coconut shell. '*Ei*, Tara,' one of the women drying Grey's feet called out, '*ei*, Tara, do you want us to put *alta* on his feet?' Tara shrugged and, holding the pitcher against her waist, started to walk away. '*Ei*, don't trample over those garlands! Those are for Grey *shayeb*.' Tara pushed the heap of garlands aside with her foot and walked away from them. Grey stopped eating and stared after her. Then, catching Julian's eye, he lowered his face and resumed eating.

As the sun went down, Nikhil woke Julian up and pushed Benu away. 'Come,' he said, 'let's go.'

'Will you play tonight?' asked Nikhil as they reached Grey's bungalow. Julian nodded. Nikhil tossed a handful of indigo powder at Julian and laughed. 'You could be as blue as that, y'know.'

The indigo form shivered in the mirror. The flute on the table shone gold near the lit lantern. 'Your hair is fine the way it is,' whispered Nikhil. 'Like a golden halo.' Gul-mohr blossoms were in his hair, a garland around his neck, flowers at his wrists and ankles. The women had drawn paisleys under his cheekbones with sandalwood paste, and they had reddened the sides of his feet with *alta*. A long, blue silk cloth was around his waist, a white silk scarf over his shoulders.

'Are you cold?' asked Nikhil, and offered the flask of honey wine. Julian shivered again as the drumbeats rattled in the darkness.

Arms around waists, two long rows of bodies in rhythm facing each other. The dancers moved close, then fell back again, their feet rising and falling with the rumble of drums, their bodies swaying unrestrained. The banana trees glistened and the bamboo groves were more restless than ever. The moon was enormous and dark gold.

*   *   *

They could not dance to his flute. The strains coiled around their feet and shackled them. The drums faded to a murmur. They stood in horror and amazement and watched him play. 'The colour of stars are his eyes,' some whispered. 'The moon is trapped in his hair.'

He is one with the night, thought Nikhil. The darkness of Krishna. Thank God for the indigo. Thank God for his madness.

The night fell on his skin indigo soft, and the moonlight encased him in translucent golden scales. Julian glittered as if carved in sapphire. Then, very slowly, he began to move in circles around the trees.

Out of the huddled bunch of children crept Benu. 'Don't look at him,' he said. 'Don't look at him. Awful, awful. That's not his skin. He has filled himself with Nag's poison, awful indigo poison. Don't look at him.' Benu ran, stumbling in the dark, back to Grey's bungalow. With a rusty knife he slashed at the ropes of the swing.

A strong gust of wind almost swept the bamboo groves to the ground. Grey held his shawl tightly and hobbled as fast as he could towards the drumbeats and the music. 'What the hell is going on? That's not how they play the drums usually. Jesus! What's going on? Damn the bloody ankle!' He spat and limped on.

'Wo-o-o-o, strike me dead, lovey!' He stopped mid-stride awkwardly, almost falling backwards, and gripped a low branch. 'Out of 'is bloody moind, 'e 'is,' he whispered hoarsely. 'Lordy, lord, he's banaaanas, nuts, crackers, stark, staring mad! The moon's done it, that's it. Yes, sir, the moon and that ruddy flute of his. Good lord —'

Julian scrambled up a tree and balanced himself at the fork of two branches. He relaxed between the branches and felt the leaves brush against him as the wind swept through them. There was nothing else; just the music, just the darkness, and the wonder in fifty pairs of eyes.

The leaves brushed the indigo powder off his body. The dancers gasped as they saw the blue powdery swirls merge

184

with the moonlight. The blue powder floated up into the moonlight and into the fluteplayer's nose. Unable to control the irritation, Julian dropped his flute, sneezed loudly and suddenly, and crashed to the ground.

'Ha-ha-ha —' Laughing, Grey stumbled in. 'Ha-ha-ha-ha, bless my soul! If that isn't my lord of Ravinspur! And what does he think he is?'

Nikhil followed a slouching Julian mutely. They reached the pond in the village and stared at the water. After the fall, Julian lay under the tree for hours, quiet and immobile. Everybody had left slowly. Grey's mocking laughter still echoed in their ears. Now, the village was as still as the pond. All the huts were dark.

Julian dropped his flute on the grass and took off his clothes and the flowers. His slender body shimmered blue. A few rapid steps, and he paused before the water. Leaping into a high arc, he dived straight into the heart of the silver disc trembling on the ripples. The moon cracked and splintered into a thousand fragments of sharp, glittering eyes, flashing, blinking, dropping. Julian's body arched under the rioting water and shot up into the air, washed clean silver-gold.

The swing lay on the red dust, the ropes cut to bits. Standing around the bullock cart, the children dug their toes into the red clay and tore leaves off bushes. Benu ripped hibiscus blossoms to shreds. Nikhil sat on the steps of the veranda. He didn't like Benu. He always felt like wrenching his little arms off Julian's neck. The Saontals had sent flowers, milk and honey that morning. The women had wanted to touch his feet one last time, but Julian chose to remain indoors. What is he doing? wondered Nikhil. The cart's been waiting for nearly an hour and we should set off before three.

At the sound of footsteps, he turned around. Julian came out of the house with Grey behind him. They stood on the veranda and looked at each other quietly for a few seconds, then shook hands. Julian walked to the cart through the group of children and tossed his cloth bag inside. Nikhil stood up and stretched. 'Thanks a lot for everything, Grey *saab*,' he said. Grey did not take Nikhil's outstretched hand.

'Don't ever come back here,' Grey said, 'and leave him alone.'

Julian reached out to pat Benu's brown head. But Benu drew back sharply. Waves of nausea hit Julian. He climbed into the covered cart.

Nikhil's hands shook as he picked up his stuff and walked towards the cart. He could see Julian's raised knees and feet. He must be lying down. The cart driver stubbed his *biri* and stood up. Nikhil scratched his head. Benu stared at Julian's feet unblinkingly. Suddenly, he bent down and reached for something.

No, no. Nikhil's head reeled. 'Julian – Julian —' Julian's body jack-knifed up in pain as the stone struck. He clutched his bleeding foot. For a split second they stared at each other, Benu and Julian. Then Benu turned and ran off into the woods.

Chapter 8

Dane ran through the dark woods slipping and stumbling. Why couldn't he run any faster? He felt as if his heart would burst. The air was damp and heavy; the ground, slippery with wet fallen leaves.

The temple at last. Oh, God. She would be there against a broken column like she always was, waiting. They would tremble as their arms tightened.

The sea was in his ears, the waves crashing and crashing, waves glowing green with phosphorus. And warm sand, warm even when shining white with moonlight. Dane cried helplessly. There were pomegranates too, somewhere, somewhere, and sandalwood, jasmine, even dolphins. Dolphins leaping from waves at night, quivering with green flames. The sea swept around, roaring, waves rising within him again and again. On the sands he was rolling, rolling, on golden, unhurting powder-glass of sand and moonlight which cut only where it should.

How did you hurt your foot, Ju? By mistake. Red soil, banana trees, coconut palms, mustard fields, cows, goats, children − one smudgy line outside the train window. Then darkness, then the flute. Olive trousers, khaki shirt and pale yellow flute. Julian played. This is the sea, he said. This is the sand. This is the moonlight, hey, wha'd'you say? he laughed. And, ha, ha, this is a pomegranate! Ju, you ass. Then the flute laughed and laughed.

The sea in his head laughed and stunned him. Black, black waves, and his fingers lost among them.

'Sakhi,' he said. 'Sakhi.' Her mouth behind his ear. The sea washed over him again.

Swimming like dolphins swim, aflame with phosphorus

and moonlight, drowning among black waves and red-brown seaweeds, riding seaward on the waves. At sunset, a pomegranate sea. Somewhere, the flute and Ju. Laughing, laughing, and 'Don't worry, Dane.' Don't-worry-Dane-Ju. Laughing-flute-Ju. His face brushed the blanket. He opened his eyes slowly to broken columns. Sunshine and warm, dry grass. He felt the cold altar under his arm through the blanket.

Holding the shawl closely around him, Julian ran up the steps of the Krishna temple. He was still there, his fluteplayer, the slim, blue form. His breathing relaxed at last. All night long, Julian had tossed and turned in bed. The sun came through the grey columns and filled the altar. Julian's shadow fell on his fluteplayer and kept the god in darkness.

It's been so long, so long. Hands among petals – he longed for their sight. Hands among flowers that had become a permanent vision in his mind.

She appeared with flowers, and knelt at the altar. Julian hid behind a column and watched her work. The fatigue of restless nights vanished. On that late January morning the stone was ice cold against Julian's cheek, but the sun on slender brown hands and flowers and blue feet felt incredibly, overwhelmingly warm. His head reeled a little, as if he was drunk on warm honey wine.

I wonder why and how rumours spread, Lorna? Howard tells me a subaltern from the cantonment, Thomas Sherley, told Roanna Lyndon about all that happened with Dane. I thought only the servants spread rumours. *Sahibs* don't, or so I'm told. Then why did Thomas Sherley talk? Men stick by men, never talk about each other, at least that's what Charles always said, and my father, too. Men protect each other, honour each other. Why then did the soldier break this unwritten code? Or aren't there any codes any more?

'How did you do this to your ankle, Cyril?' Sherley carefully removed Trevors's boots and socks as he groaned on the bed.
  'Rugby. They fell on me and I slipped awkwardly.'
  'It's pretty swollen.'
  'Broken?'

'I don't know.'

'Pulled something near my shoulder too.'

Sherley's fingers travelled expertly over Trevors's shoulders and back. Strong muscles; smooth tanned skin. Red-brown hair that curled ever so slightly where it touched his neck. Sherley wiped his sweating palms on his trousers.

'Ah, feels good, Tom.'

A beautiful ridge down the centre of his back. He felt the shoulderblades under warm skin and muscle. Skin grew warmer and warmer as Sherley's hands worked and worked.

Thick, soft hair kept touching Sherley's fingers. He couldn't prevent it somehow. Hair slipped between his fingers. Such soft skin behind the ears, white and a little salty. And just where the hair touched —

'What the hell are you doing?' A hard punch in the stomach knocked Sherley off the bed. He doubled up and gasped in pain. 'What the hell are you doing, Tom?' Trevors grabbed Sherley's hair and, forcing back his head, hit him on the jaw. Sherley tried to scramble to his feet. But Trevors's fists found his face over and over again. He couldn't see clearly any more. Just red, bright red, warm and wet. The floor was cold and stunning.

Sitting cross-legged on the sunlit lawn, Dane and Harry watched Julian split open a pomegranate. 'Ah, the caviar of fruits,' Julian sighed, 'the exquisite, decadent pleasure of eating pomegranates – like sinning almost, with its faintly bitter aftertaste. Perfect.' His mouth touched the dark red interior. 'Dane, have one.' Harry picked one up and sniffed it. 'Eat it, Winston. Gently split it open and let your mouth do the rest.' Harry followed directions clumsily, the juice staining his mouth and clothes.

'Here, Dane, open your mouth, darling, pomegranates, love.'

'Stop it, Ju – Ju – you – you —' Julian pinned Dane to the ground with his knees. 'Ju – you – damn —' Harry held Dane's arms down. Pomegranate juice ran all over Dane's face and down his throat. Julian's sticky hands forced his mouth open, Harry's hands bruised his wrists, and he struggled and laughed, deliriously happy.

'What on earth are the three of you doing?' Caroline stared at them aghast. And then, slowly, and softly, she began to laugh with them.

Dr Aloke Bose looked up in surprise as Julian walked into his examination room at the hospital. 'Is something wrong?'

'Just dropped by to see how you were.'

'I'm fine, and you look pretty healthy, too.'

'Would you care to come to the club for lunch?'

'I – you see —' Dr Bose looked embarrassed. 'We're not allowed —'

'Oh – I – er – how stupid – I mean —' Julian moved his hands, trying to explain he didn't quite know what.

'Why don't you come over to my house for lunch?' Dr Bose said.

It was a neat little bungalow about a mile away from the hospital. Mostly cane furniture, plants and sketches on the walls. Plenty of bookshelves, filled with Renaissance, seventeenth-century and nineteenth-century literature, and several volumes of beautifully bound books – Bengali literature, Julian assumed.

'Please call me Aloke,' he said as Julian forked shrimp and rice into his mouth. 'Did you like Calcutta?' Julian nodded in response, his mouth full. 'Did you see the goat sacrifices?' The shrimp whatever-it-was-called was delicious. 'You missed something fascinating. Tch, tch.' Julian served himself some more rice and shrimp.

'This shrimp stuff is wonderful. Never had it before.'

'It's cooked with coconut and other stuff.'

'Mmm.'

'The Eden Gardens?'

'Boring.'

'And the Strand?' Julian nodded and smiled. 'And Park Street?' Julian scraped the last of the rice and shrimp off his plate and licked his lips.

'Absolutely marvellous.'

'Yes, Calcutta is marvellous!'

'I meant — Yes, it's marvellous.' Julian watched Aloke Bose lift food to his mouth elegantly. 'Do you go to Calcutta often?'

'Once a year.'

'Family?' The doctor nodded. 'Dr Morel said you write poetry.' Dr Bose nodded again. 'What do you write about?' He swallowed with difficulty, gulped some water down and sat back in his chair.

'About our fear of feeling too much, fear of self-surrender, of belonging to another, about misfits.'

'Misfits?' Julian raised his eyebrows.

'Yes. Like myself. Look at me,' Aloke Bose said, 'a perfect hybrid of Anglo-Indian culture, yet fitting in nowhere! When I visit my family in Calcutta and meet friends, I'm totally alienated by their lack of sophisitication, Western sophistication, that is. They don't understand what I've become and I don't understand why they can't change. And as for the British' – he drained his glass of water – 'well, I'm just a native who doesn't belong to their clubs. They're happy that I speak the language perfectly; but that does not change anything else.' He folded his napkin into a neat square and placed it next to his plate. 'What do I do with myself if both cultures reject me after having turned me into what they want?'

'You chose to become —'

'No – my father wanted me to become a doctor; learn English, go to England, study medicine. The hospitals all over the country are looking for Indian doctors who speak English. They want us to go to England and return with our qualifications to serve them. That's all. So here I am: Dr Aloke Bose, thirty-five, and a non-person really.' Julian scratched his plate with his fork. 'And, to top it all, now my parents want me to marry some strange girl from Burdwan. Rich and beautiful is what I've been told. I wrote to my father: "Marry her yourself". The state of mind of this country amazes me!'

Aloke Bose stood up abruptly, scratched his head and sat down again. 'Do you know that there are still *sati* cases being reported, something like ten a month? Do you know how many child-sacrificers are caught every year?' He adjusted his tie and looked at his cuffs. 'And this is still a beautiful country with its sunsets, rivers, the Himalayas, rich alluvial plains, rice fields, sandalwood groves, the ancient civilisations of Mohenjo-Daro and Harappa, Graeco-Roman art that Alexander left behind, the tree under which Buddha attained nirvana, fascinating temples, folk-lore, rich poetry, and – and – myth.'

He stared at his plate. 'Invasion after invasion from the north-west,' he muttered, 'all men who wanted to control this land of mythical milk and honey.'

This is a terribly alien country, thought Julian. There are no particulars here to be pinpointed and labelled.

'I sometimes wonder why the Indians are stirring about independence all of a sudden. We've never been independent! Before the British there were the Moguls; before them other rulers, most of whom came from outside the country.'

'Aloke, don't you have to go back to the hospital?'

'Yes, yes. I'm sorry, I didn't mean to – to – say all this – I – I —'

'I'm glad you did.'

'Julian, forget all that I said. Just play your flute, and I'll cut open patients.'

'Let's go riding.' Julian walked into Dane's room. Dane lay on the bed and stared at the ceiling. 'Come on, we have two hours before tea.'

'I want to chop wood,' Dane said.

Ravi Singh spread a blanket on the low brick wall of the back yard. Julian stretched himself out on it sideways and propped himself on his elbows. A peacock feather between his teeth, he looked at Dane. Dane dropped his shirt on the grass, picked up the axe and looked at the two formidable portions of a tree trunk that stood on the ground. Jugnu, Ravi Singh and the *mali* disappeared as soon as Dane raised the axe over his head. They knew they were not supposed to witness this. Jugnu knew for sure that the collector's *khansama* would give him one of his special kababs for this story.

'If you laugh, I'll chop your head off, Ju.' Wood splintered and flew up. Julian fell off the wall laughing.

Julian watched the sharp, heavy blade dive into wood. Tiny, yellow-brown flames against the clear blue light of February. It was that time of year.

Crack. Crack.

And the logs split apart under the power of seventeen-year-old-shoulders. Don't go, Ju! But he left all the same. Left the green woods and the splinters of wood splashing up. The sun so bright as he walked away; the sun always bright at departure. And arrivals, always rainy, stormy. Leaving, so expected, coming back, such a surprise.

Crack.

Arright, we'll go fishing. Arright, arright! Shut those dogs up.

Don't let me drown, Ju, squirmed the six-year-old tadpole. Omigosh, there are fishes in here! Don't let me drown.

Don't worry, Dane, you'll be a far better swimmer than me.

You're going away again?

Here, I'll rub your shoulders. Lie down. Firm, gentle hands.

Stay, Ju.

Why couldn't he stay? Ravinspur wasn't empty any more. There was laughter, too. And blue light.

Why do you sing when it storms, Ju? What does the rain do?

I don't believe them. They're lying, aren't they? Tell me they're lying!

No more questions. There had never been answers.

Running constantly. Breathless, and still running.

Why couldn't he stay?

To hear that 'Stay, Ju'. Always to hear, 'Stay, Ju'.

'Julian, here, you give this a try.'

The peacock feather fell on the white dust along with the collarless, green pin-striped shirt. 'You think I can't, eh?' And, crack.

'Ha, ha, ha, oh, God!'

'God! This axe is too damn heavy!'

'Come on, work those shoulders.'

Crack. Crack. Crack.

Such frail shoulders. A wet, exhausted body whimpering on the altar, shaking, but still that hint of defiance. What happens to Ju?

Those dark clothes that spring. Sweeping black capes, black velvet and satin, white silk and just a touch of lavender, sometimes mauve or orchid. String ties. Hair always a little untidy in front.

And when their eyes met, he had looked away, for twelve

193

years almost. Now, squinting in the brightness.

Racing through the woods, the bright green woods. You'll never catch me, Dane. I run faster, I do! But he caught him all the same, tripped him at last, sat on his chest, pulled his hair, punched his arrogant nose. And Ju, laughing and licking the blood trickling from his nose. Said he never felt pain. Then why cry, Julian, when it storms?

'Break, you goddamn fossil.'

Splinter like the wood, Julian. Perhaps you're splintering already. Maybe this is the last run. This time you are coming home.

Julian threw the axe down and collapsed on the grass. 'Ahh, my shoul – my everything!'

'Roll over.'

These thin shoulders and this weak body. Yet they had run all over the world almost unexhausted. Dane ruffled Julian's damp hair as he groaned. Come home, Julian; I'll take care of you.

Julian pressed his face against the grass. Strong, gentle hands that never stopped pulling.

Sherley filled his plate with scrambled eggs, six rashers of bacon, four slices of toast, three sausages, two sautéed cherry tomatoes from the breakfast array in the mess. He turned around and looked at the seated, eating men. Trevors was sitting near the windows on the left. Sherley walked to the far right and sat down next to a young blond who had just picked up a crisp slice of bacon with his fingers. 'Try the bacon with your fingers, Tom,' said the young man.

'You're turning into a savage pretty fast, Metcalfe.'

'Always was. Feels great.'

'What you doing tonight, eh, George?'

'What's special 'bout tonight?'

'Just asking.' Sherley added sugar and cream to his coffee and glanced at Trevors across the mess. George Metcalfe finished his bacon, then proceeded to scoop the scrambled eggs into his mouth with his fingers.

'I'm going fucking tonight. Wanna join me, Tommy?'

'George —'

'Tommy —' Metcalfe picked up his coffee and took a sip,

keeping his eyes on Sherley's face. 'Tom – oh God – you should see your face – ha, ha – Tom!' Metcalfe threw his head back and laughed, spilling his coffee down his shirtfront.

'Why, you —'

'Come with me tonight.'

'No thanks.'

'Why not? I got two o' the best.'

'You keep 'em.' Sherley turned to his food, keeping his eyes on his plate.

'Aw, come on, Tom,' Metcalfe persisted, 'come on, come on, come on ...' Sherley ate, ignoring the nagging. 'Cyril's coming with me,' said Metcalfe, 'now you'll come, won't you, you lazy sonofabitch. You've had no real exercise at all since you've been here, you —'

'Shut up.'

'Hey, Cyril,' Metcalfe bawled, looking towards Trevors, 'come and help me fix Tommy up real nice.' Sherley wiped his mouth with the napkin. Placing it next to his plate, he folded his hands on his lap. He heard the men laugh and he knew Trevors was not looking at him. He wanted to scream till his throat gave out. A bearer came and refilled his coffee cup. Sherley added sugar and cream, and drank his coffee slowly. Then he got up and left the mess.

He sat down on the sun-warmed bench outside. Dick Farrell, holding a mug of steaming tea, came out of the mess and sat down next to him.

'Hello, Farrell.'

'Did you hear?'

'What?'

'We can't leave the premises on Holi. O.C.'s orders.'

'Why not?'

'The natives get pretty rowdy and drunk, throw colours at each other, etcetera.'

'I don't give a damn.' Trevors's voice boomed from the back. 'I'm going to the *kota* that night.'

'You better be careful, Cyril,' Farrell winked.

'She's dancing that night, the bearers at the mess are talking about it. She hasn't danced for a long time.'

'Well, you had better be careful. Don't get carried away by Metcalfe's reckless ideas.'

Sherley looked at his shadow on the ground intently. Its hair was blowing gently in the wind, too. It, too, sat with its hands between its knees.

'What are you doing, Ju?' Julian turned around, startled, from his writing desk.

'I thought you were at the club playing cricket.'

'I got bored.'

'Is something wrong?'

'No. What are you doing anyway?'

'I was writing to Jarvis.'

'To Jarvis?'

'Yes. He's seeing to the tenants' cottages and stuff. I'd inquired about that earlier.' Dane looked at his brother, surprised. 'And the mills ought to be reopened and repaired.'

'Yes, I know. I thought about that last year, but —'

'I want to talk to you about that some time.'

'Sure.' Dane scratched his head. 'Er, would you play your flute, Ju?'

He sat on a boulder near the riverside and listened to his brother's flute. Why he had wanted to hear Julian play all of a sudden he didn't know. Haunting, fragile, escalating, almost heartbreaking.

'My pomegranate piece,' smiled Julian. 'Listen.'

Dane closed his eyes as the sea swept around him. Holi — everybody was talking about Holi, the festival of colours. The madness of spring, Dr Morel called it. How would living be after the madness?

Will Ju come home to Ravinspur? Dane raised his face to the dazzling sky, eyes closed. Ju looks so peaceful playing his flute. So quaint, this music. It created a realm of its own and drew the player in, and the listener, too. The music built that realm note by note, without labour or pain. And what was this place where Ju was now? He opened his eyes. That look on his face as if Ju was lying under that old elm tree. What are you thinking of, Ju? Unicorns, he'd smile, storms. And that silly smile of his. You don't believe in unicorns! In the woods of Ravinspur I can. Why couldn't he ever disappear into that world of Julian's?

'Ju, stop.' Dane jumped off the boulder. 'Good lord.' He almost landed on several small dark bodies crouching against the boulder. What were all these children doing here? He hadn't even noticed them when they walked up to the river.

Nikhil settled the chairs in Dr Morel's consultation room and straightened up the doctor's table. He filled a pitcher with water and stepped outside to water the plants.

'Hello, Nikhil.'

'Julian —' What to say to him now? He had killed him that night. As he fell from the tree, hadn't he died? But Julian's eyes — so clear, so free of pain. Those blue-grey dawn eyes — couldn't look at them any more.

'Where've you been all these days?'

'Working. The hospital's been busy.'

'Is everything all right?'

'Sure.' Nikhil set the pitcher down. 'Julian — Julian — I'm sorry about everything — please — please —' He sat down on the steps outside and blubbered. 'I'm sorry — I'm sorry —'

'Now, now —' He patted the dark head. 'You're really being very silly —'

'Please don't hate me —'

'I like you. Now please stop crying. Look at the sunset, isn't it cheery? Now, now —' Nikhil wiped his face. 'Wait here for me; I'll be back shortly,' Julian said and walked into the hospital.

A quarter of an hour later, Aloke Bose and Julian came outside, Aloke apologising for the delay. 'So, shall we then?' Aloke asked. Nikhil looked up, surprised.

'Yes, let's.' Julian smiled. 'Come on, Nikhil, we're going to Aloke's for dinner.'

'Um, Julian, could I speak to you for a moment?' Aloke steered Julian back inside. 'This is a little awkward — about Nikhil — um — he's from the streets sort of — and I — um — don't really associate, um —' Aloke Bose looked at his shoes and shrugged. 'Y'know, people might talk —'

'About what?'

'In our country, the different stratas of society don't mix.'

'Two different races aren't supposed to mix either.'

*　　*　　*

'What a change! A fork and a knife again!' Nikhil examined the cutlery with delight. Julian began to eat with his fingers.

'Tell me about Buddhism.' Nikhil raised his eyes, startled at Julian's demand.

'Buddha – um, he was an incarnation of Vishnu. He was born in Nepal —' Aloke Bose stammered.

'No, no, not this life stuff. Where did he achieve nirvana?'

'Under a banyan tree at Gaya. The tree's still there, y'know.'

'Where's Gaya?'

'In Bihar – one of the eastern provinces.'

'Buddha's boring,' snapped Nikhil.

'He's easier to relate to than Krishna,' snapped back Aloke Bose.

'That depends.'

'Buddha preached moderation and humanity —'

'Ascetism, abstaining from every pleasure in life —'

'Not at all! He just said don't overdo things.'

'Look at those monks with shaved heads and —'

'You don't have to be like them to follow the Buddhist way of life.'

'Buddha – ugh! That fat little squat figure!'

'Nonsense! Go and look at Graeco-Roman representations or the murals at Ajanta. A tall, slender, beautiful youth; an Aryan prince.'

'How come Buddhism didn't spread in India?' inquired Julian.

'Of course it did. It became a part of Hinduism – a philosophy rather than a religion.'

'I see.'

'The chicken's delicious! Could I have some more?' Nikhil's smiled a wide childish smile.

'Are there any Buddhist monks out here, Aloke?' Julian asked.

'Oh, yes, but not right here; across the river there is one, on the other bank.'

'That one! That man was tried for two murders! There wasn't enough evidence so they couldn't hang him and had to set him free.'

'Rubbish! Nothing of the sort. He teaches in the high school there.' Aloke Bose ignored Nikhil. 'His name is Ashokananda.'

It seems like we have paused to breathe, to rest the heart. February is passing into March with a clear blue light and crisp air laden with the bitter fresh smell of these neem trees. Jacaranda and bougainvillaea – purple, magenta, yellow, white, orange – take my breath away, Lorna, as I sit here on the veranda. There are roses, too. Tiny red ones, pink-red, and large black, red-black Persian roses.

'Holi' is round the corner – the festival of colours. A time of madness, spring fever, something like that. I hear a lot about that from Meena and from people at the club.

Sometimes I feel we've come out of a cyclone, at least Julian has, and to some extent, Dane. And now they have to take deep breaths and move on.

At the club, the rumours are dying. But Roanna Lyndon must bring up what we want to forget! She sidled up to Dane and hooked her arm around his!

'Lord Dane Hartley! My, don't you look nice —' She fluttered her lashes. 'What do you think of Indian women, er, I can call you Dane, can't I?'

'Taking into consideration the temple sculptures,' Julian stepped in, thank God! 'I would say the women are —'

I tried to interrupt because I was sure Julian would say something horrifying. But —

'As I was saying, the fevered eroticism is fascinating . . .' Roanna Lyndon found herself against the wall with the Earl of Ravinspur's mildly hoarse voice pouring forth a graphic critique of temple art!

'The Graeco-Roman sculptures are at Taxila, or Taksheela, as we call it, up north.' Aloke Bose's eyes followed the mercury that moved with Julian's blood pressure. 'A little low – but that's all right. I'd say the headaches are due to too much sun. This is the Indian sun, y'know, not the Mediterranean.'

Julian rolled down his sleeve and buttoned it. A bit of thread was sticking out from the seam of the left cuff. Raising his wrist to his mouth, he bit it off. 'Too much sun, hmm. Couldn't I get used to it, though, by now?'

'After five years, maybe.'

'The sun's wonderful these days.'

'Yes, but you Englishmen can't take such enormous doses of it.'

'I can.'

'Sure.'

'Now, tell me about A-sho-ka-nanda – is that how you say it?'

'Almost.'

'How old is he?'

'Fifty-five? I really don't know. Monks always look ageless anyway!'

'Can I go and see him?'

'He's not a museum piece, Julian.'

'That's not —'

'Why do you want to meet him?'

'Don't know.' Julian shrugged and stood up.

'He doesn't care for Englishmen very much. He went through interrogation last summer. They thought he knew something about a minor bomb explosion near the high school there. My hands ached from stitching and bandaging. They found out later that it was just a bunch of firecrackers stuffed into a coconut shell, not a bomb.' Dr Bose picked up the pen from its holder and scratched a few marks on his note pad. 'Why are you friends with Nikhil? He's just a loafer.'

'So am I,' smiled Julian.

'You are the Earl of Ravinspur.'

'So what?'

'Maybe Ashokananda will take to you. He's interesting. Was in Tibet for quite a few years, in some monastery in Lhasa. Met the Dalai Lama, got converted and all that.'

'When was that?'

'Oh, years and years ago.'

'And he's cut all that from his life now?' Julian asked frowning.

'No, no, just cut it here, here and here. I don't want it short.' Julian adjusted the white sheet around himself and glowered into the mirror in his room.

'Yes, *saab*,' said the Collector's personal barber, Antony, and set to work. Dane sat on the bed and watched the pale gold wisps flutter to the white sheet spread on the floor.

'No, don't touch that part. Here, let me do it.' Julian pulled the damp hair down on his forehead. It reached below his nose. He snipped off two inches. 'That's it.'

'Crooked, *saab* —' Antony wrinkled his straight Goanese nose.

'Never mind. Thank you very much, you may leave.' Jugnu, shifting his weight from foot to foot outside the room, rushed in to clean up.

'It's still too long,' said Dane.

'I like it this way.'

'Are you coming to church with us?'

'I'm going fishing.'

'Fishing?'

'Want to come?' Julian's eyes flickered over Dane's face in the mirror.

The mirror quivered into green and blue waves. A green pool turning gold under September sun. Could I do the worms, Ju? Tiny silver flashes under green, blue, gold waves. Or was it just Julian's eyes?

Go fishing, again, after so many years. Dane felt a fast-moving piston-like urgency somewhere deep inside. He never thought he would hear that again from Julian. All that had stopped, was long over. But now, to slowly release this something so longed for, so feared. Go fishing . . .

'Dane! Hurry up.' His mother's voice was so far away, far, far away, and Julian was feeling the length of his just-trimmed hair at the back of his neck, not smiling at all, biting his lower lip, just looking at himself.

'No, we didn't catch anything.' Dane scratched his head. That silly smile on his face again, thought Caroline as she dropped croutons into the soup. 'Too many children and people, er, running around.' Julian pushed the soup aside and began to toss croutons into his mouth, crunching noisily.

'Mrs Lyndon was particularly interested in what kind of fish you wanted to catch.' Julian shrugged, giggled and tried to suppress a loud hiccup. Holding the napkin against his mouth, he hiccuped and giggled alternately. The wine sort of hiccuped out of Dane's glass as he tried to set it down on the table.

Pio, pio, saab. Tarra hai, garam hai. Maza ayega dus minute me! A group of men near the river, laughing and thrusting bottles of that stuff into their hands.

Coughing and choking after the first draught, and then the fish swam in silver flashes in their heads. Some fish! laughed Julian Oh-ho-ho, some fish this! They were all getting ready to get drunk for Holi, they said. You've got to prepare yourself to get properly drunk for Holi. The fishes were still swimming in their heads. Dane tried to control his giggles behind his napkin.

'Julian.'

Dane aimed a kick at his brother's leg under the table at the sudden sharpness in his mother's voice. 'Ouch! You little —'

'Julian.'

'Yes'm.' Julian ducked his head twice. Dane buried his face in his napkin, his shoulders shaking.

'Julian, you need a thorough spanking!'

'Hic – oops – you tried it once, remember? Hic – but remember how your – hic – palms smarted? What a – hic – hard little bottom I had – hic – y'said, remember? What a – hic – oops – hard little bottom – gosh – hic – and I knew just how to – hic – clench my arse – hic – and make it devilish hard – hic —' Chair pushed back sharply; a rustle of silk. A hard slap nearly knocked Julian off his chair. Dane stood up in shock, his chair crashing behind him. 'Mother!' Before Julian could clamber to his feet, another slap jerked his head around and flung him against the table. Grabbing the arms of his chair he stood up, his face white. Dane hurriedly started to mop up the wine and soup running all over the table. The servants were not going to re-enter for quite some time now, he knew.

Caroline's hand rose again. Julian shut his eyes and drove his hands into his pockets as the strong, slender hand flashed up.

Julian lay in bed, hands under his head, chewing his lower lip. Dane sat and cracked his knuckles. 'Stop that,' Julian said.

'Go and apologise; it's been two days.'

'Don't worry. It'll get settled.'

'She's never been so mad at you before.'

'I overdid it this time. Go to bed; it's late.' Julian turned on his side and covered himself.

At two in the morning the sound of the door opening made Julian blink. Caroline came in and sat down on the bed. Her thick satin robe glistened in the darkness. 'You're very silly at times, dear.'

'Yes.' Julian's voice was sleepy and hoarse.

'And so am I.'

'If you say so.'

'Don't get drunk with natives, dear. News travels fast in this country.'

'Certain kinds of news.'

'I have something for you. I wanted to give it to you before.'

'What's this?'

'A gate or a doorway of some kind. A miniature of some temple gateway, or something like that.'

'What's this made of?'

'Ivory.'

'It's exquisite. Look at this work!' The two-inch arched gate gleamed on his palm in the dark.

'Somebody gave it to Charles in Delhi. He wanted to give it to you, but felt silly about it.'

'Thank you, Caroline.' He leaned forward to kiss her cheek.

'Go back to sleep, dear,' she said and left.

Lighting the gas lamp, Julian examined the tiny ivory gate. A gateway in the middle of nowhere, it seemed, darkness around it, passing through it. The giant white gates of Ravinspur. And the storms that beat against them, rushed through them, crashing against windows. Then the wet, wet, dark green outside, wet, red-gold even, but wet, dark green . . . The lamp glowed behind the ivory gate.

Going away, Ju?

Keep the cap, here —

Did you like the watch Father gave you?

It's all right.

There's something written at the back of it.

Yes.

Could I see it again?

203

Here.

Amo ergo sum. Doesn't make sense at the back of a watch.

Rushing through the gates of Ravinspur.

'Julian!'

'Well, you look pretty bright!'

'It's Holi. Want to join the fun?'

Leaning over the balcony, Julian rubbed his chin. The D.M. had passed out notes to every English family in Phulgarh requesting them to stay indoors on Holi. People were laughing and throwing colours at each other. He could hear singing and drumbeats. What the hell – why not go and see what it was all about?

'Julian, d'you know that Holi was one of Krishna's rituals? It's the spring festival,' Nikhil yelled.

'The *sahib* who plays the flute!' Coloured powder smothered Julian. Soon his hair was a cloud of purple, his face and clothes, magenta, yellow, red, green, indigo, gold. Julian had never been thronged by so many people before. '*Pio, saab.*' '*Pio, dost.*' He took the offered bottle. Fire-water, the people in the streets called it, and fire-water it was.

They lifted him up on their shoulders and carried him past the temple, through the crowded streets, the bazaar. The streets were stained bright. Even the cows and dogs were green and purple. Everything and everyone was smothered by colour. It was time to wipe out winter. Reaching the river, they sat Julian down on a boulder. '*Bajao, bajao!*' 'Play for them,' urged Nikhil. Drunk and excited, they danced while he played. They touched his feet over and over again. The spring festival. They refused to feel the bone-cold sharpness in the wind.

Exhausted, drunk and happy, Julian paused near the maidan. He had crept away while they sang and danced. There were children running around in the maidan, throwing colour at each other, splashing each other with buckets of water. He could see the hospital in the distance. Lying down under a tree, he rolled over on the grass and looked up. A neem tree. Fresh, fresh, limey, bitter. His eyes grew heavy.

'Julian! Julian! Look!' He jumped up. Nikhil stood there

204

with a horde of children. The children were all yellow. 'Look, they've rubbed pollen all over themselves!' Their heads, faces, throats, bodies, arms, legs, were all glowing yellow. 'Look at their hair – golden like yours! They want to look like you, so they've covered themselves with pollen and yellow powder!'

Julian pressed his back against the rough bark of the neem tree. The children crowded around him, touching him. He couldn't move back any further. The tree was hard and rough behind him. Their pollen-covered hair hurt his eyes. 'They're trying to look like you!' It was getting difficult to breathe.

'*Arre, kya karta hai! Chalo, chalo, jao hiyanse!*' Aloke Bose's voice scattered the children. 'My God! What have they done to you? Are you hurt? Are you all right?' He shook Julian lightly.

'What – yes – yes —' Julian unclenched his hands.

'How did this happen? Why are you here? You're supposed to stay indoors.'

'I'm all right. I just wanted to see —'

'Come to the hospital; I'll check for cuts.'

'No. I'm fine.'

'Well, you should see yourself!'

'I'm fine. It's just colour, uh, Holi, uh, isn't that what you call it?' he smiled weakly.

'Yes,' smiled back Aloke Bose, 'it's also the day Buddha was born.'

Julian staggered up the drive and reached the veranda. Jugnu and Ravi Singh were serving tea. Dane, Caroline, Harry, Dr Morel, the Bancrofts and the Lyndons lowered their tea cups. 'Well – ahem – hello, everyone,' said the Earl of Ravinspur, his magenta and indigo face breaking into a smile. He tried to smooth down his purple hair which was standing on end. Mrs Bancroft blinked twice. 'As they say, er, spring is in the air, etcetera, y'know. Feeling all right everybody?'

'Oh, God, Julian.' Dane's laughter ripped away the ominous silence. 'Have you ever seen a purple cow? Ha, ha! Oh, God, Julian!'

They had to rush to Mrs Bancroft's assistance then. Choking on the Darjeeling tea, her face turned a strange hue.

'Gracious – catastrophe!' said Harry Winston as the purple cow ran indoors chased by a laughing Dane Hartley.

Jugnu ran through the slum and stopped in front of a shack. It was very dark. He moved the sack that functioned as a door and entered. 'Who's there?'

'Shh. It's me. Wake up. A terrible thing has happened. I'm cold. Can I put my feet under your blanket? Listen, today was the big dance, Shehzadi's special spring dance. She appeared in black. People gasped in shock. Who wears black on Holi? Then she took off the black cloak, and, oh! there she was in turquoise —'

'So what's so terrible about that? Get out of here and let me sleep.'

'No – wait. She sat down and broke all her glass bangles, laughing and joking with the men. And at that moment, the prince of Talkot walked into the *kota*!'

'What!'

'Yes. The prince has been lovesick and passive for so long. But he couldn't take it any more. The pain was too much. He had tried to forget as he had been commanded to do by the *nawab*. He knew a *nachnewali* is not worth his love. But, his heart was breaking like her glass bangles. He had to see for himself what was going on, why Sakhi had turned away. Winston *saab* and an officer from the cantonment were there at the *kota*. They saw it all. The prince picked up a crystal decanter and smashed it on the dance floor, and said, prove your fidelity. Dance on glass.'

'Then?'

'Lord, I couldn't believe my eyes and ears! She just walked across the broken glass, her feet streaming blood, and knifed him! With a fruit knife. Phew!' Harry wiped his forehead. Dane sat on the couch and stared at the clock. Two in the morning.

'Yes sir, I just stepped right in,' said Trevors, 'and said that we'd take care of it. We're the law anyway. I was afraid they'd slaughter her.'

'Dr Morel took her in. Her feet have been taken care of,' Harry said. Julian fingered the brass and onyx objects on the table in front of him.

'I guess they'll put her in jail.'

'No! I won't let that happen. We can't. Why can't we do something? Julian, you can. You plan it – you're good at that. You have to.' He could save her now, at last, like that doctor in Dr Morel's story, do something, somehow, not totally hopeless, oh, if only! To ride away into the mountains or the desert or the sea. This awkward madness – to just sit on it always and choke it because they would laugh. Laugh, then, laugh. Should I care? 'Julian, say something!'

'Woof, woof.'

'Kill the prince!'

'He's half-dead.'

'We have to get her out!'

'Golly, that'll be a real-life blooming adventure!' Trevors stood up and straightened his uniform.

'How – how – er – there'll be a terrible scandal —'

'We'll simply create an accident. Why, Harry, you can write a book twenty years later!'

'This is not a lark – a – a – I mean, you're just assuming that – that —'

'Harry,' Julian stood up, 'your carriage, Harry, is perfect. I'll drive it.'

'No!'

'Yes!' yelled Dane, 'yes!'

Julian began to laugh. 'God! Is any of this real?' They stared at him as he fell to his knees laughing.

This citadel of flowers is now stained with blood. No idle rumours, but a real case of attempted murder, a woman, the woman associated with Dane, made to walk on glass. Such excitement at the club over another's pain, Lorna. I'll write it down as I heard it, from the other room, word for word:

'A ghastly affair,' grunted Mr. Bancroft at the club over his double scotch probably. 'To be expected, I daresay. The dissolute lives these fellows lead, unprincipled and all that sort of thing, y'know. But Mr Winston, you acted like a gentleman.'

'An Englishman, sir,' corrected Mr MacLeish and brought his fist down on the mantelpiece. 'An Englishman.'

'We have to maintain law and order in the right way, of course. Take charge of things —' The D.M. cleared his throat.

'We'll tell the *nawab* we can't have this chopping heads business. There has to be a fair trial. The way I see it, a few years in jail. After all it was self-defence, damn it. You can't make people walk on glass. Actually, she could be acquitted, really, I mean, I mean, we have to protect her, because the *nawab* will try his damnedest to have her killed. My dear Winston, you and Trevors did the right thing by God! By the way, isn't she as beautiful as they say?'

'Oh – er —'

'But why were you there, Mr Winston?' asked Roanna Lyndon. She had slipped in between the men as usual!

'Roanna!' Robert Lyndon sounded as if he was choking. 'Good lord! What are you doing in here?'

Through the wall between our space and theirs we heard it all. Roanna had to go over to that room. She gets excited with them because she wants to be part of that side.

'The *nawab* is furious. Wants Sakhi killed and Firdausi slaughtered.' Jugnu moved his hands excitedly. The men were listening to him at last. They crowded around him at the maidan, men and women, and She, She, too. 'That scum urged the prince to go to the *kota*. It's *kismet* that the prince is still alive. Lost buckets of blood. But you see, she stuck the knife in four inches to the right of his heart. Women never know where a man's heart is situated, thank God for that! The D.M. doesn't know what to do. They've placed six guards outside the hospital to watch over her. However, the *nawab* is planning to steal Sakhi from the *sahibs* and kill her. But he won't succeed. Just you watch, Sakhi will vanish. Maybe my *saab* will ride away with her and they'll live in the Taj Mahal for ever after!'

The six guards sat and smoked on the steps of the Phulgarh hospital. One of the guards produced a pack of cards and began to shuffle. The dim gaslight above their heads provided a hazy yellow circle of light. The night was very dark and very fragrant.

Flutetones coiled around them gently. Through the bougainvillaea, jasmine, jacaranda, eucalyptus, honeysuckle, it crawled in. It hovered among the bitter leaves of the huge

neem tree. The guards looked around. Nobody in sight. But
the music was close, very close, like warm breath on their
necks. They spread out to search the grounds. They weren't
supposed to leave the hospital grounds. But this music! It had
to be found – the source of this music. Nobody was supposed
to enter the hospital grounds at night. The music seemed to
move swiftly from point to point. It would die then rise again
in slow waves. Among the gul-mohr . . . No. From the river?

'Something, something, la-la-la-la-la . . . the brave Lochinvar,'
muttered Caroline shaking her pen. A few drops fell on the
blank page of her diary.

Here's what happened at the club over lunch:

'Vanished, sir. Nothing I can do, sir. Not a clue of any kind.'

'Now, now, Lyndon,' said the Collector, 'there's got to be
some blooming explanation. What did your guards say?'

'Not my guards, sir. MacLeish's.'

'So – what do we do about the *nawab*?' the Collector asked.

'You should certainly have a chat with him, sir, and explain
the – er – y'know —' said the District Magistrate.

'You're the D.M., Lyndon, security is your business.'

'I said they were MacLeish's guards, not mine.'

'Well, I've suspended them, Lyndon,' said the Superintendent of Police, and as *burra saab* says, you are the D.M.'

'Mr Bancroft, you are the most senior officer of the Raj out
here. You ought to face the *nawab*.'

'What am I going to say to him?'

'The old boy's pretty upset, I hear. Maybe we should have
just handed her over to those savages and forgotten about the
mess,' Mr MacLeish said digging into his bread pudding.

'I refuse to go to the palace!'

'Now, now, Lyndon —'

'MacLeish sent the bloody guards – let him deal with the
damned *nawab*!'

'Robbie, dear,' Roanna Lyndon cut in as usual, 'why don't
we go off on a short vacation?'

'Mrs Lyndon, this is hardly the time —'

'Oh, don't be so stuffy, Mr Bancroft.'

'Roanna!'

'Well, Lyndon, what do the guards have to say?'

'They were drunk, sir.'

'Impossible, Mr Lyndon! My guards are never drunk!'

'They said, Mr MacLeish, that all that they heard was a damned flute, and they followed the bloody tune to the river but found nobody.'

'The guards left the hospital premises and went off to the riverside? My dear MacLeish, that's a serious business, I mean, that's not disciplined behaviour at all, dear, dear, to go chasing after a tune.'

'Collector *saab*, I have a hunch the *nawab* had a finger in this one. And now he's playing innocent. We should investigate the palace, sir, and I bet you, we'll find her head in a flowerpot or under his highness's black roses or something.'

'Will you just keep your hare-brained ideas to yourself, MacLeish! Investigate the palace! We have no authority in Talkot. Right now we have to figure out what to tell the *nawab* so that we don't look like utter fools.' I thought Mr Bancroft was going to have a stroke as he screamed at Mr MacLeish; but he didn't.

'I wonder how the earl feels about this whole thing?' Roanna Lyndon smiled and turned to me. She can be so aggravating, Lorna!

'Julian and Dane are in Agra at the moment,' I said and asked for a cup of jasmine tea, a flavour which I introduced to the Phulgarh Club. I don't like the way we are associated with everything that goes on in this town! Why they had to fly off to Agra that night I'll never know.'

'Vulcan fashion me such a cup,' sang Julian, drawing his dark cloak around him. 'Pass the bottle, Harry.' They walked away from the Taj Mahal. The moon was nearly a half slice. 'Quite perfect, isn't it?' smiled Julian.

'It's a bloody tomb,' said Dane.

'So it is.'

'And hundreds of people were probably slaughtered in the making of it.'

'Maybe, but it's still a work of art.'

'Who needs a half-acre tomb?'

'It's a symbol of love, I believe,' said Harry.

'Symbol of love – hah! Signifies death to me.'

'I say, let's not get morbid now,' groaned Harry. 'Let's just go and get drunk.'

Dane turned and looked at the Taj Mahal. The moon was so bright. But he couldn't make out the sharp silver outlines of trees, marble, the stretch of land. All blurred into a wet dark muddiness. His head throbbed.

Sticky pomegranate juice, cold stone, slippery dark eyes, sharp glass cutting into brown feet. *Lente, lente, currite, noctis equi*, Julian had said in the dark once upon a time. I want to believe in your unicorns, Julian. Take me with you when you disappear to where the unicorns are. The dolphins, glowing like panther eyes, leaping from dark waves. A warm sea jostling him, swiftly moving the sand from under his feet, and he, trying to hide in its strength and its weakness, forgetting, forgetting, not waking —

Amo ergo sum? He was ceasing to be.

And after all this, you feel you have barely untouched. Barely untouching all through long, long nights. 'Ju – sing that song.'

'What song?'

'The one you sang at the cantonment that night.'

'Now? Here?'

'Why, what's wrong with here and now?'

After three gulps of rum, Julian let out a pleasant snarl. 'Well, well – "so, we'll go no more a-roving" – this is the best rum I've ever had – "so late into the night" – want some, Dane? "Though the heart be still as loving, And the moon be still as bright." So – ah, feels wonderful! Sing along with me, damn it! Come on –

> For the sword outwears its sheath,
>   And the soul wears out the breast,
> And the heart must pause to breathe,
>   And Love itself have rest.

'Well – come on, you dummies! I'm certainly not going to provide entertainment like a – like a – here, gimme another swig.'

Dane looked at his brother with a funny half-smile. 'I'll whistle it,' he said, 'if you sing.'

' "Though the night was made for loving . . . " '
Dane began to whistle softly.

'What did I tell you? Sakhi's vanished. Listen, the *nawab* said
to the prince, you are the biggest fool. A worthless *naachnewali*
stabbed you and you sit and mope. The prince hasn't spoken a
word for a week. They even suspect he cries in secret,
dropping his tears among the rose petals in the fountain. Only
his mare, Dilruba, knows the prince's thoughts.

'The *nawab* is plotting something, maybe war, maybe peace.
But there will be corpses, I'm sure. Ah, but now there are only
pomegranate shells and broken glass. I think the prince still
wants to fight my *saab*, but in his heart a voice cries, what are
you fighting over? A woman? Where is the woman? A flute
took her away . . .'

'And where did you hear the secrets of the prince's heart?
From the horse's mouth?'

'Laugh at me – is that all you'll ever do? After all that I've
done – all the excitement I've brought into your life – all
the —'

'*Oy, chutiya,* wasting my time for months. Get out of my
sight. I know what you're looking for and you're not getting it
from me. Out – *harami kahin ka*. A – a-a-acchoooh!' A kick
followed the sneeze. Jugnu walked out of the slum. The night
wind was still sharp. But that bare stone altar always seemed
warm. It contained a warmth deep down in its core, the
warmth that lovers of old had left behind, ingrained in stone.

Julian knocked and walked into Dane's room. He tripped on a
shoe in the dark. 'Dane.' Empty bed at two in the morning?
Since they returned from Agra, Dane had been annoyingly
uncommunicative. That was unlike his brother. When Dane
was upset, he talked, raved, indulged in strenuous physical
activity. For the past few days, Dane had sat and smoked on
the veranda, turned away from cricket, horses, alcohol and his
mother. Julian walked out of the house.

Gasps, muffled, but audible from the chipped steps of the
temple. On the bare altar, stretched out on a blanket, his face
in his hands, Dane's body shook with unrestrained sobs. The

cool March wind swept the dry leaves in little swirls on the stone floor. Julian touched the dark head hesitantly. 'Dane.'

'Go away.'

'Dane.' Julian lay down and put his arms around his brother. The wind played with the dry pomegranate shells, shh, shh – a hushed sea noise, a deep, soft, sea noise; silver fish moving among seaweeds, dolphins combing the dark hair of waves. 'Dane.' He pressed his face against the soft, warm hair.

They lay there on the altar while the moon faded, the sky paled and the spring dawn blew in with the wind that wouldn't leave the dry leaves alone. It was their very first morning on that altar among pomegranate shells and flute-dreams.

PART THREE

The Gate of Dreams

Chapter 9

Crouching on a boulder near the dark Yamuna, Nikhil let the raggedy blanket slide off his shoulders. His body shivered and bent over his knees. The wind of *vasant* was always sharp. When it rained, it rained needles.

And Krishna left for Mathura. Left the garden, left them that loved. The flute – lost in the river, laughing, crying, laughing. Red-gold gul-mohr blossoms mingled with white dust rising in swirls from departing feet and chariot wheels.

He'll cross the river. He'll forget the temple, the altar, the adoration, and cross the river. The flute played false and I have nothing more to say to him. Dr Bose does all the talking. Bengalis always do this – open up unknown, unsought doors. So he'll cross the river.

Never dream under the neem tree, the bitter green of the neem tree.

Dane sat in a cane chair on the veranda, legs stretched out, ankles crossed and resting on the table in front, hands behind his head. An unbelievable shock of flowers all over. White chrysanthemums, marigolds, dark red dahlias, sunflowers, purple pansies, laburnum, jacaranda, tiger-lilies, frangipani, jasmine . . . And the glowing bougainvillaea, almost the colour of pomegranates. Dane rubbed his eyes. The afternoon sun was getting harsher.

Julian must be hooking, pulling, cutting, sweeping, driving, his slender willow sending the ball skimming over the lush green and over the boundary line. He's really got into cricket again. Should go and watch him play. What to do? Days seem to fall on their knees. And when we go back, what then?

I think I'll move to Cheveley. Next Christmas they could come to Cheveley.

217

'Hello, dear. Why aren't you at the club playing cricket?'

'Aw, just feeling lazy.'

Caroline pulled up a chair and sat down. 'Why don't we visit Kashmir in a few weeks?'

'Um, OK.'

'Sheila's going to Kashmir.'

'Again?'

'Yes.'

'Mother —'

'Yes?'

'Did you think about that dancing girl business at all? The prince made her walk on glass, asked her to prove her fidelity by walking on glass. That's hideous. Did he love her, d'you think? Or was it just hurt pride, or just hurt for hurt; can we judge them according to our rules? He ought to be shot for what he did. I feel that sometimes, and sometimes I don't know what to think or feel about him.'

'You can't do that sort of thing to people. You can't own people, I mean. Why is that incident on your mind, dear?'

Dane looked at the bougainvillaea.

'Dane,' his mother said, 'I asked you something, dear.'

'There's something I've wanted to tell you, Mama,' he said, 'I'm thinking of moving to Cheveley.'

'I'll be alone at Ravinspur.'

'Julian will be at Ravinspur.'

'How do you know?'

'I just know.'

'Is that why you wish to leave?'

'I've got to learn to live by myself, Mama, for myself. I've said a lot of things in anger, all the waiting, but now it's going to be different.'

'Oh, Dane —'

'Don't.' Dane removed his mother's hand from his hair and held it tightly. 'I love you, Mama.' He kissed her hand and held it against his throat.

'It's such a beautiful day,' Caroline said.

The March wind swung through the bougainvillaea scattering leaf-like, wine-dark petals. Dane rubbed his eyes and stood up. 'I think I'll go and watch Ju play.'

* * *

Julian removed his pads and gloves and sat down on the steps of the patio of the club. White figures were running across the pitch in the distance. The forward short-leg had missed a catch, and the long-leg fielder was running after the red ball. Julian flexed his fingers and cracked his knuckles. He had knocked the bails off with a light, backward tap of his bat. He just wanted to get out. They'd been running between the wickets up and down, up and down, up and down. There was no other place to run to or run from when you held the bat and took your stance at the crease. You had to make sure that once you stood there you had to stay there, make the place secure and yours. God, why? The constant running from wicket to wicket, absolutely having to touch that white line with your bat, sometimes a mad dash, a wild leap, sometimes stretched out on the green, just somehow touching that white line. And then the red ball again, hitting a certain brown patch and shooting up viciously, cutting in to the left or to the right, or, sometimes, just coming straight at you. And you had to hit it, hit it hard enough, keeping your bat straight enough if you wanted to be safe. Beware – don't let the ball glance off the edge of your bat. They were all waiting, half-crouched, eyes focused; hands ready to catch, legs ready to leap and lungs ready to burst: 'How's that!' That's all there was to it. Just that cry and you held your breath and waited for the index finger to go up. Then you were dead. And if you weren't, then the running again, up and down, up and down, up and down, trekking your territory, gaining, gaining, securing, owning, fighting and keeping.

'I can't believe what you just did, Ju.'

'What —' Julian looked up. Where did Dane spring from?

'Hit-wicket? I can't believe it. You did that on purpose.'

'I hate these silly white clothes.'

'Maybe some day they'll wear pink or yellow ones.'

'Yeah, pink pads and a white ball.'

'And they'll play at night too.'

'You bet. Nothing sacrosanct about cricket.'

'You're in a splendid mood.'

'I feel like smashing this bloody bat in the middle of the pitch or doing something equally obscene and tasteless.'

'Why did you knock your bails off?'

'Oh, shut up.'

A low wailing sound made them turn around. A snake-charmer's *been*? There he sat, the snake-charmer in dirty clothes, a strip of yellow cloth tied around his head. Eyes closed, he swayed a little to the waves of his music. Slowly, very slowly, from the open wicker basket in front of him a black snake surfaced to air, its head fanned out, its slit eyes glittering. Mrs Lyndon gave a low gasp as the forked tongue jabbed the air twice. The snake-charmer stopped, looked at the *memsahib* and scratched his head. 'Go on, go on,' whispered Roanna Lyndon who had had the bearers bring in the snake-charmer. The players returning from the field gathered around the snake-charmer. 'Go on,' urged Mrs Lyndon again. The snake-charmer fought his adolescent embarrassment and began to play. The men shuffled uncomfortably and looked at each other.

Julian hugged his bat to his chest and watched the cobra in its wicker basket sway from side to side. It moved only in a certain way, side to side, then back and forth, then lunging forward to strike the source of that frustrating sound, the *been*. Recoiling, then trying again and again. And the people, just staring like idiots at its stripped, impotent, delirious swaying body. A cobra – its insidious beauty still glowing, but the essence gone. Performing, performing, forced, teased, robbed of all grace and dignity by dull, stupid eyes. Unable to move in any other way, in any other direction. Back among the tall grass, or in stony places, the real dance to unfeigned music; but powerless to return, trapped in a wicker basket.

Sitting on a wooden plank at the far end of the boat, Julian smiled and wrinkled his nose at Nikhil. The warmth of the afternoon sun made him remove his *kurta*. He waved as the boat moved away into the Yamuna. Nikhil watched the slim golden-brown form glow in the criss-crossing shafts of light that entered the river's surface.

With half-closed eyes, the *majhi* looked at the *sahib*. He had heard of the mad *sahib* who played the flute. But the *sahib*'s eyes were peaceful, happy, and did not roll like a madman's eyes. Where was his madness hidden? He was crossing the river like everyone else, sitting where he should, and the warmth made him remove his *kurta*. His hand touched the waters and played with its wetness.

How would he introduce himself? Julian wondered. What was he going there for? What if Ashokananda slammed the door on his face? What was he going there for in the first place? He had stepped on to the boat so easily while a fear had moved like a piston inside him. He was losing something, he had felt. He was leaving behind something – a something that could never cross the river with him. That terrified him. But the boat waited, and the *majhi* waited with indifferent eyes. I don't think I'll go, he had wanted to say. But it would seem indecisive, vacillating. Nikhil had stood there with arms folded and head lowered. Careful – don't slip on the mud, he had muttered. And Julian had been careful and not slipped on the mud while getting on the boat.

What would he say to Ashokananda? I just came to see what you are. How asinine! Should he ask the *majhi* to turn back? They were halfway across the river's breadth. Ask the *majhi* to turn back! Calm down, now, calm down. He'll think you're crackers, ol' boy, he'll think you're bananas.

Following the directions Aloke Bose had given, Julian walked past the noisy school, the slums and the bazaar. Then through the Muslim section, past the blue and white mosque, and the fountain that now boasted tadpoles, three ducks and a moss-covered mermaid cradling a dry pitcher. No children splashed in the shallow water; they just stood around and watched the ducks. They looked at him suspiciously, Julian felt. People seemed to move away from him. Women selling corn and peanuts near the fountain pulled their *chunnis* over their faces and lowered their eyes. What's wrong with these people? wondered Julian.

Crossing the maidan, Julian looked around for the large stone well Aloke Bose had mentioned. There it was – near the banana trees. And resting his hands on the stone rim of the well, Julian looked at the small cottage with its tiled roof and the two mango trees. A goat tied to a post by a long rope tore at the grass. An energetic, prick-eared, brown mongrel dug furiously at the ground with paws and nose, tossing up swirls

221

of grass and soil. No walls, no fences, no gate; a small house in the middle of an unkempt grassy plot.

What will I say? I've come this far. His throat was parched; there wasn't even enough saliva in his mouth to swallow down the dryness. Julian untied the rope from the wood post of the well and looked at the rusted pulley from which rope and bucket were suspended.

As the bucket slowly disappeared into the dark interior of the well, Julian gritted his teeth. The intense grating, groaning, creaking of the rope and the pulley horrified him. What a godawful noise. This unbearable grating.

'Arf, arf, arf, arf!'

Julian's hands flew off the rope, and in a few seconds the bucket hit the hard dry bottom of the well with a deafening, resounding crash. 'Arf, arf, arf, arf!' Julian covered his face and bent over the edge of the well.

'Please do not follow the bucket – it is not necessary.'

'I'm sorry – I'm sorry – I'm really sorry – I wasn't out to steal anything – I was thirsty – just very thirsty —'

'Who would ever think a *sahib* was a thief?'

'I – I —' Julian straightened up and looked at the man standing near the cluster of banana trees. He wore a light brown *kurta*. He looked at Julian with narrowed, laughing eyes, rubbed his cleft chin and then his short straight nose. His grey-black hair was untidy. He can easily throw me down the well, thought Julian. Ashokananda was at least four inches taller than Julian and with shoulders that could easily wrench a hard wooden door from its hinges.

'I was just thirsty.'

'This is a dry well. Why didn't you drink from the well at the bazaar?'

'People looked at me rather oddly. Don't know why —'

'They don't like *sahibs* here in Murli.'

'I see.'

'Last year's interrogations and things like that.'

'I see.'

'I can give you water if you don't mind stepping inside my house.'

Julian handed the aluminium mug back to Ashokananda

and wiped his mouth in the tiny kitchen. One of those bucket-like stoves stood under the window; a few pots and pans on a shelf in a corner, a clay pitcher filled with water on a low table, a broom behind the door and an old Tibetan prayer wheel hung from a nail on the wall. The room they had crossed through had contained a single rope bed – a *charpai*, a rush mat, a bookshelf spilling over with old books and an oil lamp on a table.

'I have to inspect my tomatoes,' said Julian's host. 'By the way, my name's Ashokananda.'

'I'm Julian.' He followed his host out to the kitchen garden.

'Oh, my God!' Julian couldn't help himself. 'Cauliflowers, cabbages, onions, potatoes and tomatoes – all these vegetables!'

'And that – a green pepper bush, and that – basil, and there – a lemon tree,' pointed Ashokananda. He paused and looked at Julian's clothes. 'So where did I pick up the language, *sahib*? Long story, tell you some time. But now – what are you doing in Murli?'

'Murli?'

'Yes, name of the place. Means flute, y'know, flute.' Julian stumbled over a ginger cat that had appeared from nowhere and found its way between his feet. 'Ah, ah, the tomatoes look good, almost ready.' Ashokananda crawled between the rows of tomato bushes, parting leaves and examining the tomatoes. 'Well, *sahib* —' Ashokananda stood up. 'Where are you from?'

'From Phulgarh. Crossed over two hours back, I'd say.'

'Why?'

'Wanted to see the other side.'

'The other side.'

'Yes.'

'You're not a civil servant.'

'No – merely visiting, sightseeing, vulgar tourist, etcetera,' Julian smiled.

'Yes, curiosity is vulgar.'

'I'm not just curious; I want to know —'

'A change of clothes – if you think that's all it takes to become like the other —'

'I like these clothes.'

'You look very nice in them.' Ashokananda smiled for the first time, a wide, affectionate smile, showing even white teeth. 'Yes, you look very nice indeed.' Julian moved his hair back from his damp forehead.

'I – I better be getting back now. Thanks for the water.'

'I teach at the high school from eight to twelve, weekdays.'

'Oh.'

'Welcome to Murli, *sahib*.'

The boat responded gaily to controlling hands. The water bounced up and swirled around. Julian lay flat on the wooden planks of the boat and closed his eyes. He had taken his *kurta* off again. The *majhi* observed the *sahib* carefully this time since his eyes were closed. A faint smile on his lips, and a happy, excited, tired face, like a boy's when he goes to bed after a crazy afternoon of kite-flying.

When the boat bumped into the muddy bank of Phulgarh, Julian opened his eyes and saw Dane and Nikhil. The Yamuna was a molten lava stream under the setting sun. Julian took Dane's outstretched hand. 'Is the sun going down on me, what?' Julian muttered as his brother pulled him on to shore.

'I really don't know what to do about this.' Caroline walked into Julian's room waving a gilt-edged card. Julian looked up at his stepmother from the floor. He was half-propped on his hands, his body stretched out fully, his feet touching the wall. 'What on earth are you doing, dear, in this rather awkward position?'

'Push-ups.'

'Push-ups?'

'Yup. Feel like it.'

'Shouldn't you be getting dressed for the club dinner?'

'I will. One – two – three – four – phew – five – six – seven – Jesus – I'm not cut out for this stuff —'

'You poor darling, tch, tch.' Dane strolled in elegantly dressed and blew a kiss at his brother's prostrate form on the floor.

'Shut up, you bastard.'

'Oooh.'

'Eight – nine – oh, God —'

'Dane, take a look at this.'

'What is it?'

224

'We have been cordially invited for tea, at the palace; the *nawab* will be brokenhearted if we are, in any way, unable to attend.'

'Ten – eleven —' Julian fell flat on his face. 'Caroline, ah, shouldn't break hearts —'

Dane stared at the card blankly. 'I'm not going,' he said.

'Don't be silly,' said Julian, rolling over and getting up, 'just think – you'll meet the son.'

Julian hesitated before the open gates of the Lord Bentinck High School. The guard in his khaki uniform observed the *sahib* with a remarkable lack of curiosity. Julian cleared his throat, put his hands into his cream cotton trouser pockets and walked into the school premises. He was pleasantly surprised as the guard clicked his heels and saluted.

Well-trampled lawns; orange brick buildings with long black shadows of age; volley ball courts; an enormous clock which showed ten minutes to twelve. Julian did not go up the steps. From the edge of the lawn he could see dark heads leaning over wooden desks, impatient nail-chewing, bored faces looking out at the dusty white road which stretched to the river.

There weren't very many trees or flowers here. Murli was pretty much dry and barren compared to the lush greenery of Phulgarh. Murli – flute, Ashokananda said. Murli should be green, all green, and warm, and golden.

Wonder where Ashokananda teaches – upstairs or down-stairs?

Clang! Clang! Clang! Clang! And then shouts and laughter and running feet. A storm of bodies burst through all openings and swept around Julian, jostling him, tripping him, making him gasp. The little tornadoes, all screaming and shrieking, ecstatic at escaping. They were free of thought at last. Nothing, no one, could force them to think now.

'So here you are, *sahib*.' Ashokananda stood on the steps. Before Julian could respond, a young man came running out of the building and grabbed Ashokananda's arm and turned him around. Julian could sense the urgency in the young man's manner, but he couldn't hear a word. An arresting face, he thought. Dark hair, dark eyes, but skin tone that screamed 'white' in spite of the tan. Ashokananda seemed to be calming him down. Then they turned towards him.

'This is Eric Donovan.'

'Julian Hartley.' Julian grasped the slim nervous hand and wondered at the agitated dark eyes. 'Do you teach here, too?'

'Yes, chemistry.'

'We break for an hour for lunch. Would you like to come with us to the canteen, *sahib*?' asked Ashokananda.

'I don't want to go to the bloody canteen!' burst out Eric Donovan. 'I'm going to Al Khusru's.' And with that he marched off.

'Well, that's that,' laughed Ashokananda, 'I can go home in peace now.'

'Is something wrong?'

'Oh, no. Eric's just – I mean he has rather a volatile temper. But I'm at your disposal now, *sahib*. What do you want to do?'

'Well, I'd like to go to Al Khusru's, too, if that is permitted.'

'It's a tomb. Eric sits and broods there.'

Murli was a much smaller town than Phulgarh, Julian learned from Ashokananda as they walked past the slums. 'That's Al Khusru's tomb,' pointed Ashokananda at a hexagonal, red sandstone structure on top of a mound in the middle of an uncultivated, unpopulated stretch of land. As they neared, Julian could see the inlay work and the intricate friezes. There was a shallow tank in the small courtyard and Eric Donovan sat on its edge, chewing his nails. 'We won't bother you, Eric,' said Ashokananda and escorted Julian into the tomb.

Julian looked up at the domed ceiling and saw an enormous beehive. Sparrows and pigeons allowed the saint's spirit no peace and quiet. The stone floor and the burial spot were richly encrusted with droppings. 'Look at the walls,' said Ashokananda, 'those engravings – they aren't just decorative, they are verses from the Koran.'

'Is this like a mosque?'

'More like a shrine really. People come here to ask for things, not just pray.'

'Aren't there any temples here?'

'Yes, as a matter of fact, a Krishna temple and a Shiv temple; but nobody believes in those two any more. Al Khusru is known to grant prayers, make wishes come true. A complying saint is always more attractive than an indifferent god.'

'You bet.' Julian traced three feet of engraving on the wall with his fingers. 'Can you read this?'

'No.'

'What do you teach?'

'History.'

'Ancient Indian history?'

'No – nineteenth-century and current political developments.'

'Ancient Indian history is really fascinating.'

'You mean the ancient civilisations?'

'Well, yes, and also the early religions, like – like – Buddhism, for instance.'

'Buddhism was a later development really.'

'This thing about the tree at Gaya has always intrigued me – y'know, the banyan tree under which Buddha sat and received enlightenment.'

'Intrigues you, eh? Well, what do you want to do – go and sit under it or uproot it and examine the soil and roots?' Julian scraped off some dried bird dropping with his shoe. 'Now let's go and cheer up Eric,' said Ashokananda after a slight pause.

Eric Donovan still sat on the rim of the tank, sullen and fidgety. Next to him lay five sandwiches on a sheet of brown paper. He looked up at them as they walked outside. 'Hey, Ash, want a sandwich?'

Munching on chicken sandwiches, they looked at the crows hovering around. 'I say, Mr Hartley,' smiled Eric Donovan for the first time, looking very attractive, 'take a look at this bloke here – Ashokananda: the first ruddy Buddhist monk, I'll bet, to feast on chicken sandwiches! Say, Ash, you'll un-nirvana your end at this rate!' Julian was a little shocked at the young man's brazenness, but couldn't help smiling all the same.

'Are you a Buddhist monk?' he inquired with his most innocent smile.

'Not a practising one,' replied Ashokananda.

'Were you in a monastery or something at some time?'

'He was in Tibet, Mr Hartley. Even shaved his head!'

'And how about you, Eric?' asked Julian, 'what are you?'

'Me? Oh, I'm just trash, just trash.' Eric Donovan stood up and wiped his mouth with the back of his hand. The cautious politeness in his voice stunned Julian momentarily. 'Nice meeting you, Mr Hartley. Inhale Buddhist poppies. *Au revoir.*'

Julian stared at Donovan's departing figure. A lithe, carefree walk, almost defiant, and an odd resentment emanating from every breath he exhaled into the blue-gold afternoon air. 'Did I say something wrong?'

'No. That's just Eric.'

'Why?'

'He's Anglo-Indian, and only twenty-three.'

'Where's his father?'

'In Calcutta – Fort William, I think.'

'And his mother?'

'Nobody knows. His father took him away when he was two years old, and he was brought up by his aunt in Bangalore.'

'Is it difficult for him to find work?'

'No, not really. It's just that he'll be treated like an outcast by both races.' Ashokananda looked at the sparrows pecking at crumbs. 'And what shall we do with our children who hate us, *sahib*, what shall we ever do?'

As Meena washed my hair this afternoon, I remembered a certain afternoon in Ravinspur when Dane had washed my hair. After hours of begging, I had let him do it. In that lovely peach and grey bedroom, 'Please, Mama, please, please, please, please . . .' A twelve-year-old insistence that was hard to quell. Actually, it had all started with Julian. Julian bathing in the lake under the waterfall, soaping his hair into a white soufflé, and Dane trying to get his fingers into that foamy richness. Don't. Julian had pushed Dane away. But Dane, adamant: must feel soapy hair, must, must, must. So: please, Mama, please, please, please. Go and wash your own hair! No – it ain't as much fun.

And soon, at Ravinspur: no Dane. Julian? Who knows?

Julian seemed happy, but a little puzzled about something at dinner. He told us he'd visited the town on the other bank and met a Buddhist monk. He felt, as he talked to the monk, that the monk knew of him, somehow. He looked at Julian as if he knew why he had come to visit, as if he was expecting

Julian. How could he expect Julian? Is it some kind of spiritual foreknowledge? I've always wanted to meet someone like that ever since Charles told me of the Belgian (or was it Austrian?) Buddhist monk he had met in Delhi who spoke of Lhasa and yaks and living in the Himalayas. Like Charles, Julian meets all kinds of people. I wanted to hear more about this monk, but of course Julian had to rush off to the club.

Accident: As Julian rose to leave, he reached for his watch. Watch not in his pocket. Gaping hole in pocket! Julian's lost Charles's watch. It's been handed down from Charles's great-grandfather. A family heirloom gone. Things! Soon the children will leave. Left with empty rooms and echoes.

Nikhil removed the thermometer from his mouth and handed it to Dr Bose. 'No fever,' said Aloke Bose and regarded Nikhil's unhappy face. 'No fever. Smile.'

'Why are you speaking to me in English?' asked Nikhil.

'Simply because my Hindi is atrocious, and you don't follow Bengali very well.'

'I still feel ill.'

'There's nothing wrong with you.'

'D'you know that Julian went to see that Buddhist dummy?'

'Ah, yes, I heard about it.'

'From whom?'

'From Ashokananda.'

'What d'you mean?' Nikhil sat up. 'Was he here?'

'No. I went to Murli, first, to tell him that so and so might pay him a visit, and later, to find out what happened.'

'I'm not sure Julian would like your interfering habits.'

'He won't know.' Aloke Bose lit a cigarette.

'Really?' Nikhil glanced at his hands and rocked on the chair. 'Really?'

'Surely you're not going to carry tales.'

'What did you tell Ashokananda about Julian?'

'Nothing much.' Aloke Bose drew a few circles and triangles on his note pad.

'I'd like to know what you said.'

'Merely that he likes hearing about mythology, and – and – mystical stuff, and, uh —'

229

'Did you tell him that he plays the flute?'

'So what?'

'I don't think you should see Ashokananda again.'

'Just who do you think you are telling me —'

'Julian won't like it.'

'You little —'

'Julian likes me.'

'I know a few things about you that'll turn him off.'

'Julian trusts me, he really does.'

'You work here, remember.'

'Under Dr Morel.'

'I could get you sacked.'

'Julian might get very upset about certain things.'

'I can have you beaten up, y'know.'

'I'm sure. But I still don't think you should cross the river again, at least not while Julian is still in Phulgarh. Thanks a lot for checking my pulse, etcetera.'

Julian paced on his balcony, tugging at his hair behind his ear. Where could the watch have gone? Where did he drop it? He had never really thought much about it, but he had never wanted to be without it. 'That's it,' he said out loud, 'it's out of my life for good. Why do I like the dratted thing so much now that it's gone? Blast! Why did I have to lose it?' At one in the morning, Julian sat down on the bare floor of the crescent-shaped balcony.

Crunching gravel in the dark made him crane forward. The dim patio light fell on Eric Donovan's dark head.

Julian ran downstairs before Donovan could knock, or ring the bell. Surprised, Donovan stepped back. 'I – I'm sorry. I – I just came to return, uh —' He held out Julian's gold watch.

'Oh, I say! Thanks a lot, but how —' Julian closed his fingers around the watch and looked at the young man biting his lips.

'I should have brought it back three days ago. I'm sorry. I thought of stealing it actually —' Donovan stopped in shock. 'I mean – I mean – oh, God!' He covered his face and sat down on the steps. Julian fingered the gold chain and wondered why the patio light was so dim. 'I – I wasn't going to keep it, please believe me. It's just that —'

'Where did you find it?'

'Near the tank at Al Khusru's. I went back there after dark. It was lying there, shining brighter than the moon.'

'I'm surprised nobody took it.'

'Nobody goes there after dark. It's haunted, they say. And people only go there on Thursdays. That's when Al Khusru grants wishes – that's the belief. Anyway, I realised it was yours, because there was "C.H." engraved at the back of it.'

'So why didn't you keep it, Eric?'

'It's the stuff that's written at the back – I hated it.'

'*Amo ergo sum*?'

'That's awful. I didn't want it any more. I'm sorry, I guess I'm just trash.'

'Don't be silly, Eric.'

'I'd better go now. The boat's waiting.'

'Eric,' Julian caught Donovan's elbow, 'come for dinner tomorrow. I'd like you to meet my brother.'

Caroline smiled warmly as the young man took her hand. What a good-looking boy, she thought. Such beautiful dark eyes. Wonder if he has a photograph of his mother in his wallet. But – oh-o – don't ask about family or childhood or . . . Julian's voice rang in her ears. What a perfectly charming situation. What on earth were they going to talk about?

Before dinner, over stuffed mushrooms, they talked about horses. 'Come riding with us,' insisted Julian. Through dinner Julian talked about storms, then about Scheherazade.

'So, Eric,' smiled Caroline nursing cognac on the veranda, 'tell us something about your work.'

'Oh, uh, I teach chemistry.'

'And how long have you been at Murli?'

'Nearly a year.'

'And before that?'

'Delhi.'

'Say, Eric, you play bridge?' Julian reached for the cards.

'I hate it.'

'So how long were you at Delhi?'

'Here, let's play poker then.'

'Where's your family?'

'Poker's fun. Come on.'

'Is your family in Delhi?' asked Dane.

'Actually, let's go for a walk,' said Julian, rising. 'Lovely night. Just look at that moon.'

Two days later, being Sunday, Eric Donovan came over in the afternoon. 'Hello there, Eric.' Dane grasped his hand. 'The horses are ready. There's this spirited bay stallion . . .'

What are they talking about? wondered Julian, watching Dane and Eric from a distance. After the horses lifted their heads from the water trough at the bazaar, Eric and Dane rode back towards Julian. 'Ever been to the temple?' Julian asked.

'No. Don't like crowded places.'

'Won't be crowded now.'

Leaving their horses at home they walked to the temple. 'Take your shoes off,' Julian told them as they walked into the empty courtyard. Dane hesitated for a few seconds, but seeing Eric and Julian slip off their shoes, did the same. 'See this well here?' Julian touched the stone rim. 'If you come at dawn, you bathe here. And then,' he steered them up the steps, 'you kneel at this altar, pick up the flowers – here, kneel – and hold them like this, and then say whatever it is you want to say, to Krishna.' Dane looked at his brother's profile. 'And if you kneel here long enough you might even hear his flute!'

'If you kneel here long enough to hear that flute,' said Eric, 'your knees will be a beautiful bruised blue.'

'He's sort of shy,' said Dane after dinner. 'I like him.'

'Don't ask him anything about his family again.' Julian lit a cigarette.

'Don't have to. He told me.'

'Told you?'

'Yes.'

'Told you?'

'Yes.'

'He never said anything to me.'

'You're too old, Ju.'

'Why, thank you.'

'I mean, he feels comfortable talking to me. You always look so removed.'

'What did he say?'

'Well, it's private.'

'What's the matter with his father?'

'Stationed at Calcutta now. His aunt brought him up, father's sister, that is. She died when he was seventeen. Left him some money.'

'What about his mother?'

'That's the sticky part.'

'What do you mean?'

'He was born in Simla. I think she was a servant or something like that. I didn't ask. I couldn't. He's been with his aunt ever since he can remember. Lived in Bangalore, went to school there. Then he went to Calcutta, and went to college there.'

'So why did he just start spilling the past?'

'It was awfully awkward. I – I asked him if he'd ever been to Ireland.'

'Ireland?'

'Well, he's Irish.'

'Your powers of deduction will never cease to amaze me.'

'Aw, shut up. Then he said, no, he was only half-Irish anyway, and I said, oh, and he said, the other half is Indian. So I, like the oaf I am at times, went ahead and said that I'd never have guessed he was half-Indian. He laughed. I said, my mother liked your dark eyes. He said his father's eyes were a watery blue, an' his aunt's were grey. An' then it all came out.'

'And you like the oaf you are sat and listened.'

'You're jealous, aren't you, that he chose to open up to me instead of you?'

'A little, I guess.'

'There's a girl somewhere.'

'He even told you that?'

'He's sort of shy.' Dane removed the cigarette from Julian's fingers and stubbed it.

Julian placed the watch next to the tiny ivory gate on the bed and lay down in front of the two objects. He saw his pillow through the ivory arch. Both gleamed white in the dark. He lifted the watch and laid it on the other side of the gate and looked at it through the white passage of ivory. When he

233

woke up next morning and got dressed, he put the watch in one pocket and the ivory gate in the other.

'So you're going to Kashmir,' Nikhil said as Julian peeled an orange and threw the peels into the river.

'In two weeks, yes.'

'Staying on a houseboat?'

'Guess so.'

'Y'know, the Mogul emperors escaped to Kashmir during the summer. It was their private utopia. No place could have such beauty except a terrestrial paradise, another Eden. An impossible manicured perfection.' Nikhil paused and held out his hand. Julian gave him half the orange.

'Well, go on.'

'Kashmir – there are no harsh summers there, no destructive rains, no bitter winds. No lack of flowing streams – don't I sound like a court poet, in Akbar's court perhaps?'

'A bit.'

'No sorrow there, no pain, no want, no misery. No lack of nature's beauty, no drying flowers or fountains, no unsmiling faces, no voices that do not sing. No orange as sweet as this, Julian – do you know why?'

'Why?'

'Because you gave it to me.'

'Let's not get too carried away.'

'Well, back to Kashmir. Some poet or emperor once said, "*agar firdaus zamin ast, hamin ast, hamin ast, hamin ast.*" "If there be paradise on earth, it is here in Kashmir." '

'Paradise is pretty easy to create,' Julian said. 'Haven't you heard?

> Ah, with a book of verse beneath the bough,
> A flask of wine, a loaf of bread, and thou,
> Thou beside me singing in the wilderness,
> Ah, wilderness is paradise enow!

'It's "thou" that's essential, y'know. Without the above-mentioned "thou" wilderness can't become paradise, though.'

'Yes, yes, laugh at me, Julian. Wait till you see Kashmir!'

'Go on, let's hear some more.'

'You're impossible! I'm trying my best to paint utopia. No

234

other place can compare with Kashmir! Trying to compare it with something that exists is futile, impossible. Oh, it's so difficult to write or speak paradise!'

'Why, you're doing splendidly. The place you've described is *ou topos* indeed.'

'No! It's utopia!'

'Why did you leave Kashmir?'

'Why must you go to the other side?'

'To learn about paradise.'

'That lunatic knows nothing.'

'I always feel he knows too much. Talk to you later – here comes the boat.'

Standing before the stables Sherley reached into the left pocket of his breeches and removed an envelope. He stared at it for a while. His name and address were written in green ink, the handwriting a little shaky. He opened it and read the letter. A letter from his sister as usual, one every eight weeks, telling him everything that was happening at home, and asking him how was India and how he was.

How are you, Tommy? How are you? . . . are you, Tommy?

What's your problem, Tommy? said Metcalfe. What's your problem? . . . your problem? . . . problem?

Where could there be peace and relief and quiet? To be away from those voices.

The horses were stamping and neighing inside. It seemed as if the light wind was making the sunshine bounce. He ran into the stables, saddled Brick, and led him out. A long ride, and no voices.

Reaching Phulgarh, Sherley followed the river.

Nikhil leaned against the neem tree and saw Julian become smaller and smaller as the boat cut deeper and deeper into the river's breadth. He closed his eyes and felt the warmth of the sun on his eyelids. I'll wait here till he comes back, he thought. The tread of hooves on the grassy shore made him turn. His cheek pressed against the rough bark of the neem tree, he looked at the rider.

Soldier Green Eyes, oh, soldier Green Eyes, must you step in when I'm so empty?

Sherley flushed. Nikhil turned to the boat in the distance. Julian's blond head was still discernible. 'So where's his lordship off to?' Sherley asked, fidgeting with his shirt cuffs.

'Want me, soldier?' Sherley felt as if he had just lost his legs in a cannonblast.

'This is Brick,' he said.

'And you're soldier Green Eyes.' Nikhil reached and felt the reins.

'Where did you learn English this well?'

'It's a long story. I'll tell you at the construction site. Work's been abandoned again. There's nobody there.' Nikhil guided the horse gently.

'What do you want, *sahib*?' Ashokananda sat on his doorstep and lazily cracked his knuckles.

'Does it hurt to call me Julian?'

'*Accha*, Julian.'

'Eric came over to Phulgarh a few times.'

'Yes, so he told me. He likes your brother. He likes you too.'

'Why was he so upset the first day that I met you at the school?'

'He had an argument with the headmaster.'

'Are you really a Buddhist?'

'Does it matter what I am?'

'I'd just like to know something about the philosophy from someone who's part of it.'

'It's not a philosophy; it's an ideology.'

'Why d'you say that?'

'Because it begins to run your life after a while. If Buddhism was a philosophy it wouldn't have codes that were meant to control you.'

Julian removed the ivory gate from his pocket and set it on the grass. 'See this,' he said, 'this could have its ideology too. My father bought —'

'Where did you get that?' cut in Ashokananda.

'Oh – er – my father —' Ashokananda rushed from the steps and snatched the ivory gate from Julian.

'Oh, God! Meng Men, Meng Men!'

Julian sat speechless while Ashokananda buried his face in his hands.

'Meng Men,' Julian repeated slowly, 'what the hell is Meng Men?'

'You said your father – your father – where did he get this? How? How?' Ashokananda grabbed Julian's arm.

'I believe he bought it off some boy in Delhi.'

'Charles *saab*!'

'Uh, yes, his name was Charles —'

'Tall, dark hair, grey eyes, and he was in his mid-thirties when he came to Delhi?'

'He was nearly thirty-seven, yes.'

'He had a way of biting his knuckles sometimes.'

'Y-yes.'

'A tiny scar on his chin.'

'From his fencing master, I believe.'

'Charles *saab* – Meng Men —'

'You knew my father?'

Ashokananda closed his eyes.

'What's Meng Men?'

'A monastery near Lhasa. This ivory gate is the miniature version of the gate of Meng Men.'

'Does that mean something, Meng Men?'

'The "gate of dreams", or "the gate through which dreams pass".'

'Is that where you got it?'

'No. I visited the monastery long after I sold it to your father.' They looked at each other quietly for a few minutes.

'Please tell me,' said Julian. 'Please.'

'When I was twelve years old,' said Ashokananda, 'I ran away from the orphanage at Ranchi. I managed to get hold of a shoeshine boy's box – I stole it, actually – and worked and wandered around. After six months, I ended up in Gaya. A lot of Buddhists and Hindus come to Gaya during Holi, which is also the time Buddha was born. There were all these monks all over the place running around in their long robes and whispering to each other. And among them was Etienne Perreaux, better known as Lochana, a 42-year-old Belgian who had made his way to Tibet in search of nirvana. I'd found out that begging near that sacred tree was very lucrative. Limping around as usual, I held my tin can under Lochana's nose one day. And he laughed at me! I didn't like that at all.

237

Then he grabbed my neck and said, "If you work for me, I'll see to it that you're well-fed." That's how it started. *Sahib*, this is a very long story —'

'If you don't mind telling me, I'd very much like to hear.'

'Well, I began to work for Lochana, y'know, cook and clean, basically. Then, slowly, he began to teach me English. He spoke five languages: French, English, German, Hindi and Tibetan; and he also knew Latin, Greek and Sanskrit. He taught me Sanskrit too. We kept travelling from place to place and I kept learning about Buddha, Tibet, China, Japan and Meng Men, the monastery Lochana came from.

'He talked of Meng Men as if it was the valley of dreams, sort of a fairytale place where there is only the tinkling of bells, soft footfalls on candlelit stone floors, mists that only lift for brief summers. He talked of children running after sleepy-eyed yaks; the market-place where yak-butter candies melt in the sun; and he also closed his eyes and recreated the almost unending winters when Meng Men broods under oceans of snow . . .'

And Julian saw, too, startled, fascinated; he saw Meng Men through the tiny ivory arch on Ashokananda's palm.

'Then we reached Delhi after five years of travelling around India, Burma and Nepal. Lochana stayed at a wealthy gentleman's house. He'd have visitors every day. They'd talk to him for hours and hours, while I ran around serving tea, fruits and sweets. One day, in walked two *sahibs*. One was tall and handsome, the other, of average height and a little overweight. They came to see Lochana six times. I asked him why the *sahibs* came. He said, "Because they are curious." I came to know their names from the other servants in the house: the dark-haired one was Charles *saab*, the red-haired one, Alan *saab*.'

'Sir Alan Mellors!'

'You're probably right.'

'Good God.'

'Charles *saab* gave me a silver coin and smiled when I served him tea. So I liked him. Just before their last visit to Lochana, Lochana told me that he would be leaving for Tibet in a week and that he had made arrangements with the gentleman we were staying with so that I'd receive a proper education and be able to have a better life. I was furious. I did not want to be abandoned this way. I'd come to love Lochana like the father I'd never had. I begged him to take me with him. I insisted I wanted to take the vows and become a novice monk. He refused. He said he couldn't take me there. I want to be a lama, I said. I'd have to do it on my own, he said. He couldn't "take" me there. Go there on my own! I thought that was preposterous! How would I get there on my own?

'Anyway, Lochana was as firm as a rock. My tears did no work at all. The final blow was the ivory gate. Lochana handed this to me and said, "Here's the gate to Meng Men. Remember me through this." The bastard, I thought. Not only is he abandoning me, but he is making sure that I'll never get over this awful moment in my life by planting this constant reminder in my hands.

'What did I mean to him? Nothing. So why should this stupid little item have any emotive value for me? I'll sell it and get some money. So I ran after Charles *saab* as he was stepping into his carriage and offered it to him. He examined it carefully for a few minutes, then paid me twice the amount I'd asked. The horrid little thing was out of my life. And seven days later, so was Lochana.' Ashokananda tossed the ivory gate up into the air and caught it.

'And then?'

'What then? For the next ten years I ripped myself apart for having sold Lochana's gift. I've got to get there somehow, I cried day after day. I worked with a forger for two years. I just wanted money to get to Tibet —'

'But what about the gentleman who was supposed to take care of you?'

'I ran away from there the day Lochana left.'

'So you missed your college education!'

'No, I didn't. With the money I made from the forging business I put myself through college. Then I got a job as a secretary – worked for an East India Company man for a year. I couldn't bear it any longer. I had to reach Meng Men. I planned to set off. But, oh, I fell in love – with my employer's wife! Her husband was a bore, she said. So I played "secretary" for one more year.

'I lived in Meng Men for ten years. Lochana, I learned,

239

never made it back to the monastery; he died on the way.

'Meng Men – Meng Men was the place of Lochana's stories. Meng Men was —' Ashokananda shook his head slowly. 'No, I did not want to live there for ever.'

'What was there to come back to?' Julian could not contain the agitation in his voice. 'What was there to come back to if Meng Men was the valley of dreams?'

'The sun's about to set, *sahib*. Go home now. Here's your – here's the ivory gate.'

Caroline looked at the tiny ivory gate on her stepson's palm and leaned back among the pillows.

'I want to give it back to him. Would you mind very much?' Julian asked for the second time.

'Why? Because it reminds you of your father and —'

'You don't understand! I never hated him.'

'You never loved him.'

'I liked him; that's more important than love.'

'And why do you wish to give this away?'

'Caroline, you should have seen the man's face! It was as if he had recovered his soul. It's his anyway. Rightfully, it is his. The look on his face will haunt me for ever if I don't give it back to him.'

'Julian —'

'Do you understand what I'm saying?' Julian stood up and went to the window. 'I have to return it.' The night was so soft, it was unbelievable; the warmest, softest feathers under the wings of a black swan.

'What about Ravinspur, Julian?' Caroline asked, adjusting her pillows, 'who will you give away Ravinspur to?'

Sherley slid off his horse and walked towards Nikhil sitting on a pile of bricks at the construction site. The sun made the place look very dry and bare. It was the only place in Phulgarh that had been stripped of its greenery. 'I've bought Brick,' Sherley said, 'now I have my own horse. Would you like to ride him some time?'

'Not unless you give him to me,' Nikhil said with a laugh.

'Give him to you! He's my dear beloved friend.'

'What am I?'

240

Sherley cleared his throat. 'Trevors came to see me, y'know. He was a gentleman about the whole thing, Cyril was. Just wanted to reassure me that he'd never talk about what happened. Over and done with. Now that I've got a transfer everything's OK. He's been a good friend to me in spite of all. Can't expect him to understand or accept everything. He's put up with my vile moods all this time.' Sherley lay down on the brick wall. 'Shook my hand an' all.' Nikhil looked at the soldier's lower lip pulled between his strong, white teeth. His mouth always appeared firm till he opened it to talk. Then the lips would be dragged between teeth or twisted in wry smiles or just move in unrhythm with the words that slipped out. Dark, dark hair, burnt cinnamon, and firefly eyes. Strong, toned muscles. No frail, delicate elegance in these shoulders.

'I'm leaving for Madras soon.'

'Let's go back to the river.'

'Thinking 'bout his lordship?'

'Don't be silly.'

'So do you think it's him when it's me?'

'I don't like this place. Let's go.'

'Tell me.' Sherley grasped Nikhil's arm.

'What's the matter with you?' Nikhil tried to break away.

'I wish I knew, love. I'd sing about it like 'canary' then. Tell me about him.'

'What about him?'

'Didn't like you enough, eh?'

'He likes me all right. He's different, that's all.'

'He's "different" all right!' laughed Sherley.

'You don't understand. He's not that way. When he was younger, he was just experimenting, that's all. He's really very nice.'

'Cold.'

'Not at all.'

'Towards me he is,' Sherley said.

'That's just how he comes across.'

'He doesn't like me.'

'Oh! But you hated him ever since you set eyes on him.'

'Wasn't hate. That came later.'

They walked to the river, slowly, holding hands, separating, holding the reins, leading the horse, keeping the horse between them.

'Strange, when you're drawn to something, someone, you consider it weakness, and fight it, and turn your desire into hatred. Then you're strong again, because you can hate. Violence and anger towards yourself, towards another. But I, Tom, when I love, I will call it love, I thrive on my longing, I reach and I reach and I reach in every way possible, I turn my longing into that which is most intimate and ultimate, and choose to burn for ever. If longing kills me, fine. If I can just touch once, I can dream for a lifetime, or maybe I'll die at the instant of touch.'

'If I touch, I must have.'

'Having! It's the being that matters. He's leaving soon, I think.'

'What will you do?' Sherley asked.

'Nothing,' Nikhil said.

'I've got a transfer to Fort St George.'

Those eyes were so green, so green. Green pools under green of the jungle. Green as neem leaves quivering under rain clouds. Green as Will Grey's elusive parrot. Lotus leaves on Dal lake. But what of those eyes like blue-grey clouds over the mountains from which half the rain has fallen? Like blue-grey dawns over the Yamuna?

Leaning against Brick, Sherley watched Nikhil scratch marks on the bark of the neem tree on the river bank. 'Can you swim?' Sherley asked suddenly.

'Sure.'

'Go and swim,' said Sherley.

Julian smiled at the *majhi* and jumped off the boat. The river was sunset warm. He was glad he hadn't found Ashokananda at home. He held the ivory gate in his hand as he waded waist deep in the water. God, the river was so warm!

Slipping a little on the mud, Julian scrambled to shore. 'Go and swim,' he heard and looked up. A dry white shirt was handed to him. 'I'm wet,' he muttered.

'Dry off.' He wiped his face and hair hurriedly. Then he slipped into his own clothes which the *majhi* held out. 'Hello,

Nikhil,' he said to a pair of lost dark eyes. 'Nice horse, Sherley,' he said, handing back the shirt.

Dane sat on the front steps. Eric can't talk without moving his hands. Talks with his hands almost, putting shapes to words and ideas. 'Why don't you come to the club with us tonight?' he said.

'No, please.'

'Why not?'

'Don't like crowded places.'

'Classrooms are pretty crowded.'

'That's different. Anyway, I'd really like to go to Kenya and —'

'Hunt lions?'

'No! It's just beautiful country. And then I'd like to go to Alexandria.'

'Alexandria?'

'It's the way your brother described the city – I just want to go there now! And Japan, too.'

'Funny, Ju once said he'd like to go to Kyoto. He was only nineteen then, and y'know, I remember this quite vividly. He was in the corner of this lake at Ravinspur, under the waterfall, bathing. He was, er, is, I guess, a little eccentric. I was swimming around and pestering him as usual. And he said, as he rubbed soap in his hair, that he wanted to be in Kyoto, sleep on the grass at night, breathe apricot and cherry blossom air.'

'You're lucky you have a brother like him.'

'Actually, for years and years, I thought I was rather unlucky to have inherited a brother like him; especially when the woman I'd become totally infatuated with left me for him.'

'What happened? Did he fall in love with her?'

'Julian in love! Oh, no, no. The affair lasted two weeks; he left for Europe tired and bored.'

'Did she come back to you?'

'I didn't want her back. But no, she went and married the Marquis of – never mind – a very wealthy man of forty-five.'

'Have you ever been in love?' Eric asked. Dane looked at Eric's dark eyes for a few seconds, then at the squirrel running across the lawn. 'I'm sorry,' said Eric. 'I – I saw this girl a year ago, y'know, I told you that. But — she's Indian, and her family's fairly well-off, and she looks at me like — like — oh, I don't know! There's this trace of fear or something in her eyes all the time as if I don't have anything inside me.'

'Where is she?'

'In Delhi.'

'Why did you come here?'

'I just got sick of the whole thing.'

'How did you meet her?'

'She practically fell into my arms — from a guava tree!'

'A guava tree!'

'Well, I was walking across my Dutch employer's lawn with all these important papers when I heard a yelp. A girl was somehow clinging to a nearly-breaking branch of a guava tree. Guava trees aren't too sturdy. I rushed to help her. She sort of fell on me!'

'What was she doing there?'

'Her father worked for my employer, too, and she's pretty friendly with his two daughters.'

'You should go back to Delhi, Eric.'

'I think I will. Y'know, she punched my nose; my nose actually started to bleed!'

'Now, why would a proper young lady do something like that to an equally proper young gentleman?'

'Proper? Well, um, I kissed her.' Dane couldn't check his amusement any longer. 'Don't laugh at me!' yelled Eric, 'stop it!'

'Oh, Mr Donovan, you'd better go back to Delhi and have her kiss your nose back into shape!'

'What's this about noses?' came Julian's voice from the back.

'Oh, we're just talking about imperfections,' said Dane.

'Can I join the club?'

'What imperfections could you possibly have, m'lord?'

'Oooh, haven't you heard yet, Eric, what a rogue and peasant slave am I?'

Ashokananda sat cross-legged on the little patch of grass before his house with his eyes closed. 'Why did you leave Meng Men?' Julian touched his knee.

'You can't live there for ever. Saps you entirely. You're dying slowly and you don't even notice it.'

'How can you say that! Meng Men – that's like a place of rebirth!'

'There isn't always rebirth,' smiled Ashokananda and opened his eyes, 'you've got to want to be reborn.'

'But you had everything there.'

'*Sahib*, I did not want to spend my life staring at a stone idol, waste my body in a place where thought and action are unnecessary.'

'Sounds like bliss to me. I have a sort of a pipe dream, y'know, that when I'm old I'll go off to some faraway place, Kyoto maybe, and go off in an opium cloud!'

'Before I reach that stage I'd like to do something constructive. I've always wanted to teach. I don't exactly like teaching here, but I've enjoyed teaching at schools in Agra, Lucknow and Calcutta. Actually, I'm here because Murli's removed from the unrest that's started in the eastern states. I know it's going to sweep the country soon, but I'm a little too old for all that. I'll help in my own way.'

'I understand how you feel, but please don't get hurt, I mean, please don't —'

'So you've heard.'

Julian looked down. They watched the goat rip leaves off a hibiscus bush. The sun dropped behind clouds that lined the horizon. A sudden gust of wind tugged hard at the creepers that climbed the walls of the cottage.

'What's that smell? Did you get that? It's the headiest fragrance I've ever – y'know, I've caught that in Phulgarh, too, many times at night.'

'That's called *raat ki rani*, "queen of the night" – look there, those white flowers.'

'Sort of smell you'd get in Meng Men, I'd imagine,' smiled Julian.

'There were no smells in Meng Men – I mean, no smell of flowers,' said Ashokananda sharply. 'You could smell grass in the summer, yak-butter in the market-place, unwashed children running around in tattered strips of blankets. In the monastery – well, there was incense. Can't bear incense any more – reminds me of unaired rooms.'

'I like sandalwood incense,' said Julian.

'That has a fresh smell. The incense they burned at Meng Men was suffocating. Come to think of it, paradises are suffocating, cloying. Gardens of bliss, they transfuse you with inertia.'

'I guess I have a different view of paradise.'

'Create a mental paradise and indulge in it intellectually. Abandonment in gardens turns you into something other than your self.'

'What's my self anyway other than what I'm supposed to be?'

'And what are you supposed to be, *sahib*?'

'What is Kalki and *kalyug*?'

'Ah – ha – ha – ha! In our corrupt age Krishna becomes the destroyer. All that hogwash. All depends on how you choose to see things, Krishna or Kalki, one and the same thing, but we see them as different. How you perceive, Julian, that's what's important. How you perceive the flute, the fluteplayer, your self. Hogwash. It's getting dark, *sahib*, go back now. The *majhi* gets restless waiting after sunset.'

The river was purple streaked with copper. What was I doing painting myself blue and playing the flute on a tree? What have I been doing for the past few months, for years and years? The fragrance still lingered. Hogwash? The *majhi*, singing in a low monotone, glanced at the *sahib* casually a few times. Where was the *sahib*'s madness that the people talked about?

Julian went up to his room two hours after dinner and sat on his bed in his turquoise silk robe. Looking at the flute on his writing desk, he bit his lips. Before he could remove his eyes from his prize possession, Dane walked in without knocking.

'Ju – I just wanted to tell you that I'll be moving to Cheveley after we go back.'

Julian tried to stiffen his back and shoulders to stop his body from shaking as his brother left.

Eric jumped off his horse and held the reins of Julian's mare as

246

he dismounted. 'Thank you for everything,' he said, 'I've been having a wonderful time.'

'Don't thank me – you spend all your time with my brother.'

'Yes, but I'd have never met your brother if it hadn't been for you.'

'Eric, have you ever thought of going to England?'

'Well, yes, but I don't think I want to go there.'

'Why not?'

'Just don't want to go.'

'Um, well, come and sit over here.' They left the horses to Ravi Singh and sat down on the steps of the veranda. They could hear Dane running up the stairs. 'Look, Eric, you said you've had some business experience —'

'I – I helped manage my Dutch employer's apple orchards, I mean I handled paperwork, I wasn't there on the estate.'

'My estate manager at Ravinspur wishes to retire and I can't really refuse. He's pretty old; been with us for forty years. Would you consider working under him for some time and then taking over?'

'What? Me?'

'Well —'

'How can you trust me? I nearly stole your watch.'

'Will you think about this? I'll talk to you again when I get back from Kashmir.'

We're leaving for Kashmir tomorrow – all of us. I can't write in this any more. I have to let go. I wanted to say certain things, wanted to work through certain things for myself; I've done so. In my mind I established a communication that seemed impossible – talking with you, talking, really, with myself. I had to talk but not out loud. Also, I feel it so strongly now – we have all established touch. I'm breaking off suddenly, I know. But's that the only way. Or I'll never let go. Goodbye, Lorna.

'Mama.' Caroline closed the diary and turned from the writing desk.

'What is it?'

'Nothing.' Dane shrugged. 'Wondered what you were doing?'

'Do you know anything about Lorna, Dane?'

'Lorna? Julian's mother? No more than you do. The portrait in the library – the woman in the mauve dress with trees and clouds in the background. Riding accident and death. Why do you ask about her?'

'Oh, it's nothing. Wonder how well she knew Julian? Just idle curiosity.'

Sherley lay on the grassy bank, his chin on his knuckles. Nikhil lay on his side and watched the cows and goats being ushered home by figures along the horizon. 'Y'know,' he said, 'we call this the cowdust hour.'

'We call this twilight,' said Sherley.

'They're in Kashmir now, did you know?'

'You're obsessed with him.'

'So what?'

'Two different worlds. Can't come together ever.'

'Our worlds can collide – they did! Such satisfying violence, madness. But you're right. Our worlds can never . . .' Nikhil looked at the river. 'A terrifying safety of never coming together. Only touching – the shock of accident.'

'Why are you so taken with his eyes?'

'The colour of stars; like the light of water.'

'Hah! Ever seen eyes as green as mine?'

'I like yours – earth colour.'

Sherley reached and touched Nikhil's hair, then turned to the river again. 'Do you know what was between the dancing girl and the brother?'

'Nothing. And you shouldn't have caused all that trouble. It's all over now. There were no worlds there. Just something undefined and a sort of thoughtlessness, I mean free of thought,' Nikhil said.

'I wonder why we think all the time?'

'So that we don't feel. Think and you'll feel less.'

'No!' Sherley sat up.

'Yes! I haven't thought for years.'

'You think of him all the time!' Sherley caught Nikhil's shoulder.

'No. I feel, I feel.'

'You're crazy.'

248

'Sure,' Nikhil said, 'sure. And the only ones for me are the crazy ones, those that burn and live and die and know and do not know and feel, feel, feel, all at the same time, all the time.'

'I just want peace and quiet,' Sherley said.

'I want the fire, earthfire, windfire, the fire among the waves.'

'What of the ashes?' Sherley asked.

'They'll burn, too,' replied Nikhil.

Julian returned from Kashmir quiet and unsmiling. Dane couldn't stop talking about his plans for Cheveley. Caroline tried not to reveal her tension while referring to the *nawab*'s invitation to tea in three days. 'What'll you wear, Julian?' she asked him the night before.

'What'll I wear?'

'Are you going to wear a grey suit?'

'A grey suit?'

'Is there any need to repeat everything I say? Wear a light blue suit; goes with your hair.'

'I'll wear a blue suit; perhaps Dane should wear pink.'

'I don't feel right about visiting the *nawab*.'

'We can't refuse, Caroline. It would look rude.'

'It might be a trap of some kind.'

'What's he going to do — behead us over a silly rumour?'

'I heard something awful at the club. The servants are talking, too. There was a secret execution — someone beheaded — at the palace.'

'Don't be ridiculous — an execution! Did the Collector find a head on his doorstep?'

'The Collector's *khansama* said something to ours about the *nawab* wanting satisfaction. Someone's blood had to be spilled to restore honour, faith, I don't know what. And Jugnu knew all along what's been going on. So Meena tells me. That dratted boy! He spread all the stories at the bazaar.'

'Must we believe servant-talk, Caroline?'

'Where do you think they would throw the head?'

Ashokananda touched Julian's shoulder. 'Why do you look at the river? Tell me, how was Kashmir?'

'Is it true that Krishna threw his flute into the river?'

'The flute. Yes.'

'Why did he do that?'

'You can't keep certain things for ever. Some things you have to let go, because their purpose seems to be over. You have to break a relationship when it's not taking you any further, when it's not growing any richer. But your moving away, your discarding doesn't remove the link from your life. Only apparently it does. When you are ready again, it returns. Look at the ivory gate. I thought I had lost it for ever, thrown it away in anger. Look at the circle it has taken to come back to me.'

'I guess I'll never figure this one out,' Julian laughed.

'There's no need to. The flute, Julian, you can't control it, it can't control you, if you only play and not think of mastering, but instead of perfecting an art. When something attracts you and draws you, give in to it, give to it, take what it gives, but don't try to take it over, control it, possess it. We talk of the love of things, love of people, and say, I want. Always a power-play, desire and power, unnaturally joined. Let the flute go, it will come back newer, richer. You will feel the loss like death. And you will return to your first world again, in pain, as you should.' Ashokananda shook his head and smiled. 'Do I talk like a pseudo-philosopher, *sahib*? Don't believe me.'

'I like believing you,' Julian said.

They couldn't believe their eyes when a black Daimler groaned up the drive at four. Feroze stepped out elegantly and bowed. As if entering Cinderella's pumpkin coach, they slid into its leather interior. 'Hell, it's better than the viceroy's car,' said Dane adjusting his tie. Caroline felt her emerald earrings lightly and raised her eyebrows. Julian looked down at the dark red rose-bud on his pearl-grey lapel, glanced at his pearl cufflinks, and crossed his legs. Feroze turned around from the front seat and said, 'Only half an hour, countess, lordship, your honour,' with a charming half-smile. The driver patted his red and gold turban twice and shifted gears.

Musk and roses, and a very mild weedy stench wafted around them as they were escorted to the marble terrace overlooking the lake. 'Ah!' breathed the *nawab* over the countess's hand. 'Lovely, lovely! What beautiful children.' He has a pretty firm grip, thought Julian. Why were Dane's hands in his pockets? 'My son,' said the *nawab* of Talkot. 'My son, Salman.'

He bowed his head ever so slightly and sat down after them. What exquisite handcrafted shoes, Caroline sighed inwardly as Salman crossed his legs. Dane kept his eyes fixed on Julian's lap. Julian quickly glanced at his crotch. What the hell's the matter with the idiot? His fly was buttoned. For heaven's sake, look somewhere else.

'Kashmir!' sighed the *nawab*, 'ah, Kashmir! Was it not exquisite, countess? The paradise on earth!' Thank God for Kashmir, thought Julian, relieved, and picked up his cup of tea. The countess and the *nawab* traversed the land of bliss for the next hour. Caroline saw a little glow inside her head, the little glow with which the journal had burned to ashes in the kitchen stove.

Julian wrinkled his nose slightly as the weedy stench from the lake wafted around them again. He remembered a fresh leafy odour the last time they had sat here after the *shikaar*. Dane was fidgeting with his cuffs and looking at the lake. Is he getting the funny smell, too? And Salman – Julian suppressed a smile and looked at the prince's exquisite shoes. Good night sweet prince! What a stage-set.

'And now,' the *nawab* clapped his hands, 'music.' As four men in yellow clothes began to play, 'Folk tunes,' said the *nawab*, 'cheerful.' He didn't bother to name the instruments. 'Well, Salman,' he raised an eyebrow at the prince, 'you haven't said a word. Why don't you show his lordship and his brother our new Arabs, and of course your Dilruba?' For a few seconds the prince of Talkot looked at his hands. Then he stood up.

'I hope you will like our horses,' he said in that clear unaccented English he had spoken that night.

Julian felt sorry for the young man suddenly. 'I've heard about your black Arab mare, your, er, highness,' he said with a smile.

'Please call me Salman.'

Four horses were escorted into the sandstone courtyard before the palace. Dane and Julian drew their breath in sharply. Salman rubbed his face against the black mare's and stroked her mane. 'Those three are still rebellious, you see,' Salman said, 'have to be broken in.'

'They're gorgeous.' Julian tried to pat an impatient white stallion.

Dane desperately wanted to hate the young man who was now trying to stroke the restless chestnut mare's neck. But there was such a helplessness about him, Dane felt. I've got to hate him. He did something really awful. He hurt her terribly. I should break his face this very minute. I should — Salman turned and looked at Dane. Does he recognise me from the cockfight? Dane wondered. What has he been told about the fair business? I wanted to kill him. We thought he would want to kill me. But something's broken inside his eyes, something utterly smashed and lost. I feel I've gone through worse than death. Does he feel that too? Must be terrible for him to stand there and act polite to me, almost as terrible as it is for me. He should hate me, too. I wish I could hate him right now, at this very moment.

'Shall we go back now?' Salman gave Dilruba a parting slap on the flanks.

Mild commotion greeted them on the terrace. Caroline sat white-faced, clutching a handkerchief to her nose. The *nawab* paced around apologising profusely. The servants kept leaning over the railings and whispering.

'Is something wrong?' Julian asked.

'Oh, God! Awful!'

'I'm so very sorry, so very, Allah, I'll have them all strangled or castrated! So sorry, so sorry —'

'What is it?'

'The corpse – there's a corpse out there! My God, it's true!' Caroline covered her face.

'What is?' asked Feroze.

'Nothing, nothing. Now, Caroline, calm down,' Julian patted her hand, 'and shut up for heaven's sake,' he added under his breath.

Children laughed and screamed on the steps that led to the lake. They were throwing stones at something. Among fresh pink lotuses and their broad dark leaves floated a muddy form, swollen, hog-like, entangled in the lotus stalks. 'Gross, gross.'

252

The *nawab* held an attar-scented silk handkerchief to his nose. The stench touched them only intermittently, as and when the breeze swept their way. 'Gross. How dare he drown himself in our lake! How dare he! Feroze!'

'Y-y-yes, *nawab saab*.'

'Call Zafar Khan at once.'

Minutes after Feroze disappeared, Zafar Khan appeared on the steps from where the children were throwing stones. 'Zafar!' Julian had never heard such a high pitch in the *nawab*'s voice before. 'Take care of that monstrosity right now!' he ordered in English.

'*Nawab saab*?' Zafar Khan looked puzzled.

'*Laash hatao*!' screamed the *nawab*, and Zafar Khan, after one look at the lake, slapped his forehead.

'So sorry, so sorry,' the *nawab* turned towards them, 'I beg you, forgive this awful thing, Collector must not hear. *Hai Allah*! How could this have happened? Everything spoilt! Everything ruined! O-o-o —!'

'So much misery in our land,' sighed Feroze, 'wretches throw themselves in lakes, beg to be beheaded.'

'That doesn't have a head?' Caroline gasped.

'We could always check,' Julian said.

'Gross, gross! Let's just ignore.'

'Yes, let's just ignore the whole thing.'

'Oh, gross!'

For a fleeting moment, Julian felt as if the prince suppressed a smile before motioning to the musicians.

'Ah, ah, thank Allah for music. Ah, Feroze, jasmine, Khayyam, Khayyam.' The *nawab* sank among velvet cushions. Feroze sprinkled the essence of jasmine from a tiny crystal bottle.

'Back to normal again,' said Salman, and sat down.

'Your lordship,' Feroze handed Julian a glass of wine, 'your lordship, I hear you play the flute exquisitely. Would you not play for his highness? It would soothe his soul at this moment of agony.'

'How do you know I play the flute?' Julian set the glass down, spilling wine on the brass table.

'News like this spreads like cholera,' the young man smiled and handed Julian a black and gold flute.

'Yes, please play, your lordship, please,' murmured the *nawab*.

Julian turned the flute over in his hand and felt the smooth cold surface. The copper translucence of the sky was being wiped away by an opaque indigo. 'I – I c-can't quite —' stammered Julian.

'Please, m'lord, please.'

Julian jerked his head back at the sharp coldness of metal against mouth. No warmth of bamboo or its tangy smell. Forcing his mouth to the flute and unstiffening his fingers, Julian closed his eyes. Awkward and harsh, the first few notes. The musicians began to respond slowly, hesitantly on their strings, for they had never heard such alien notes before.

Salman sat with clenched fists. Julian opened his eyes briefly and caught the stare. Hooves beat in his head. Echoing stone. What did the prince see now? A *sahib* in grey with a flute. The blueness of night. A creature that had never known day on an altar of flowers, with a magic flute. A *sahib* in grey. In silver-grey, silver-blue in the night colour of stars. He would never guess, would he, without the setting?

Dane took the offered hand as they rose to take their leave. Meeting those dark eyes, he gave a watery smile. Shaking hands, as they must according to all rules, were they now trying to pinpoint a certain something they had never quite been able to grasp? It was an odd feeling about an odd emptiness. Neither knew what it was; and 'it' was as vague as 'it' always is. Had they ever been in a position to choose? Decisions had been made long before choices became clear. The winner had taken nothing, for there was nothing to take. Right now it was just the absence of presence, a nothingness. Hate mattered so little in the long run.

'Well, Eric, what have you decided?'

'Um,' said Eric Donovan, standing outside the school gates and shaking his head, 'um, let's go to Al Khusru's. I like being there.'

Sitting on the rim of the tank outside the tomb, Eric rubbed his eyes. 'I don't think I want to run away.'

'Run away?'

'You're offering me an escape really. I've got to live with this and work things out in my own way. Running to England and living under your aegis will not really help. Won't change what I am. Do you understand at all what I'm saying?'

'Eric —'

'I belong here!' Eric got up, walked to the arched entrance of the mausoleum and walked back. 'Some day they'll accept us, accept that I – we – belong here, on this soil. I'm not going to run away.'

Julian stood up and caught Eric's shoulder. Eric pulled away. 'Eric, if you ever want to come to England, please write to me. Keep in touch.'

'I will. Thanks. You're lucky to have a brother like Dane.'

The children were in the river again, and they would be there just a little longer, Julian knew, till the sun went down. Sitting on a boulder, he smiled. They were throwing stones. Throwing stones. A tiny finger touching his wrist. Anger in dark eyes. Small brown hands showering him with petals. A river of petals, a cold cutting wind. Garlands, drums, moon on the waters. Black and white marble floors, red, red clay, bamboo groves, hibiscus, gul-mohr, coconut water, laughter among branches. Hands among petals, turning, turning; bodies frozen by flutetones; sandalwood paste, a green parrot, rice on banana leaves, honey wine and indigo, indigo, indigo.

What before? What after? Funny, the past's all so clear, and gone so suddenly. All the gloves, canes, hats, capes, shoes, ties, bats and balls, laughter, anger, fear, even fear. The past has a way of disengaging itself; falls off the cliff sort of. Ceases to matter.

Before, there was a fear, unidentifiable. After, a fear's lost, still unidentifiable. Fell into the river maybe.

The gates are wide open. Always have been. Empty rooms?

To be what one is not, to be not one but many. Cut up the self and let each fragment have its own little dance.

Lost my centre somewhere, fighting something. Only tried to create something. To create something. And something's lost in the process; lost, yet not lost. Don't know quite, but as if something's not lost but changed, like corals and pearls. Not a fading, but a changing.

255

May those that love me try to forgive what I have done. May those that I love forgive me.

'*Saab, saab! Bansuri bajao!*' Fingers around his ankles, and a thrusted flute. '*Saab, bajao, saab!*' Such laughter and demand, such clear desires. The flute again, and a madness. And so what? Only till the sun goes down.

Behind a boulder they stood and watched. 'Don't look at him that way,' Sherley said.

'You don't understand.' Nikhil moved away a few feet.

'Come with me to Madras.' Sherley caught Nikhil's wrist. Staring at those green eyes, Nikhil blinked. He saw only the light of water.

'So, *sahib*, why so quiet today?' Ashokananda handed Julian a plate of rice and vegetables.

'It's getting hot these days.'

'Time for you to sail back home.'

'I'm not sure I want to leave.' Julian felt the temperature of the food with his fingers and began to eat slowly.

'That's how I felt when I took my vows at Meng Men,' said Ashokananda. Julian ate without lifting his eyes from his plate. 'Is my cooking edible?'

'Oh – this is awfully good. Thanks for feeding me. I was starving.'

'Hunger's easy to take care of.'

'Yes —' Julian stopped eating and looked up. 'What do you mean?'

'Would you like some water?'

Copper smears began to stain the banana trees and the sky beyond them. They had sat quietly looking at the landscape. Neither knew what the other had been thinking for so long a time, and neither felt any curiosity. 'You've crossed the river quite a few times,' said Ashokananda.

'And I've crossed back too.'

'Yes, cross back. Mountains or rivers – one has to cross back some time. You get lost, then you go back to the beginning and search for that which made you cross over.'

'Odd, isn't it?'

'Maybe. It's necessary to pause and breathe.'

256

Julian removed the ivory gate from his pocket. 'Here,' he said, 'I want you to have this – it's yours.'

'I can't believe this!' Caroline extracted a silver vase from its wrappings and set it on the brass table in front. 'Presents from ⊥he *nawab*.'

'Interesting,' Dane said. Julian felt the intricate work on its surface.

'Open yours, Dane.'

'Aw, you open it.' They blinked at the gold dagger set with rubies and emeralds. 'It's pretty sharp. Christ!' Dane ran his thumb lightly along the blade.

'Probably wants it through your heart,' laughed Julian. 'Let's look at mine.' He ripped the tissues away and lifted the *nawab* of Talkot's farewell present.

'Don't drop it!' Dane grabbed the crystal flute that slipped from Julian's fingers.

'Oh, look, there's a card with it,' Caroline said, 'this one's specially from the prince.'

Nikhil sat on the steps of the temple and waited for sunrise. It was so cool, the grey stone and the watery sky. The river in the distance was very flat and silver. Footsteps made him look down at the courtyard.

'Hello, Nikhil.'

'Julian —' Nikhil swallowed and tugged at his hair. 'Heard you're leaving soon.'

'Yes. Haven't seen you for some time.'

'Want to watch the sunrise?'

'Yes.'

Under a foamy pearl sky the air gathered the bitter freshness of neem trees that grew outside the temple.

'I didn't want to – I didn't want to –' Nikhil bit his knuckles – 'I've done a lot of silly and selfish things.'

'So what?'

'I've been happy, too, for a very short while.'

'That's all that matters.'

'I love you, Julian, I always will. What we had was unique.'

'I don't think we ever had anything except a common image.'

'How can you say that? All that I did —'

'All that you did was for yourself, and all that I did was for myself. We depended on each other for self-satisfaction.'

'You never felt – you don't care about me – never did – never felt a bond – I can't believe that! Why, Julian? Because I'm a native and you a —'

'Stop it. Why are you trying to pick a fight, now, after everything? What is it you want now? A quarrel? So that you can be satisfyingly miserable and run to Sherley and present your broken heart? Well, I won't allow you that pleasure. I've been through as much heartbreak as you have. You think I didn't suffer? I lost myself to the point where return was death. You led me and I was only too happy to follow and even lead. I'm not blaming you. You haven't done anything wrong. But I won't get into a silly quarrel about give and take and winning and losing, because we are not breaking up like lovers break up. I'd like to think of us as dreamers together, coming out of a dream only to enter another. But you won't allow that. You want your clichéd unhappy end. There is no end, as I see things.'

'Where's this new philosophy coming from? From the other side? From that Buddhist dummy?'

'What would you think if I say from your William Grey?'

'You were my dream, Julian.'

'Then as dreams pass, so shall I, painlessly.'

'I waited for you for years —'

'Where – at the temple?'

'Yes, at the temple. And you did come.'

'I'm not your god, Nikhil.'

'That's not what I said. I never wanted an altar between us. I wanted us equal.'

'You pushed me on to that altar and then wanted equal power. Isn't that unfair, to me? You cannot force a man to be a god and then want the god to be yours only. You can't want to be free and want to hold someone. We were never equal. You never wanted us equal. You wanted a god you could adore, control, rebuke, forgive. I was happy to be that, for it took me away from things that I hated. But it was yet another trap, a trap I created with you. In that we were equal. You got what you wanted, so did I – self-satisfaction. I don't blame you. I won't quarrel with you. I like you. Don't you blame me and pity yourself.'

Julian reached out and took Nikhil's hand. 'Strange fascination, Nikhil, for the alien, yours and mine. Why reduce it to a plebeian spat? Y'know, we've never even held hands, and you claim we have loved!'

'Loved with my mind, Julian. Touched with the flute – from my hands to yours. That awful flute always between us.'

'Yes, now you know. A flute between us. But that's how you wanted us.'

'Never any closer, closer than ever, is that what you mean as dreamers?'

'Tell me, how does one forgive a god?'

'If you laugh at me I'll cry.'

'If you cry, I'll laugh more.'

'I'm sorry about everything, Julian.'

'You are being very silly, y'know.'

'What were we to each other, Julian?'

'Krishna and Kalki, Kalki and Krishna!'

'I don't want to listen to this any more. Do you dislike Tom Sherley?'

'Does it matter?'

'He's just —'

'Look – he was just very irritating a few times, that's all.'

'Could I tell him that you don't dislike him?'

'You can tell him whatever you want. Look – here comes the sun.'

'Look at the river, Julian, look at its light!'

Children thronged Julian as they reached the river. '*Saab, saab, bansuri bajao,*' they demanded.

'Oh, God.' Julian made no attempts to extricate himself from the mesh of arms and legs.

'And now what are you going to do?' Nikhil sighed.

The women turned and smiled at their *pagal sahib*. 'Is he going to play?' they whispered to each other. Julian sat down on the grass and let the children mess his hair, touch his skin, smell his clothes. '*Bansuri bajao.*'

'No. No *bansuri*,' Julian said, laughing. 'I'll sing – *gana!*' He whistled a few bars, and to Nikhil's surprise, began to sing.

> Full fathoms five thy father lies,
>   Of his bones are coral made,
> Those are pearls that were his eyes.
>   Nothing of him that doth fade
> But doth suffer a sea-change,
>   Into something rich and strange.

Nikhil saw clothes float away as the women left their work. Julian sang the song over again.

Something rich and strange. That's what I sought and that's what I found. Nikhil turned away. The sea-change, the sea-change it floods over. Rich and strange and mine for moments only, and then just alien, alien, alien, alien, alien . . . What have I loved, what have I loved?

'Come for a walk.' Julian nudged Dane as they stood lighting cigarettes on the veranda.

The woods were warm and dry. Leaves and twigs crumbled and snapped under their shoes. 'Let's go somewhere else,' Dane said.

'I like the temple,' said his brother.

Dane kept his eyes off the bare altar. 'What are those figures on the walls?' he asked.

'Scenes from the life of Krishna. Want to hear a story?'

Dane listened, surprised. How does he know all this. 'And the flute,' continued Julian.

'Why d'you play the flute, Ju?'

'And then he threw it into the river . . .'

'Ju —' Dane sighed as his brother's voice echoed within the ruins. A few pomegranate shells rubbed against the stone floor as the light breeze moved them. Dane, he heard, Dane! And laughter. Barely, barely untouching; untouching warmth. He sat down on the cold altar. 'Ju —' Julian sat down.

'During the great battle he was a charioteer . . .'

'Julian, shut up.'

'When everything was settled . . .'

'Julian.' Dane caught his brother's shoulder. 'You coming back to Ravinspur?' Julian looked for a moment into those indigo eyes.

'Yes,' he said.

'Why? Tell me.'

'I don't know — to refocus. To look at things differently. When you get lost you go back to square one.'

'What's that supposed to mean? Will you stay?'

'Perhaps.'

'You can come and visit me at Cheveley.'

'Why are you moving to Cheveley?'

'To refocus, like you said.'

'Dane —' Julian stood up and walked to the empty alcove.

'What are you doing?' Dane followed his brother. Julian stepped into the empty space.

'There used to be a statue here, y'know,' he said.

'There are cobwebs all over you, Julian. You hate cobwebs and spiders.'

'Ravinspur will be empty.'

'It was, for a long time.'

'Don't,' said Julian.

'Don't what?'

'Don't go to Cheveley.'

The afternoon sun was so bright, and loud, loud with voices, felt Dane. Wheels and horses rushing out through the gates of Ravinspur. A slender figure in a black cape running down the wide steps; hands in dark leather gloves adjusting a hat on a blond head; lazy swing of legs into a carriage, a wave; and, 'see you next year, maybe.' Please, Ju . . . Ah, hooves and wheels had always clattered over 'Please, Ju'. And now, did he have the right to smile?

'Say what I used to say, Julian.'

'You know where to hit back, don't you?'

'So do you, Julian.'

'Damn you, Dane.'

'Damn you, too.'

'You hit me too hard that night by the river.'

'You cried, too, Julian. That's all I wanted.'

'Why?'

'Because.'

'For all that's happened —'

'I don't give a damn.'

'Please, Dane, stay.'

'There's a remarkably large and hairy spider hanging over

your head. Next Christmas at Cheveley, m'lord, you're cordially invited. This'll be my last year at Ravinspur.'

'You'd better make sure the chimneys are cleaned; we were nearly smoked out the last time we were there,' Julian whispered.

The silver vase worried Caroline. It's the shape, she decided. Urn-like. What flowers would go with it? Not roses. Maybe tulips. No. Maybe azaleas. Hmm. No. Flowers wouldn't look nice in it. They just wouldn't. What to put in it then? Looks nice on the mantelpiece. But what to put in it?

'Caroline.' She turned and saw her stepson standing at the foot of the stairs with a blade of grass in his mouth. 'Caroline, I'm leaving in a few days.'

'Leaving? I – I thought we were all leaving in two weeks.'

'I'll be at Ravinspur when you arrive.' Chewing the blade of grass, Julian went up the stairs.

Why am I worrying about what to put in the silly vase? thought Caroline. Why put anything in it at all? Maybe it's just meant to hold nothing.

Julian walked through the narrow crowded streets of Murli sensing the same discomfort around him. Suspicious eyes, and bodies moving away. Children looking away.

When he had told Ashokananda that he was leaving in a few days, the older man had smiled and lowered his eyes. A Buddhist monk! A Buddhist monk with an ivory gate and lazy eyes.

The river lay in front glazed gold by the sun. The *majhi* threw his *biri* on the mud and stood up. Julian bent down to roll up his trousers.

'Julian.' He straightened up. Ashokananda was running towards him.

'Oh, I say —'

'Here —' Ashokananda held out the ivory gate.

'No, no, it's yours. You keep it.'

'No, I can't. It's meant to be yours.'

'No, it isn't. It's —'

'Please, Julian, please take it back.'

'Why?'

'It has completed its circle with me. Goodbye, *sahib*.'

Julian sat in the boat and smiled at the two inches of whiteness. The *majhi* glanced at the *sahib* and wondered where the madness was hidden.

Nikhil stood under a neem tree and watched Sherley ride away. Nights were warm now, and the river so dark and lightless.

Never dream under the neem tree. Soldier Green Eyes, oh, soldier Green Eyes. Only the light of water quenches a thirst. What now? You have crossed the river. The wheels wait and the horses tear at the ground. Where the flute, the music, the player? Only a dark garden. Ah, perhaps it should be a dark garden, night-loved to night colour, the darkness of Krishna. And the only light, the light of water.

Coda

Caroline felt the surface of one of Julian's suitcases with her forefinger. She could hear him in the dining room laughing as he tipped the servants. What had happened? Will I ever know? She smiled at the bougainvillaea outside.

They came to India. They lived in a house covered with bougainvillaea, a house with a white veranda and crescent-shaped balconies. There was a river, and in that river children ripped at the water and women washed clothes.

Into a vermilion coach they stepped and rushed past wheat fields and entered rose-gold evenings. Then there was a terrible storm, and Julian arrived all wet, with that look in his eyes. After that, came the flute.

Dane stood on the steps as Jugnu and Ravi Singh carefully placed Julian's luggage at the back of Harry's carriage. Harry had wanted to get a car, but Julian insisted on going to Delhi in the carriage. Sort of like it, y'know, he had laughed. Been quite a help, don't you think?

Dane looked at the bougainvillaea. He'd never be able to think of India without seeing bougainvillaea. Magenta bougainvillaea against a copper sky. And sticky pomegranate juice on hands and mouth. The sun was savage bright. He blinked and rubbed his eyes.

And what about that flute and Julian? Did he find Ravinspur in a flute?

Walking through rows of tables and chairs of the empty mess, Sherley felt his white cotton undershirt at the throat. It was cool and dark inside, and so quiet now, between lunch and tea. Only faint clinks and shuffling feet somewhere there beyond the counters. Wonderful place, Fort St George. Voices rang in his ears. Hot though.

Never mind the heat, ol' chap, never mind the heat. 'Cause there's always rain, and blue-grey clouds.

How play cricket again?

Good ol' Brick, wild chestnut Brick. Mine the red manes.

Can connect nothing with nothing.

Soon everybody will march to Simla, like before, for the summer.

They say you see dry brown mountains, cotton fields, sugar-cane stand still outside the train windows as you go south.

Even alone is all right; just to stay unexhausted by hate. Ah, our flawed faces! Don't haunt me, face.

Far, far away, and wait again. Follow soldier Green Eyes, won't you?

No matter, no matter. Time and space I'll grab, and like you said, not think much, not think. When the stars come out, forget worlds, laugh and play. Under the sun, throw off your shirt and – and – not think, and you'll be free.

Nikhil ran and hid behind a boulder as he saw Julian in the distance walking towards the river.

Julian felt the cool breeze from the river on his face. There was a boat near the other side. So empty today. Not a soul here. The bamboo flute in his hand was warm. He got that fresh tangy odour again as he held it against his face.

No! Nikhil wanted to scream. No, no. Don't, please don't. The river swept the flute away. I can never reach it now, never. Against the dark stone, Nikhil's body shook. Left with a dream, a shadow, a love frozen in stone. All that I have – a little rushlight to lead back to splendour. I tried to create it, tried, tried.

Julian walked away.

The flute did not sink. It simply slid further and further towards the heart of the river.

Abacus now offers an exciting range of quality fiction and non-fiction by both established and new authors. All of the books in this series are available from good bookshops, or can be ordered from the following address:

Sphere Books
Cash Sales Department
P.O. Box 11
Falmouth
Cornwall, TR10 9EN.

Please send cheque or postal order (no currency), and allow 60p for postage and packing for the first book plus 25p for the second book and 15p for each additional book ordered up to a maximum charge of £1.90 in U.K.

B.F.P.O. customers please allow 60p for the first book, 25p for the second book plus 15p per copy for the next 7 books, thereafter 9p per book.

Overseas customers, including Eire, please allow £1.25 for postage and packing for the first book, 75p for the second book and 28p for each subsequent title ordered.